IN HER NAME: FINAL BATTLE

By
Michael R. Hicks

Copyright © 2012 by Imperial Guard Publishing, LLC
ISBN: 9780984673063
IN HER NAME: FINAL BATTLE

For Benjamin and Samuel.
May all your dreams come true.

WHAT READERS ARE SAYING

Drawn straight from some of the reader reviews of *Final Battle*:

"The final chapter of the IN HER NAME series is an amazing conclusion. Sometimes during the reading I asked myself how the narrator could find a solution for the difficult knots in the plot but there was always a wonderful surprise ahead."

"I have read many science fiction books in my 61 years but this series is without doubt the best. I cried more laughed more and cheered more than I have with any other series I have ever read."

"Once again Michael R. Hicks teaches us about our own humanity & enriches our lives through his writing. Reza Gard never fails to impress me with his brains & brawn! I have become addicted to all the action & intrigue, love & loss, but most of all the emotional connection I feel with every character. This is the perfect compliment to complete this trilogy. I'm looking forward to reading the prequels!"

"By the time most authors get to the end of a series of this length they have accidentally backed themselves into a lot of corners they can't get out of easily. That does not happen here. This is a very satisfying and exciting conclusion to a wonderful series."

"Michael Hicks packs an enormous amount of words into each page which added a depth to his tale that's rare and fully enjoyable to me. It's that weight and the richness that made the work so enjoyable for me."

"When I finished this book I was almost crying and wanted more..."

DISCOVER OTHER BOOKS BY MICHAEL R. HICKS

The *In Her Name* Series
First Contact
Legend Of The Sword
Dead Soul
Empire
Confederation
Final Battle
From Chaos Born

"Boxed Set" Collections
In Her Name (Omnibus)
In Her Name: The Last War

Thrillers
Season Of The Harvest

Visit *AuthorMichaelHicks.com* for the latest updates!

ONE

The world was strangely white, so unlike the darkness of Death, so unlike the place where the First Empress's spirit had waited all these generations for Her awakening, and where only he, among all mortals, had ever been. He could not imagine the power, the wonder that must come to the Empire upon Her return, and his heart stopped beating for a moment as he thought of Keel-Tath's spirit encased in Esah-Zhurah's body. He would have given anything, everything he had ever had, to see her in the white robes and slender golden collar, high upon the throne, the most powerful Empress his people had ever known. His only regret would be that he could never again call her by her birth name.

In the whiteness that was now the Universe, he saw strange shadows hovering above him like odd birds fluttering above a snow-covered field. Their jerky movements were accompanied by noises that were sharp and purposeful, but not threatening. Were they other spirits, perhaps?

But he knew that this could not be; the place of the banished was forever dark and cold, and all those who dwelled there did so in eternal solitude. Or did they?

The world seemed to turn slowly, the white turning to gray, the strange noises drifting away into silence.

He slept.

* * *

If any time had passed, he was unaware. Dreams of life, and things that were beyond life as any other human had ever known, came to him, played their parts upon the stage that was his slumbering mind, and left to wherever such dreams go. While he would never be able to recall the exact moment, at some point he became aware that he did, in fact, possess a body. He gradually became sure of this because of what his mind perceived with gradually increasing clarity: pain. It was not the sharp, excruciating pain of a weapon cutting flesh, the kind of pain that he had been trained and toughened to withstand, to endure; it was the slow, throbbing pain of his body struggling to heal itself. This pain also was something he was well accustomed to. But this was deep, to his very core, and he realized in that instant that he was still alive.

The shock of that realization was sufficient to send enough adrenaline through his sluggish body to bring him to the threshold of consciousness. He opened his eyes. He was still in the white place, but saw no shadows.

"Reza," said a voice, so softly that he could barely hear it. "Can you hear me? Squeeze your right hand if you can. Do not try to talk."

Not questioning the instructions, Reza tried to carry them out. Sluggishly, he traced the nerves from his brain to his right hand, commanding it to close. Nothing. He concentrated harder, ordering his hand to obey. At last, he was rewarded with a slight twitching of the muscles in his forearm, causing his fingers to move fractionally.

"Can you feel this?" the voice asked with barely contained excitement. Reza felt a gentle pressure around his fingers, the squeeze of another's hand. He replied with another feeble movement of his fingers.

In his vision, he saw a shadow appear above him that gradually resolved into something that, after a moment, he recognized. It was a human face.

Nicole.

He tried to speak her name, but somewhere in the complex chain of physical operations that made speech possible was a breakdown. His lips, feeling swollen and numb, parted. The tip of his tongue curled toward the roof of his mouth, behind his teeth, to its accustomed position for making the "n" sound. But that was all he could do. His lungs were too weak to force enough air into his larynx to make the sound of her name. He tried again, hard.

"Ni...cole," he breathed faintly.

"Please, *mon ami*," she said softly, placing a finger gently against his lips, "do not waste your energy trying to talk. We will have plenty of time for that later."

She smiled, and Reza saw tears brimming in her eyes. It took him a moment, but it finally struck him that she looked exhausted, haggard. Her face was pale and drawn, her normally flawless ivory skin creased and sallow. Her eyes were bloodshot, with dark rings beneath them.

She mourns, he thought absently. But that was at odds with the light that shone in her eyes now. They were joyful, relieved.

"You will be all right, now," she said. It sounded to Reza as if the words were more to reassure herself. "We were very worried about you for a while. You were hurt very badly."

"How... long?" he asked, ignoring her pleas to conserve what little strength he had. His range of vision began to constrict, the periphery of his world turning to a dull, featureless gray until all he could see was Nicole's exhausted face.

She hesitated for a moment, and Reza sensed a general feeling of unwillingness to tell him the truth. His senses were terribly dulled, blunted like a rusty sword, but they told him that much.

"Six months," she said finally, her eyes questing, hoping the news would not send him into shock. When she saw that he was not fading on her like he had so many other times over the last months, she went on, "It has been six months since we left Erlang. After you got Eustus and Jodi to *Gneisenau* – however it was that you did it – the surgeons worked on you for many hours." Her smile faded with the remembrance of how agonizing that time had been. She herself had to be anesthetized, to shield her from the pain that Reza was feeling as the surgeons worked on him, trying to reconstruct his shattered body. "You never came out of the anesthesia, never fully regained consciousness," she went on. "Until now. You have been in a coma all this time." Her own recovery from the psychologically-induced trauma had taken two months, and the news that she was being forcibly retired from combat duty sent her into a bout of depression that she had still not entirely recovered from.

"You... all right?" he whispered.

"I am... better, now. I know I must look awful, but I have not been able to leave you." She looked down at her hand holding his. "I had a great deal of leave built up, so I decided to take some. To be here for you, when you woke up."

Reza's heart ached for her. He sensed the long, lonely hours she had spent at his bedside for months, wondering each moment if the next he would be dead, or would never wake up at all. "Thank you, my friend," he sighed.

"I could not leave you here alone," she whispered. Tony had understood, and had supported her after *Gneisenau* had returned to Earth on Fleet HQ's orders. He himself had spent many hours beside her, beside Reza. The two men had not seen each other in a long time, since the wedding that had made Tony and Nicole husband and wife, but there was a bond of trust between them that went far beyond the measure of their acquaintance.

"Erlang?" he asked as his strength began to wane, his range of vision narrowing again.

"The Mallorys, and what few Raniers are left, are well," Nicole said, still marveling at how that was possible. While the cities and major townships had been totally destroyed with grievous losses among the population, the vast majority of Erlangers – almost exclusively Mallorys – had survived. The Kreelans, after retrieving whatever it was that they had come for, had mysteriously departed without inflicting further harm. "Several convoys of ships have taken them the things they need to help rebuild. Ian Mallory sends his hopes for your recovery, and his thanks."

She did not add that he had also petitioned to be a witness in Reza's defense at the court-martial that had long since been planned for him. He was charged with multiple counts of murder, including those of President Belisle of Erlang and Chief Counselor Melissa Savitch, as well as high treason against the Confederation.

Reza sensed that there was something deeply wrong, something that she was not telling him, but his body demanded that he rest. "I am glad that Ian lived," he said quietly

The last thing he felt before his eyes closed was the gentle warmth of Nicole's lips pressed to his.

* * *

Tony Braddock was a troubled man. Someone to whom he owed his own life and that of his wife was in a dire situation, and there did not seem to be any way for him to help. While he had told Nicole that Reza had been charged with murdering President Belisle, Counselor Savitch, and an Erlang Territorial Army soldier, plus what he took as nothing more than a gratuitous and hate-inspired charge of high treason, he had not told her how extensive was the evidence against him. Not only did Colonel Markus Thorella claim to have been a witness (by remote, naturally), the man had also produced an especially damning piece of evidence in the form of a recording of the soldier's and Belisle's murders. The holo had been validated by the court in the last months, meaning that it had been declared devoid of tampering, was genuine, and would be admitted as evidence in Reza's court-martial. The alleged murder of Counselor Savitch was based entirely on Thorella's say-so, but considering the other evidence in hand, Tony Braddock knew that almost any military or civilian court would convict Reza out of hand. Politically, as the war went on and worsened, they could ill-afford not to. The public wanted a scapegoat for the pillaging of their civilization, and they would have one. And who better than Reza, who was caught between two worlds?

Worse – *How could it be worse?* Tony asked himself – since so much time had passed and no one was sure if Reza would ever come out of the coma, they had dispensed with the pre-trial preliminaries that might have given him some sort of due process, at least in terms of technicalities. Most of the witnesses for his defense had been released to fleet duty, their sworn testimony recorded for the proceedings. But it was not the same as in-person testimony, Braddock knew, especially when Reza's chief accuser,

Colonel Thorella, had conveniently been ordered to a posting on Earth after he had somehow explained away the annihilation of his own regiment on Erlang.

While Tony had no proof, he had no doubt that there were some dark forces moving things along. He suspected Senator Borge and his increasingly large and vocal militant following of having a hand in it, but there was no way to prove it. And even if that were true, what could he do? Go to the president and accuse Borge of subverting the legal process in the military?

He smiled bitterly. Even with evidence as solid as Kilimanjaro, that would be foolhardy, at best. Borge had few remaining political enemies except the president and a few older and more powerful senators who still remembered what democracy was like, and who cherished the ideal above the rhetoric of their office.

And there were still a few young fools like Tony Braddock.

He rolled over, careful not to disturb Nicole, sleeping beside him. She seemed so much better now, after the months she had spent recovering from whatever had come over her, all the while distraught over whether Reza would survive. Tony had found it maddening sometimes, but he had done everything he humanly could to be there for her, to comfort her and try to lighten her burden. He knew she had been, and still was, deeply depressed at being assigned a non-combat position, but he was relieved that she had finally been taken out of harm's way. She had done more than her share, and it was time for them to have some time together as man and wife, and perhaps to ask themselves again if they were ready to become father and mother.

He heard her whisper Reza's name in whatever it was that she dreamed. His heart used to darken out of jealousy, wondering if perhaps she did not really love Reza more than she did himself. But over time, his fears had subsided. She loved Reza, yes, but as a sister might a brother or close friend. Perhaps there had been a time when she had wanted it to be something more. But he knew, from both Jodi and Nicole, that Reza would never have accepted anything more than platonic love from her or any other human woman; Reza's heart lay elsewhere, deep in the Empire.

Braddock had also listened to Jodi tell him of her suspected "psychic link" between Nicole and Reza, but he had never believed it until Admiral Sinclaire himself had told him of what had happened to Nicole on *Gneisenau's* bridge when Reza was wounded.

Braddock would have to learn more about that, and many other things, come morning, he thought, as well as bring an old friend some very bad news. He would go and visit Reza, not as a friend, but as his legal counsel in a trial that he knew could only result in Reza's execution.

* * *

"...and that's where you stand, Reza." Having finished outlining his friend's situation, Tony sat back in the chrome chair next to Reza's bed, feeling drained. A week had passed since he had first resolved to visit Reza, but the doctors had refused any visitors other than Nicole, who seemed to be a catalyst in Reza's recovery. But after seven days the patient's condition had improved enough that the doctors had finally allowed Reza one additional visitor. His defense counsel.

Reza showed no reaction, but continued to stare out the window as he had the entire time Tony had been talking.

Braddock frowned. "Reza, did you hear anything that I just said?"

"Yes," Reza said, at last turning to face him, his face an unreadable mask. "I heard and understand."

Braddock's temper flared. "Dammit, Reza, they're not just trying to throw the book at you, they're trying to dump the whole library on your head! Everyone who knows you knows that you would never have committed these crimes, but the court will–"

"I did, Tony," Reza said quietly, his eyes glinting in the light.

Braddock's mouth hung open for a moment. "What?" he said. "What did you say?"

"I killed Belisle and the Territorial Army soldier," Reza went on, his voice not showing the keening in his blood. "The killing of the soldier was unfortunate, an act of self-defense, but I killed Belisle with forethought." He paused, noting the blood draining from Braddock's face. "And if I had to do it again in front of the Confederation Council itself, I would. He was an animal, a murderer. Had I not killed him, or had the Kreela not come and destroyed the city, many of Erlang's people would even now lay dead at his hands. As for Melissa Savitch, her death was Markus Thorella's deed. And I shall yet find a way to avenge her."

"Can you prove that Thorella killed her?" Braddock asked, seeing his case to defend Reza foundering as surely as a scuttled ship. But perhaps there might be enough to hang Thorella for murdering Savitch. At least that bastard could swing beside Reza on the gallows.

"None but my word."

"That's not good enough, Reza."

Reza nodded gravely. In the world in which he had been raised, the world of the Kreela, one's word was a bond stronger than steel, a commitment backed by one's very life. Among those of this blood, among humans, however, it often meant little or nothing. Especially if one stood accused in a court of law. "I would have taken his head, as well, had he not outwitted me," Reza told him, describing Thorella's scheme and what exactly had happened in Belisle's office. "He shall not deceive me again."

No, Braddock thought, *he won't: you will be a dead man and he will go free.* "Reza," he said, leaning forward to emphasize what he was saying and shocked that Thorella's accusations were even partially true, "confession is only going to earn you a quick trip to the gallows. The only way I can help you is if there are some mitigating circumstances, maybe by having some Mallorys testify as to Belisle's misdeeds. We might be able to get that charge reduced to a crime of passion in the UCMJ, or even dropped altogether if we can get the Council to cede jurisdiction to Erlang."

Reza was warmed but amused by his friend's determination to keep him from the hangman's noose. He shook his head. "My friend Tony, you know far better than I that the Council will do no such thing. They cannot. I killed Belisle and the soldier, but not Melissa Savitch. To try and convince anyone otherwise would be to lie. And what of the charge of treason?"

Braddock shook his head, wishing that this were all a bad dream and that he would wake up in a warm bed next to Nicole. Even if he could get the murder charges dropped or reduced, the treason charge would not be let go. "How could you have done this Reza?" he asked more to himself than his doomed friend. All Tony could do now was to ensure that due process was given and the procedures themselves were legal. "You don't have a prayer with the judges. You may as well have just stayed there and died."

"I tried," Reza said quietly.

Braddock frowned. "The only other alternative I can think of is to ask the president to pardon you. I mean, since you are the only real authority on Kreelan affairs, maybe–"

"Impossible," Reza said quietly. "I am accused of capital crimes, Tony, two of which I am guilty by my own admission. How can it be that your society, which claims to hold justice so high, could simply allow me to go free? I do not well understand the politics of the Confederation, but I do not see how even the president could manage such a thing without devastating repercussions. He would not pardon me; he could not. And I do not wish it. I knew what I was doing when I took Belisle's head. I simply did not intend to survive to receive the punishment I must under Confederation law."

"You could escape," Tony said quietly. He was not suggesting it as a counsel, but as a friend. He knew that Reza would not have done what he did without good reason, but that would not hold up in a court, especially if

Reza confessed. "It would be easy for you," he said. He knew as well as anyone that Reza could disappear like a ghost if he wished.

Reza shook his head. "And go where, Tony? To the hills of this planet? To the desert? Even if I could whisk myself to Eridan Five and dwell among the saurians there, I would not. What would be the point? Even without a trial, I am an outlaw among your kind, having forsaken the cloth of the Corps and the Regiment, and I cannot return to my own people without disavowing the oath I made that banished me. And that is something I can never do, even at the price of my own head."

Braddock did not say anything for a while. He felt like his guts had been ripped out and stomped on.

"What about Nicole?" If Reza had resigned himself to death, then so be it. There was nothing more he could do for him. Now he had to worry about Nicole. His wife. "How will she handle your death?" Tony asked, imagining the metal cable tightening around Reza's neck, Nicole writhing in agony as it happened, filling her with the same grisly sensations that Reza would feel. "What is this bond, or whatever it is, between you going to do to her?"

Reza had been devoting a great deal of thought to that, but he had no answer. He simply did not know. Even the memories of the Ancient Ones that only seemed to unlock themselves in his dreams had left him no clue. "I do not know," he said helplessly. "There is no way to undo what has been done."

"Does this link still exist?"

Reza shook his head. "I do not know. I have not sensed her since I awakened, but that means nothing. The Blood that flows through her is much diluted, for there is little enough in me. The bond has always been little more than a filament between us. Perhaps the shock of what happened broke it..." He shrugged helplessly at Braddock's uncertain expression, his own heart filled with fear on her behalf. "Tony, if there was any way at all to guarantee her safety, I would do it. But I just do not know."

"Sometimes, when she dreams, she speaks in a strange language. Would that be the language... your people speak?"

Reza nodded. "It would be the Old Tongue," he explained, "the language used in the time of the First Empress. She would only speak it if the bond was unbroken."

Braddock's heart sank. He was afraid that would be the case. "She spoke that way last night."

Reza closed his eyes, his heart beating heavily in his chest with grief. "Then I fear that whatever I feel, so shall she."

"She'll die, Reza."

Opening his eyes, Reza looked his old friend in the face, his own twisted in a mask of emotional agony. "I know," was all he could say.

* * *

"Now tell me, Markus," Borge said cheerfully, "isn't this far better, even after having had to wait so long?"

Markus Thorella smiled as he cut a strip of sirloin that was among the usual delicacies served at Borge's table. "Yes, your Honor," he said honestly. "I have to admit that I thought you were wrong all this time, but now..." He shrugged. "I was wrong. Publicly humiliating Gard has been more fun than I possibly could have imagined."

In many ways, an outside observer might have thought that the two were like father and son. It was a comparison that would not have been lost on Borge, although Thorella would have chosen to ignore it. Borge had sponsored the younger man, getting him out of trouble when required – as in the nasty incident on Erlang – while developing him into the political and military tool that he needed. He was daring, ruthless, and bloodthirsty, all characteristics that suited Borge's needs most satisfactorily. It had been a lengthy struggle to keep Thorella from following his passions when he should have been following orders, but it had been worth it. Borge's plans demanded such an individual, and the time was drawing near for him to put Thorella to his ultimate use.

The fact that he would eventually have to kill Thorella was entirely beside the point. He could never allow such a powerful weapon to exist after its usefulness had ended.

"So," Borge asked, "tell me, how goes the war?"

Thorella looked startled. "You haven't heard?"

Borge shook his head as he carefully set down his fork. He was not in the mood for surprises. He never was. "What's that supposed to mean?" he said. "Is there something the General Staff hasn't been telling us?"

"I don't know, Senator. But Admiral Zhukovski–"

"That Russian bastard," Borge hissed under his breath. *I'll make Zhukovski eat gravel one day*, he vowed to himself. "He's a meddler and a fool."

"Well," Thorella went on, "my little network found out that there's been something strange going on. Zhukovski's people apparently believe that the Kreelans have slacked off heavily in the last few days in their overall offensive, and a lot of their fleet units have mysteriously disappeared."

"Are you telling me that those witches are retreating?"

"I don't know, sir," Thorella said carefully. He was not about to stick his neck out on the basis of someone else's information, no matter how valid it might be. "But that was the word I got. Unfortunately, I assumed that it would have already made its way to the Council by now."

Borge nodded. He was furious, boiling inside, but not with Thorella. The Council should have been informed immediately, and he was determined to find out why it had not. "Not your fault, colonel," he said graciously, actually meaning it, "not at all. But I am afraid that this will cut our dinner date a bit short."

"I understand, sir," Thorella said, relieved that Borge's wrath would be directed away from him. Without hesitation, he rose from the table after Borge and followed him to the hall that led to the front door of the senator's mansion.

"Be standing by, Markus," Borge said. "I may need your services very soon."

"It will be my pleasure, your Honor," Thorella replied, shaking the older man's hand before he put on his cap and opened the door to leave. The smell of coming rain was strong in the night air. "You know where to reach me."

As the younger man walked to his waiting speeder, Borge returned to his study to contact his staff. They all had a great deal to do tonight.

* * *

"Blast it," the president said, "how did he find out? The entire bloody Council and Senate is up in arms, screaming that the Executive has withheld vital defense information from them without due cause. Borge has asked for an emergency Council session this morning, and no doubt putting my head on the chopping block will be the topic of discussion." He had no doubt what the result would be if Borge somehow managed to push through a vote of confidence.

Zhukovski shrugged. "Is not so difficult that he found out, given nature of information," he said. "Anyone gets idea that Kreelans are backing off, word spreads like fire, and to devil with security."

"That does not help us, Evgeni," Admiral L'Houillier said, exasperated. "The fact that your people came up with some analysis like this on the war and were not able to keep it secret–"

"What do you propose I do, admiral?" Zhukovski retorted before his superior could finish. "Shoot my entire staff, their families and friends? Everyone wants war to end, and is willing to pass on good news to others, rules and regulations be damned. But leak of Kreelan 'withdrawal,' as good Senator Borge might say was, perhaps, premature."

"Meaning?" the president asked sharply.

Zhukovski called up a galactic map on the table's holo system. "Information that Borge received was initial analytic conclusion," Zhukovski explained in his rumbling voice. "Young analyst of mine saw pattern of sharply increased losses among Kreelan ships and ground forces in battles over last few days, without apparent reason. Further, she found that far fewer Kreelan ships are now in human space than week ago, and offensives on and against many of our colony worlds have suddenly and inexplicably collapsed." He frowned. "It is as if Kreelans have suddenly lost will to fight. This is information she initially reported informally to me, and I presume is same information received by Borge."

"I sense a large 'but' coming up, Evgeni," L'Houillier said.

Zhukovski turned his good eye on the senior admiral, nodding his head gravely. "Indeed, it is so. Analyst continued her good works, and discovered what I believe to be Truth, with large T." The other two men were silent. "Her analysis of STARNET reporting shows that large number of Kreelan warships have passed through trans-Grange and Inner Arm sectors on what looks like converging vectors."

"Well, where?" the president said impatiently. "Dammit, Evgeni, spell it out!"

"We have only been able to plot location to spheroid of about eight-thousand cubic light years, centered toward galactic hub, past Inner Arm rim worlds." He sat back, waving his hand dismissively. "But that is immaterial."

"Why, Evgeni?" L'Houillier asked him.

Zhukovski eyed him closely. "Because, my dear admiral, if projections of my analyst – completed as of this evening – are correct, as I believe they are, no fewer than three thousand Kreelan warships are massed in that sector for what can only be final chapter in this war: total destruction of humanity. And those are ships we know about. There could be more. Many more."

The other two men sat silent, dumbstruck.

"Three thousand," L'Houillier whispered finally. "Evgeni, that is impossible! How could they mass that many ships, and so quickly? We do not have half as many warships in our entire fleet!"

"Exactly my point," Zhukovski said as he took another sip of the over-sweetened tea. "Why Kreelans suddenly die like flies in combat, like drunkards or fools, I do not know. But with three or four thousand ships, even drunkards or fools can destroy Confederation Navy and every colony populated by *homo sapiens*."

"Lord of All," President Nathan whispered, "what shall we do? Evgeni, even if you are completely wrong – which, unfortunately, I doubt – if that information were to reach the press, we'll have an interstellar panic on our hands. The government will collapse."

"Borge will not hesitate to use it against you, Mr. President," L'Houillier said. While he was supposed to be apolitical, the Grand Admiral had no illusions about Borge's own lust for power, and had no doubt that he would use any tool available to further his own cause. "Nor can we legally keep the information from the Council, even if there were no leaks."

Nathan nodded. His political position had just disappeared, vanished into a bottomless morass. But that was not his real concern; the people of the Confederation were. "I'll have to strike a bargain with him."

"Better to be bitten in throat by venomous snake," uttered Zhukovski, not relishing the president's position. He himself despised Borge and his sycophants, avoiding them whenever possible. Unlike L'Houillier, he made no effort to disguise his personal or political likes and dislikes.

"Believe me, Evgeni," the president said, "I would much rather jump into a pit of such snakes than give Borge this kind of leverage." He thought of how long he and Borge had been friends, before Borge had changed, been consumed by a lust for power that had made him into something alien, despicable. *It's strange*, Nathan thought, *how well I thought I once knew him. I wonder what ever made him change into something so evil?* "But I don't have any choice, do I?"

The two military men looked at each other, then at the president – their commander-in-chief – for whom they had worked for many years. They could not exactly call each other friends, but they were close and respected one another.

"No, sir," L'Houillier said flatly, wishing there was some other way out, "you do not."

"And what of the Kreelan fleet?" Nathan asked. "Is there anything we can do?"

"I have already taken liberty of calling operations officer," Zhukovski said, exchanging a look with L'Houillier. The woman, competent though she was, was a political animal who would jump at any chance to get ahead. "I gave her 'hypothetical' scenario to model on command computers, to see what best fleet reactions would be." He winked at L'Houillier. "I explained that Grand Admiral was most interested in such extreme cases to get more money for fleet expansion, and would be most grateful. Results should be available in another hour."

"Evgeni, you are incorrigible," L'Houillier said with a wry smile. "You are worse now than as a midshipman."

They were silent then, each of them turning Zhukovski's grim news over in their heads.

"Well," the president sighed, "I guess there's not much for it. Thank you gentlemen, and please keep me apprised of the results of the simulations. If you'll excuse me, I have some calls to make."

The two Navy officers got up, saluted, and left the president as he called in his aide and began to prepare to meet Borge's onslaught.

"You realize, admiral," Zhukovski said quietly as the two of them walked down the corridor to the elevators, "what simulations will say?"

"Of course, Evgeni," L'Houillier said glumly. "Despite Laskowski's best efforts to show that she can come up with a plan for victory, the computers will show that we are about two thousand ships short. Even if we concentrated every battle group in a single place to defend against a massed Kreelan attack, we would still be outflanked and destroyed, no matter how poorly the enemy fought."

As they made their way back to Joint Headquarters, Zhukovski wondered about the Kreelans' sudden lapse of fighting spirit. He made a note to ask someone who might just know.

* * *

Reza stood perfectly still in the center of the room, naked except for his collar. His long black hair was again carefully braided in a cascade down his back, a startling contrast to his pale but now healthy looking skin. Starting with his left little toe, he began to flex each muscle in his body, working up his left leg to his waist, then back down his right leg. Then he began to work on his abdomen, then his upper body. He noted with dismay how weak he had become, how quickly his muscles tired, but that only fueled his determination to rebuild both his body and his spirit. It was all he could do, and so it is what he did.

He performed the exercises of body and mind that he had learned as a boy and young man, taking himself to his present limits, slightly beyond, then resting. Even though he was a prisoner shortly to be condemned, the hospital still viewed him as a patient, and so he had no trouble getting the food he needed for the repairs his body was making to itself. At one point, he had even considered asking for his Kreelan clothing to be returned to him to wear, but there was no point; the shape of his body had altered so much that nothing would fit, or so he believed. If necessary, he would wear no clothes at all rather than disgrace himself in ill-fitting armor.

He was just completing the first cycle of calisthenics, vaguely similar to human tai chi, when a knock came at the door. He closed his eyes, looking beyond the metal confines of the room as he ran an impromptu test of his weakened psychic abilities.

Evgeni Zhukovski, someone he had not seen in many years. And he had a very, very troubled mind. He put on a plain white robe for the admiral's benefit.

"Come," he said as he turned toward the door.

He heard the electronic buzz as the security lock was released, and Zhukovski quickly pushed through with his good hand.

"Welcome, admiral," Reza said, taking Zhukovski's hand. "This is a pleasant surprise."

"I wish I could say same, Reza," Zhukovski said sadly. "You as man condemned does not appeal to me. Counselor Braddock has told me of your situation. I wish there were something I could do. I am sorry."

Reza nodded. Zhukovski understood him.

"I know this is unfair, Reza," Zhukovski went on as the two of them sat at the tiny table in Reza's room, "but something has come up, and I find I must ask your help."

"I will try," Reza told him.

The admiral nodded, and over the next few minutes explained what he and Admiral L'Houillier had discussed the previous night.

After he had finished, Zhukovski said, "Well, how do you think?"

Remaining silent, Reza stood up and walked to the armored window that looked out over a tree-filled courtyard. It was also backed with an invisible force field. While he was still technically a patient, he was very much a prisoner, at least in the minds of his keepers.

"Something has gone wrong with the Ascension," he said quietly, his fists clenching at his sides to keep them from trembling with anxiety. "The Empress is in distress."

"What does that mean?" Zhukovski asked. "Is she sick? Dying?"

Reza shook his head. "It is not so simple as that," he told him. He had never spoken to anyone of the Empire, save for what he had told Nicole and Jodi. But now, after hearing what Zhukovski had told him, he felt the old admiral had a right to understand. "The Empress is really two entities, one of flesh, the other of spirit. Her body is that of a warrior who is determined in life to be the vessel for Her spirit. When the reigning Empress is near death, the Ascension takes place, and the spirit is passed from the old Empress – whose body then dies – to the chosen vessel. That process has not been interrupted in over one-hundred thousand Standard years... until now."

Zhukovski was shocked not so much by the event itself, but by the longevity of the unbroken chain. *One-hundred thousand years*, he thought to himself with amazement. So long ago, early humans had not even scrawled primitive paintings upon the walls of their caves, and these aliens already had a global, perhaps even interstellar, empire. "What could have caused this?"

"I cannot be sure, but it must have something to do with what took place on Erlang. You see, there is another, a third entity, that of the First Empress, whose spirit fled to what you might call Purgatory many, many centuries ago. It was said in legend that someday Her spirit would return to us; that, joined with the reigning Empress, She would grace Her Children with the ancient powers which had for so long been lost to us." He turned back to Zhukovski, a look of genuine fear on his face. "She has returned. I know this to be true. But something has gone wrong."

Zhukovski did not know what to make of Reza's explanation, Kreelan religion holding little interest for him, and the rest sounding like fantasy from ancient legends. He was interested only in its effects. "Is this why they fight so poorly?" he asked. "They are... preoccupied with these events?"

"'Preoccupied' is hardly the word, admiral," Reza told him, fighting the nausea that rose from his stomach. *Esah-Zhurah*, he wanted to cry out, *what has happened?* "The will of the Empress is their will, their motivation, their reason for existence. They are not telepathic as you might understand it, but there is a psychic bond that links every heart in the Empire together unless, as in my case, it is intentionally severed by Her hand. If the Empress is in distress... if the vessel of Her spirit has died prematurely... they will not know what to do. They will be lost." With difficulty, he managed to find the chair opposite Zhukovski, slumping into it like a dying man.

It was difficult for even Zhukovski's natural cynicism to stifle his growing excitement. "If what you say is true, now could be our opportunity. If we struck at them, at their homeworld..." He slammed his fist against the table. "But we do not know where to strike! We know where their ships are gathering, which must be around their homeworld, but our information is not yet accurate enough."

"Do not ask me to help you find the Homeworld, admiral," Reza told him, his voice no more than a hoarse whisper. "For even if I knew how to guide you there, I would not."

Zhukovski shook his head. "I would never ask you such a thing, Reza," he said apologetically, alarmed at how old Reza suddenly looked, how tired.

How afraid. "I am sorry that you are caught between humans and Kreelans like deer between charging tigers. I do not envy you. But as human, I can only hope worst for your people, that your Empress is dead, that they will be helpless before us for just this once."

Reza nodded sadly, his fingers caressing the eyestone on his collar, on which was engraved the rune of the Desh-Ka. He bit back the tears that burned his eyes, for he knew how uncomfortable it would make his guest, bearer of bad tidings though he was. "Please do not wish Her dead," he whispered. "Wish the Empire all the ill will your heart may conceive, but do not wish my Empress dead."

Zhukovski leaned back in his chair. "Reza, I know Empress is leader of your religion and government, as it were, but—"

"She is also my wife," Reza rasped, his green eyes burning with fearful longing. "She was to ascend to the throne. If the Empress lies dead, so, too, does she."

The admiral felt a sudden pang of shame and guilt for his words. "I am sorry, Reza," he said sincerely. "I... I did not know. Please, forgive me."

Reza nodded slowly, his eyes falling closed, his mind turning inward to wonder about Esah-Zhurah's fate, his heart calling out to her. In vain.

Evgeni Zhukovski laid his hand on Reza's shoulder for a moment before he got up and left the room, quietly closing the door behind him.

* * *

Nicole awoke from her nap with a start. Her chest felt as if it was being held in a giant vice, making her heart thunder in her ears and her lungs heave against air that had suddenly become as thick as water. She was not in physical pain, but she sensed a hurt far deeper than any lance could make, an echo in her brain from someone calling her from far away.

"Reza," she said aloud.

"Nikki?" she heard from the other room. "Are you okay?" Jodi's concerned face peered through the door.

"*Oui*," she said with more energy than she felt. "I am all right."

Jodi was not convinced. She came in and put her hand on Nicole's forehead. "And I think you're a lying sack of shit. You look terrible."

"Complimentary, as always," Nicole murmured, trying to brush Jodi's hand away. "Please, Jodi, do not pester me."

"Pester, my ass, woman," Jodi said, straightening up. She had been staying with Nicole and Tony while she completed some of the non-resident courses for the Command and General Staff College. She was still on flying status, occasionally going to the Fighter Weapons School for refresher training and to help beat the new crop of fighter jocks into shape for the real thing, but she spent most of her time with Nicole, who was still on medical leave. She knew that Nicole resented someone keeping an eye on her, but that was just too bad. "You just don't know how good you've got it. There are a lot of people who'd pay to have me telling them they're full of shit. Now that I think of it, that's what the Navy does."

"You are impossible," Nicole said, managing a weak smile. "Now, get yourself out of my way. I need to visit Reza."

"Need to?"

Nicole sighed. "I *wish* to. Is that good enough?" Jodi was still frowning. "*Merde*, commander, get out of my way!"

"Aye, aye, ma'am," Jodi saluted as Nicole made her way past her to the bathroom. "Mind if I tag along? Maybe those stupid jarheads guarding him will let me through this time..."

The trip into the city did not take long. Someone from the twentieth century would not have recognized New York City, or any other major city of that time, for a very simple reason: they no longer existed as they once had. Earth had largely been depopulated in the twenty-second and twenty-third centuries through a combination of famine, regional warfare, and then mass exodus soon after interstellar travel had finally been made practicable. It was only after humans had finally begun to explore the worlds in their galaxy up close, discovering just how inhospitable most of them were, that they realized what a priceless treasure their own birthplace had been. In the twenty-fourth century a program was begun to revitalize Earth as something more than a breeding ground for *homo sapiens*. While much of what had been done in centuries past could never be undone, the new caretakers did the best they could, and in their hands Earth had been reborn. Humans still lived here in great numbers, but with swift and clean transportation available to go anywhere on the globe, they were able to widely disperse themselves, minimizing their impact on the again thriving world. The great cities, which had been so instrumental both in humanity's early development and in the catastrophic consumption of its resources, had gradually been dismantled into smaller townships and villages, and much of the land returned to a natural state that had brought back the luster to planet Earth.

The automated shuttle dropped them off at the central entrance to Kennedy Memorial Hospital before speeding off to fetch more passengers. They made their way through the warmly lit corridors and elevators to the penthouse level: the isolation ward.

"Captain," the Marine in charge of the security detachment said politely as Nicole showed him her ID. "I hope you didn't come for a smile, ma'am. He hasn't been very happy since Admiral Zhukovski left this morning."

"Admiral Zhukovski was here?" she asked, looking at Jodi, who only raised her eyebrows. "Do you know what about?"

The Marine, a first lieutenant, laughed. "No, ma'am," he said. "Admirals usually don't confide their business to the likes of us. We're just the hired help around here."

Jodi took the opportunity to thrust her ID forward. The Marine verified with a quick retinal scan that she was who she was supposed to be, then checked his approved visitors list, which was very, very short. "Sorry, commander, but I can't let you in. You're not on my list."

"Oh, come on–"

She shut up as Nicole gestured for her to be silent. "Lieutenant," Nicole said, "Commander Mackenzie is a very close friend of Captain Gard." The Marine started to shake his head, but Nicole persisted. "I know it is against the rules to let her in, but the last time she saw him was in sickbay on board the *Gneisenau* when we all thought he was going to die. I would appreciate it if you would consider letting her in long enough just to greet him. I will vouch for her conduct."

Jodi could see that he was hesitating. "Please," she said. "Just for a minute."

The lieutenant looked at the other five Marines, all enlisted, who made up the guard detail. They were astutely looking in any other direction but at him and the two Navy officers. *Why is it*, he asked himself, *that this always seems to happen on my watch?* "All right," he relented, "but so help me God, commander, if you–"

"I'll be a perfect angel, lieutenant," she said. "I promise."

"All right," he went on, "I'm sure I'll live to regret this. Step into the lock, please." The two women stepped into the security lock that was both a physical safeguard against escape and a scanner that looked for concealed weapons or other contraband. Satisfied, the lieutenant passed them through. "Five minutes," he said pointedly Mackenzie.

She nodded, then opened the inner door.

Reza stood before them, bathed in sweat from the exercises he had been doing to focus his mind. Other than his collar, he was again naked.

"So much for modesty," Jodi said lightly. "At least you know how to greet a girl in style." Without hesitating, Jodi embraced him, sweat and all. "I'm so glad to see you. That you're all right," she said, kissing him on the neck, on the lips.

"And you, my friend," he said, returning her embrace with moderate pressure, his effort rewarded with a light popping sound from her ribcage.

"Your Marine friend out there gave me a few minutes with you," she told him, surprised that his strength had grown so quickly. "Nicole sweet talked him for me. But I can't stay long."

"So true," Colonel Markus Thorella said as he stepped through the security lock. "I just had a little discussion with our Marine lieutenant outside. I don't think he'll be making any other security breaches again for quite some time."

"I take full responsibility for Commander Mackenzie's presence, colonel," Nicole said, cutting toward him like a destroyer. "The lieutenant—"

"Spare me, please, Carré," he snorted. "The lieutenant is my concern, not yours. He was negligent, and he'll pay the price."

Jodi felt the muscles in Reza's back flex like steel springs. With feline grace he separated himself from her embrace. "You should not have come here," he hissed, his blood singing in his veins as he prepared to attack.

"Reza, no!" Nicole shouted as she tried to get between him and Thorella, bracing herself to protect someone she hated so much from someone she so loved.

But she need not have bothered. As Reza's fury peaked, something inside him seemed to break, as if his brain was no longer able to command his body. His eyes wide with surprise, he collapsed in a heap on the floor, completely paralyzed.

"What the fuck did you do to him, Thorella?" Jodi snapped as she knelt next to Reza, feeling for his pulse. It was there, his heart beating rapidly to clear the adrenaline from his system. His eyes were still open, but they stared straight ahead, unblinking. "What did you do?"

"Not a thing, commander," he said, a surprised smile on his face. "And I would remind you not to address me like that ever again. I don't care if you like me or not, but I am a superior officer."

"Then let me say it, Markus," Nicole growled like a leopard, her nose not an inch away from his, "what the fuck did you do?"

"I already told you," Thorella said, obviously pleased with whatever had happened. "While I know you won't believe me, I did absolutely nothing. It just appears to me that your traitorous friend there has not fully recovered. Such a pity."

"Reza, can you hear me?" Jodi said urgently, looking into Reza's glazed eyes. The pupils were dilated wide open. "Nicole, I think you'd better get the doctor in here. There's something—"

As she watched, Reza's pupils suddenly began to contract to something close to normal for the light in the room. He blinked and tried to speak.

"Well," Thorella said merrily, "I do have to leave now. I just wanted to check on our temporary guest, pending his trial and execution." He stepped back toward the door, then turned around as an afterthought. "And Commander Mackenzie, please don't stay more than sixty seconds after this door closes behind me, or I'm afraid I'll have to have you arrested." He smiled, and was gone.

"Nicole–"

"I know, Jodi," she said, kneeling down beside her as Reza began to recover from whatever had happened to him. "You had better do as he says. I will take care of Reza."

"But–"

"Go," she said. "He means it. We can ill afford more trouble now."

Furious, Jodi did as she was told. As she stepped through the outer lock of the holding cell, she noticed the Marine lieutenant standing at stiff attention, eyes boring a hole in the far end of the corridor, staring after the retreating Marine colonel who had just promised to destroy the younger man's life in the military. "Lieutenant," she said to his pale, emotionless face, "I'm terribly sorry. I'll see... I'll see if there's anything I can do..."

He said nothing, did not even acknowledge her presence.

Feeling like a fool and plagued with guilt, Jodi turned and walked away, the sound of her boots on the marble floor echoing hollowly in her ears.

TWO

Commodore Denise Marchand was quietly elated but openly confused. Her tiny scouting squadron, consisting of the heavy cruiser *Furious* – her flagship – and three destroyers, had stumbled upon a much superior Kreelan force of three heavy cruisers forty-three hours earlier. Much to her surprise, the Kreelan ships had not only failed to engage her, but had split up and run without making anything more than half-hearted attempts at defending themselves. Not by nature a cautious sort, Marchand had split her force, sending two destroyers after one cruiser, the *Furious* and the remaining destroyer after another, while temporarily ignoring the third enemy vessel. That was as much prudence as she was able to muster at the time.

In a matter of minutes, the first Kreelan cruiser had been reduced to a flaming hulk by torpedoes from the two pursuing destroyers, which immediately wheeled about to rejoin the flagship and her escort, which were still racing after the second fleeing Kreelan vessel. Not long thereafter, that ship finally came within range of the guns of the pursuing *Furious*, which wasted no time in breaching the enemy's hull with a series of accurately placed salvos. The enemy cruiser exploded in a swirling fireball.

Then Marchand turned her attention to the surviving Kreelan cruiser, which had wisely used the time bought by its companions to try and escape, for now it was completely outnumbered and outgunned.

But this ship, or its commander, was different. While it hardly showed the fearless courage normally shown by Kreelan warships, its captain fired back, keeping both the *Furious* and the darting destroyers from nipping too closely at her heels as she fled deeper into Kreelan space.

Marchand was still wary of some sort of elaborate trap, but that would be totally out of character for the enemy. The Kreelans did not run, nor did they normally play games of cat and mouse. At least, not until now. Besides, she thought, why would anyone sacrifice two cruisers – three, if she caught up to this one – in exchange for a cruiser and three destroyers?

No, she told herself, this was something else, and it fit with the recent intelligence reports of sharply decreased resistance on the part of Kreelan forces everywhere.

"Commodore," the flag communications officer reported, "we have an answer from Fleet."

Eager to see what headquarters had to say in response to her request to follow the enemy cruiser into what was, except for the silent scoutship patrols, unknown space to human ships, Marchand called up the message on her console: *Pursue enemy at own discretion. No supporting forces available. Godspeed.*

It was just what she wanted to hear. She had been in the Navy – and had survived – for nearly twenty years. She was tired of always being on the run, turning her stern to run away from what always seemed to be a superior enemy force, or rushing to save some colony from destruction, only to arrive a little too late. While her squadron hardly constituted a major battle fleet, they were good ships with good crews, and this time she was determined to take the fight to the enemy.

"Captain Hezerah," she asked of the *Furious's* captain, "what's the range to target?"

"One-hundred fifty thousand kilometers and steady," he said instantly. "Zero closure rate." At flank speed, the human squadron was making only enough speed to keep up with the Kreelan, not enough to overtake her. "Commodore," he said quietly, "we won't be able to keep this up much longer. *Tai Mo Shan's* main drive is near the breaking point, and our own core passed the red line three hours ago. If we don't slow down soon, we may never get home."

Marchand frowned. She had known this was the case since *Hotspur*, one of the other destroyers, had blown a deridium converter over twelve hours before. Somehow, her engineers had kept her going, but that would not last for much longer.

She looked at the red icon that was the Kreelan ship they were hunting, wondering for the thousandth time why it had not jumped into hyperspace. The only reason she could imagine was that there was something wrong with the enemy ship's hyperdrive. For the pursuing human squadron, that was both a blessing and a curse. Had the ship jumped, Marchand would have been forced to turn back. It was impossible to actively track a ship in hyperspace, and this entire area of space was uncharted. Marchand could not afford a jump that might drop her squadron back into normal space in the center of a star. On the other hand, drawn out, high-speed chases through normal space were hard on ships and their crews. And in

Marchand's grim estimation, any ship losing its main drive this far into enemy territory would have to be written off the naval registry as another casualty, for they could hardly expect to return home.

"We're so close," she whispered angrily through her teeth. "Are they still headed for that nebular formation?"

"Yes, ma'am," Captain Hezerah replied uneasily. "Right for it." In all his years in the service, he had seen nothing quite like it. Like a giant fog bank in space, or some gigantic ball of wispy cotton, it hung before the racing ships like a siren's lair on the seas of old. Much sensor probing and more discussion had not given them any more understanding of it than that it appeared to exist; it was real. He dearly would like to chalk up the remaining cruiser to the squadron's score, but there was something unsettling about the cloud toward which they were heading, something unnatural that sent a shiver up his spine. He silently wished that Marchand would call an end to the chase. He did not want to take *Furious* in there.

In the main viewer there was a sudden flare where the Kreelan ship – otherwise invisible to direct observation – raced in front of them.

"Captain!" shouted the chief gunnery officer. "Looks like they had a core breach! She's losing way!"

"Thank the Lord of All," Hezerah breathed. "How long till she comes in range?"

"If their projected deceleration curve holds up, thirteen minutes, sir," the navigator replied.

"Will she have reached the nebula?" Marchand asked quickly, her eyes fixed on the little red icon in the holo display that was now ever so slowly losing ground to her own pursuing hounds.

"On the current velocity curve, she'll come within about three-hundred thousand kilometers of it by the time we're in range."

"Close," Hezerah muttered.

"Order the destroyers to flank her at their best speed," Marchand ordered her operations officer. The destroyers could make slightly better speed than the larger cruiser, and Marchand felt it worth the risk of pushing their drives past their already strained limits. "They are not to get within range, just keep her penned in. I don't want her to get away from us now. Captain," she said to Hezerah, "you are to commence firing as soon as we are in range."

"Aye, aye, commodore," he said. Anything to keep from having to go into that so-called nebula, he thought.

The minutes crept by as the human squadron, the destroyers now pulling ahead and slightly to the side, gained on the fleeing Kreelan ship.

The human sensors recorded the debris the enemy cruiser left behind, silent mementos of the explosion that destroyed enough of her drive capacity to leave her far too slow to escape, to make it into the looming mist. It reminded the humans of how easily they could become marooned in this strange area of space.

Marchand watched with barely contained impatience as the main battery range rings on the holo display slowly converged on the enemy ship. At last they overtook the fleeing prey, flashing a set of gunnery data that was echoed throughout the ship's weapons stations.

"In range, captain," reported the gunnery officer.

"Commence firing!"

The lights on the bridge dimmed to combat red as the energy buffers of the main guns siphoned off all available power that was not used by either the ship's drives or her shields. Seconds later, the energy was discharged into space in the form of a dozen crimson blasts from the cruiser's main forward batteries, stabbing out toward the ever-slowing enemy ship.

"Three direct hits," the gunnery spotter reported. She need not have; the extra long range and precise resolution of her special instruments were not required in this case. The Kreelan ship had long since come into view on the main screen at a medium magnification, and the hits were plainly visible.

"Fire!"

Again the main batteries fired, and it was obvious that the gunnery section had found the Kreelan cruiser's range. Every crimson lance hit home, flaying the enemy ship's vulnerable stern into flaming wreckage. The stricken ship began to yaw off course, a secondary explosion setting her tumbling about her long axis. A sudden flurry of shooting erupted from turrets along her battered hull as the human ships came into their line of fire, but the firing was erratic, poorly aimed. She posed no threat.

"Fire!"

The third salvo blasted the cruiser amidships, breaking her back. The stern section, two of the six drives still burning bright with power, broke free of the shattered midsection to drift uncontrollably until it exploded in a fierce fireball. The sleek bow section, still resplendent with the runes with which all Kreelan ships were decorated, tumbled end over end, trailing incandescent streamers that were the ship's burning entrails.

Captain Hezerah was about to order the *coup de grace* when the chief gunnery officer spoke up. "New contact! Looks like a small cutter or lifeboat separating from the bow section."

"What the devil?" Marchand asked, watching on the viewer as the tiny ship separated from the twisted wreckage of the cruiser. It wasted no time, heading straight toward the nebula at flank speed.

"Commodore?" Hezerah asked, waiting for her instructions. The guns were trained on the cruiser, waiting to finish her off. The escaping cutter was another matter. Unless they took it under fire right away, it had every chance of making it into the nebula.

Marchand had no time to consider. Something strange was afoot, and she was determined to get to the bottom of it. "Captain, you may finish off the cruiser," she told Hezerah shortly. Turning to her operations officer, she ordered, "Have *Zulu* intercept the lifeboat, or whatever it is. She is not, repeat not, to open fire on it. I want it – and whoever might be on board – in one piece if at all possible."

"Aye, ma'am." The man turned away and quickly relayed her orders. Like a greyhound on the scent of a rabbit, the destroyer *Zulu* hauled her bows away from the dying cruiser to pursue the much smaller prey.

But as the *Furious* quickly finished off the remains of the Kreelan ship, it became clear that *Zulu* would not be able to get close enough to the escaping lifeboat to fix her with a tractor beam.

"Dammit," Marchand hissed *Nothing could ever be easy,* she thought acidly, *or even just difficult but straightforward.* More and more, she wanted that ship, and whoever or whatever was on it.

It suddenly had become an imperative for her, an obsession. It was a hope for explaining the strange twists of fate that had brought them farther than any humans had ever been into this sector.

To the flag operations officer she said, "Tell *Zulu* to maintain contact and continue to close, if possible."

"They're to proceed into the nebula, ma'am?" he asked, his eyebrows raised. Their sensors had not been able to penetrate the milky whiteness, the likes of which no one had ever seen before. They would be running blind.

"Negative," Marchand sighed. She was well aware of the dangers, and was not about to risk one of her ships in there. She had another idea. "She is to proceed to the mist's edge only. And have the other destroyers patrol around the nebula. I don't want us to be surprised from the far side. Captain Hezerah."

"Ma'am?"

"Take your ship to the mist's edge," she told him. "And have the Marine detachment commander report to me immediately in my ready room. I have some work for them to do."

As he carried out her orders, Hezerah silently thanked the gods that he would not have to go in there.

He also said a silent prayer for the Marines who would.

* * *

"This stinks," Eustus muttered as he stared at the unbroken whiteness that was all either he or the pilots of the ship's cutter could see. He'd never seen or heard of anything like it in space. It wasn't a nebula, which was a lot denser than normal space, but nothing remotely like this. It was like flying through a cloud in atmosphere, with noticeable resistance against the vessel's screens and hull.

"Tell me about it, Top," the pilot in command, an ensign on his first tour, replied. "Talk about flying by the seat of your pants." None of the instruments that were normally keyed to the universe beyond the small hull were showing anything, the mist effectively isolating them from any points of reference except what the ship carried on board. The pilot knew only his relative velocity, distance, and bearing from *Furious* since the time they had launched. And if there were a gravity well in here – a planet or dwarf star, for instance – even the ship's inertial readings would be rendered useless and they could find themselves completely lost. After they had entered the mist in pursuit of the Kreelan boat, they had quickly lost all contact with the *Furious* and the destroyers. He had no idea at all what was in the space around them except where they had just passed, which by definition was empty, relatively speaking. "There could be a frigging planet hiding in here and we wouldn't know until we hit it."

"Yeah, well, maybe that's the idea, ensign," Eustus replied. "And maybe there *is* a planet in here somewhere."

"That makes me feel a whole lot better," the ensign answered nervously. He was a good pilot, but this was the first time in his short career that he had piloted a boat entirely on manual. For once, he was happy that the cutter had such a big forward viewport, for all the other times he had complained about it being too much of a distraction. "At least I don't have to do anything more than play taxi driver," he went on. "You jarheads are the ones who get to play touchy-feely if we find something. Providing, of course, that we don't smash ourselves into whatever it is first."

Eustus grunted agreement, thinking back over the turn of events that had landed him here. Three months after they had returned from Erlang, Eustus had been ordered back to fleet duty, never having seen Reza recover from his coma. Assigned to another of the Red Legion's battalions, his company had been parceled out to Marchand's "Roving Raiders" as they were sometimes known, and he had been sitting aboard the *Furious* with the rest of his troops for the last few months, waiting for action that never seemed to come.

Until now, he mused silently. And not only was this one of the most hare-brained and dangerous schemes he had ever been part of, but he had the dubious honor of having to take charge of it. Captain Dittmer, the company commander, had been seriously injured four days before when her pistol discharged while she was cleaning it. While Eustus had never had anything against Dittmer and had gotten along well with the woman, her level of tactical proficiency had never been demonstrated until then, and Eustus and the others who had seen combat had not exactly been impressed. While technically Eustus was outranked by the four platoon leaders (the company did not have an executive officer replacement yet), all of them were "ninety-day wonders" straight from Officer Candidate School, and none had any combat experience. In light of those facts, Commodore Marchand had made him a brevet captain and put him in charge of the company for this grand, suicidal tour.

Without thinking, he touched the locket that Enya had given him, that now hung around his neck. As wearing any kind of jewelry while in duty uniform was completely against regulations, he kept it hidden just below the neckline of his tunic, taped to his dog tags. *At least she's safe at home*, he thought. She had returned to Erlang to help her people rebuild, and had promised to wait for him, to have a home ready for the two of them. If Reza's word were true, as Eustus had always believed it would be, the Kreelans would never again bother Erlang.

He turned to look down the length of the cutter's passenger compartment, now in its modified configuration as a troopship. Since the commodore was only willing (thankfully, Eustus thought) to risk one cutter on this mission, Eustus had been forced to leave half his company behind. Worse, the two platoons now crammed into the cutter had hard vacuum gear but none of the powerful space armor like Eustus and Reza had trained with at Quantico so many years ago. He bit the inside of his lip as his eyes swept across the anxious faces of his people. If they ran into anything bigger than a bunch of rock-throwing, blue-skinned female neanderthals, he thought, they were in big, big trouble.

"Tai," said the copilot, a female petty officer, to the pilot, "check this out."

Not able to keep himself from butting in, Eustus said, "What is it?"

The pilot shook his head. "Don't know. Looks like a partial signal return from somewhere ahead."

"The lifeboat?"

"No," the copilot said decisively as she studied the signal. "The signal's too scattered. If it's hitting anything, it's got to be pretty big."

"Like how big?" Eustus asked, peering at the multicolored lines wiggling across her sensor display, unable to make sense of it.

"Like that big," the pilot said quietly.

As if they were emerging from an ocean fog bank, the clinging white tendrils that had surrounded the cutter for the last few hours suddenly dissipated: before them lay a planet, basking in the radiance of the surrounding globe of mist.

The pilot's eyebrows shot up at what the sensors were telling him. "This thing has an atmosphere that looks like it should be breathable," he said wonderingly. "One point two standard gees, oceans, cloud formations, the whole nine yards. All that, and no sun to warm the place. Maybe the mist does it somehow."

"Jesus," Eustus whispered, wondering if somehow the Kreelans had engineered this. "How could this be?"

"Beats me," the copilot said shortly, "but there's our friend." The lifeboat was clearly visible on the sensor display, which now was functioning normally within the confines of the hollowed out sphere within the mist. "Looks like they suffered some damage clearing their ship," she went on as she worked the instruments. "Scorch marks and some dents along her hull. Stabilizers look like they've been smashed up pretty good."

"Can we catch them?"

The pilot shook his head as he took in the information that was now flooding onto the viewscreen, which was really a massive head-up display showing flight and combat information provided by the ship's computer. "They'll make the surface first, but we'll be right behind them. From the size of the boat, there can't be more than a few blues aboard."

That was the least of Eustus's worries. "What about on the planet? Can you read anything?"

The copilot shook her head, frowning. "Nothing in orbit, no ships or satellites at all, anywhere in here. On the surface, I can make out what looks like non-natural structures. But there aren't any indications of habitation: no hot spots, no movement. Nothing. Looks like a damned ghost planet."

"Then why the hell were they so intent on getting here?" Eustus asked himself aloud. "What could they have hoped to gain?"

The pilot shrugged. "Maybe it wasn't always this way," he said, speculating. "Maybe they thought there would be some help here."

"And everybody just vanished?" the copilot snorted. "Come on, this is the Kreelans we're talking about here."

"True," Eustus said, "but something really weird's going on, been going on. Think about it: first, three heavy cruisers act like destroyer bait. Then they launch a lifeboat under fire – something I've never heard of, even in the tall tales you hear in the bars. And then they – whoever *they* are – head for what looks like a completely abandoned planet in the middle of whatever the hell this white stuff is." He shook his head. "As much as I hate being in here, I think the commodore may be right. There's something, or someone, in that boat that we need to know about."

"Well," the pilot said, "in about four and a half minutes you're going to get a chance to do exactly that." He glanced up at Eustus. "Better strap in, Top."

"Roger," Eustus said, quickly taking his seat – a flimsy affair compared to what the Marines' regular dropships had – and buckling in. A minute later, he and his troops all had their helmets on, weapons checked, and were ready to go.

"Stand by," the pilot announced over the intercom channel. "One minute."

Eustus could feel the slight perturbations in the ship's gravity controls as they balanced the internal artificial gravity against the rapidly increasing natural gravity of the planet. The scientists said that it was impossible to feel anything like that, because the equipment was so sensitive and sophisticated that it damped out the tiniest flutter. But Eustus could feel it, no matter what the scientists said.

"The enemy boat's down," the copilot reported. "I've got two targets moving away from it toward one of the structures, looks like an opening to a subterranean tunnel... Damn, lost them. Looks like you get to play hide and seek."

"Gee, thanks," Eustus replied sarcastically over their private channel. He did not need his troops to hear the very real fear in his voice. Following Kreelans into a tunnel on what looked like the only indigenous Kreelan world humans had ever discovered, knowing nothing about this place or whom they were chasing, was not Eustus's idea of fun, even without the creepy mist they'd flown through.

"Ten seconds," announced the pilot tensely as he guided the cutter as close as he dared to the yawning archway through which the escaping Kreelans had disappeared. "Ready... we're down! Disembark!"

The cargo doors on each side of the cutter hissed open, and Marines poured from the ship to take up a security perimeter. Eustus leaped from the forward passenger door, a tight squeeze with his armor and weapons, but landed lightly for someone so heavily loaded with gear.

As the last Marine jumped from the hold, the doors slid shut and the ship pulled away from the ground with a bone-tingling thrum. A few seconds later it was circling overhead, its two twin pulse guns snuffling the air and ground for targets.

Eustus quickly surveyed his surroundings. They had landed in what looked like a huge, open plaza. It was not earth under his feet, but intricately sculpted tiles that seemed soft and pliant, not at all like the stone they appeared to be. All around them was what looked like a great terrace, climbing in massive steps to reach dozens of meters into the sky. Each level was decorated with runes and symbols that meant nothing to him, but that – had he had the time to marvel – he could not but help find intrinsically beautiful. Above them, strangely, the sky had a slight magenta hue, and well hid the featureless white of the strange mist that surrounded the planet and mysteriously gave it light and warmth.

In front of them was a great stone arch that Eustus instinctively knew must have been built before humans had discovered fire. *How tiny we are in the scheme of things*, he thought suddenly, momentarily overwhelmed by these constructs of a people who had been plying the stars long before a human hand had ever put down the first words on a clay tablet. *How insignificant, how mortal we are, and yet we are here, perhaps at the mouth of a temple built to alien gods.* Perhaps this was where the throne of the Empress stood, or maybe this was where the pulsating crystal heart had been taken. Perhaps...

"The Kreelan boat's empty, Top," Grierson, the First Platoon leader, reported.

With a twinge of regret, Eustus called his attention back to the here and now. There was work to do. "Okay," he said. "Schoemann, leave a squad back here to cover our ass. The rest of us get to check out the tunnel of love here. First Platoon's got point."

The two platoon leaders, while inexperienced, were not hesitant or incompetent. With a minimum of orders and in short order the two platoons were moving into the mouth of the tunnel, with a small but potent force left behind to guard their avenue of escape.

"I hate underground work," someone grumbled on the common channel.

"Stop bitching," Eustus snapped, his skin prickling as they worked their way in. "Keep your links clear unless you've got something to report."

The floor, the rounded walls and ceiling, were covered with runes like the great terrace outside. While he could not say exactly how, he was sure there was some kind of purpose to them; they were not random or just for aesthetics. In the illumination, which itself seemed to come from within the walls, as if the surface of the stone gave off its own light, the lines of runes twisted and turned elegantly, precisely, reminding Eustus of a sculpted tree he had seen once. A bonsai, it was called, he remembered.

Trees, he thought. *Trees...*

"Of course," he said aloud as the realization struck him. "Trees. Family trees." Raising a closed fist as a signal for his troops to halt, he knelt down to the floor. His suit light gave him a better look at the writing in the stone that seemed never to have worn, despite the sense of ages having passed since this place was built. He could not read the runes, but he could see how some of the characters repeated in the entries of a branch, much like names or parts of names of predecessors given to the newborn to carry on a tradition that had begun thousands of generations before. He noted where some branches ended, the last of the line having died, perhaps in some battle along a distant frontier, or against humans.

But there was one thing that struck him as terribly odd. All the entries in a branch seemed to have only a single root name, not two, as there would have been in any human genealogy for the mother and father of a child. All the names here, if that is really what they were, were of females, he realized, the mothers and daughters. All the countless sons that had been born in the time of these engraved scrolls must have lived and died only to preserve their race, for no record had been kept of their passing.

"Top?" Grierson asked tightly. "You okay?"

"Yeah," Eustus said slowly. "Yeah. Let's move out."

They moved cautiously up the great tunnel in time that was measured in the harsh breathing and rapidly beating hearts of forty-six humans in a decidedly alien place.

"I've got something!" the Marine on point called. She was carrying a tracking device that was occasionally known to work, and now it was telling her that someone – or something – had passed this way not long before. "Heat trace on the wall." She examined it carefully, not sure what she was seeing. "Looks like a hand print."

"Well," Eustus said, "we seem to be going in the right direction. Let's step it up a bit. We can't afford to let them get away now."

Moving now at a trot, the Marines hastened through the great tunnel as it burrowed deeper into the earth and then leveled out. Eustus was struck by a sense of déjà vu, remembering the tunnel that had led him and Enya to the crystal heart.

"Hold up!" the point Marine reported softly.

"What is it?" Grierson demanded.

"We've got an intersection," she reported from her position, well forward of the others. She was the sacrificial lamb on this outing. Two other Marines followed behind her at an interval of a few dozen meters to report if anything untoward happened to her, hopefully in time for the main group behind them to react to the threat. "Another tunnel, same size as this one, crossing at a ninety-degree angle. Looks like more of the same in both directions. I don't have a read on anything from the tracker. Cold scent."

Eustus had been afraid of that. "Grierson, I'll take your third squad ahead. You take the left tunnel with the rest of your platoon," he ordered. "Schoemann, you take the right tunnel. Try to keep from splitting up any more than you have to, and let's just hope that our communications don't get screwed up any more than they are already." They could just barely read the squad that had been left outside. "Hurry people, we've got to catch these ladies."

Quickly the Marines split into three groups and started down the tunnels. Eustus hoped for a break soon, or they were sure to lose their quarry.

He did not have long to wait.

"Top!" the new Marine on point called excitedly. "I've got a trail! There's blood on the floor up here!"

"Keep your eyes open!" Eustus ordered sharply as he and the others moved at a run toward the corporal who was standing in the corridor ahead of them, barely visible at this distance. "Grierson! Schoemann! Get back here on the double!" he ordered over the company net.

Eustus, who now led the squad of charging Marines, could see the corporal kneeling on the floor, his weapon trained ahead of him. Hearing the approach of the reinforcements, he turned his head toward them.

That was when Eustus saw the shadow detach itself from the wall where the tunnel bent to the right. Even at this distance he could see it for what it was: a Kreelan warrior.

"Down!" he screamed into his helmet even as he raised his rifle, his finger already pulling the trigger. "Get down!"

The young Marine reacted instantly, diving for the floor as he rolled and fired down the tunnel, but it was an instant too late. Even as the Marines began to pour a volley of blue and red energy bolts toward their enemy, the shrekka that howled from the dark warrior cut across the corporal's chest, opening his heart and lungs to the cool air.

Eustus dived for the stricken Marine just as a second shrekka swept in from the chaos a split second after the first, slicing deeply into his upper thigh. The shrekka's blades were so sharp that, at first, he felt no pain. He hit the ground hard, one hand pressing against his leg, the other vainly trying to aim his rifle.

But what caught his attention was the apparition that clattered past him, right for the Marines who knelt and lay behind him, firing into the smoke and dust-filled tunnel to cover him and their fallen comrade. Freed and given the gift of motion by the cutting blades of the first shrekka, the dead corporal's munitions bandoleer and its six grenades skittered along the floor. As if looking at it through a microscope, Eustus could see that one of the grenades had somehow been armed.

"Grenade!" he screamed, throwing himself to the far side of the corporal's body in the forlorn hope that his still warm flesh might provide some protection to his own body.

The other Marines gaped at the deadly bundle that came to a jarring halt in their midst.

The armed grenade exploded, setting off the other five. Fire and thunder filled the tunnel just before it collapsed, burying the shattered corpses the blast had left behind.

* * *

The first thing Eustus noticed was the smell of blood. He wrinkled his nose and was rewarded with the rupture of the brittle crust of coagulated blood on his cheek that released a fresh flow down the side of his numbed face. He opened his eyes, unsure what he would see, and not sure if he wanted to see it. He knew there would be a lot more blood pouring out of his body than the little trickle from his cheek. There must be.

But, while he ached like hell and was completely deaf, he had suffered no major injuries except for the gash in his leg left by the second shrekka, and blood oozed slowly from the wound as it throbbed with pain. With trembling arms he pushed himself up onto his elbows, shedding dust and rocks like a sand crab emerging from a windswept beach. He looked from side to side, but the faceplate of his helmet, while more or less intact, was opaque with dust and a spider web of cracks. Reluctantly, with fingers like lifeless sausages, he undid the bindings, letting it fall from his head to the rock-strewn floor with a clatter that he felt more than heard.

The light that had glowed from the walls did so now with only a fraction of its former power, which, when he saw what he had been lying in, was probably for the best. Willing himself to hold back the nausea that fought to overcome him, he rolled out of what was left of the corporal who had been the first among them to die. But even in death, he had managed to help save another Marine's life, miraculously absorbing much of the explosive force of the grenades.

Of the others, there was no sign. The tunnel had collapsed completely behind him, burying anyone else who might possibly have survived the explosion. Worse, there was no way for him to contact the platoon leaders: his comm link, as with everything else except the blaster at his hip and the knife strapped to his leg, had been smashed into useless junk.

Pulling himself unsteadily to the support of the tunnel wall, Eustus sat down, legs straight out, and took a look at the gash in his thigh. If he could keep it from bleeding too much more, he might be all right. Although it was deep, it was still only a flesh wound, having severed no major veins or arteries. He opened his first aid kit and rummaged around for the only thing left that was not bent or crushed: a tube of liquid bandage. Ripping the cloth of his uniform from around the wound, he brushed the dirt from it as best he could before squirting some of the gray paste into and around the gash, noting how lucky he was that the shrekka had not simply taken off his entire leg. The patch job was not going to win any medical awards, he admitted, but it should keep him together until he could get out of here.

And that, he thought dejectedly, was not going to be an easy feat. Knowing that he would probably need it again, he put the bandage tube into one of his cargo pockets.

"Well," he said to himself, his own voice barely audible through a persistent ringing in his ears, "I guess I'd better get moving." He had no illusions about digging his way through the tons of rock and debris behind him, and he had serious doubts about any survivors out there being able to dig through to him. They had no heavy equipment, no blasting charges (*I think we've had enough of that*, he thought darkly), and – most importantly – no time. While Commodore Marchand had been keen on catching the survivors from the Kreelan cruiser, she was loath to have her squadron stay here for too long. The Marines had been given exactly twenty-four hours to conduct their business and return before the Roving Raiders roved on without them. He also had to hope that the other Marines and the Navy boat crew would wait until the last minute in the hope that someone from in here would make it back out. But they could not wait forever, and Eustus had no idea how long he had been unconscious. If he was going to get out of here, he was going to have to find another way to the surface. And quickly.

Shedding the burden of his horribly abused armor and other now-useless gear, Eustus gathered himself up and began shuffling deeper into the corridor, toward where the Kreelan had launched her attack. He held his blaster at the ready, but felt vaguely ridiculous in doing so. His aim was so unsteady that he would be lucky not to shoot himself if he had to fire, and there was no way to tell if the weapon would still work without testing it. And that would give away his position for sure if his enemy were still about.

Slowly, painfully, he worked his way through the shambles of the once-beautiful tunnel, peering through the gloom toward its fateful bend.

As he got closer, he lowered his pistol. The Kreelan's shrekka was not the only weapon to wreak havoc in the passageway. The fusillade from the doomed Marines' guns had collapsed this section of the tunnel, as well. While not completely blocked, it was choked with huge sections of ancient stone that had been blown from their long-held positions in the walls and ceiling, and littered with countless other fragments of black obsidian and cobalt blue inlay.

But he saw no bodies. While it was true that any one of the huge stones could conceal several crushed warriors, he felt uneasy. He raised his pistol again, holding its wavering muzzle before him as he stepped into the maze of fallen slabs. He struggled from rock to rock, clambering up on top of a massive stone, scrabbling across it, and dropping down to the debris-strewn floor before starting the process over again.

After letting himself down from a crazily canted slab, he was sizing up the next climb when he caught movement out of the corner of his eye. Forgetting about his ripped leg as he reached for his holstered blaster, he turned toward the movement and dropped into a crouch. At least, it would have been a crouch had his leg not collapsed under him. Cursing in pain, anger, and fear, he fell into a heap among the sharp shards of stone, cutting himself in a dozen different places. His pistol fell from his grip, clattering to the ground in a puff of dust.

Sitting motionless, helpless, he stared uncomprehendingly at what had startled him: a hand. A huge Kreelan hand, with the biggest set of talons he had ever seen, protruded from the gap formed by the huge slab as it rested on another, smaller chunk of rock. The hand moved, clawing at the rock, as the owner sought to escape from her prison.

"Holy shit," Eustus breathed, able now to hear his own curses beyond the slowly fading ring in his ears. Ignoring the pain in his leg, where blood again seeped from the partially stripped bandage, he moved closer to the hand and the dark aperture leading to the tiny prison of stone. He saw a pair of eyes glowering malevolently at him from a face that was shadowy, indistinct in the dim light. With an angry grunt the Kreelan assaulted the slab, pushing against it with all the leverage she could muster in her cramped position. He watched in awe as the enormous slab lifted as the warrior strained within, rising a few centimeters, then a few centimeters more.

But it was not enough. With a cry of anguish, the warrior gave up and the stone slammed home again, dust shaking from it like tiny flakes of snow. He could hear her harsh and ragged breathing through the persistent buzz in his ears.

He was tempted to just turn and leave her there, to die of thirst and starvation, or perhaps bleed to death if she was injured. But he knew Reza would not have approved. The Kreelan had done no more than her duty, he supposed, whatever that might have been. No, he told himself, it would not cost anything to put her out of her misery quickly. The Kreelans had killed many of his people, for whatever reason, but they had never sought simply to inflict pain on humans, as through torture; that seemed to be reserved for humans to do to themselves.

Turning away from her, he looked for his blaster in the rubble, cursing the fact that all of it appeared black and angularly shaped. He shuffled through the mess, kicking and prodding for his weapon. At last, he saw the stubby pistol, resting next to a smaller slab that had fallen from the wall. As he reached down into the odd bits of chipped stone to retrieve it, his thigh screaming at the effort, his fingers brushed against something soft, something definitely not stone. Curious, he took up the pistol with his other hand and began to brush away at whatever lay beneath the black gravel.

It was the face of a Kreelan child.

"This can't be," he murmured, shaking his head. In all the years that humans had fought the Empire, no one had ever encountered a Kreelan child. They were as mysterious as were the males of the species, of which Eustus had also been one of two humans to ever see, at least in mummified form. He wondered if the light might be playing tricks on him, but as he continued to brush away the dust and chunks of rock, it was clear that it was a child. But the face and shoulders were all he could uncover, for the rest of her body was covered by a fallen slab. It was smaller than the one entombing the adult behind him, but it had been large enough to crush the life from the child. Or had it?

Knowing that he was just wasting his own very limited time and strength, he carefully let himself down beside the child, leaning over her to see if he could see her breathing. He saw a bit of fine dust on her upper lip stir. Again. And again. She was still alive. He put a hand on her forehead and peeled back one of her eyelids. He was not sure what he might see, but he thought it might give him some clue as to how badly she was injured; there was a lot of blood on her face and head. Aside from the irises looking oddly dark and round in this light, he noted nothing that he could make heads or tails of.

"Kar'e nach Shera-Khan?"

He was startled by the plaintive voice that issued from the hole beneath the slab where the warrior was trapped. He had never heard the Kreelan language spoken, even by Reza, and certainly never by an enemy. "What did you say?" he asked, not knowing what else to do.

"*Shera-Khan*," the warrior said, her hand pointing in the girl's direction. "*Kar'e nach ii'la?*"

"She's alive," Eustus said quietly. *My God*, he thought, *what the hell is going on here?* Eustus had learned during his time in the service that you sometimes had to act on instinct. But there were other times when, regardless of how quickly you had to act, even one moment of concentrated thought was crucial. And this was one of those times.

Eustus sat for a moment, pondering this new situation. It did not take him long to come to a conclusion and decide upon a course of action. Commodore Marchand's hunch had been right: there had been something important on that ship – this girl. Eustus did not know why she was important, but the Kreelans, especially the warrior whom he now took to be her protector, had gone to the greatest lengths to keep her alive, despite their present condition of general confusion, which itself remained a mystery.

He had to take her back with him. The only question was how.

"Well," he said, struggling to his feet, "there's only one way to find out." Shuffling to the side of the slab that pinned the girl to the floor, he leaned over and grasped the exposed edge with his battered hands, doing his best not to rip open the wound on his leg.

He pulled. Nothing.

Grimacing, he pulled harder, feeling his muscles and tendons pop and crack with the strain, until the stone just barely moved under his grip.

But that was all. He tried one final time, but it was just too heavy, and he let it settle back into place with a sandy grinding noise. The girl did not cry out, and he thought that perhaps the stone merely pinned her, and had not crushed any of her limbs. But until the stone was removed, there was no way to know for sure.

Panting like a dog, he sat on the slab that had just thumbed its nose at him. "I'm sorry," he apologized to no one in particular, "but that's just a bit... too heavy."

The trapped warrior pointed at him. "*Sh'iamar tan lehtukh*," she said, hammering her hand against the stone that pinned her. She pointed at him again, then gestured with her hand for him to come, then pounded against the rock.

Then she pointed at the girl. "*Shera-Khan.*"

"Yeah," he said. "Sure. If I helped you get out of there, even if we both could move that rock, the first thing you'd do is gut me like a pig." He shook his head. "I don't think so."

The warrior was adamant. "*Shera-Khan!*" she cried. While Eustus knew nothing of their ways and language, he had no doubt that a deep and frightful anguish lay behind the warrior's voice. He knew that her job must have been to protect the girl, to see her safely to wherever they were going, and that she was failing. Had failed. And if he let her out of her confinement, he had no doubt that she would kill him without a second thought and carry on with the girl.

On the other hand, he had come to realize that she might be his only hope of making it home. By his own admittedly unreliable estimate, it had taken over half an hour just for him to hobble down to this part of the tunnel, a distance of less than fifty or so meters, and clamber over a few slabs of rock. At that rate, how long might it be before he finally found his way out of here? Hours? Days? And how long had he been unconscious? Most likely, it would take him more time than the hours the boat would wait for him to return. And the warm stickiness he felt down his right leg told him he was still bleeding, a process that was already exhausting him and, if not stopped, could leave him dead. The bandage helped, but it was just that, a bandage, and not designed to hold up to what he was trying to do. Unfortunately, the more sophisticated medical tools in his first aid kit that could have sealed the wound permanently had been destroyed.

That settles it, then, he thought. "All right," he said, knowing that he was going to regret this. "I'll help you get out of there so you can help the girl." He pointed at himself, then the rock, and nodded, hoping she would understand. "In exchange," he went on, "you help me out of here and back to my ship." He pointed into the darkness and her glowing eyes, then at himself, then upward, toward the surface. He saw her blink, but that was the only acknowledgment he received.

Gritting his teeth at the pain in his thigh, he struggled up from the smaller slab pinning the girl and took the few steps back to where its larger cousin held the warrior trapped. Taking a deep breath, trying to still his mounting apprehension, he stepped within range of her hand. She did nothing. Accepting that as a positive sign, he planted his injured leg on the ground, hoping it would support him long enough to get this over with, and set his other foot against the wall. He gripped the edge of the rock with both hands and said, "Now!"

He pulled against the stone with all his might, his face contorted in a rictus of effort. Nothing was happening.

He was about to give up when he heard a savage cry from beneath him and the stone shuddered, rising upward.

"Push, damn you!" he spat through clenched teeth, pulling with his arms and upper body as his leg pushed against the wall with all the strength he had left. The slab continued to rise up and away from the wall, gaining speed as its center of gravity shifted to their advantage. Suddenly, it was standing on edge, and with a final shove the Kreelan warrior sent it crashing over and onto the floor. Eustus flung himself out of the way to avoid being crushed by its ponderous bulk. He lay on the floor, his lungs burning from the exertion, his leg a mass of pain as he waited for her to come and kill him.

But he waited in vain. Behind him, he heard her groan again, a sound that was followed by the crash of another slab falling to the floor. Rolling over, he saw her kneeling by the child's side, her great hands gently touching the child's face. Beside her lay the stone that she had pulled off of the girl.

He pulled his hand away from where it had been holding his thigh. It was slick with blood. "Damn," he whispered to himself as he was struck with lightheadedness. He waited a moment longer for the Kreelan to do something, and when she did not, he half crawled, half dragged himself to where the girl lay deathly still.

Looking at her small body, he saw that her injuries probably were severe. Her armor was creased and pierced by the shards of rock that had been blasted from the wall and then fell on top of her when the tunnel collapsed, and there was a lot of blood from a number of wounds in her head, chest, and legs. As he had guessed, while the slab that had fallen on her had undoubtedly produced its own injuries, at least it had not crushed her arms or legs, or anything else he could see. She might still live, but she would have to get medical attention fast.

He reached for the tube of liquid bandage in his pocket, eliciting a fierce glare from the warrior, whose muscles visibly tensed. "I'm going to try and help her," he said softly, holding his hands up, one empty, the other with the partially used tube. "This won't do much, but it might help stop some of the bleeding." The Kreelan watched suspiciously as he put some of the gray paste on the girl's head where the skin had been broken. Then he managed to get the woman to help him unfasten the girl's armor, letting him squeeze the bandage into some of the more serious wounds.

"Oh, man," Eustus breathed as he peeled away the tattered black undergarment that he had been accustomed to since basic training when he first saw Reza in one. "She's got some broken ribs," he said softly, being careful with the bandage. "Probably some internal injuries, too. We've got to get her to a doctor." The warrior only stared at him uncomprehendingly. "Isn't there a doctor here? Anybody?" He gestured around them, then at the bandage, then at the girl.

The Kreelan pointed at herself, the girl, then Eustus, then swept her arm around them, then pointed to the three of them again.

"So," Eustus said miserably, "it's just us chickens, I guess." He bit his lip, thinking. "Then we've got to get her to the ship. You've got to help me get her to the ship or she's going to die." He tried to convey the thought through a series of gestures, but the warrior only stared at him. He tried a different set of gesticulations. Nothing. No reaction.

He was about to try something else when she drew out a wicked looking knife that she held over the child's heart. Eustus knew what was about to happen. Unable to save her, she was going to kill the child, and then herself.

"Wait!" he said, grasping her hand and trying to move the knife away. But her hands were huge and powerful, and he might as well have been wrestling with a two hundred-kilo silverback mountain gorilla for all the effect he was having. "Dammit," he hissed angrily at her stubbornness, "I wish Reza was here."

"Reza?" the warrior whispered. "*Reza tu'umeh sameh ka'ash?*"

"You know him?" Eustus asked, shocked. "Reza Gard?"

The woman's eyes closed as she put a hand on her armored breast as if to keep her heart from stopping. The knife fell away from the girl's chest. Eustus watched in shock as she knelt there, her body trembling as if she were crying. She spoke softly, as if saying a prayer, mentioning Reza's name several times.

Suddenly, he understood. "He's not dead," he told her, cursing their inability to communicate. "He... listen." Her eyes remained closed. He grabbed her shoulders and shook her. "Listen! Reza didn't die. Look." He gestured to himself "Reza, right?" Then he took her knife from where it had fallen on the ground, pretending to thrust it into his chest. She turned away as if she had been struck. "Dammit, pay attention to me!" Eustus shouted angrily, shaking her again. She whirled around, ready to strike him, but he ignored her, repeating his enactment of the sword spearing through Reza's armor. He fell over like he was dead and closed his eyes.

Then he opened them again. "He didn't die," he told her again. He pulled himself painfully back up to a sitting position. "He was hurt really bad," he told her. "Look, this is Reza," he set a rock between them. "Reza. Doctors worked on him for a long time." He took the bandage tube and squeezed some of it on the rock. "It took a long time for him to get better, but he recovered." Eustus took the rock and stood it up like a doll, marching it around between them. "He's alive," he told her again. He pointed to her, to himself, then swept his arms around them.

"He's alive right now. Right now."

The light of understanding finally dawned on her. "Reza," she said through trembling lips. Then she pointed to the girl. "Reza."

"No," Eustus said, waving his hands. "She's not Reza. Reza's out there," he pointed upward, "on Earth still."

The warrior's eyes brightened. She pointed upward as Eustus had. "Reza?" she asked hopefully.

Eustus nodded. "Yes. He's on Earth, though, not here, not on the ships up there." He pointed at the girl again. "That's not Reza." He took a guess. "That's Shera-Khan."

The warrior nodded, as if copying his gesture. He did not know that she had learned it many years before from a very young human boy. "Shera-Khan," she repeated. "Reza. *E'la tanocht im.*" She gestured at her loins, and then at Eustus's, and then at the girl. "Esah-Zhurah. Reza. Shera-khan."

Eustus sat back, feeling like someone had slammed him over the head with a club. "She's his daughter," he said numbly. "Esah-Zhurah is her mother and Reza is her father. And Esah-Zhurah almost killed him. Jesus." He looked at the girl, shaking his head in sad wonder. "And he never even knew about her, did he?" On impulse, he reached out and pulled up one of the girl's eyelids again. There had been something strange about the iris, and now, taking a closer look in the dim light, he saw what it was: the child's eyes were green like Reza's, and the pupils were round, totally unlike the cat's eyes of the Kreelans. The "normal" Kreelans, that is. He had not noticed it before, mostly because he had not expected to find anything like that. But now...

"Listen," he said, wishing that she could understand what he was saying, "I can get you to Reza, and to some doctors who might be able to help Shera-Khan, but we've got to hurry. We've got to get to the surface and the ship that's waiting there – I hope – before it leaves." He gestured at the three of them, then upward. "Reza," he said again, pointing up.

He did not need a translator this time. The warrior understood perfectly. With infinite care, she gathered the child in her arms and stood waiting while Eustus staggered to his feet.

"This is really going to suck," he said, mimicking one of his older – and deceased – brothers as he tried his best to follow the warrior down the tunnel. He stumbled after the first few steps. His vision was turning gray as his leg beat at him with lancing pain. He only made half a dozen steps more before he collapsed, exhausted and bleeding.

He could only watch as she returned for him, and he felt himself plucked from the floor as if he were a mere paperweight before she draped him over her shoulder. The floor began to pass by in a blur with the woman's powerful strides, and her rhythm felt to him like waves rolling on the ocean. Eustus closed his eyes.

Darkness.

THREE

Vice Admiral Yolanda Laskowski sat back in her padded armchair, infinitely pleased with herself. It had taken her three times longer than she had originally estimated, but she had found a solution.

No, she corrected herself. She had found *the* solution. Working alone with the battle computer that was her only true friend, the only one she had ever felt she could really trust, she had finally found an answer to Evgeni Zhukovski's "hypothetical" scenario (which she knew quite well was more than hypothetical). The projected outcome, while not exactly a landslide in humanity's favor, nonetheless predicted victory. She had found a way, in theory – and with the help of some very special weapons – that a human fleet might be able to win.

While she had been forced to use a number of unverifiable assumptions in the decision matrix that the computer used to generate the result probabilities, she felt her assumptions were close enough to fit the available data. The Kreelans were in headlong retreat, and were ripe for a full, devastating pursuit.

She stood up and took her place behind the podium at the front of the briefing room.

"First," she began in her briefing to L'Houillier and the senior members of the General Staff, "this scenario is only valid as long as the Kreelan forces do not demonstrate their historical fighting potential. If at any point in the first phase of the operation they regain their will to fight, for lack of a better description, our odds drop to near zero." Heads nodded around the table. No one needed the battle computers to tell them that.

"Second, we must have complete surprise. Even in their present state, their fleet potentially could mass enough firepower to beat back the most determined attack we make. Just in measure of known numbers – and the STARNET figures are almost certainly conservative by a factor of at least fifty percent – the engagement will leave us outnumbered by one point seven to one. Only strategic and tactical surprise can balance out that inequality.

"Third, our commitment has to be total. I input every armed ship either currently afloat or ready to put out of drydock into the attack, giving us a total of two-thousand, eight-hundred, and forty-seven vessels. That includes Navy combat vessels and every armed coast guard and auxiliary ship with hyperlight drive that could be assembled in a forty-eight hour period, using midnight Zulu time tomorrow as H-hour."

She called up the holo image of space that extended from the human-explored Inner Arm sector, inward toward the galactic core. "This," she pointed to a red spheroid that appeared among the star clusters like a malignant tumor in a mass of neurons, "is the zone where the Kreelan fleet is gathering, which the scenario assumes to be the approximate location of their homeworld. As you can see, it has diminished somewhat in size since it was first identified, but we still do not know the precise location of their massing point." She paused, looking at L'Houillier, then Zhukovski. "That is the last, and most crucial, assumption I have had to make: that somehow we will discover that information before our fleet sails."

"I accept your assumptions, admiral," L'Houillier told her, but he was looking at Zhukovski. "As for the last one, we will see what can be done."

The Russian admiral said nothing, but stared impassively at the red corpuscle in the holo display as if he had not heard his superior.

"Please go on," L'Houillier said quietly.

"Sir," Laskowski said, nodding. Their exchange had not gone unnoticed. Zhukovski, her chief rival, was coming under some kind of pressure. Good. "The operation itself is fairly straightforward, with two simultaneous attacks, one in support of the other. The objective of the first attack is to engage and tie down the Kreelan fleet. It is not to destroy the enemy in a decisive manner, but to prevent it from engaging the ships taking part in the second attack. The objective of that effort will be the physical destruction of the Kreelan homeworld or worlds."

Faces among the staff suddenly became deadly serious. "Planet-busting," as it was often called, had always been more of a theoretical issue than a practical one. For one thing, humans had never encountered a Kreelan world. For another, many believed that it could not be done without involving a tremendous number of ships in an extended bombardment.

"A task force of seven ships," Laskowski went on, "will approach the Kreelan system from a different vector than the main body. They will be armed with kryolon and thermium torpedoes."

Laskowski felt an electric thrill run through her body at the mention of the device and the effect it had – stunned silence – on her audience. The kryolon torpedo was nearly a legend, a weapon that had been theoretically perfected years before, but that had never actually been used in anger. It was a star killer that caused a star to go nova, obliterating any orbiting planets. Their existence never confirmed to the populace or the military at large, the few weapons that had actually been constructed had remained in carefully protected secret bunkers on faraway asteroids, a suitable target for them never having been identified.

Until now.

"Three ships will launch their kryolon weapons at the system's primary star," Laskowski went on before anyone could interrupt, "while the others will seek out and attack any inhabited planets or moons in the system with improved thermium torpedoes." Thermium torpedoes had been developed with the help of research done on what was left of Hallmark. While not nearly as cataclysmic as the kryolon weapons, they would destroy the atmosphere of any Kreelan-held worlds. And these weapons had been tested against a real planet, an already-destroyed human colony. In a way, Laskowski thought, the Kreelans had sown the seeds of their own destruction.

She looked around the room. "Any planet attacked with one of these weapons will suffer the loss of its atmosphere, at a minimum. And the kryolon weapons launched into the star will trigger a massive flare that will destroy any units of the Kreelan fleet remaining in-system, as well as any planetary bodies that may have survived or escaped the thermium attacks." She paused dramatically, savoring her moment of triumph. "If all goes well and the intelligence estimates of the Kreelan population in-system are within expected parameters," she glanced significantly at Zhukovski, who pointedly ignored her, "we should be able to destroy most, if not all, of the entire Kreelan race."

Everyone in the room was quiet, considering the significance of her last words. To destroy an entire species was certainly nothing new to Mankind. Humans had eradicated thousands of unique forms of life on Earth and on colony worlds, and had even attempted over the centuries to eliminate some varieties of their own species. But to openly pursue the goal of annihilating an entire sentient race, regardless of the damage and loss of life it had incurred upon humanity, made some people uncomfortable. It hearkened back to the times of "racial purification" and "ethnic cleansing" that had been carried out by despotic powers against other humans in the darker times of Earth's history.

L'Houillier frowned. He wanted the war stopped and human lives saved, but the potential risk of what Laskowski presented was unfathomable. It was not an issue of hypothetical morality regarding the intentional annihilation of another sentient species. That, to L'Houillier, was not a concern in this case: the war must be brought to an end, and if the Kreelan race had to be exterminated, so be it.

But there was the question of repercussions. Who was to say that the ships gathering beyond the Inner Arm were but a token showing of the entire Kreelan fleet? How many colonies did they have beyond their homeworld from which another vengeful campaign of large-scale destruction could be waged against human worlds? The Kreelans, for reasons fully understood only by Reza Gard, did not engage in campaigns of wanton destruction, obliterating entire colonies without at least giving them the chance to fight back; they came looking for a fight for fighting's sake, and the humans had been forced to oblige them. But could they take the chance that the Kreelans would not retaliate in kind if the thermium weapons – let alone the kryolon star killers – were used? They had demonstrated with Hallmark that they could obliterate an entire world, and if those means continued to exist after the Kreelan homeworld was destroyed, Laskowski's plan could open the door to an interstellar Armageddon that would leave every human colony nothing more than a mass of molten rock.

He suddenly remembered Zhukovski's recounting of his conversation with Reza, recalling how long-lived had been the Kreelan civilization. *Over one hundred thousand years since the current Empire's founding*, he thought. And how many of those thousands had they been in space? Or developing weapons, a worthwhile pursuit for a race that thrived on warfare? How many planet-killers might the Kreelans have? And what other hideous weapons of mass destruction might they possess? The thought sent a chill up his spine. Glancing at Zhukovski, L'Houillier could see that his intelligence officer had come to similar conclusions. His perpetual scowl was deeper than usual. He was practically grimacing.

Laskowski was waiting with barely contained excitement for what L'Houillier would say about her plan. She had taken certain defeat and turned it into victory, coming up with a plan that dealt a massive and mortal blow to their enemy. While it was really more a consequence of the weapons she wished to employ than some kind of grand master strategy, the thought that humans could pay the Kreelans back in blood for human lives lost in the century-old war was one that she relished. *Vengeance*, she thought, *would surely be sweet*.

"Admiral?" she asked finally, becoming annoyed at L'Houillier's extended silence.

"It is impressive, Yolanda," he said finally, "and I wish you to pursue detailed planning along this line as a contingency–"

"As a contingency?" she blurted, unable to restrain herself. "Sir, with all due respect, this can give us victory! We have the opportunity here to destroy the Empire! We–"

"And that," L'Houillier said firmly, forcing himself to forgive – this once – her near insubordination, "is why you are to prepare contingency plans for an offensive. However, I think I see potential risks here that you may not have taken into account. For example, what happens to the scenario if there is a significant influx of Kreelan ships into the fray? Or if the target system is protected by automated defenses that do not rely on this 'psychic link,' as Admiral Zhukovski has related to us from Reza Gard, and is therefore not subject to whatever has caused their state of confusion?"

"But sir," she said, shaking her head, "the Kreelans could not possibly have more ships than I calculated into the probability matrix. And as for automated defenses, we've never seen any evidence of–"

"You are not answering my questions, admiral, unless you know for certain the size of the entire Kreelan fleet, which I doubt anyone does," L'Houillier said coldly. "The question, admiral, was, *what if?* That is the purpose for a scenario in the first place, is it not?" Laskowski, belatedly realizing her error in trying to tap-dance around L'Houillier, nodded sheepishly. "I ask you again: what if?"

"The operation would fail, sir," she said quietly.

"Casualties?"

"Depending on when the balance of forces shifted against our fleet, up to ninety-nine percent of the attacking force that had been committed to battle would be lost."

Which would be the entire human fleet, Zhukovski thought bitterly. Every armed vessel that could be gathered together in a forty-eight hour period, as Laskowski had put it.

"Repercussion extrapolation?" L'Houillier asked.

"Based on what little we know of their psychology and motivations, anywhere from fifty to one-hundred percent." Laskowski took a deep breath. She had not expected this... inquisition. "Using the Hallmark case as a benchmark, the matrix yields a minimum of twenty colonies destroyed in toto within six months."

"And what is maximum?" Zhukovski growled.

Laskowski looked at her feet. "All human inhabited domains: planets, moons, asteroids, orbital and deep space stations, and any surviving ships." In other words, the Kreelans were expected to destroy humans anywhere they lived, breathed, and used technology that could be identified and tracked. Any survivors would have to live at not just a pre-atomic level of civilization, but pre-electricity.

"Lord of All," someone whispered.

L'Houillier looked up at her. "I know you were given this task on the side, Yolanda, unofficially," he told her, "and you did an excellent job. But we must have another option. That is your task from me now. Find me that option, one that does not leave the fleet open to destruction and our homeworlds utterly defenseless if something goes wrong, as it inevitably does in such matters."

Making one last try, Laskowski said, "But the negative angles are all at the extremes of the matrix, admiral. I admit that the probabilities are not negligible, but the potential gain is more than worth the risks involved."

"That is not for us to decide," L'Houillier said. "That is for the Council and the president."

"Yes, sir," Laskowski responded tightly. You fool, she thought sullenly. Your only viable option is right in front of you. And if you won't listen to me, I know someone who will.

FOUR

Jodi smelled a rat, and it smelled suspiciously like Markus Thorella.

ACCESS DENIED.

The study cubicle's main screen displayed the words in blood red letters. Those two words had become her constant companions during the last half-hour of her informal – and strictly unauthorized – research.

"Eat me," she murmured, glaring angrily at the terminal. Had she bothered to look at the local time display in the lower right margin of the screen, she would have noticed that almost nine hours had passed since she left the hospital after Thorella's intrusion and Reza's mysterious fainting episode. And that was why she was here. It was just too convenient, she had told herself as she stalked out of the hospital, almost unconsciously heading for the General Staff HQ research center where she had spent most of her waking hours the last few months, studying for her doctorate in applied military theory. Reza was probably the most superb physical specimen the human race had ever known as far as endurance, strength for mass, and sheer toughness. He had only very recently awakened from a coma, true, but that did not seem enough to her to explain the spell that had visited him the moment he demonstrated aggression toward Thorella. And Thorella's own behavior: it was if he had been taunting Reza, deliberately trying to provoke him, to see... what?

"To see if something would work," she had thought aloud to herself as she strode into the building, startling the guard at the entrance. Working on the theory that Thorella was somehow exerting an unnatural influence over Reza, Jodi had begun to dig.

And, hours later, the gems she had found. She glanced down at the tiny storage card that now held all the information she had retrieved in the course of her travels through the center's vast databases. She had not hit the mother lode yet, had not found the answer to her underlying question, but she had discovered a cornucopia of "nice to know" items.

"Know your enemy" was the route she had initially taken in her quest, and Jodi had begun prowling for any information she could find on one Thorella, Markus Gustav.

At first, she had been disappointed. Born into a wealthy Terran industrialist family, Markus Thorella had been an excellent student in his primary and secondary schools, and quickly demonstrated his prowess at team and individual sports, as well. He was never in trouble with the law, attended church regularly with his parents, and even worked frequently as a volunteer, donating his time to a local hospital as an orderly. On the face of it, he looked like every parent's dream: bright, almost brilliant, physically superb, and selflessly dedicated to those around him.

That person, Jodi told herself, was definitely not the same Markus Thorella that they all knew and loved.

Then she found out about the crash. For Markus's fourteenth birthday, his parents took him on a cruise to the Outer Rim, to a group of worlds that had been – for the most part – free of Kreelan attacks over the years, a place where tourism was still a thriving industry. In a freak accident while departing Earth orbit, the starliner had somehow collided with another ship that had been inbound. While such collisions were extremely rare, they did sometimes happen, and when they did, they were disastrous. Over fifteen thousand people lost their lives that day. Only eighty were finally rescued from residual air pockets in the shattered hulls; the collision had occurred so suddenly and unexpectedly that none of the passengers or crew of either vessel had been able to reach a single lifeboat.

One of the survivors had been Markus Thorella, who had been terribly injured. According to a subsequent press account of the incident, the body that bore the clothes of Markus Thorella had been reduced to little more than a pulsating lump of flesh.

And that is where Jodi began to run into dead ends. Curious as to what happened afterward, during his physical reconstruction and therapy, she could get no closer than a hospital record certifying his release more than a year later. Everything in between, everything, was either barred from her or listed as "information unavailable." That is when her unofficial research methods began to pay off. Using an unlocking program she had acquired from a young graduate student eager to impress her (too bad it had to be a guy, she lamented sourly), she began to worm her way through the passages that blocked access to Thorella's past.

The program finally turned the key to the information she wanted, and she was literally deluged with data ranging from Thorella's daily urine tests to the books the nurses read to him during the early phases of his recovery when his eyes were still regenerating in their sockets. While a medical student might have found interest in such things, the only thing she cared about was the DNA fingerprint.

The results, when she found them, did not surprise her as much as she would have liked. According to the official records, the DNA sample could not be firmly identified as belonging to Markus Thorella. The reason, she found out after doing some backtracking through press and a few restricted government files, was because all of Markus Thorella's previous medical records – from his schools, the two hospitals he had visited since he was born, and the Thorella family physician – had mysteriously disappeared. However, since the boy had been in possession of Markus Thorella's identity card and other personal effects when he was found in the starliner's wreckage, everyone assumed he was Markus Thorella. On top of that, no one could positively identify him physically because his entire body – including fingertips and teeth – had been damaged beyond recognition. When the surgeons rebuilt him, they used some old holos that the schools were able to provide. When they were finished, he again looked like Markus Thorella.

But was he? Jodi asked herself. Had the physical and emotional trauma of the crash altered his personality? Or had he always had a sadistic streak that never showed up in any of his early psychological profiles? Or was there something else?

As she followed the history of the "new" Markus Thorella, she discovered that he had become incredibly rich after the death of his parents. Since they had died and he had no surviving family members to contest the estate, he was awarded the entire Thorella inheritance. He was instantly worth hundreds of millions of credits. But in Earth's jurisdiction, he still had to have a legal guardian at that age.

The guardian's name turned out to be Strom Borge. The name rang a bell with her, but she could not quite place it. She knew she had seen or heard that name before, but where?

Running a search, it did not take long to find out. Strom Borge was a Terran Senator to the Confederation, member of the Confederation Council, and chairman of a dozen major committees within the government. The hairs at the back of her neck tingled.

"Now I remember you," she murmured to herself. He had been the leader of the group opposing the confirmation of Reza's citizenship after returning from the Empire, and had been in favor of the radical psychotherapy procedures demanded by Dr. Deliha Rabat, another of Jodi's personal favorites.

But there was something else. She had seen that name earlier this evening, during her research. Running another search on Borge, Strom Anaguay, she excluded all references after the crash and before Markus Thorella was born, limiting the search to the first fourteen or so years of Thorella's life. In but a few seconds, she had her answer.

"Jesus Horatio Christ," she breathed as the information scrolled up on her screen. Borge had been on the starliner with the Thorellas. He had been a friend of the family for some years, or so the records indicated, and he was frequently to be found in their company. Along with his son, Anton Borge.

Twenty minutes more of digging through increasingly compartmented files in the research center's data network for Anton Borge's DNA fingerprint confirmed what she suspected: "Markus Thorella" was Strom Borge's biological son.

She sat back, imagining to herself what must have happened. Borge, an aggressive and ruthless politician, had received the support and friendship of the Thorella family, who themselves had much to gain from Borge's rapidly growing political influence in the defense sector, since the Thorellas owned one of the largest shipbuilding firms on Terra.

But the genial relationship between the parents was not shared by the two boys, who apparently loathed each other. Not surprising, since psychologically Anton Borge was the complete antithesis of the Thorella boy: while they were in fact similar physically, Anton was arrogant and hateful, never failing to make those around him miserable. Arrested on a dozen charges ranging from petty theft to sexual assault against a seven year old boy, he always managed to avoid punishment because of his father's influence.

When the collision occurred, Strom Borge probably acted with his noted ruthlessness to take advantage of the situation. As evidenced by the hospital records, Borge's son must have been hideously injured in the crash. The question then, was what really happened to the Thorellas? Did Emilio and Augusta Thorella die outright, or did Borge murder them? Their bodies were never recovered. And what happened to the real Markus Thorella? If Strom Borge was able to somehow put the Thorella boy's clothes (what was left of them) and his identity card on his own mutilated son, Markus Thorella's body must still have been on the ship and more or less intact. Again, was he already dead, or did Borge kill him, perhaps tossing the body into a blazing compartment on the ship to hide the evidence of his crime?

Another thought nagged at her: how had Borge and his son managed to keep their true relationship a secret? Borge had obviously gone to great lengths to conceal the true identity of "Markus Thorella" by somehow destroying or confiscating all of the Thorella boy's medical records (and, she found out, the records of his parents, too, to prevent any DNA tracing). Not surprisingly, the official investigation into the disappearance of those records ended rapidly and prematurely, no doubt under the shadow of Senator Borge's influence.

But aside from all the possible paper trails that he had deftly covered up, how had his son reacted to suddenly becoming someone else? The boy was certainly old enough to know that he was not Markus Thorella, and all it would have taken was for him to call Borge "Dad" in the wrong company and someone might have become suspicious.

The answer was in a name that Jodi knew all too well: Dr. Deliha Rabat. Jodi reviewed the medical records again. She was looking for some clue as to why no one had suspected that Strom Borge and Markus Thorella were really father and son. Borge's wife wasn't part of the equation, since she had been killed in a Kreelan attack on a colony world not long after Anton was born. But then Jodi discovered that "Markus Thorella" had undergone psychotherapy at the hands of the young and ambitious Dr. Rabat, who treated him for emotional trauma. The reports showed that the newly reconstructed Thorella boy was having delusions that he was actually the son of Strom Borge.

Imagine that, Jodi thought acidly.

While she did not understand all the technobabble in the reports, she did see the effects of Rabat's treatment: the "delusions" rapidly disappeared. In the end, the boy retained all the awful traits of his true self, but came to believe that he was the sole survivor of the Thorella family and heir to all its wealth, and whose best friend in the galaxy was Strom Borge.

Not surprisingly, the young Dr. Rabat soon left the hospital for her own research lab, funded entirely by the Thorella estate and endorsed by Senator Borge, the estate's executor until Markus Thorella's coming of age.

"How very, very convenient," Jodi muttered. She hated Thorella, despised him, but she saw now that whatever evil had been in him before had been twisted even more by his scheming father and his sycophants. With the unwitting help of the hospital and the conniving of Dr. Rabat, Borge had transformed his own son into an incidental fortune that had financed his own interests. By the time Markus Thorella was handed the papers for the estate, he was already two years in the Marine Corps and safely out of Borge's hair. The good senator was left to oversee matters while the "son of his dear, departed friends" went off to war.

"Fucking bastard," Jodi hissed as she continued her scanning.

She discovered that their relationship did not end there, by any means. Reading over the official military records that mentioned Markus Thorella – she had not been able to gain access to his actual Marine Corps personnel files – she soon came to see that he had acquired a reputation as a hatchet man, as ruthless or more so than his secret father. And the enemies he was sent to fight did not have blue skin: not one single time in his career was the unit in which he was serving sent into the line against the Kreelans. Instead, he spent his service time engaged in police actions on various worlds, bashing in human heads in places like Erlang that had somehow earned Borge's ire.

That information, in turn, led her to discover the connection Borge had with those places. Millennium Industries – which originally had belonged to the Thorellas, but had long since come under Borge's control – had holdings or interests on every one of the planets where Thorella and his goons had been deployed: Erlang for precious and strategic minerals; Kauchin in the Outer Rim for cheap, undisturbed, labor; Wilhelmstadt for high tech items; the shipyards around Manifest. And a dozen more. From what Jodi could tell, every ship, weapon, or defense system built in half the Confederation contributed to the senator's coffers. If he wanted, Jodi did not doubt that he could build his own battle fleet; he already owned a sizable portion of the merchant marine. But all of it fell under the ownership of Millennium Industries, and any investigation short of the outright data penetrations that Jodi was conducting (which were completely illegal) would show Borge only as a minor shareholder and acting chairman of the umbrella company.

Jodi shook her head in wonder. Borge was using both his political position and his influence with the military – she hoped unwittingly – to boost his own power, employing his biological son as an agent any time he needed a dirty job done. And he was getting away with it at an untold cost in terms of human lives and suffering.

And in the case of Erlang, she discovered, President Belisle had not only been a tyrant, but he had also received kickbacks from Millennium Industries, presumably as a payoff to keep the Mallorys in line and ensure that Millennium got its cut of Erlang's mineral production. But, according to the figures she saw here, Belisle had not only failed to keep production at an acceptable level, he had lately been demanding more and more money from Millennium for his cooperation and silence. But when Reza appeared, soon assisted by Melissa Savitch, the role of Millennium – and Borge – in the rape of Erlang and the Mallorys could have become public. Borge had not sent Thorella there just to bring the Mallorys to heel and take care of

Reza; he had been sent to kill Belisle, and had murdered Savitch because she happened to be in the way.

"They set you up, Reza," she murmured. That was the only way Thorella could have gotten any valid imagery of Reza killing Belisle, because Reza would have killed the good colonel, too, had he had the chance. Thorella had known what Reza would do, and he had set a very good trap for him, using Belisle as bait. In one stroke, Borge and Thorella were able to both get rid of Belisle and frame Reza for murder. And now, even though the Mallorys, who were now legally in charge of Erlang, insisted that the Confederation government not only drop the charges against Reza but give him a medal for what he had done, Borge somehow had bought enough influence to make the charges stick.

But they could not try him until he had recovered from his coma. And that was where she began to run into real problems. While the worm program she had been running was more than a match for the basic security codes that had been put on the older files, the more recent ones having to do with the Erlang incident and its aftermath were much better protected. In her last half hour at the research center, she had only been able to gain access to one document: the list of medical personnel who had participated in Reza's care over the last six months. And she was not terribly surprised to learn that one of the most frequent visitors had been Dr. Deliha Rabat.

She glowered at the screen, willing the current ACCESS DENIED warning to go away.

Trying again with the last bypass algorithm the worm program had been written to attempt, the words disappeared.

"All right," she said eagerly. "Maybe we're getting somewhere."

But what echoed on the screen was not at all reassuring:

VIOLATION OF SECURITY LOCK
128904-34-23341
USER 527-903-482-71 ACCESS SUSPENDED
SECURITY MANAGER ALERTED
REMOTE STATION DISCONNECT

The screen suddenly went blank and the terminal refused to respond to her frantic hammering on the keyboard.

"Oh, shit," she muttered. She quickly tossed everything but the data card with all the information she had downloaded into her shoulder bag. The card she put in her boot. It would not escape anything more than a cursory search, but it might make the difference.

Opening the door just a crack to see if anything unusual was going on, she saw that the center, crowded as always, remained quiet. She made her way toward the main lobby at a brisk walk, her eyes alert for any sign of trouble.

Because she was in trouble. She just did not realize yet how much.

FIVE

L'Houillier's eyes opened unwillingly at the urgent beep coming from the General Staff comm link beside his bed. Beside him, his wife rolled over, burying her head in her pillow in a reflex she had developed over many years of being married to a Navy officer constantly on call.

He rolled over and slapped the machine, nearly knocking it from the nightstand. "L'Houillier," he said groggily. Unlike many of his contemporaries, the ability to become alert immediately upon awakening had always eluded him.

"Forgive intrusion, admiral, but something most urgent has come up."

Zhukovski, L'Houillier thought. *Of course. Did the man never sleep?* "I'll be there in thirty minutes, Evgeni."

"Pardon, admiral, but matter cannot wait thirty minutes," Zhukovski's voice shot back. "I am on my way to you. Five minutes."

Before L'Houillier had a chance to protest, Zhukovski had terminated the transmission. "*Merde*," he muttered.

"Evgeni again?" his wife asked, fully awake.

"Who else?" L'Houillier said grumpily. She could fall asleep in five minutes, be awake instantly, and fall asleep again without missing a beat. The same cycle took him hours, if he could manage it at all. He was terribly jealous.

"I'll start the coffee and tea," she said crisply as she got up, donned a robe, and disappeared out of the room.

Forcing himself out of bed, he had just managed to go to the bathroom and put on his own robe when he heard Zhukovski hammering on the front door, pointedly ignoring the more pleasant doorbell.

A few minutes later, L'Houillier was indeed awake, and not because of his wife's special version of Navy coffee.

"Evgeni, this is fantastic," he said as he reviewed again the message from Commodore Marchand aboard *Furious*. "A willing Kreelan prisoner and a child they think belongs to Reza Gard?"

"So Commodore Marchand reports, sir," Evgeni said as he took another sip of the excellent tea proffered by L'Houillier's wife. For Zhukovski, that was enough incentive to rouse his commander from sleep for an impromptu visit. "We have great opportunity here, admiral. But we can do nothing without translator."

"Gard, you mean?"

Zhukovski nodded. "Correct, sir. This is our chance to find out more. We must bring all of them together."

"What if the Kreelans – or Reza – do not wish to help?"

Zhukovski shrugged. "Then we have lost nothing but time courier ship needs to bring prisoners to Earth."

L'Houillier did not hesitate. "Make it so, Evgeni."

* * *

The situation in the sick bay on board *Furious* was tense, Eustus thought, but it was under control. For the moment. The huge warrior stood a silent vigil over the Kreelan child, watching with the greatest trepidation every move made by the ship's surgeon as she began to work on the girl.

Eustus remembered little between passing out in the tunnel after the warrior started carrying him and waking up here on the *Furious*. But he had apparently managed to keep the Navy boat and the surviving Marines from shooting the Kreelan woman and the child, and Commodore Marchand had been ecstatic about their capture.

But no one on the ship who'd seen the warrior was under any delusions that she was truly a prisoner. Wisely, no one had tried to take her weapons. Even if someone had, her physical strength and her rapier claws would have wrought havoc in the close quarters of the ship before she could have been brought down. But there were no human weapons here, no Marines or armed sailors. The sickbay had been sealed off, the surgeon and two assistants tending to the girl as the warrior looked on, while Eustus was left to the accurate but less-than-tender ministrations of one of the automated aid stations that could easily repair the damage to his leg. But a platoon of fully armed Marines in battle armor waited tensely outside the door.

The surgeon was busy pulling away the lower part of the black undergarment to check on the girl's legs.

"Lord of All," she whispered. The two nurses gawked in astonishment.

"What is it?" Eustus asked just as Marchand's voice cut in over the intercom with the same question. The commodore, along with half the ship's officers, was glued to a screen in her ready room, watching the video feed from the operating theater.

"This isn't any girl," the surgeon pronounced. "We've got ourselves a male child here, people."

"Jesus," Eustus breathed. It was certainly a day of firsts.

The warrior looked at Eustus uncertainly, her great hands flexing in a gesture Eustus knew well from Reza. She was nervous, anxious.

"It's all right," he said quietly, hoping that a reassuring tone would suffice for words he did not know. "We just expected a girl, is all."

She frowned, but seemed to relax slightly. If a figure as imposing as she could be said to relax.

The surgeon worked on the boy for nearly two hours, doing the best she could to repair the damage to a kind of body she had never worked on before. She spliced bone and muscle, fused blood vessels closed. Thankfully there did not appear to be any injuries to the child's internal organs, the functions of some of which the surgeon wasn't sure.

"All right," she said finally, wiping her arm across a brow that had been sweating profusely the entire time, despite the nurse's best efforts to blot it away, "that's it. I think he'll make it."

There was a burst of applause from the comms terminal as the officers and crew gathered around similar sets throughout the ship offered their congratulations. At first, the warrior was terrified that something had gone wrong. Eustus quickly reassured her that the boy would live, reaching out a hand to hold hers. That, and the smile on his face, was enough to reassure her that the child was safe.

It was perhaps the first victory in the war in which a life from the opposing side had been saved, and Eustus could only hope that what they had accomplished here today would set a precedent for the days yet to come.

SIX

President Nathan slept fitfully, alone in the president's quarters in the Council Building. His wife slept without him, as she often did, in their home in the country. He missed her and she him, but the affairs of state, as it had so many times in the many years of their marriage, took precedence over their personal lives. It was a sacrifice that very few of his countrymen truly appreciated.

The previous few days had been an unending political nightmare as he sought to fend off repeated attacks by Borge and his growing retinue of virulent supporters. While Nathan agreed that the current situation presented a historic opportunity, the military had not yet given him a plan with which he felt comfortable, a plan that did not expose every single colony – even Earth itself – to possible counterattack and destruction. For probably the first time in his life, Nathan was truly afraid, not for himself, but for his people. The decision he made had to be right. The consequences were simply too awful to contemplate if he was wrong.

But that was not good enough. The Council was rapidly swaying toward Borge's arguments that the time to strike was now, and that they should strike with everything. Borge was quietly branding anyone who opposed the idea as a traitor, and had come within a word of calling Nathan a coward in the middle of the heated debate. Actually, he had done better than to state it explicitly. He had painted a picture with related words, leaving it to the listener to see the final portrait, false though it might be. Nathan was determined that Borge would not have his way, and so far he had managed to maintain enough support for his administration to thwart the ambitious senator's machinations.

Imagine, Nathan had thought, mutely horrified, *what would become of the democracy that had ruled the Confederation for the last century if this man came to power*. Borge had made no secret of his reactionary attitude toward the military and scientific communities, not to mention what he thought – and claimed he would do – with regard to his political rivals. The man was nothing short of a megalomaniac, the kind who is spawned only in times of intense political crisis and in places resonating with corrupting power. In his mind, he had so much to gain by stepping up to Nathan's position; and in Nathan's mind, humanity everywhere had so much to lose. He would have arrested Borge if he could, just to shut him away from the power he so craved and would do anything to gain more of. But Nathan could not do that. He had lived his life by the constitution he had sworn to uphold, and he did not feel himself above the laws that guided the common man and woman in this time of perpetual crisis.

And that was the source of Nathan's frustration: his inability to effectively combat Borge, for the senator was an enemy every bit as tenacious and far more inhuman even than the Kreelans. Nathan vowed to fight him tooth and nail in the Council chambers and wherever else he could claim as a battleground, but he knew that unless something drastic happened very soon, he would lose. It was inevitable. In his dreams, the president of the Confederation hoped for a miracle.

He did not hear the stealthy footsteps of the man who entered his room. The electronic guardian, the eyes and ears located throughout the large apartment, lay dormant, deactivated. The guards downstairs were alert, at their posts, but saw nothing. In the president's bedroom it was dark, but the intruder had no difficulty seeing. This was what night vision lenses were made for.

The dark form paused for a moment at the president's bedside. A smile passed across the intruder's face under the black mask as he considered his next move, one that he had rehearsed numerous times. He silently extracted a wicked looking dagger that had been fashioned by Kreelan hands, but whose most recent owner had been human. It was Reza's dagger, his most prized possession.

He moved close to the bed. He wanted to see Nathan's eyes. The intruder nudged the slumbering president. The older man's eyes snapped open wide.

The blade flashed down in a lethal arc as Nathan's mouth made an "O" of surprise. He raised his arms in a defensive gesture that was too slow, too late. The knife, which was made of the sharpest and most durable metal known, speared Nathan's chest directly over the heart, slipping through his ribs to rupture the vital muscle that pulsated beneath. A small ring of blood appeared on the sheet, but that was all.

With a gasp and shudder, the president of the Confederation, and democracy itself, died.

The intruder stood and watched the dead man for a few moments, savoring the feeling of the kill. He was sorely tempted to massage the massive erection in his pants to fruition, but he knew from experience that it would have to wait. This time. There had been others when waiting had been unnecessary. And he was sure there would be still more.

His erection grew harder. It was time to leave.

With the barest sigh of his rubber-soled boots on the plush carpet, the man made his exit. After he left the building through an exit that the guards thought was secure, the electronic guardian reactivated, its internal memory already adjusted to account for the moments it had been fooled: the horrified guards watched as Reza Gard appeared out of thin air, plunged a knife into their president's heart, and then just as quickly disappeared as the alarms began to sound.

* * *

While she did not realize it at the time, walking home very likely saved Jodi's life. She normally took the transit shuttle from the government complex to the rural hub four kilometers away that, in its turn, served the outlying areas where Nicole and Tony had their house. But after what she had discovered at the research center, she needed some time to think about what she had learned and had decided to take one of the many nature trails that wound their way through the countryside. It was dark, of course, but the sky was clear, the stars and waning moon lighting the way. Besides, she was not afraid. Even had she not been competent in Aikido and the street-style fighting Tony Braddock had taught her, she still could do more than her share of damage with the pocket blaster she carried under her tunic.

She was actually enjoying the cool smell of the night, the sounds of the crickets chirping and the high chittering of the bats that flew from the trees in search of their evening meal.

Fear did not take hold until she was within sight of the house and saw the three security skimmers pulled up in front.

"Not very subtle, are you?" she murmured to herself as she moved behind a fortuitously positioned hedge to conceal herself from the half dozen Internal Security troops wandering around the front yard. "Shit," she whispered.

In the doorway, she could see Tony gesticulating angrily at what must have been the head IS man, who gestured back. She could hear their voices, but they were still too far away to make out. But she did not doubt the reason for the IS presence here: her "research" had set off some big alarm bells.

Then she saw the gun. Silence suddenly descended on the house.

"Jesus," Jodi gasped. The IS man had pulled a gun on Tony, a junior senator and member of the Council, no less! "What the fuck is going on?" she murmured as she forced herself even lower behind the hedge.

The rest of the security troops wasted no time, pushing roughly past Tony on their way in to search the house, no doubt for Jodi. Tony had been trying to fend them off, she thought, because they probably did not have a warrant to search the house. But a gun against an unarmed man was quite persuasive, if not exactly legal.

"Don't do anything stupid, Tony," Jodi pleaded under her breath.

Braddock just stood there quietly, his arms raised, his face twisted in a mask of fiery anger as the IS man held his gun leveled at Tony's chest.

Suddenly, Jodi heard a female voice from within the house, screaming angrily at the intruders in what could only be French. *Nicole.* They had probably been in bed when the storm troops came knocking, Jodi thought, and Tony had gotten up to answer the door. Surprise.

But the biggest surprise was the sight of four IS men herding Nicole out the door, dressed only in her robe, then stuffing her into one of the skimmers. The leader nudged Tony along with the gun, pushing him roughly into the vehicle beside Nicole.

Then the IS people got into the skimmers and left, except for two men they left behind. After their comrades departed, they went into the house, closed the door, and turned off the lights. To wait for Jodi.

She felt her stomach drop away into infinity. Had she arrived a few minutes earlier, they would have caught her. Had she arrived a few minutes later, they would have caught her. Someone, presumably the God she had never really believed in, had been looking out for her. She could only hope that Nicole and Tony would be all right.

For now, she had to look out for herself, because she knew that if the security forces captured her, Borge's secret would never see the light of day. She would silently, tragically, disappear. She looked at her watch. Twenty-three hundred. She had about six more hours of darkness.

Six hours to find help.

* * *

"What in the hell is going on, senator?" Tony Braddock demanded angrily. He and Nicole sat on the opposite side of a security shield, guarded by four IS agents with drawn weapons. Senator Borge sat on the other side, his face a mask of sorrow.

"Please, Councilman, captain," he said solemnly, "this situation is not as I would like, but events have taken place that demand the most extreme action." He looked at them gravely.

"And what is this 'situation?'" Nicole asked coldly.

Borge nodded. "Earlier this evening, less than an hour ago, to be more precise, Reza Gard escaped from the detention facility at the hospital. Shortly thereafter, he murdered President Nathan."

"That is not possible!" Nicole said incredulously, jumping to her feet. "Reza would never do such a thing!"

"I wish that were the case, but there is evidence to the contrary." He nodded to his aid, who activated a holo recording showing Reza materializing in Nathan's bedroom. Moving close to the bed, he withdrew a knife and, after only a moment's hesitation, plunged it into the president's chest. The alarm went off a few seconds later, and Reza disappeared from the room as mysteriously as he had come.

"I don't believe it," Tony said firmly. "This is some kind of a hoax or a frame-up. Reza gave his word to Nicole that he would not try to escape, and he would never have broken it. You've got the wrong man, senator. I don't know how, but you've got the wrong man."

"Besides," Nicole asked, grudgingly retaking her seat, "what does this have to do with us? Are you implicating us as accomplices?"

Borge shook his head as if he were mortified at the thought. "You two? Heavens no. But Commander Mackenzie is another matter. She attempted to see Reza again tonight, even after her earlier little... tiff... with Colonel Thorella." He looked at them significantly. "I would like to know why. Internal Security knew, of course, that she was staying with you, and that naturally was the first place to look."

"This is ridiculous–" Nicole growled.

"Even if this is all true," Tony interrupted hotly, "does that give you the right to hold us at gunpoint in our own home, without so much as a search warrant?"

"I don't think you understand the gravity of the situation, Councilman Braddock," Borge said slowly. "In accordance with constitutional law, I legally inherited the powers of the president just as Nathan took his last breath. I will not allow his death – his murder – to go unpunished. I apologize for the zealotry shown by the IS agents at your home, but I am taking no chances, and I will spare no effort to get to the bottom of this. You two are friends of both Captain Gard and Commander Mackenzie, and are our only leads to them. I hope that you are able to put aside your personal feelings in this matter – and I realize that will be terribly difficult – and help Internal Security find Reza Gard and Commander Mackenzie."

"And if we do not?" Nicole asked.

Borge looked at them with eyes glowing with barely concealed ferocity. "I will have you both cited with contempt and thrown in prison until you decide to cooperate." He leaned forward, his hands spread before him. "Please," he begged, "please do not make this any more difficult than it already is. The president was a good friend of mine for many years, and to me his loss is a very personal one. Captain Gard is implicated in his murder, and Commander Mackenzie was in the wrong place at the wrong time. If he is innocent, and she is not involved, fine. We will find who is. But I want answers, my friends. Quickly. And I will have them, one way or another."

Nicole and Tony looked at each other helplessly. There was little they could do. And the image of Reza driving the knife into Nathan's heart was more than convincing, at least to anyone who did not know him. He had powers that were arguably supernatural, and both of them knew that Reza could easily do what the video had shown.

Until Tony remembered what Reza had said about what had happened on Erlang with Thorella's little holo act. Who was to say that they weren't witnessing a repeat performance? But he kept that to himself. Right now, Borge held all the cards in this particular deadly game.

"What do you want us to do?" he asked quietly.

* * *

Jodi was running out of time. She had made her way as quickly as she could back into the subterranean complex that made up the city's core. She realized that it would be more dangerous for her there, but she needed information, and that was the only place she could think of to get it.

The news, when she saw it broadcast on the holo banners in the main mall, stunned her. President Nathan was dead, murdered. Reza Gard, having escaped from the hospital, was the prime suspect, and Commander Jodi Mackenzie was believed to be involved. There was her picture, for all to see, on at least a dozen banners that were in her direct view.

The only thing that saved her was that the mall was so crowded with people seeking out the capitol's nightlife. Most of the wanderers ignored the holo banners. They ignored the broadcast. They ignored her. For the moment, at least, it appeared as if she could still move about. But that was not going to last for long.

She moved quickly to a vid terminal, putting her back to the crowd and the gruesome images of the president's death that were finally getting some attention: more and more people were stopping and staring.

"God," she whispered, "what in the fuck's going on? What am I going to do?" Her hands were shaking. *Come on*, she shouted at herself. *Think.* She needed shelter and information, maybe a new identity. Transportation. Money. More than all that, she needed to find Reza. She knew the escape story was garbage, but where did that leave him? And how could she possibly find him? She could not make it more than a few kilometers by herself. She needed help. But with Nicole and Tony out of the picture, whom could she turn to who was close by? She couldn't use any inter-city transportation or she'd be picked up for sure.

Something nagged at her memory. A name. Someone she knew, someone close by. For a while, it refused to come to her, instead fluttering just beyond her recollection, taunting her.

Tanya. Tanya Buchet.

The name sent a shiver up her spine. She closed her eyes and slumped against the wall of the booth. Of all the people in the world she would have to turn to, why did Tanya have to be the one? It just had to be someone who probably still hated her guts after all the years since they had last seen each other. Maybe even as much as Jodi hated her. They had not parted on the best of terms. But Tanya had everything that Jodi needed.

"Oh, Lord," she moaned. "Why her? Why that fucking bitch?"

After a moment, her mind was made up. She had no other choice. Calling up the directory, she quickly found Tanya's address. It was the same as it had been all those years ago. Glancing at the flow of people behind her, she darted to the rear of a boisterous group of Marines making their way back to one of the local barracks, using them to mask her escape through the nearest exit to the surface level.

* * *

The tiny suburb called Hamilton had changed little over the years. Jodi had last seen it while in her late teens, when she was still in school. She had befriended the daughter of a wealthy family that normally lived in Europe, but that had given their young daughter a cottage here, only a few kilometers from the capitol, where she could live during the school year. It probably would have come as no surprise to her parents to learn that she was seldom alone there. She was brilliant, beautiful, and cloaked by a touch of darkness that Jodi and many others had found irresistible. She was Jodi's first lover, and without doubt the cruelest.

Sensing Jodi's need for her affection, her approval, Tanya Buchet had kept her almost as an emotional slave, alternately tormenting her and pleasing her as she might an animal in an experiment. Jodi finally realized the extent of her plight when she found herself holding a blaster to her own skull, having discovered that her first love had been cheating on her. With the cold muzzle of the gun pressing into her temple, Jodi suddenly thought how much better it would be to kill Tanya instead, but she had let it go as only an unpleasant – if gratifying – thought. She had moved out that day, and it was not long after that the Navy whisked her away for what Jodi had hoped would be forever.

But forever hadn't been as long as she'd hoped. Walking up the steps to the cottage, she saw how well it had been kept up. In fact, except for the growth of the trees and new paint, it had hardly changed at all.

Her spine crawling with dreadful anticipation, she rapped on the door of what had once been an emotional Hell. *If there is a God*, she thought, *please let Him be with me now.*

There was no answer, no indication of anything or anyone stirring within. She hesitated, then knocked again, louder this time.

The old wooden door suddenly opened without a sound, swinging back on well-oiled hinges. Startled, Jodi took two steps backward, nearly falling down the steps in surprise.

The woman who stood in the doorway was stunning, clothed in a black dress that was as elegant and beautiful as it was plain. Her long brunette hair framed a flawless ivory face, the hazel eyes appraising, predatory. The smile, when it finally came, exposed perfect teeth behind full, sensuous lips.

"Jodi," those ruby lips said, exposing the husky voice that had come with womanhood, "how very nice to see you."

* * *

Now, sitting on the sofa in the small parlor and holding the cup of tea she had been given, spilling half of it in the saucer from her shaking hands, Jodi faced the witch of her adolescent years.

"Believe me, Tanya," she told the woman, who sat quietly in the chair opposite, her unblinking eyes focused on Jodi's, "I'm not here because I want to be."

"Jodi, dear, you didn't come all this way just to hurt my feelings, did you?" Tanya replied evenly, shifting herself to reveal a little more leg from under her dress.

"No, of course not," Jodi replied hastily, consciously looking away from Tanya. She would not, could not, let herself be drawn into that spider's web again. "I didn't even know you'd still be here. Even now, I can't believe you are."

"And why shouldn't I be? This has been my home. I go to the family estate in Europe sometimes, when I feel like it. But Hamilton and New York serve my purposes adequately. I sometimes board students here who attend our old school."

Jodi suppressed a shudder at what must happen to the students here.

"Didn't you ever do your civil or military service time?"

Tanya laughed. "Of course not, dear! Who do you think is going to make the only daughter and surviving member of the Buchet family play soldier in this silly little war? I'm one of the five richest people on this entire planet, probably in the entire Confederation, and have been since just after you ran away. I'm quite content to let you little generals run about and play war games with the Kreelans. My interests lie elsewhere."

Jodi gritted her teeth, forcing back the response that fought its way to the surface. "That's obvious enough," she muttered instead. "What about your parents?" she asked. "What happened to them?"

Tanya waved her hand, dismissing the issue as if her parents had never been of any consequence. "They got themselves killed on a transatlantic flight. I don't remember the details, really. It's not important now." Like a wraith, she uncoiled herself from her chair and came to sit beside Jodi on the sofa, putting her arm across the sofa back behind Jodi's neck. Jodi could feel her own body reacting instinctively to Tanya's nearness, sensing her warmth, smelling the alluring scent of her perfume. "What is important," Tanya whispered, "is you. Tell me, why are you here?"

Downing the last of the bitter tea that she suddenly hoped was not drugged, Jodi set the cup and saucer down on the coffee table and turned to face her nemesis-benefactor. Tanya's gaze held hers. Her lips were so close...

"I need your help, Tanya," Jodi told her, forcing out the words while looking Tanya in the eye. She had conjured up the sight of Nicole and Tony being held at gunpoint by the IS, and the anger that uncoiled in her chest gave her the strength she needed to resist Tanya's magnetic gaze.

"I thought as much," Tanya said, a smile touching her scarlet lips. "I suppose it's not every day that I have a chance to speak with someone who conspired to kill the president."

"That's total bullshit," Jodi spat. "Reza Gard did not kill the president and I didn't help him get out of the hospital. We were both set up: Reza because the real murderer needs a scapegoat and me because I found out something I'm not supposed to know."

One of Tanya's eyebrows arched. "Really? And just what might that be?"

"It's a long story," Jodi said uncomfortably, suddenly wondering why she had come here. More and more, she felt as if she were in a trap. The words suddenly came to her: *Come into my parlor, said the spider to the fly...*

"Well, dear," Tanya said, casually examining one of her perfectly manicured blood-red nails, "I have plenty of time."

Jodi bit her lip. "Please, Tanya. I have nowhere else to turn, no one else to go to. There's a lot riding on this, a lot more than just my life. There's something terribly wrong in the Confederation government. I think I know who murdered the president, but it wasn't Reza Gard."

"Well," Tanya said, looking up from her nails to pin Jodi with her gaze, "I'm sure President Borge would be happy to hear about it."

Jodi felt her black skin go pale as the blood drained from it. "*President Borge*," she whispered. She closed her eyes. She was too late. "Dear, sweet Jesus."

She felt a cool hand against her face. "Jodi," Tanya asked with what almost sounded like genuine concern in her voice, "are you all right?"

"No," Jodi choked. "The Confederation's fucked. We're all fucked, now that that bastard has gotten what he wanted."

"Tell me," Tanya said softly, "why do you say that? Borge has been a friend of our family for many years. I know him quite well."

Somehow, that did not surprise Jodi. Their personalities seemed to go hand in hand. *God*, she thought, *what do I do?* She had no choice but to tell her. "I think Borge had President Nathan murdered, and I think I know who he used as an assassin." And then she began to tell Tanya about her time at the research center, about Borge and Thorella, and all that she had learned there.

When she finished, Tanya was quiet for a long time, looking out the window at the dawn sky. She was a night person, Jodi remembered, forsaking the light of the sun for the moon and stars. Like a vampire.

When she finally spoke, Jodi almost didn't recognize her voice: it was wooden, dead.

"I knew Markus Thorella," Tanya said. "Our parents were very good friends, actually. I had always liked Markus." She smiled bitterly. "He was everything a young girl could have wanted in a boy. I remember the accident, too, how horrible it was. I used to visit him in the hospital every Tuesday, when my parents would let me fly over to visit him. But when he finally woke up, he had... changed. He was quiet, sullen. Arrogant. But I didn't let that stop me. He had been through a lot. I would not abandon him. We were friends."

She stopped talking, her words drifting into the silent void that the room had become. Jodi felt her skin crawling at Tanya's revelation. The picture of Borge's evil, horrible as it was, was becoming ever clearer.

A single tear slid down Tanya's cheek, glistening in the morning light. "I kept seeing him even after he left the hospital," she went on, more softly now. "That's when I first met Senator Borge. He seemed like such a nice man. Much like Markus's father had been. I spent a great deal of time with them. That's why Mama and Papa bought me this cottage. Just so I could be closer to them. To him. My friend, Markus." Her voice dropped to a whisper. "The friend who raped me when I was fifteen." She smiled then, an evil, hateful smile that floated on a sea of anguish and pain. "But who could I tell? Who would believe me? That Markus Thorella had raped his best friend? No one would have believed it. I was no saint, even as a child, but Markus was. Had been." She shook her head. "I said nothing, because I still thought he might... love me. But my body was all he wanted, and he took it whenever and however it pleased him. He made me do things, terrible things. And when he was old enough to enroll in the academy, he left without a word. He tossed me aside like rubbish. And now you're telling me... that it was not even him."

Jodi was now beginning to understand her own past. In her anger and self-loathing, Tanya had taken out on everyone else the love/hate she had felt for Markus Thorella. He had warped her, had emotionally and physically raped her, and she was trying to purge herself of the demons he had left inside her. And there had been no one for her to confide in, no one who would believe her accusations because of the legacy of the real Markus Thorella, whose word had once been honorable and true. She had never told anyone what had happened until this day. Jodi had been one of her victims, and doubtless there had been many more, some probably not as lucky as Jodi had been. But the greatest victim of all had been Tanya herself.

"I will help you," Tanya said quietly after the tears had passed. "Tell me what you need."

* * *

"Pray to your God that I never rise from this table, doctor." For the hundredth time, Reza tried to free himself from the restraints that held him firmly to the cold stainless steel operating table. But as his determination crossed a magic threshold, he lost his strength, his will. He sagged back before the power of the restraints, exhausted. The electrodes pressed into his skull tingled as his head thumped gently against the table. He felt like Samson after losing his hair to Delilah's hand; he could call upon neither his psychic nor his physical powers to extricate himself from his bonds.

"This is my god," she replied as she worked the set of consoles that encircled him like hungry, flesh-craving electronic gargoyles. She shook her head in wonder at the data pouring from her instruments. "What a magnificent specimen you are." She turned to him and smiled. "We're going to become very close, you and I. Closer than you can possibly imagine."

Reza closed his eyes and tried to concentrate, but he could not channel his power. Normally, he could have simply willed himself to be somewhere else, and he would be gone. But she had done something to him, something that interfered with his most basic neural processes. He was helpless before her, and the only thing greater than his anger was his shame. He could not even commit suicide.

"I was going to do to you what I had originally suggested when you returned from the Empire," she explained, "to give you a deep-core probe. But I'm glad that things turned out differently. That would have been such a waste.

"You see, I've always hoped for an opportunity like this, and I've planned for it all these years. A deep-core, of course, depends on the external analysts being able to interpret the data that comes from the target brain. That means you need people who know the language, the culture, and who can understand the imagery that the target brain is projecting. We never recover everything, of course, but under ideal circumstances, we can successfully interpret up to thirty or even forty percent of the core data."

"And this is all you get for the price of the victim's sanity?"

"It's a small enough price," she said confidently. He felt her hands adjusting something on his head, almost as if she were checking the ripeness of a melon. A throb filled his skull, like a noise so low in pitch that it could not really be heard, but only felt. "But I've done better since then. Much better.

"Now," she explained, "instead of a gaggle of analysts struggling to understand the massive output of even the most diseased and atrophied brain, I can actually link my own cortex into the data stream as an on-line interpreter, drastically improving the recovery rate, bringing it up to nearly one-hundred percent. In effect, I will know everything you know, will feel everything that you feel. And these computers will record it all for later study in a format any qualified analyst can understand." He saw her face above his, looking down at him with eyes bright with anticipation. She wore a tiara of cerebral implants. "You're looking at the one person in the Universe who in a few minutes will know more about you than any other."

"You are a fool, Rabat," Reza warned. "You do not comprehend what you are about to trifle with. My brain, as my body, is alien. You shall not find there what you expect."

She smiled condescendingly. "Don't flatter yourself so much, Reza," she told him as she made some final adjustments on the small console in front of her. "I am the one who will be in control, not you. And I will also be the only one of us who will walk out of this room when we are finished." She ran a hand over his forehead as she looked down at him, an expression of consideration on her face. "It's a shame, really, to use you up like this. When we're done here, you'll be nothing but a drooling vegetable for Thorella to dispose of." She shrugged. "But they were going to kill you anyway. At least I convinced the senator – the *president* – that we could still get very valuable information from you."

"How generous of you," Reza hissed.

"We're going to start now. Just close your eyes and try to relax." Suddenly he felt a dizzying sensation, as if a thousand tiny jolts of electricity were coursing through his body. "What I'm doing right now," she said in a very clinical voice, as if she were speaking to a patient rather than a victim, "is scrambling your voluntary nervous system. You won't be able to twitch a muscle unless the computer commands it. A security precaution on my part, obviously. You see," he saw her smiling above him again, "you've been carrying a tiny implant around inside your head since just after you came back from Erlang. I took the liberty of implanting it while you were in your coma. A rather ingenious device, if I do say so myself." Reza felt a curious tingling behind his right ear, a scraping sound that seemed to come from inside his skull. She held up a tiny white capsule that was stained with blood. "This is what's been keeping you under control. Any time your brain waves reached a certain threshold, this acted like a jammer, influencing the key areas of your brain to reduce your adrenaline levels and critical neural signals. It has also been busy transmitting data on your brain activity all this time, allowing me to make much better calibrations for this experiment than otherwise would have been possible." She paused as she ran a skin sealer across the small wound, dropping the tiny device into a waiting bowl. "This is also why you were in a coma for so long. I wasn't ready for you until now, and it gave Borge the time he needed for his own plans."

Completely paralyzed and unable to speak, Reza silently wondered if she really believed that Borge would let her live; long enough to boil the essence of Reza's thoughts down to data understandable by her computers – and in turn by Borge's people – but no longer. If she did not know everything, she knew enough. She was a liability. And Borge did not tolerate liabilities.

"But when Thorella comes for you," she went on casually, ignorant of his silent monologue, "the capsule might make things look a little odd when you're... discovered. Not to mention that it interferes with the cerebral interaction we're about to induce."

Reza had no difficulty imagining a scenario. It would be much the same as when they brought him here. He suddenly had collapsed, unconscious, in his hospital room, and the next thing he knew he was here. In the near-vegetable state he would be in after Rabat finished with him, Thorella could hand him a weapon – Reza might have enough gray matter left to understand how to hold one – and put him in any setting he thought fitting. And then he could simply gun Reza down at the end of some concocted hunt, walking away with the laurels of a hero. Easy. Clean. Simple.

"There!" she said. "That's all done. Now we can get to work." She looked deeply into his eyes. "I've waited for this for a long, long time." On impulse, she leaned down and kissed him full on the mouth. Then her hand touched a control on one of the computers surrounding him, and suddenly the cold metal and machine world around him disappeared.

* * *

Deliha Rabat stood at the edge of a great plain, upon which stood a city that only one human had ever visited.

"Where are we, Reza?" she asked in wonder.

"This is the Homeworld of the Kreela," he answered from behind her. "That is the city where the First Empress was born, and where I first fought for the woman who would become my love."

She noted with pleasure that he was not speaking Standard; he was speaking Kreelan – the Old Tongue she knew now – and she understood it. She suddenly forgot about the city as her mind began to receive the first trickle of Reza's thoughts, his knowledge. She looked around her, at the mountains, the magenta sky, at the Empress moon above. The trickle soon turned into a torrent, filling her with all the images and memories of an alien lifetime. She felt the knowledge pouring into her, a fountain that seemed endless. She drank all that he had to offer her, and still demanded more. All that he knew was hers. *Everything.*

"No," she heard his voice say. "Not everything."

"What do you mean?" she demanded in a tongue she had never before spoken. "Give it to me! I want it all!"

"I warned you, doctor, but you would not listen. And now you shall pay the price for your vanity. Behold!"

She whirled around. Behind her should have been the mountains surrounding the valley that was the birthplace of the Empire so many eons ago. But as she watched, the great peaks disappeared behind a veil of fire, a wall of boiling scarlet flame that looked like bloody lava. "What is it? Tell me!"

"It is the Bloodsong of my people, human," Reza answered contemptuously, "the song of Her will. You and your machines can only comprehend the barest essence of the Way, of our lives. You can catalog the sights, sounds, smells, even the language of Her Children. But you do not understand our soul, or the power of the Empress, the power of Her spirit that dwells within us all. The Bloodsong is what unites us, all who have ever lived since the death of the First Empress. You wish to understand us? Then you must face the fire!"

"No!" she screamed as the wall of flame roared closer, devouring all that lay before it in a symphony of exploding trees and scorching rock. "I'm turning this off!" she screamed as she tried to flee back to her reality.

"Too late," Reza bellowed, and she felt his hands pinning her arms. She saw the silvery talons of his armored gauntlets pierce her flesh, felt the warm trickle of blood running down her arms. She struggled in vain. His breath was hot on her neck. "I warned you, you fool!" he shouted in her ear. "And now shall you know the truth! You wanted everything, and now you shall have it!"

As the wall of flame grew nearer, towering in the sky to blot out the glimmering Empress moon, Rabat could hear another sound above the din of the advancing apparition: voices. Thousands of them. Millions. All calling to her. They were angry, enraged. She looked into the flames and saw their terrible claws reaching for her, their mouths opened wide to reveal the fangs waiting to tear out her throat. Her skin began to blister in the heat, and she could smell the stench of her hair as it smoldered and then suddenly burst into flame.

She screamed, and kept on screaming as her skin and flesh began to boil away. Her eyes bulged and then exploded from her skull as the flames roared over her, the ethereal claws of the ancient warriors tearing at her flesh, at her soul, devouring her spirit as the world around her turned the color of blood.

* * *

"Reza! Jesus, are you all right?"

He felt hands moving along his body, tearing away the monitors and probes.

"Where is she?" he rasped. "Rabat."

"Looks like the good doctor's had it," Jodi said quietly. She had to look away from the body. The woman's face was frozen in a nightmarish grimace of agony, her hands clutching her breast as if her heart had exploded in her chest. In fact, as a coroner would ascertain some time later, it had.

Shaking her head, she turned her attention back to Reza. "Come on," she told him, helping him up from the table. She had managed to figure out how to turn off the suppressor field holding him to the table. The rest of the machines had apparently malfunctioned when Rabat died. She kissed him, then held him tightly. "I'm so glad I found you," she whispered, trying not to cry.

He smiled as he wrapped his arms around her, holding her shaking body gently as he kissed her hair. "I am, too, my friend."

After a moment, she unwillingly pushed him away. "We've got to get our asses out of here right now," she told him. "We're both in really deep shit."

"What has happened?"

"You're up on a rap for murdering the president, I'm your accomplice – helping you to get out of the hospital, no less – and Markus Thorella isn't really Markus Thorella at all. He's Senator – now President – Borge's son and an impostor. That's the scoop in a nutshell. Aren't you glad to hear it?" Jodi helped him to his feet and handed him some clothes. "Internal Security is crawling everywhere like a bunch of ants, and they picked up Nicole and Tony for questioning."

"What?" Reza asked incredulously as he pulled on the blue sweater and black pants that Jodi had brought for him, then some boots. Obviously, his uniformed days were over. Jodi was not wearing hers, either. "How could they?"

Jodi snorted. "Easy. Borge's the president now. I don't think he plans on doing anything with them except to try and lure us in, but I don't think they'll go for it. Anyway, he's declared martial law across the entire continent, which makes things that much more difficult for us."

When Reza was dressed, Jodi handed him a blaster. "Here," she said, "you're going to need this later. I already had to use it on the way in." She led him out and down a corridor that was deserted except for three bodies and the stink of burned flesh.

"How did you get in?" Reza asked. "How did you even find where they had taken me?"

Jodi shrugged. "An old friend of mine is helping us. She has... connections."

"Can you trust her?" Reza asked as they moved through a portal and into a tiny lobby. The research center where they had taken him was in a distant rural settlement that Rabat had thought would be sufficiently isolated to avoid any unwanted scrutiny. And, with Reza under her control, she had convinced Thorella and Borge that a lot of guards would just raise the visibility of the facility and the risk of exposure. And so, there had been only three guards. Had been.

"I don't know for sure," Jodi replied. She hopped into the pilot's seat of the waiting skimmer, closing the hatches after Reza had climbed in after her. "She certainly has a score to settle with our friend Thorella, though." She looked at Reza as the skimmer responded to her deft touch, quickly becoming airborne and heading east. "It doesn't really matter, anyway," she told him. "I had no one else to turn to."

Reza frowned. He was missing something. "But why would Borge be after you?" he asked.

Jodi smiled. And then she told him the entire tale of the man who would be president and his misbegotten son.

SEVEN

President Borge did not rage. He appeared calm and cool, despite the massive confusion that swirled around him as the entire security network of planet Earth worked to find and kill – Borge had decided to dispense with any remaining pleasantries – Reza Gard and Jodi Mackenzie.

But there was a slight problem: they both had disappeared. Mackenzie had not been seen since the afternoon before, and Reza had broken out of Rabat's little torture chamber earlier this afternoon. Fortunately, her death and the deaths of the Internal Security agents there only sealed the lid tighter on the two fugitives' coffins. He would have had to kill all of them eventually to ensure that no one even peripherally involved in his designs could ever reveal what they knew. While he had no evidence in hand, Borge instinctively knew that Mackenzie must have been responsible for rescuing Reza from Rabat. Captain Carré and Councilman Braddock had been under constant surveillance since their release and had not been caught helping either of the two fugitives. Borge had decided that there was no point in keeping them in custody, especially since there was always the chance that they might prove incidentally useful.

The problem of Mackenzie, however, remained. How had she escaped the dragnet that had been thrown over the city since his security people had been alerted by her delving into his past and that of his son?

She must have had help, he decided. But from whom? And why would anyone help her when every form of public media carried the story of her aiding and abetting Reza Gard in his bloody escape from the hospital before "killing" Nathan (Thorella had arranged to have a particular Marine lieutenant and a few of his troops die in Reza's "breakout")? He knew Carré and Braddock would have helped the fugitives, but they had been effectively neutralized. Who else was there? His intelligence people and researchers had combed the files for anyone who had been associated with Gard and Mackenzie, but those relative few had all been ruled out. Reza did not have any other known associations on Earth, as most of the officers and enlisted members of the Red Legion only returned from their regiment as corpses sealed in boxes.

The search for people who had known Mackenzie, however, yielded a surprise: Tanya Buchet.

Borge shook his head. *Tanya, of all people.* He had known her since she was a child, and had often looked upon her as an adopted daughter. He had never known or suspected that she and Mackenzie had known each other. Borge had called her about the matter personally, and had been reassured that she had not seen Mackenzie in nearly twenty years, and if she had, she would have shot her herself.

He had eliminated Tanya Buchet from his list, leaving him a blank screen. Not a single lead presented itself. Borge silently fumed.

Colonel Markus Thorella entered the confusion of the Internal Security Command Post. Ignoring everyone around him, he made his way straight to the new president.

"It had better be important, Markus," Borge warned ominously. Despite his outward appearance of calm, his mood was homicidally ugly.

"It is," his secret son said quietly. "We need to talk. Privately."

Borge scowled. He looked at the anthill-like activity swirling about him. He could do nothing but wait. And it would not really matter if he waited here, alone but for his thoughts, or talking to the Marine standing before him. His son. "Very well," he said.

After the door to Borge's makeshift ready room closed behind them, he said, "All right. What is so important that you had to interrupt the hunt?"

Thorella snorted derisively, but he was not about to tell the president what he really thought of the incompetent IS troops and their "hunt." No, if Gard and Mackenzie were going to be found, he would have to do it. And he thought he had a good idea where to start. But that was not why he had come here.

"I was just talking to the fleet operations officer," he said, leaving out the slight detail that they had been talking while in bed. "She said she came up with a plan on the staff battle computers for beating the Kreelans. Decisively. She explained it to me, and it sounds like it could be done. But L'Houillier and Zhukovski didn't buy off on it. Neither did Nathan." He smiled. Slightly. "I think you ought to hear it from her yourself. Very soon. The Navy has a lot of information – a lot more now than they even had a few days ago – and she thinks she can pinpoint the location of the Kreelan homeworld. And, if her plan looks like it would work, we could take out the Kreelan fleet and homeworld in a single, massive attack."

Borge nodded, his eyes narrowed as he thought. If what Thorella said was true, the potential for making history could not be underestimated. The man who won this war would have power beyond measure, and everlasting glory in the pages of history. Indeed, this was worth his attention, even over and above what was going on in the room next door. "And those bastards have not bothered to bring this to my attention?" He did not mention that he had put off both officers while he conducted his witch-hunt for Gard and Mackenzie. "I want a briefing as soon as possible from this operations officer of yours," he ordered briskly. "After that I want to see the two admirals. I won't stand for this kind of behavior."

"There's something else you should know," Thorella said quietly. "A fleet squadron patrolling out beyond the Rim is bringing home some interesting cargo." He smiled again. Chillingly. "Two Kreelans, one of which they say is Gard's son."

Borge's face twitched into a smile. *Surely, this was a joke*, he thought. But he could tell from the younger man's face that it was not. "Incredible," he breathed. The opportunities were immediately obvious. "How do you suggest we proceed?"

That is what Markus Thorella had always loved about this man. He asked for his opinion, and even listened to him. A better father one could not have, adopted or otherwise. "Gard is going to find his way off-world somehow," he told the president, "despite the best efforts of the Internal Security Service." Borge frowned at his son's disdain, but he did not say anything. The ISS was not known for its brilliance in the field. "Once he does," Thorella went on, "it's going to be almost impossible to track him down."

"Unless we give him a destination he can hardly refuse?" Borge prompted.

Thorella nodded, handing Borge a stylus pad on which he had already outlined the operation. "If we want this to work," he told Borge, "we have to get on it right away..."

* * *

Several thousand kilometers away, on an estate fifty kilometers south of what had once been the city of Paris, was a private subterranean spaceport large enough to house the single vessel that had belonged to the Buchet family for over one hundred years: the *Golden Pearl*. She had not been moved from her berth in fifteen years, not since Tanya's parents had died. Tanya herself had only infrequently visited the old estate, and things there were not quite as pristine as they once had been. Things had been cared for, of course, from the massive bounty of wealth left by her parents, but the place lacked the look and feel of habitation, of an owner's love and pride.

Fortunately for Reza and Jodi, the *Pearl* had also been cared for, the ship having been tended and kept in perfect running order by the technicians who periodically were paid to visit from Le Havre and Brest. The two of them did not have the time nor the inclination to tour the estate itself, but if it was anything like the ship on which they now found themselves, Jodi could not believe that Tanya did not spend more time here. The ship was a work of art both in terms of engineering and creature comforts. Having quickly studied the most important of the operations tutorials, she quickly realized that this ship, despite her age, must still be one of the fastest ships in human space. It was a badly needed bit of luck.

But she found herself lamenting the fact that they could not take a more leisurely cruise. The ship was a traveling wonderland of luxury, a relic of the pre-war age when grace and refinement were more important than batteries of guns and torpedoes. Of course, at some point during the war she had been fitted with a complement of those, as well, along with a series of increasingly sophisticated upgrades to her electronics.

But the weapons were irrelevant in the ship's history and her mission of pleasure. A presidential yacht could not have offered as many graceful appointments as the *Pearl*. The ship could accommodate fifty guests in luxurious suites. *No hot-bunking on this tub*, Jodi thought. Guests ate their meals in a lavish dining room, with the food served on real silver and china. They could find entertainment ranging from casual conversation in the sitting room to plays on stage. According to the ship's log, the *Pearl* had even once hosted a performance of the Bolshoi Ballet Company.

Jodi had never realized just how rich the Buchet family was until she had come aboard this ship with the entrance codes Tanya had provided. She smiled to herself. It was too bad things hadn't worked out with Tanya, she thought. It would have been nice to marry rich.

Tanya had said she would join them as soon as she could, but that there was some unfinished business she had to take care of. Jodi was not entirely comfortable taking her along, but she was obligated to, for a lot of reasons. She just hoped they were the right ones. She also hoped that Tanya was not intending to do anything foolish. If she did, she would be on her own. Jodi would not be able to help her.

When she finished the pre-flight preparations, Jodi headed aft to find Reza asleep on a leather sofa in the library. She covered him with an immaculately decorated afghan. She could tell that even it had received its share of care over the years, for it smelled clean and fresh, without a trace of the stale reek of age. When his eyes fluttered open, she said, "Go back to sleep. We've got a while longer before we go."

Reza mumbled something unintelligible and did as he was told. Leaning down, she kissed him softly on the lips, then left him to rest.

Back in the cockpit, she went through the ship's abbreviated checklist again. The weapons, above all, were ready. While the yacht's armament made it no more formidable than a Coast Guard cutter, it could still deliver a sharp sting to anyone not being very careful. In addition to the four twin laser barbettes arrayed around the hull, she had two torpedoes in a ventral launcher for more serious situations.

She just hoped she would not have to use them at all. Compared to what was probably arrayed against them, it was little more than a last great act of defiance.

Sitting at the pilot's station, she switched on the data scanner. She had programmed it earlier to sweep any channels it could access for information pertaining to herself or Reza, as well as Tanya, Nicole, and Tony. She hoped the latter two were all right, but all she could do now was pray to a God that she was starting to believe in. She had been having too much luck to believe otherwise.

The computer had graciously prioritized the tidbits it had come across in the last hour or so. And after viewing the first one, Jodi did not need to see any more.

"Ladies and gentleman," announced some talking head news anchor Jodi did not recognize, "we have just received a startling announcement from General Staff Headquarters." The screen cut to the face of someone Jodi knew only from thin gossip: Admiral Laskowski.

"Commodore Marchand," the fleet operations officer said, "in command of the Seventy-Third Reconnaissance Squadron, with her flag aboard the cruiser *Furious*, has reported the capture of two Kreelans, a warrior and a child." The view cut to the two faces, then scenes of the two aliens in an isolation cell. While Jodi was no expert in things Kreelan, there was no mistaking the sheer exhaustion in both of them, notably in the older one, who was incredibly haggard. Worse, their faces were black, just as Reza's wife's face had been the day of the battle for Erlang.

"More significant than the capture itself, however, is that the child is a male, the first living Kreelan male to ever be discovered." There was an animated murmuring in the briefing room a few thousand miles away as the reporters and other attendees assimilated this bit of information. A few people raised their hands for questions, but the admiral ignored them.

"Even more startling," she went on after a suitable pause, "is that we believe the child is the product of the union–" she made it sound like a dirty word, "–between Reza Gard and a high-ranking Kreelan warrior."

The conference room went as silent as a grave. "This is not a joke or a publicity stunt, ladies and gentlemen," the admiral cautioned darkly. "Some of Commodore Marchand's people have been able to establish rudimentary communication with the adult warrior that led to this conclusion." Jodi was suddenly treated to the image of Eustus Camden gesturing to the warrior, and evidently receiving some kind of – to Eustus, anyway – intelligible response. "And the child's overt physiology bears out the claim." Another shot of the child's face.

"My God," Jodi whispered as she leaned closer to the display. "His eyes..." There could be no doubt they were Reza's eyes, the same penetrating green as the boy's mother had when Jodi saw her on Erlang.

Except for one detail near the very end, the rest of the press conference went by in a blur to Jodi, whose mind was still captivated by the face of the child born to parents of two races. The only other thing that she heard and understood was the destination of *Furious* and her living cargo: Erlang.

* * *

Markus Thorella was tired, his body and mind spent in what he considered a good day's work. He opened the door to his apartment and switched on the lights. The furnishings and other adornments, exactly opposite Borge's tastes, were spartan and plain. He spent little time here or in any of the five other dwellings that he held the keys to on as many planets, using it only as a place to rest and recover for the next day's work.

He carefully hung his cap on the hook that silently slid from the wall to accept it, then made his way to the living room – it might have been comfortable had it been furnished – and the waiting bar for a well-earned drink.

He stopped when he saw the glass of scotch sitting in the bar's outlet port.

"Scotch, straight," a female voice purred from the direction of the darkened bedroom. "Just the way you like it. Plain and boring, like you. Turn around, Markus. Slowly."

The back of Thorella's scalp crawled. "I know that voice," he murmured to himself. Turning around, he saw the woman emerge from the shadows. She held a blaster trained on his stomach. "Tanya," he said, a wry smile touching his lips. "It's been a long time."

"I'm so flattered that you recognized me... Anton Borge," she said quietly.

Thorella's smile cracked. "What's that supposed to mean?" he asked innocently. Tried to. He felt the weight of the knife in his uniform sleeve. "The senator has been a good friend of mine since my parents died," he said, "but he's hardly my father."

Tanya shook her head, the anger glowing in her eyes as she stepped further into the light. "Don't play games Anton. I hated your guts when we were children, and I can't say I shed any tears when I found out you'd died in the crash. And then what your father managed to pull off. And what you did to me..."

"Anton Borge is dead, Tanya," he said decisively. "Whatever Jodi Mackenzie told you – it was her, wasn't it? – was garbage. Lies." His voice softened. "I'm sorry that you felt hurt when we... broke up. But that was a long time ago–"

"And I've been living with it ever since," she snapped viciously. "I loved Markus, and you were jealous. I know you were. And after the crash, when I helped him – you – recover, what was my reward? To be raped like an animal until you grew tired of using me and left. It was the perfect crime, Anton. I was so blinded by my feelings for Markus that I never knew that I had been destroyed until you walked away. You took my soul, you bastard. You stole it. And what did your father do to Markus?" She stepped closer, the barrel of the gun unwavering. "Was Markus already dead, or did the good senator murder him?"

"I don't know what you're talking about." The knife slid unseen into his palm. "I am Markus Thorella. If you want to believe otherwise, that's up to you. But I suggest you leave now, or I'll have to call security." He moved toward the comm panel over the bar.

"He killed him, didn't he?" Tanya said almost to herself, her eyes boring into Thorella as he reached for the controls on the wall. "He murdered Markus and stuffed your beaten body into his clothes. And with his power, he bought silence and secrecy, even from his own accursed son." Her finger tensed on the trigger. "Goodbye, Anton."

As Tanya squeezed the trigger, the illegal Kreelan knife that Thorella always carried flew from his hand as he dodged away from the blast of her weapon. He rolled to the floor as the wall behind him exploded in a flash of sparks and the stench of molten plastic, and watched with satisfaction as Tanya slumped to the floor, the knife buried to the hilt just above her right collarbone. The gun fell from her lifeless arm and clattered onto the floor.

"You silly fool," Thorella said as he regained his feet. "You should have just killed me when you had the advantage. But you had to act out your ridiculous little passion play." He smiled. "And now it's going to cost you."

Tanya was already pulling herself toward the gun, the knife a searing pain in her chest as the handle dragged along the floor. A thin trickle of blood seeped from her lips; her right lung had been deeply punctured. She moaned, but did not cry out.

Thorella casually kicked the gun aside. "I'm afraid you already had your chance, Tanya," he said quietly. "Now it's my turn." He knelt down and roughly turned her over. His hands squeezed her breasts, then ran down her stomach to linger between her legs as she struggled weakly against him. "I'd very much like to relive old times," he glanced up at the SECURITY ALERT light, activated by Tanya's blaster firing, "but I'm afraid I just don't have the time."

He knew he would have to work fast. Gripping the knife's protruding handle in one hand, he clamped his other around her throat. "You see, I need to know where Reza and Jodi are, and you're going to tell me."

"Go fuck yourself, you murdering bastard," she hissed through bloody spittle. Working behind the cover of her injured body, one of her hands groped for the tiny transmitter hidden in her belt. A trembling finger pressed the single button on the device's face.

"That's not a very nice thing to say, Tanya," Thorella said with a blazing smile. His hand constricted around her throat to silence her. Then he began to saw the knife back and forth through her bleeding flesh, slowly.

Her mouth opened in a soundless scream.

* * *

"Where the fuck is she?" Jodi whispered to herself. The ship was powered up and ready to go at thirty seconds notice, the clamshell doors to the *Pearl's* docking bay open to the cloud-flecked skies of what was once central France.

"We cannot wait much longer, Jodi," Reza said from the cockpit ramp, startling her.

"How do you feel?" she asked, recovering quickly. She felt like her bare ass was sitting on a cushion of needles.

"I am alive... thanks to you." He sat down next to her, his gaze seeing through her.

"What's that look for?" she asked uncomfortably.

"You care for her, don't you?" he said. "Even after all that has happened, after all this time."

Jodi was silent for a moment. "I was in love with her once, Reza," she said. "And that's something that never really leaves you, I guess, no matter what happens." She frowned. "I think that at one time she was a good person, before Borge and his son corrupted her, suppressed or destroyed what was good in her. I wish I could have known her then."

"Perhaps," Reza said thoughtfully, "you gave her the chance to restore her honor."

Jodi was about to tell him of the news she saw when a voice interrupted them. It was Tanya.

"Jodi," the voice said as a holographic image of Tanya's face appeared on the screen, "if you're hearing this now, then you'll know I can't be with you. I had an old score to settle with a mutual friend of ours, but things haven't gone right and I won't be able to make our rendezvous. You and your friend will have to go on alone in the old *Pearl* to wherever your final destination might be. She's always been a good ship. She's yours, now, and everything else that belongs to me: you're the sole beneficiary in my will now." The recorded image of Tanya's face looked reflective for a moment before it went on. Tanya's real face lay a few thousand kilometers away, contorted in mortal agony. "There are so many things I'd like to say, Jodi, but... the only thing that might matter now – for what little it's worth – is that I'm sorry for what happened between us, for what I did to you. I can't make the past right again, and I won't have a chance to explain everything the way you deserve, but I wanted you to know." A bittersweet smile. "Good luck, Jodi. And goodbye."

The image vanished.

Jodi was silent, staring at the space where her one-time lover had spoken what she knew were Tanya's last words. "She's dead, isn't she?"

Reza nodded solemnly. "I grieve with you," he said quietly, his hand on her shoulder. Her hand covered his.

"Well," Jodi said in a raspy voice, taking her hand away to the more familiar territory of the control console, "I guess we'd better get this tub moving before more trouble shows up."

"Have you decided where we are going?"

"Yes," she said decisively. "Erlang."

As the *Golden Pearl* powered up for its first flight in years, Jodi told Reza of the son he never knew he had.

EIGHT

She's dying, Eustus thought as he looked through the force field screen and into the brig where the two Kreelan prisoners were being held. The warrior lay on one of the cell's two beds that protruded from the wall, her massive frame overwhelming it. While her eyes were closed, Eustus was sure that she knew he was here, watching them. The boy-child, Shera-Khan, knelt next to her, gently stroking her hair with his red talons.

Eustus took in a deep breath. "All right, private," he said to the Marine at the brig controls, "open the door."

"Are you sure, gunny?" the commodore asked from behind him. "You don't have to do this." Eustus turned to the small knot of officers behind him. Without uttering a word, he only nodded his head.

Commodore Marchand nodded to the private at the door controls, who in turn exchanged a glance with the four other Marines who guarded the entrance. Their weapons snapped to the ready. The hum of the force field dropped away, and the force field warning light surrounding the portal went off. Inside, Shera-Khan stood up and turned to watch. The great warrior did not move.

"Okay, gunny," the private said in a hushed voice.

Eustus stepped into the cell, the force field snapping up behind him just as his feet cleared the doorway. For a long moment, he and Shera-Khan regarded one another in silence. The fact that they had managed to get this far was nothing short of miraculous, Eustus thought. He would have given anything to have seen the look on the faces of the cutter's crew and surviving Marines back on the planet in the mist when they opened the door, only to be faced with a giant of a Kreelan warrior holding a child in one arm and Eustus slung over her shoulder. According to the crew's report (Eustus having been unconscious at the time), the warrior had simply leaped into the passenger bay like she belonged there, pushing people out of the way to make a place for herself and the injured child after she carefully set Eustus down on the deck. Everyone had been too shocked to even think of shooting, and the flight back to the *Furious* was spent in silent awe.

Once aboard the cruiser, little had changed. Commodore Marchand perceived the situation correctly and realized that the warrior wanted them to help save the young one's life, just as she had saved Eustus. The two prisoners and the injured gunnery sergeant had been spirited to sickbay, where they had saved Shera-Khan. The boy's recovery, Eustus had noted with little surprise, had taken astonishingly little time. He was on his feet just four hours after surgery, and then he and the warrior were escorted by a platoon of Marines to the brig.

Now, looking at the boy, Eustus could not shake the tingle of excitement that came from the realization that this was the son, the flesh and blood, of Eustus's best friend. Looking into the boy's fierce green eyes, Eustus could see the fire that he had known to be in his father's, and an intellect that Eustus could not even guess at.

"I thought you might like some food," he said awkwardly. The boy had eaten nothing since his recovery, despite the best efforts of the intel officers and the cooks. Eustus finally convinced the commodore herself to allow him to try. After all, he had explained, he was the only one aboard who had ever known the one real Kreelan expert: Reza. He slowly set a tray of food down on the shelf that protruded from the wall near the head of the warrior's bed.

The boy's eyes flicked to the food – two slabs of raw meat (syntho, of course) and two mugs of the alcoholic concoction Reza had taught him to make – then back to Eustus. Then back to the food. Eustus could tell that he was starving, and not just from the last two days. Something told him the boy had probably not eaten for a lot longer than that.

"Go ahead," he urged as he stepped away. "Try it."

Shera-Khan made no move to sample what Eustus had brought him until a single whispered word escaped the lips of the warrior lying nearby.

"*N'yadeh*," she said. *Eat.*

The boy turned and bowed his head to her, and Eustus saw that her eyes, sparkling with silver, were open and fixed on Shera-Khan to ensure he obeyed. He saluted her with his left fist over his chest, uttering something that Eustus could not make out. The warrior said nothing, but closed her eyes as the boy turned away to regard the food more closely. Then, his decision made, he reached for one of the chunks of meat.

Eustus watched as he carefully carved it with the claws of his shaking hands, slicing the meat into finger-wide strips. Only when it was completely cut did he begin to eat, his eyes all the while fixed on Eustus.

Slowly, with his hands at his sides, Eustus backed up to the far wall and took a seat on the floor, watching as Shera-Khan inhaled his food. The boy sniffed at one of the mugs. Glancing at Eustus, he hefted it to his lips and swallowed some of the warm, bitter ale that had been Reza's favorite drink. He made a quiet humph of evident satisfaction before drinking down the rest.

In but a few minutes, both pieces of meat were gone, consumed by the boy's hunger and the whispered order of the warrior. That done, he turned to her with the other mug, offering her a drink. Drawn to the heady scent of the ale, the warrior tried to lever herself upright, but only managed a few centimeters before her strength gave out. Shera-Khan tried to lift her head, but she was too heavy for him to move.

"Let me help," Eustus offered, coming slowly over to them, his arms before him, palms up. *See,* he thought, *no weapons.*

Shera-Khan narrowed his eyes, but did not try to hinder Eustus as he knelt down beside him. With trembling hands, Eustus cradled the great warrior's head, lifting her enough that she could swallow some of the ale the boy held to her lips.

As Eustus gently lowered her back onto the bed, the Kreelan warrior's eyes met his. Her lips seemed to struggle, and then formed two words that Eustus would remember for the rest of his life.

"Thank... you," she said softly. He stared blankly at her for a moment, too shocked to speak.

"You're... you're welcome," he breathed finally. She motioned almost imperceptibly with her head in acknowledgment before her eyes closed again, a grimace of pain flickering over her blackened face.

"I wish I knew what was wrong with her," Eustus muttered to himself.

"She mourns," the boy beside him said softly.

Concealing his shock at the boy's knowledge of Standard, Eustus asked in a carefully controlled voice, "What do you mean, 'she mourns?' Who is she mourning for?" An explanation for how – and why – the boy had learned humanity's primary language would have to wait.

The boy turned his blazing green eyes to him. "She mourns for the Empress," he said with a voice far, far older than his years, with a sadness that gripped Eustus's heart, "who now sleeps in Darkness, Her heart and spirit broken by Her Own hand." The boy shivered, as if sobbing. "The hour that should have been the greatest in our history, the crowning glory of our people, cast us instead into chaos and ruin. Her voice no longer sings in our blood, Her spirit is silent. Behind a barrier of fire, She lays dying of guilt and grief. And so, too, shall we die."

"What do you mean?" Eustus asked. "Who's going to die?"

The boy looked up at him, a stricken expression on his face. "All that has ever been, all that is, all that will ever be, shall be no more the moment Her heart ceases to beat, Her last breath taken. With the First Empress was our Way destined. With Her heart stilled shall it end, and Her Children shall perish from the world."

Eustus glanced up just in time to see Commodore Marchand disappearing, no doubt for the comms center and a patch through to sector command. She had no more idea of what the boy was talking about than Eustus did, but the significance of those words was apparent enough. Something was seriously wrong in the Empire, and if it could be exploited to the Confederation's advantage, they might have a hope of winning this war.

Eustus was about to ask more questions, to press the boy for what he meant, when Shera-Khan curled onto the floor, trembling. Without thinking, Eustus reached out to him, taking him into his arms as he might have any bereaved human child. And then, when what he had just done struck home, he realized that this was not an alien enemy, implacable and unstoppable, but the son of his best friend.

"Shera-Khan," he said, "would you like to meet your father?"

The boy stiffened against him. "The priestess told me of this," he replied hesitantly, "that you had made signs to her while on the nursery world that my father was alive. But how can it be so? The Empress's blade cut through his heart."

"No, no," Eustus said, holding Shera-Khan so that their eyes met. "He didn't die in that battle. He was terribly wounded, yes, but he survived. He's still alive, on Earth." He paused. "He doesn't even know he has a son, that he has you."

Shera-Khan did not know what to believe. He desperately wished his father to be alive, but he could not understand how it could be so. His mother would never have let the humans take him had there been a breath remaining in his body.

The great priestess suddenly spoke, her voice little more than a murmur.

"The priestess bids you to take us to him," Shera-Khan translated for her. "To Reza. My father."

* * *

As he looked out over the apron of the New York flight terminal, Tony Braddock silently wondered how many times he had been at places like this. Dozens, hundreds, perhaps? But he had always been the one about to step onto a waiting shuttle, impatient loadmasters herding their human cargo aboard as if they were ignorant cattle, which perhaps they sometimes were.

But today, as he had on several previous occasions, he was bidding farewell to the woman he loved. They would see one another again as the Armada sailed into enemy space, but he couldn't shake the feeling that she was leaving him.

Nicole stood beside him, her mind focused on the anthill of humans and machines that had been working around the clock for the past two days. They were moving millions of tons of materiel and hundreds of thousands of people in support of the great armada that at this very moment was assembling in the skies above the Earth and a hundred other worlds that were home to Humanity. Her fighter, one of dozens that still crowded the ramps at this late hour, was fueled and ready. The crew chief, a man she had never met before, stood impatiently by.

He looked at her, and wondered if he were not a fool for not knocking her to the ground and carrying her away from this madness. She was hardly in shape for a fight, he told himself. The business with Reza – Braddock still refused to believe it – had eaten at her like a cancer since Reza's escape several days ago. Her bond to him was yet unbroken, he was sure, but where it would lead her, God alone only knew.

And then the new president had announced the formation of the great fleet to carry out Operation Millennium. The call for "every able-bodied flight officer and rating" to serve on the horde of warships and auxiliaries that was about to sail into Kreelan space had drawn her inexorably, like a bee to an intoxicating nectar. They had argued about it, but only once: Tony had learned early on that after Nicole had decided something, there was no appeal. She was a fighter pilot, she had told him firmly, and would not be denied the chance to participate in the Confederation's finest hour. Tony knew it was more than that: it was an opportunity, no matter how slight, of somehow finding Reza. She stood a better chance of finding him somewhere among the stars than anywhere on Earth.

Braddock, too, would be setting sail with The Armada, as it was now being called. Borge had insisted on going aboard the flagship, and had told the Council in not-so-subtle terms that anyone who did not accompany him was a coward and a traitor. The sycophants, of course, ever ready to seize any opportunity to implant themselves further in Borge's rectum, had hailed the action as a stroke of patriotic genius. Braddock and his few remaining compatriots were compelled to join the parade, regardless of their own opinions of the foolhardiness of the expedition. While Braddock had not had a chance to speak with Zhukovski directly, he had seen the resigned look on his face when Borge announced in a joint civil-military meeting that he and his entourage were going along. L'Houillier had hung his head. There was little doubt in Braddock's mind as to who would really be in charge of the operation. Braddock's greatest surprise was that Borge hadn't sacked both L'Houillier and Zhukovski, until he realized that the megalomaniac was keeping them as scapegoats in case of failure.

Like a dark cloud temporarily obscuring the sun, Tony found himself hoping the flagship would not return home.

"It is time," Nicole said quietly, washing away the dark thoughts in Braddock's mind. Across the apron, the crew chief was holding up his wrist and pointing. *Time to go.*

Tony kissed her, and they held one another for a brief moment. "Take care of yourself, Nicole. Please. I'll see you as soon as I can."

She nodded, squeezing him tighter. "I love you," she said before letting go.

"Je t'aime aussi," he replied.

She smiled, then turned to go.

He watched as she climbed into her ship. The crew chief made sure she was strapped in before he climbed down the crew ladder, saluted her, then headed off to the next waiting fighter.

Nicole waved one final time to Braddock, then her Corsair lifted off, soaring skyward. It grew smaller, dwindling with distance. Then it was gone.

"*Merde,*" he whispered after her. *Good luck.*

NINE

"Gunnery Sergeant Camden reporting as ordered, ma'am."

Commodore Marchand acknowledged his crisp salute with a nod. "Please, gunny, sit down and be at ease."

Eustus glanced uncomfortably at the single empty chair at the end of the conference table. The other chairs were filled with the squadron's senior officers and the commander of *Furious's* Marine detachment.

"Uh... yes, ma'am." Stiffly, he took his seat, sitting bolt upright as he faced Marchand at the opposite end of the table. He had never been in the flag conference room before, and, under the circumstances, this was not a good time for a first visit. Some hours before, he had been a brevet captain. He had subsequently been reduced to his real rank in the aftermath of the day's news.

There was a moment of awkward silence as Eustus watched the officers mentally adjust themselves to his presence in the room. After the report of President Nathan's murder at the hands of Reza Gard, Eustus – guilty by association as a friend of the renegade – had quickly found himself ostracized from the ship's company. Since then, he had spent nearly all his time with the two Kreelans, for – ironically – they were the only ones aboard who didn't seem openly hostile to him.

"Gunny," Marchand began, "no doubt you've heard the rumors running through the ship regarding a possible fleet assault into Kreelan space."

"Yes, ma'am," Eustus replied uncertainly. There had been a lot of rumors through the ship since the Kreelan prisoners had been brought aboard, rumors that had become more fanciful and fierce with every turn of the watch since the news of the president's death.

Marchand nodded. "Well, as it turns out," she went on, "such an operation is in progress, and it's codenamed Operation Millennium. Even as we speak, ships are assembling throughout the Confederation for a sortie into the Empire for what Fleet HQ hopes will be the decisive blow against the enemy's fleet and their homeworld." She paused. "We have been given the opportunity to play a leading role in that operation, and that is where I need your help."

Eustus fought to suppress the trepidation he felt at what he knew must be coming. His fellow Marines, not to mention the squids, had branded him a traitor because he refused to believe the reports of Reza's involvement with the president's death and the other murders that had been committed in its wake. The morale on the ship had taken a nosedive after Marchand announced the news. Nathan had been a very popular president, and his death was not taken lightly. And now, Eustus knew with an instinctive certainty, he was going to be offered some way of "redeeming" himself before God, Corps, and Country. "Uh... sure, ma'am," he said. "What can I do?"

"The plans for Millennium have been underway since shortly before President Nathan's death," she told him gravely. "And Reza Gard's actions and his escape have endangered that operation. If he reaches Kreelan space to warn them, everything we have been preparing for could be lost. We have received orders to stop Reza Gard, by, as quoted in the orders, 'any and all means necessary, without limitation or exception.'" Marchand fixed Eustus with a calculated glare. "A plan was devised at Fleet HQ for getting the information we need, gunnery sergeant, but the success of this plan depends entirely upon your loyalty and devotion to the Confederation cause, regardless of the consequences to you personally."

Marchand's words were more than shocking. Eustus felt violated, raped. The very foundation of his existence had been loyalty to the Confederation, to humanity, and not least of all to the Corps whose uniform he wore. They were asking – no, telling – him that to be considered worthy, risking death for all these years was not enough. His mere association with Reza and his alleged crimes were enough to strip Eustus of all dignity, reducing his past sufferings and accomplishments to nothing. Offering his life to his nation was not enough. No, he had to do something more.

Ignoring the hot sting of tears that he felt boiling in his eyes, he said through clenched teeth, "What are my orders, ma'am?"

Marchand nodded. "High Command allowed extracts of your initial report on the prisoners, specifically that the boy appears to be Reza Gard's offspring," Marchand's mouth wrapped itself around the word with difficulty, as if it were an enormous, rotten apple, "to be released to the press after President Nathan's murder. Internal Security apparently was unable to capture Gard and Commander Jodi Mackenzie, who as you know is believed to have aided him. Security believes they escaped together off-world, and the information was broadcast in hopes of luring them to a chosen location: Erlang."

Enya, Eustus thought instantly. Lord of All, he thought helplessly, what is happening? And what do they want me to do, kill Reza and Jodi? He waited, dreading her next words.

Marchand understood what he was thinking. "You're the only one who can get close to him, Camden, close enough to either stun him or kill him. Either result will satisfy your orders. The same applies to Commander Mackenzie."

Eustus blinked. "But they haven't even been tried," he whispered hoarsely. "How can I be ordered to kill – *assassinate* – someone who hasn't even had a trial to determine their guilt or innocence?"

"Their guilt or innocence is not your concern, gunnery sergeant," Marchand warned stonily. "The president and the Council decided his fate and that of Mackenzie based on overwhelming evidence that no court could ignore. Now, I don't particularly care for your opinion on the matter. You have received your orders. The only question is, will you carry them out?"

Eustus sat quietly for a moment. *What if I'm wrong?* he thought. What if Reza *had* killed the president? Didn't they used to say that the best spies were the ones you never suspected?

No, he decided, at least not in this case. But even that did not matter. Reza was a Marine, trained to fight and kill his nation's enemies. But he was not a murderer, an assassin. Reza was a brother to him, and had offered his own life to protect Eustus countless times, and Eustus had returned the honor. On top of that, Reza was his best friend. Reza had never betrayed him. And Eustus simply couldn't accept that either he or Jodi had betrayed the Confederation.

The people around this table, he thought, throughout this ship, had belittled his sacrifices, his honor as a Marine and as a human being. Considering Marchand's offer, it was easy to make up his mind. Reza, even more than the Corps, had taught him the meaning of honor, and of being true to one's self regardless of the consequences. Eustus had offered his blood over the years to show his loyalty to the Confederation; he would not offer up his soul.

Straightening up in his chair, his eyes boring into Marchand's, he said, "Commodore Marchand, I respectfully submit that I cannot obey the orders you have given me. Ma'am."

The faces in the room turned to chilled stone.

"You know what this means, don't you?" she said in the hush of the room.

"Yes, ma'am."

Marchand leaned back in her chair, eyeing Eustus like some kind of offending insect. "You've got one chance to reconsider, Camden," she said icily.

"Negative, commodore," Eustus said firmly. "I cannot–" he hesitated, "– *will not* – help you in this. It's illegal and it's wrong."

She looked down at the table in disappointment. "Very well," she said quietly. Turning to the commander of the Marine contingent, she said, "Captain, please place Gunnery Sergeant Camden under arrest and throw him in the brig. Charges..." She paused, looking up at Eustus. "Charge him with high treason, as ordered by Confederation High Command."

"Aye, aye, commodore," the Marine officer said stiffly. With a signal from her console, two Marines appeared at the door to the conference room. This situation had been anticipated. "Marines," the captain ordered, "escort Gunnery Sergeant Camden to the brig." She glanced toward Marchand, who nodded. "Throw him in with the Kreelans."

"Yes, ma'am," the corporal in charge of the detail replied sharply.

Eustus stood up, saluted the commodore, and left with the guard detail.

Marchand turned her attention to the comms display facing her chair and hidden from everyone else's view. "I don't like this, General," she said sternly. "Camden is a good Marine."

"No one asked you to like it, commodore," replied the newly frocked Brigadier General Markus Thorella, Special Assistant to the President. "Just carry out your orders and be as predictable as Camden was." The smile disappeared behind a mask of vengeful conceit. "We have gone to great lengths to ensure that Reza Gard and his accomplice will head to Erlang and into your waiting arms, and you are to let nothing – I repeat, nothing – interfere with the execution," he smiled at the word, "of that mission. After that, you only have to hold him until the fleet rendezvous at Erlang and then transfer him to the flagship for his execution. And Mackenzie's." He stared at her. "Have I made myself clear, commodore?"

"Perfectly," she grunted, furious with this lackey's arrogance toward someone whose date of rank and command experience vastly outweighed his own.

Thorella nodded. "You will receive further instructions as necessary," he said tersely. "Thorella, out."

END TRANSMISSION blazed across the screen beneath the Confederation insignia.

Infuriated, Marchand slammed her hand on the control console, shutting down her end of the link.

"Bastard," she hissed.

* * *

Aboard the starliner *Helena*, Thorella leaned back in his ready room chair and smiled. Looking out the floor-to-ceiling viewport of his personal command ship, he saw over five hundred starships spread over thousands of cubic kilometers of space, all preparing for their final jump to Erlang where they would rendezvous with nearly three thousand more Confederation ships. It was the greatest armada in human history. And *he* was a key part of it. The thought exhilarated him and gave him a burning erection in his trousers.

But the part of the plan that he liked best was that he would finally get to see Reza Gard die. He had no doubt that Gard would try to escape; in fact, Thorella was counting on it. He knew Gard could do it on his own, but Thorella had decided to improve the odds, putting Camden on the inside and Carré on the outside, after convincing the president to order her put back on flight status. Between those two and Mackenzie, not to mention the two Kreelans, Thorella was perfectly confident that Gard would escape. And then he would joyfully hunt them down – Gard, Mackenzie, Camden, and Carré – and see them to the gallows. At last, after all these years, he would have them. He would have them all.

As he watched the ships of the armada wheel across space, his mind seduced by power, his right hand freed his throbbing member from the confines of its fabric keep. Alone in his ready room, his heart hammering in time with his hand, Thorella saluted the fleet that he knew would someday be his.

TEN

As the *Golden Pearl* slid through the whirling bands of light that were the only perceptible reality of hyperspace, Jodi contemplated the future, both for herself and for the few real friends she had in the Universe. For all of them, it looked unalterably bleak. Reza an accused murderer, with Jodi named as his accomplice; Nicole's career irreparably damaged by her association with both of them; and poor Tony, who might have someday gained enough political clout to really do the Confederation some good, politically devastated by the whole trumped-up scandal. *Things are looking pretty shitty for the home team*, she thought.

Checking on the *Pearl's* instruments to see how long they had before dropping back into reality, Jodi wondered if coming to Erlang was such a good idea. There was nothing, really, left on Erlang except the survivors who, like so many humans on so many worlds, were trying to pull themselves up from the rubble left in the wake of war. She thought they might have some friends there, but would they welcome the two fugitives with open arms or with the muzzles of pulse guns?

But those were better odds than they might face anywhere else. The news of Nathan's death had been broadcast on every human communication channel, and it was unlikely that, with the possible exception of the Erlangers, anyone who had been exposed to the propaganda – and that would be nearly everyone in the Confederation – would be willing to help them.

Besides, she thought, now that Reza knows that his son might be on his way to Erlang, there was no stopping him. While he spoke little, his few words conveyed to her the overpowering love he felt for his wife, and for the son he had never known. That alone, she thought, was something to really make one believe in God or the Devil, depending on how you looked at it.

What was the boy like? she wondered. She, along with the rest of humanity, had never seen anything other than an adult Kreelan female. She had heard Eustus and Enya describe the mummified remains of the adult males they had seen in the burial chamber on Erlang before the Kreelan attack there, but it was not the same. This was a living child, the blood of the man who had become a part of her life years ago, and who had shared his body and his soul with an alien, an enemy of Jodi's people. She remembered the woman's face, reliving her agony. From what Reza had said, it now appeared that Esah-Zhurah, too, was in mortal danger, as was her entire race. She wondered at the magnitude of an entire civilization suddenly dying out, with no survivors or descendants, and felt a sudden tremor of empathy for them.

"Christ in a chariot-driven sidecar," she muttered to herself, shaking her head in wonder. "What the hell am I thinking?" She glanced at one of the instruments on the copilot's side, noticing that Reza had slipped into the chair beside her without a sound. Anyone else might have been startled or surprised; Jodi had long since become accustomed to it.

"Five minutes to normal space and Erlang," she told him, noting that his face barely looked human, his features oddly contorted into a human mimicry of Kreelan expressions. He was reverting, she thought to herself, becoming a Kreelan again for what would probably be the last days – or hours – of his life. And of hers. "You feel okay?"

"Yes," he answered, then was silent as he stared out the viewscreen at the glowing starfield. "Jodi," he said after a moment, "I have decided to take a boat down to the surface, leaving you free to escape back into hyperspace. I can think of no way of getting a chance to see my son except by surrendering." He looked at her, his alien eyes sad now. "I would spare you the fate that will surely befall me."

"And where the hell am I supposed to go, Reza?" she asked, more hurt than angry. She needed him to need her right now. "I know Borge's dirty little secrets, remember? I don't think he's going to just let me walk away once he has you. I know the *Pearl's* a nice ship and all, but I really don't want to spend the rest of my life flitting around the galaxy in her, alone." She shook her head vigorously. "Look, brother, we're in this together, we stay in this together. If nothing else, we can hold hands as we swing on the gallows."

Reza nodded, knowing what she would say. He reached over and gently squeezed her hand.

The warning klaxon suddenly blared, announcing that the *Pearl* was about to drop back into real space. Beyond the wraparound viewport, the streaks of light suddenly quivered, then quickly began to contract and weave, soon becoming discrete points of light. Then they saw the glimmering bulk of Erlang.

But the planet's beauty was suddenly eclipsed by a Confederation destroyer that was sailing close enough to see the seams in her armor. The sight sent a chill up Jodi's spine. She instinctively reached for the weapons controls, but Reza stayed her hand.

"No," he said firmly. "They have been waiting for us."

"You knew?" she asked incredulously.

Reza nodded. "We have been led here," he said as he turned his attention to the destroyer.

There was nothing to do but go forward. With a deft movement of her fingers across the console, Jodi brought the *Pearl* away from her near-collision course with the warship. On the scanner, she noticed that there were three more Confederation ships, a cruiser and two destroyers, orbiting the planet.

"Well," Jodi muttered as an indicator winked in the display, "it looks like you're right about them expecting us." She opened a channel.

"Inbound vessel," a voice announced from an unfamiliar face that immediately appeared on the console, "identify yourself immediately!"

Jodi felt another tingle as she saw the lock-on indicators on the *Pearl's* defense display. The destroyer was tracking them with its main guns, at point blank range.

"This is Commander Jodi Mackenzie, piloting the *Golden Pearl*," she replied coolly, "serial B78-4C97101K, bound for Erlang."

The officer on the destroyer answered immediately. "Commander, you are hereby ordered to rendezvous with the cruiser *Furious*, where you and Captain Gard will be placed under arrest." He paused. "Any attempt to escape or reach the planet's surface will be met with the instant destruction of you and your vessel. Do you understand?"

"Yes," Jodi replied coolly. "We understand and will comply."

Beside her, Reza's green eyes were fixed on the gray-hulled cruiser that was even now drawing toward them. The ship that held his son.

* * *

Their reception aboard the *Furious* was little short of openly hostile. Fitted in the airlock with wrist and ankle binders that would explode if tampered with or opened without the proper electronic key, Jodi and Reza were marched separately, each inside a box of Marines armed with stunners, to the brig. Aside from the rhythmic stomping of their footsteps, the corridors were devoid of activity, the crew having been evacuated from the corridors the escort would use to get the prisoners to their destination.

A sense of uneasy anticipation had taken hold of Reza, not out of concern for his own welfare, but for his son, if he truly existed. For all the years Reza had been in the Empire and all the years since, he had never dreamed that such an honor – a child – could ever be his. But the Change that he and Esah-Zhurah had undergone those long years ago must have made it possible. And it was the fate of that legacy that most concerned him now, even more than his burning fear of what had befallen Esah-Zhurah, for he knew in his heart that in his son lay the key to the survival of both civilizations.

His only hope now was that the humans – he thought of himself as Kreelan again – would allow him at least to see the boy, if not speak to him. His hands clenched with nervous tension as they approached the slate gray armored doors to the brig.

The shielded doors opened as they approached, sliding back into the walls like the shifting jaws of a snake. Reza was led first through the security baffles and into the inner chamber. Along the rear wall were three cells, one of which was occupied.

"Reza!" Eustus called through the force field barrier.

But Reza did not hear him. His eyes and his mind were fixed on the Kreelan child who stood at Eustus's side, staring with equal fascination at Reza, his father. As if he were adrift in a river, Reza sensed himself being pushed and prodded into the cell. Standing within arm's reach of one another, father and son looked into each other's eyes, gauging their similarities, their differences, the miracle of their own unique existence.

Behind them, Jodi pulled Eustus to the side. Their time to speak would come, but not just now.

Slowly, Shera-Khan knelt before his father. Bowing his head, he saluted Reza. "Greetings, priest of the Desh-Ka," he said in the New Tongue, "my father."

"Greetings, my son," Reza choked, tears streaming down his cheeks. "What is thy name?"

"Shera-Khan, my father," the boy replied solemnly.

"Rise, Shera-Khan, my son," Reza said. "Let me look upon you." The boy stood and looked up at Reza, who offered his arms in the traditional greeting of warriors. Shera-Khan accepted, and the two touched one another for the first time, both afraid that the other was an illusion, a cruel hoax played by Fate. But the blood that trickled from the tiny punctures made by Shera-Khan's claws and the strength of Reza's grip on his son's arms convinced them both that each was very real. "Blessed be Her name," Reza whispered. "How much of thy mother do I see in thy face."

Shera-Khan trembled in mourning at his mention of his mother.

"The Empress now is she," he told Reza, sending a burning flare of apprehension through Reza's heart. "Oh, Father, She lays dying. Broken is Her heart, silent is Her spirit. We are lost!"

Instinctively, Reza pulled Shera-Khan close, wrapping his arms around him as his mind grappled with the boy's words.

It was then that he heard another voice, old and familiar, speak to him in the language of the Old Tongue. "Come to me, my son." Turning to the left, toward the far wall of the cell, he saw the great warrior who had been so much a part of his life, who had given him her legacy of knowledge and power, who had given him her love. "Tesh-Dar," he whispered, rocked by her state of mourning and her weak condition. Holding Shera-Khan close at his side, he swiftly knelt beside her, taking her great hands in his, her skin cold to his touch. "My mother."

Her wise eyes took in his face, and she smiled in the Kreelan way, an expression of joy in such an hour of sorrow. "Reza," she whispered, "my son, you are alive. The animal..." She stopped herself. "No. Your *friend's* words were true." She pulled him close to her, his head to her breast, and smelled his skin, his hair. Running her hands across his braids, pausing at the seventh that had been severed and where the hair had ceased to grow, she said, "Great was my fear, my child, that the human's words that you yet lived were false, that the sword of your love did take your life. I would have killed him, had I not sensed that he spoke truly." In but a few words, she described to him how Eustus had saved her and Shera-Khan, and how she had discovered that Reza was still alive, or at least had been given the hope that he was.

"And that has been my only hope, my son," she told him painfully, "for Shera-Khan, for the Empire. For without you, we are doomed."

"What has happened?" Reza asked quietly, watching with alarm as Tesh-Dar struggled for breath. Beside him, Shera-Khan pressed close, his body shivering with a grief no human could ever imagine. Reza would have felt it, too, except that his connection to the living Empress had been severed. He had lived the years since then in acute spiritual loneliness, but he had also been spared the horrible fate of the peers.

Tesh-Dar closed her eyes, and Reza feared that she had lost consciousness, perhaps for the last time.

But then she began to speak of the legend of Keel-Tath.

* * *

Long ago, so the legends say, after Keel-Tath cursed Her people for their treachery and what She believed to be the murder of Her lover, the First Empress was filled with anger and grief, sorrow and melancholy. The breath of life no longer appealed to Her, and so it was that She decided to hasten Her soul unto the Dark Place, where She could lament Her fate in solitude, forever. With a trembling hand, she raised a dagger over Her heart to steal away Her life, and that of Her people.

But a young priestess, Dara-Kol of the Desh-Ka, beseeched the heartbroken Empress for a chance for Her Children, now fallen from grace, to redeem themselves in Her eyes. So passionate was the young priestess's plea that Keel-Tath, Her wisdom overpowering Her distress, granted the young one's wish.

Gathering around Her a host of the now stricken males, the Imperial Guard, Keel-Tath returned them to their former grace and glory. "My guardians, My companions, shall you be, throughout Eternity," She proclaimed. The warriors fell to their knees in devotion to Her, their voices as one pledging their eternal honor to Her name, in life and in death.

Turning to Dara-Kol, who alone had had the courage to venture into the Empress's presence after the Fall, She produced a crystal heart. It was a work glorious to the eye, which was the greatest and last gift from Her lover. "When I rest," She told the young priestess, "this shall be the key to My awakening. For the one who holds the good fortune to find it, and has the courage to brave the host of guardians, the one who lays a living hand upon My heart shall awaken My spirit and My call to thee.

"But the Curse shall not be broken," She warned, "until My heart again feels the warmth of love. If I rise in spirit without such love, damned shall we all be to everlasting Darkness."

Dara-Kol fell at the Empress's feet in thanks, even then mourning the passing of the First Empress from the Spirit that bound their people together, the loss of Her power, Her magic. Her love.

Keel-Tath looked upon Dara-Kol and told her, "Rise, My child. For you shall be the First of the Last. In your blood shall flow My blood, that you may lead your people in their quest for redemption." Keel-Tath took the young woman's hand, and with the knife she carried at Her side caused their palms to bleed, then bound them together. "Your spirit shall bind with those who may follow in your footsteps, so that the wisdom of the living Empress shall be ever greater, as shall Her power. One female shall be born each great cycle, born with white hair and strong spirit, one who may ascend to the throne. I vow that this succession shall not be broken before the day the Last Empress receives Me into Her heart. This shall be My Promise to you, to My Children."

Dara-Kol closed her eyes, feeling the power of Keel-Tath as Her blood mingled with her own. She trembled with fear and anticipation, of longing to lead her people to their redemption. "And how, Empress, are we to find you?" she asked.

Keel-Tath answered softly, as if from afar, "That, daughter, shall be thy quest."

When Dara-Kol opened her eyes, Keel-Tath, along with the males who had pledged to guard Her forever, was gone. All that remained was a single braid of Her hair upon the floor, the Seventh Braid that joined Her to the spirit of the Empire. And as Dara-Kol watched, the braid fell into dust, to be carried away by a sudden tempest that swept through the great chamber and away into the great forests beyond.

Alone now, no longer a high priestess but the living Empress, Dara-Kol heard the anguished cries of Her people in Her blood, and She wept in Her heart for their loss.

* * *

Tesh-Dar shuddered under Reza's hands. "And so it happened, my son," she went on, "that Esah-Zhurah was fated to be the Last Empress before Keel-Tath's return." The pain in her voice deepened. "But Esah-Zhurah's soul was dead, for she lived in the belief that she had slain the keeper of her heart, that she had killed you, Reza. Black with mourning has been her body since the day you left us, and blacker still was her spirit after the day her sword pierced your breast. And when the Ascension took place, the old Empress passing Her flame to Esah-Zhurah, the new Empress took the glowing crystal heart in Her hands, for it was time for the last part of the Prophecy to be fulfilled, for Keel-Tath's return to the Blood." She moaned at the memory, her great hand constricting painfully around Reza's. "Never have I known such pain, my son, as when She cried out, as if Her heart had been torn from her breast. Then she fell to the dais of the throne and lay still.

"The Empire shuddered, my son," she went on quietly, her eyes fixed on a place that Reza knew contained only agony, a Kreelan incarnation of spiritual Hell. "Billions of voices cried out in fear and pain as Her voice suddenly was stilled in their blood. And in the palace on the Empress Moon, the crystal heart, lying dark beside Her, began again to glow. But this time it was not as a summons, but as a warning. For all who attempted to approach the wall of blue light that it cast around Her body died, vanishing in a shower of sparks and the stench of scorched flesh." She closed her eyes. "By the thousands did they perish, all the peers who witnessed the ceremony, all who tried to reach her. All of them. Gone."

"And you, my priestess?" Reza asked quietly.

Tesh-Dar grimaced, turning her mournful gaze toward him. "I would have joined them, so stricken with grief was I, save that I was entrusted with the life of your son. Since the day of his birth, Shera-Khan's welfare has been my honor and responsibility. Had I allowed either of us to be drawn into the fire, all my life would have counted for nothing but disgrace in Her eyes. Shera-Khan and I alone survived. Of the high priestesses and warriors, they are no more, their spirits having fallen into darkness as their bodies burned to ashes in the light. I left with Shera-Khan, closing the doors to the throne room and forbidding anyone to enter, hoping to spare any more the fate of those already dead and gone. It was then that I left the Homeworld for the Nursery where Shera-Khan was born, where your human... friend... found me, for in my bereavement I knew not where else to go, for I believed you long dead." She shook her head sadly. "But even the nursery was empty, the Wardress having evacuated all of her charges when Her voice was silenced, her fleet returning the children – even the males – home. All that remained there were the Books of Time, dead stone recounting the lineage of a dying race."

Reza felt the meaning of her words settle upon his heart, oppressive and undeniable. He could not imagine the strength of will it must have taken for her to resist the urge to reach for the Empress. And the deaths of the high priestesses, the greatest of the Empire's warriors, meant that...

"I shall be the last," he said slowly, the full weight of the responsibility he bore settling upon his shoulders. When Tesh-Dar died, he would be the last of the warrior high priests and priestesses.

"True are your words, my son," Tesh-Dar said, gently stroking his face. "For when death takes me, you alone shall be the last of the warriors to bear the mark of the ancient orders. You alone have the gifts that have been passed down from generation to generation. You alone have the honor to lead the peers in this darkest of hours. You and your love are the last hope of the Empire, for all that we are and have ever been shall be lost if the breath of life is allowed to pass from Her body. Breathes does She still, but millions die each moment She sleeps in Darkness, in mourning, their crying souls lost in eternal Darkness. And in the moment Her heart stops and Her spirit passes into the Beyond, the Empire shall be lost forever – and all of us with it."

Reza watched as her eyes closed and her breathing slowed. Her hand loosened from his as she fell into sleep, exhaustion finally claiming its due. Leaning forward, he kissed her tenderly on the forehead.

"Sleep, my mother," he whispered. Beside him, Shera-Khan had fallen into a troubled slumber. The pain of reliving those horrible hours as thousands had cast themselves into the wall of blue fire in the desperate hope of reaching the Empress had drained what few reserves of strength the boy had. Reza laid him gently on the other bed, his blood burning with a cold fire at the Way that had been laid before him, the final steps of a great journey that had begun millennia ago.

Beside him, Jodi placed her tunic over the boy. Reza felt her hand on his arm.

"Will they be all right?" she asked quietly. Eustus had told her what he knew and what had happened to bring them to this strange crossroads, and Jodi had found herself filled with empathy not only for the boy, but for the dying warrior, as well.

Reza looked at her, and she was shocked by the stricken, almost desperate look in his eyes. "No," he said, his voice hoarse with emotion, "they are dying. All of them."

Eustus looked confused. "What do you mean?"

"Unless I can find a way back to the Empire," Reza told him, "the Empress... my wife, shall soon die. And with Her shall die our entire race. The Empire of Kreela shall be no more."

Jodi and Eustus exchanged a glance.

"Reza," Jodi said tentatively, not sure just how he might react to what she was going to say, "I'm not sure that would be... such a bad thing, at least for humanity. I mean, we've been at war with the Empire for nearly a hundred years. They killed your parents, remember? There aren't many people who would shed any tears if they all... died."

"It doesn't really matter," Eustus added quietly. "Marchand told me that a fleet's assembling for an assault into Kreelan space. While she didn't say as much, I imagine that some genius at Fleet HQ finally figured out where the Homeworld is, and now they're going after it. And whatever trouble the Kreelans are in is just icing on the cake."

"When is this attack to take place?" Reza asked sharply.

Surprised by his friend's intensity, Eustus took an involuntary step back. "It must be soon," he answered cautiously, looking at Jodi, whose face bore an expression of concern, "but she didn't bother to fill me in on the details, Reza. I'm only a grunt, remember, and a 'traitor,' at that."

"After all these years," Jodi murmured to herself, "we've finally got a chance to beat them." Looking at the warrior who lay dying, and the stricken child beside her, she said, "I'm sorry Reza, I really am. But if we've got the chance to put it to them once and for all, I'm all for it. We must be pulling every ship that can hold air for this battle, and when our fleet gets to the Homeworld and finds the warriors like this, they're going to kick their asses. I just wish I could be there to see it."

"You do not understand the dangers," Reza said ominously. "Every ship in the Empire is converging on the Homeworld by now, all the warships of a race that has visited more stars than are visible in the night skies of Earth. And while they are disheartened and disorganized, all will fight to the death to protect the Empress. The human fleet will die along with the Empire, and all those human worlds that depend on starships for their survival will be cast into a dark age that may last for centuries. It will be a disaster the likes of which humanity has never known." He shook his head. "The only hope is for me to reach the Empress in time."

"And then what?" Eustus asked. "Are all the warriors going to spring back to their feet just in time to blow our ships out of space? No," he said. "No, I don't think I want that, Reza. I'm sorry."

Reza looked at him as if Eustus had slapped him. "You doubt me," Reza whispered incredulously. "Have I ever led you astray, lied to you, in all these years? I tell you truly, my friends: if the fleet attacks the Homeworld as you have said, it shall meet its end. But if I can reach Her, save Her, there may be hope for us all. You see, as Empress, She cannot destroy the heritage of Her only son, the child of Her very blood: Shera-Khan is half-human, and *She will end the war*. But only if I reach Her in time." He looked at them pleadingly. "You must believe me. I cannot do this alone. Please."

"Reza..." Jodi began, feeling helpless and fated to lose the best friend she had ever had, even over and above Nicole. "I... I don't doubt you," she said, "but I can't help you, even if everything you say is true. I'm a Confederation officer, Reza, and the Kreelans are my enemy. I know I'm here because I'm accused of crimes that I didn't commit, but that doesn't mean that I'm ready to do the real thing. What you're talking about is treason, and... I just can't. I'm sorry."

"Me, too," Eustus said hoarsely, feeling like he wanted to die. "I'm sorry, Reza." Eustus turned his eyes to the floor in shame.

* * *

In Erlang's skies, the human fleet gathered. Enya watched the tiny lights as they flicked into normal space, sometimes individually, sometimes by the dozen. The Council of Erlang had been informed by the commodore aboard the *Furious* of what was happening, and had also been told that the new president and the entire Confederation Council would be aboard the flagship that would lead the great armada into enemy space. And President Borge had invited – decreed was more like it, Enya thought darkly – Erlang to send a representative along on this "most glorious of occasions." Under the circumstances, with thousands of Confederation warships soon to be orbiting their home, the still-struggling inhabitants of Erlang were hardly in a position to refuse.

Enya had immediately volunteered. She was intelligent and strong-willed, and was more aware than most of the risks their people were taking in carrying the war to the Empire. It also gave her a chance, no matter how slight, of seeing Eustus before fate would have a chance to steal him away from her forever. Little did she know that he was under arrest on charges of high treason.

The shuttle from *Warspite* screamed in the night air, its engines howling like a hurricane as its three sturdy landing struts made gentle contact with the ground. The hatch hummed open and a helmeted crew chief poked his head out the door.

"Good luck, lass," Ian Mallory said over the continued roar of the shuttle's engines. He took Enya in his arms and hugged her tightly. "Godspeed."

"Thank you, Ian," she replied, returning his affection. He had been her father since she had lost her own. "I'll not be away for long." Kissing him on the cheek, she gathered up her single bag, a worn but respectable leather traveler, and darted into the shuttle.

With a final look around to make sure the hatch and ship were clear, the crew chief pulled himself back inside and the door slid shut behind him. As the people around it waved farewell, the shuttle's engines roared with power and it began to lift from the ground. It was barely above the trees when the landing gear retracted and the ship accelerated rapidly out of sight, leaving nothing behind it but a glowing contrail that quickly faded.

High above, The Armada continued to assemble.

Eleven

"*Merde*, but this will not work!" L'Houillier sputtered angrily, slamming his fist down on the table. "This insanity has cost us fourteen ships already from collisions around Erlang, and there will be three times as many ships appearing in the target zone. And those blasted politicians strutting around this ship like a bunch of cheap whores, pandering to that... that..." L'Houillier's vocabulary failed to provide him an acceptable descriptor for the new Commander-in-Chief.

Sitting across from him, Zhukovski added to the fleet commander's gloom. "And that is without interference from Kreelans," he muttered. In all the years that the two had been friends, this was the first time that Zhukovski had seen L'Houillier lose his temper. Fortunately, it had been in private, in Zhukovski's stateroom. Had such words been uttered beyond the Russian admiral's electronically screened quarters, or within earshot of the wrong people, Borge would have acted quickly to see that L'Houillier – or anyone else, for that matter – quickly found his way into retirement. Or worse.

There seem to have been a lot of 'retirements' recently, Zhukovski noted bitterly of the virtual purge that had taken place among upper and middle grade Navy and Marine officers. He was amazed that he and L'Houillier had avoided the axe this long. *Perhaps*, he mused, *Borge has something special planned for us.*

"There is little we can do, admiral," Zhukovski went on, pouring another vodka for the two of them, "at least without exploring less pleasant... alternatives."

L'Houillier looked hard at his intelligence officer. "I would be lying to you if I said I had not experienced similar thoughts, Evgeni," he said quietly, "but to say more – let alone to do more – is treason of the worst sort. The Confederation does not need a military dictatorship, or for the military to decide on a civilian leader."

"Even now?"

L'Houillier nodded. "Even now. You know how I feel about this man and his minions, but I swore an oath, as did you, as did every member of the

Confederation Defense Forces, to uphold its constitution and its legally established leaders. Borge succeeded Nathan legally, and that is that."

"I wonder," Zhukovski said aloud.

"What is that supposed to mean?" L'Houillier asked sharply.

"Being curious as cat – which is prerequisite for intelligence officer – I have taken liberty of conducting some... historical research into fearless leader's background."

"Evgeni!" L'Houillier hissed. "You had no right or authorization to do that! Using your position to gain access to classified–"

"Admiral misunderstands," Zhukovski gently interrupted him, putting up a hand to silence his friend and superior. "Public domain information only. No access to classified materials made," his eyes darkened. "None necessary."

The Grand Admiral frowned, still not liking it. The thought of what would happen to them should any of the current civilian leaders discover that a military officer had been digging into the background of the president...

But, as Zhukovski had known it would, curiosity got the better of him. "Well?" L'Houillier asked finally. "What did you find out?"

Zhukovski smiled. He knew his admiral well. "What I did not find out was probably more important," he said. "But of uncovered information, I found of great interest fact that Fearless Leader at one time was friend of Thorella family."

"The industrialist?" L'Houillier interjected. "Thorella's shipyards built half the ships I have served on."

Zhukovski nodded. "*Da*. Same family. Rich, powerful. Died in collision over Earth over thirty years ago. Terrible tragedy." He looked significantly at L'Houillier. "I found press report that says son of Borge died in accident, also."

"I did not know he ever had a son," L'Houillier said quietly.

"Is not widely advertised fact, it seems." Zhukovski took a sip of the cold vodka, feeling it warm his insides against the cold wind that blew in his heart. "And that is where tale becomes strange. You see, public records about Borge and Thorella families are almost blank for roughly year after accident. Very odd to say for one of Earth's richest families and popular young politician, especially when such tragedy is involved."

L'Houillier's brow creased. "Wait just a moment, Evgeni," he said. "I remember that there were many reports on that accident, and on the Thorellas, especially. I do not recall reading about Borge, specifically, but it was so long ago I probably would not remember, anyway. But I am sure the press was full of things."

With the smile of the angler who had hooked his prize, Evgeni began to reel L'Houillier in. "And that is my point, admiral," he said. "I remember much being in press, too, even as young weapons officer on destroyer patrolling Rim. It was 'Big News' at time. But now, most information is gone from available records. Disappeared. For example, article about Borge's son was text only, and last name was spelled wrong."

"Are you suggesting," L'Houillier asked incredulously, "that someone has somehow tampered with the information in the Central Library?" The Central Library had been created nearly two centuries before as a storehouse of human knowledge and information. Over the years, the various client states and colonies had come to rely on it almost exclusively for their information needs, and most smaller information libraries were not in themselves unique, but were abridged versions of the Central Library that carried a smaller quantity and narrower scope of data. The funding of the library was ostensibly from multi-source government appropriations to keep it "bias-free," but there were many significant individual contributions, as well. The Librarians had become a quasi-religious sect, guarding the integrity of the information under their care, and were expected to operate the Library with standards of intellectual and moral purity that would have astonished the most conservative of religious monks.

Zhukovski nodded grimly. "Library has been tampered with, admiral," he said. "I cannot tell how much or when, but things are not as they should be, and common factor seems to be Fearless Leader."

"Evgeni, if this is true, our... our entire history, the core of our knowledge... everything could be corrupted." L'Houillier was horrified at the thought.

"I believe that few records I found were missed for some reason: typo in text, bad picture that did not register on scan, and so forth," Zhukovski said. "I discovered other holes in information regarding past of close associates of president, information which is routinely reported by press or government register, but that is either gone entirely or selectively edited. There is no doubt. Originals are perhaps behind locked files, but in open domain where they should be? *Nyet.*"

L'Houillier sat back in his chair, looking out the port of his friend's room at the starfield of ships that were gathered, a third of the fleet that was about to strike at the Kreelan homeworld. But who, he wondered silently, was the enemy now? And what was he to do about it?

"There is also matter of Reza Gard to consider," Zhukovski said quietly, interleaving his own thoughts with L'Houillier's.

"What do you expect me to do, Evgeni?" L'Houillier asked tiredly. "We have gone through this before. I know you are convinced that he is not guilty, but that is out of our hands. We cannot override the Council's decision. Reza and Mackenzie will face a civilian tribunal and no doubt will be executed." He shrugged. "I do not like that kind of justice any more than you, my friend, but we are faced with less and less authority these days."

"Vote was not unanimous," Zhukovski said. "Perhaps we should speak to opposition–"

"One vote hardly qualifies as 'opposition,' Evgeni, and you know it. I admire what Councilman Braddock has done as much as you, but his days are numbered, as well. Borge will not tolerate him for long, and he will no doubt join our other redoubtable colleagues in 'retirement.'"

"Even more reason to consider other alternatives."

L'Houillier rolled his eyes. "You never give up, do–"

The comm panel beeped, accompanied by a blinking red light. L'Houillier slapped it with his hand. "*Oui?*" he barked.

Admiral Laskowski's face appeared on the panel. Out of sight from the comm panel's view, Zhukovski made an expression of exquisite disgust.

"The prisoners are about to arrive from *Furious*, sir," she said. "The president ordered–"

"I am aware of the president's orders, admiral," he snapped. It must be an effort for her, L'Houillier thought, to conceal her sentiment that the old Grand Admiral was long past retirement, holding a position that she was rightfully entitled to. *Well*, he thought sourly, *she would just have to wait a bit longer, now wouldn't she?* "I shall be down at once." He snapped the circuit closed.

Zhukovski was already on his feet, straightening his uniform, setting his face into its accustomed stony expression. "Since I was little boy, I always like to see parade," he said. "But not this time. Not today."

"Nor I," the Grand Admiral said quietly as he stood up to follow Zhukovski from the room. Pausing at the door, he looked back at the partially emptied bottle of vodka and suddenly wished that he could sit here and finish the rest of it, rather than participate in the spectacle that Borge had prepared.

Sighing, he relinquished the thought. *Maybe when I retire with a bullet in the brain*, he told himself bitterly.

* * *

Admiral Laskowski fumed at L'Houillier's brush-off. *Your day of reckoning is coming, old man,* she thought angrily. She knew he had been President Nathan's military pet, but it was a new administration, a new leader, and she was already on the inside track. For now, she would have to bide her time and be patient.

She was just about to head out of the Combat Information Center, or CIC, for the president's ceremony when she saw the sailor manning the STARNET terminal suddenly stiffen. He was obviously reading an incoming message, probably from one of the scoutships that were probing ever deeper into Kreelan space.

While she technically wasn't in charge of the watch – the officer of the deck was a full commander who was otherwise occupied on the far side of the dark, sprawling compartment – she was the senior officer present and had the privilege to poke her nose into whatever might be going on.

Curiosity drawing her onward, she walked over to the rating who was now staring in wonder at the STARNET display. "What's going on, sailor?" she asked.

The man turned to her, a look of awe on his face. "They found it," he said in little more than a whisper. "One of the scoutships – SV1287, commanded by Lieutenant Weigand – found the Kreelan homeworld!"

A tingle of excitement ran up Laskowski's spine. "Are they sure? Have you gotten confirmation?"

"There's none needed, ma'am," the sailor told her, his voice now laced with excitement. "Look at the plot: there are thousands of ships in the system they found. *Thousands!*"

Laskowski's eyes grew wide as she looked at the display sent in by the aptly – if informally – named *Obstinate.* She knew Lieutenant Weigand only by reputation, but in about ten minutes she would make sure that he was Lieutenant *Commander* Weigand. She quickly scanned the report: he had taken some incredible chances, doing a series of jumps along the vector of one of the Kreelan battle groups he had picked up. Hoping to emerge from one of the jumps close enough to pick up readings from any inhabited systems along that vector, he finally struck not just gold, but platinum. There were nearly three thousand combat vessels – the same number she had predicted, she thought smugly – in that system, and spectral analyses and neutrino readings indicated an incredibly advanced civilization was present. Most of it was concentrated on a planet and major moon in the system at a distance from the sun where water could exist as a liquid, and thus support carbon-based life. There were other targets in the system, including the asteroids, but the fourth planet from the star was obviously the primary target, along with its orbiting moon.

There was no mistake, no room for doubt. *They had found it.*

"My God," she whispered. Turning to the officer of the deck, who was heading her way to see what was going on, she said, "Commander, I want this information to be held closely until I say otherwise. No one – *no one* – else is to see or hear of this report until I have a chance to discuss it with Admiral L'Houillier. Is that clear?"

"Aye, ma'am," the commander replied crisply.

Satisfied, Laskowski turned on her heel and hurried out of CIC. But she had no plans of telling L'Houillier, at least not until *after* she had told the president himself.

* * *

"Tony?" Enya called above the murmur of the crowd. "Tony Braddock?" Her shuttle had arrived scant moments ago. After being led away from the landing zone by the courteous crew chief, she found herself among the crowd of dignitaries and other military and civilian personnel who had assembled in the *Warspite's* starboard landing bay.

"Enya!" Tony shouted, waving his arm for her to join him. He stood off by himself, his glum face brightening at her appearance. "What are you doing here?"

"I was chosen to represent Erlang on the Council," she told him, her eyes wide at the sight around her, the hundreds – thousands? – of people filling the great ship's landing bay.

But the sight of Tony Braddock and the look on his face diverted her attention to the here and now, as well as reaffirming her suspicions about the dark nature of the gathering of people around her. Looking around quickly, deciding that it was safe amid the background noise, she quietly told him, "We were told to supply a representative for the expedition or be cut off from all Confederation aid. Borge's hands around our throat are as tight as ever."

Braddock nodded grimly. "You aren't the only ones. He made the same speech to the entire Council, telling us all that anyone who doesn't toe the line is going to be cut off. Or worse."

Enya shook her head incredulously. The Kreelans had done damage enough. Now, humanity had inherited a maniacal leader, as well. "Where is Nicole?" she asked, hoping to brighten the conversation.

Tony frowned. "I don't know. They have me billeted with the rest of the politicos, and I haven't been able to spend much time with her since we left

Earth." He craned his neck around, his eyes searching. "I haven't spotted her in the crowd, but I'm sure she's here somewhere."

"What is going on?" Enya asked. "Why is everyone gathering together like this? Is Borge going to address everyone, or what?"

Braddock was incredulous. "You didn't know?"

"Know what?" From the look on his face, she was sure she was going to regret finding out.

"They're transferring some Kreelan prisoners from the *Furious*," he paused, "along with Reza and Jodi Mackenzie. They were captured on their way to Erlang."

"I had heard a rumor, but didn't believe it. You don't believe it, do you?" she asked him. "I know that Reza is different from anyone I've ever known, but he would not have killed Nathan. I just can't accept–"

A glance and a frown from a nearby councilwoman caught Braddock's eye.

"Yes, I know," he said, raising his voice to make sure the eavesdropping councilwoman heard, "it amazes me that President Borge is even going to bother with a tribunal."

"Tony?" Enya said, confused at his turn of his speech, but stopped when his hand gripped her arm tightly, almost painfully.

Braddock watched out of the corner of his eye as the councilwoman turned back to her conversation, apparently satisfied. Then he guided Enya to the open space beneath a nearby Corsair's wing. "Enya," he whispered after they'd moved out of earshot of their neighbors, "you've got to be very careful about what you say and who hears you. Since Nathan died, the changes on the Council have been nothing short of terrifying." He glanced around quickly, and she recognized the look from her time in the resistance: he was making sure the area was secure.

"Almost all the old members of the Council – everyone who supported Nathan and his policies – are gone," he whispered. "Since he declared martial law after Nathan's death, Borge has dismissed most of the Senate and Council. He's installed sympathetic supporters or simply eliminated representation for some worlds in the legislature. Some of them, the most vocal opponents, have died suddenly and inexplicably." He looked around again. The crowd had grown larger, closer. "The checks and balances system is gone. Even the judiciary has been subverted since Savitch was killed. We've got a dictatorship with a rubber-stamp body masquerading as a democracy."

"And what about you?"

A look of shame crossed his face. "I've tried to make a stand for the things I've felt are really important, but it's no use," he said wearily. "My only hope is to try and gain enough support in an underground movement to restore some kind of order to the government. In public, I have to appear as just another lackey, or I face the same fate as the others. Then none of us will have any hope."

Enya took his arm. "Don't be ashamed," she told him. "Sometimes there is no alternative but to dress like the enemy so you can defeat him." She, of all people, knew the truth of that. She had worked against Belisle's corrupt government on Erlang by masquerading many times as a Ranier. Some of the things she had to do...

He managed a grim smile. "That's what worries me," he told her. "I don't want to become the thing I'm trying to destroy."

"May I have your attention, please!" a voice suddenly boomed over the PA system. Braddock recognized it immediately: Voronin Hack, the Council's Master-at-Arms and ceremonial mouthpiece. The crowd quieted down immediately. "Ladies and gentlemen," his smooth baritone voice continued, "honored guests and dignitaries... the President of the Confederated Alliance of Humanity!"

A massive cheer went up as Borge took his place at the podium, the white presidential robe billowing about his ample stomach, his face flushed with supreme confidence. He raised his hands to the crowd, basking in their adulation.

The applause, Braddock noted sadly, was enthusiastic and sincere. There were no guns at people's backs, no cue cards or faked admiration. With the exception of those on the Council or in the upper circles of the military, few people here knew or understood the implications of the transformation that had occurred in the Confederation government at Borge's hand. Most of them saw him as the inheritor of Nathan's tragic legacy, as the man who had pursued a humble life in the unglamorous world of creating and guiding the law, but who now was determined to end the war and bring peace to the galaxy.

After what was to Braddock an interminable interlude of applause, Borge finally gestured for the crowd to be silent. Slowly, unwillingly, they began to comply.

"Fellow citizens of the great Confederation!" he declared as the crowd at last was still. "Fellow humans, hear me:

"For many long years we have suffered and died at the hands of the alien enemy, losing our loved ones, our children to the claws of this insidious infestation that has swept across our galaxy like a plague. Campaign after campaign have we fought, not for glory or bounty, but for our very survival." His voice deepened, his tempo slowed as he went on, "For nearly a century have we lost world after world, colony after colony invaded, burned, destroyed. Neither man, nor woman, nor child has been spared this agony, this devastation."

He looked down at the podium, as if in communion with the now-thoughtful members of the audience, as if offering a silent prayer to those who had died in the century-long invasion. "But, my friends, the tide has turned," he said, looking up, casting his gaze upon the crowd before him. "The aliens have lost their strength, their will to fight," he told them. "They have run in full retreat from our worlds, fleeing to the sector of space from which they were spawned. We may never know the nature of the divine intervention that has driven them from our homelands, but know you this..." He paused, his brow wrinkling in righteous fury. "They cannot run far enough to escape our vengeance!"

The assemblage broke into a roar of cheering and whistling, voices taking up the challenge that Borge had laid before them.

Borge patiently waited for the tremendous reaction to subside, the shower of voices finally falling into silence within the great cavern of the landing bay.

"And seek vengeance we will, my friends," he promised them. "That is why we are gathered here this day, why tens of thousands of sailors and Marines, Coastguardsmen, and so many others have gathered in these three great fleets that shall sail as one toward the enemy's shores, the greatest armed force the galaxy has ever known." He was interrupted by more cheers and applause.

"As many of you know," he continued, "the Armada set out without us knowing the exact location of the Kreelan homeworld, only a comparatively vast area of space where we knew the enemy must be hiding." There were low murmurs in the audience, particularly among the naval personnel: many of them had thought it was insane to start the operation without knowing exactly where to strike. "My friends, just before taking the podium," he went on quietly, the thousands before him now utterly silent, "I was informed that one of our brave scoutships has pinpointed the location of the Kreelan homeworld, and has confirmed that their own battle fleet is assembling for a knockout blow against the Confederation." His fist suddenly hammered on the podium. "But *we* shall strike first! *We* shall strike at the enemy's heart with all our might, and for the first time in a century carry the battle into the enemy's territory. *We* shall end this terrible war with a single crushing blow, and *we* shall lead humanity to victory!"

Despite how much he hated Borge, Braddock found himself swept up in the religious fervor that washed over the audience in the landing bay like a tidal wave, carrying away all doubt, all reservations, all fears of what the immediate future held. Borge's words were irresistible to men and women who had fought and lost again and again in a war that had begun when their great-great-grandparents were children. Nearly everyone in the bay had lost a friend or relative, a spouse or a child, to the Kreelans. Their thirst for blood ran deep, and they were willing to sacrifice everything for a moment of that soon-to-be finest hour promised by Borge's words.

Beside him, Enya watched with wide eyes as the normally professional and disciplined Navy and Marine people around her applauded the president's speech with maniacal intensity.

They have no idea what might be in store, she thought suddenly, realizing that whatever intelligence information the human fleet had come up with, it could not have told them very much more than where to go looking for trouble. *And they don't care*, she thought. Coming from a planet and class of people that had been ravaged by humans for far longer and with much greater thoroughness than the Kreelans in their single attack, Enya had difficulty relating to the near-riot boiling around her. Even Braddock appeared to have been seduced by the president's passionate speech.

"Yes, my friends," Borge went on after the crowd regained its composure, "we shall seek out the enemy, wherever *he* is." The stress on the pronoun was unmistakable, and with a sudden chill, Enya realized whom he meant. "Years ago there came among us a man, who had once been a boy of human blood, but who was no longer entirely human. Raised by the alien horde, he was used and corrupted, molded into a weapon more insidious than any we have ever known. This man fought his former hosts well and with courage, earning our trust and respect, getting us to open our hearts to him, making us vulnerable." His eyes swept across the audience. "And then he betrayed us, all of us, by murdering in cold blood the one who had led humanity for so long and so well, a man most of you knew as the commander-in-chief, the president of the Confederation: Job Nathan." He wiped an imaginary tear from his eye. "He murdered the man who was my close friend for most of my adult life.

"But this alien prodigy was not alone in his treachery," Borge went on, his voice tight with barely suppressed rage, a performance that would have been the envy of a Broadway star. "For he was aided and abetted by another of our own kind, a woman who betrayed her uniform and her race to help this murderer escape from justice." He looked toward a group of Marines in dress uniforms carrying weapons that were anything but ceremonial. They were formed up next to the embarkation ramp of a newly arrived shuttle. "Bring out the prisoners," he ordered.

The Marine officer-in-charge rendered a sharp salute before turning toward the shuttle. "Bring out the prisoners!" he repeated sharply.

The hangar deck was so quiet that Enya could hear her heart beating. Even the deep thrum from the ship's drives seemed to have gone silent.

From the shuttle could be heard the sound of the chains that had been cuffed to the prisoners' hands and feet. Each prisoner also wore a thin band of metal around the neck with a small electronic control box: high explosive collars.

There was a collective gasp as Jodi, Shera-Khan, and Reza appeared in the light of the bay. Tesh-Dar, too weak to walk by herself, leaned heavily upon her adopted son, all the while casting a baleful eye on the human animals all around her, trying to force their stench from her nostrils. She felt the cold metal of the human device around her son's neck and her own, and instantly regretted consenting to having it put on; but the humans would have harmed Shera-Khan, and she knew that neither Reza nor herself could have kept the child from harm.

"There is no other way," Reza had told her grimly as he accepted the lethal necklace himself. It had seemed to her for a moment that he was surrendering, but the flame in his eyes burned brightly still, she had seen. The Power was yet within him.

Shera-Khan also had his arm wrapped around Tesh-Dar's waist to lend his slender body for her support. He was not afraid of the animals that peered at him with their strange pale faces, for he walked in the presence of a great warrior priest, his father, and Tesh-Dar, who was a living legend of the sword. He could not understand his father's command that they obey the animals and submit to this spectacle, but he did not question it; Reza's word was the word of the consort of the Empress, the only one among Her race permitted to kneel upon the pedestal of the throne. He was the most high of Her Children, the single warrior who had no peers.

Jodi, while cast in the same light as the other three, walked alone. The humiliation she felt at being paraded before these people and those who watched from all over the Confederation through the vid paled in comparison to the sadness in her heart at having had to deny Reza her help in his greatest hour of need. She had loved him dearly as a friend, and loved him still; but she could not help him. She knew that she would go to her death convicted of crimes she had never committed. But she could not betray her people.

She walked ahead of the others, her head upright, with her eyes fixed on the evil man who wore the robes of an angel. Borge.

Reza felt the crushing weight of the emotions of those around him. It was a burden so great it threatened to smother his spirit but for the cold flames that burned for vengeance against those who had betrayed not only him, but all of humanity. Tesh-Dar was an easy and welcome weight about his shoulders. Her musky scent, pleasant from memory, was reassuring, as was that of his newfound son. He tuned out the burning hatred of the thousands of souls around him and focused on the small comforts his physical senses provided him of his Kreelan family, wishing he could sense them in his spirit, as well. But he could not, even this close to them, any more than he had been able since the day he left the Empire.

It is strange, he had thought after speaking with Tesh-Dar, *that their blood is cold and silent as the Empress sleeps, but my blood still sings its mournful solo as it had since that day long ago.* His powers had not waned since the tragedy of the Ascension, and he was left to wonder at whatever miracle sustained him. He remembered the dream of the First Empress, as he lay dying from Esah-Zhurah's sword, remembered the fire in his veins as he imagined Her blood mingling with his. Others might have thought it a dream, but he knew that it was not.

The prisoners slowly shuffled their way toward the dais, past the rows of sailors and Marines, legislators and judges, the men and women whom they had served and had served with for years. But now the prisoners weren't friends or comrades, only criminals who had committed the gravest crime against humanity in all of history.

"In the name of God," Enya whispered. It sounded like a shriek in the silence of the bay, and she said nothing more. Beside her, Braddock's only reaction was a twitching muscle in his jaw.

Finally, there were no more steps for the prisoners to take; they had reached their destination. Standing before the dais, all of them glared upward at the leader of the Confederation.

Borge wasted no time. "It would take too much time to read all the crimes with which you have been charged, so the court has waived reading all but the most vital: murder and conspiracy to commit murder." He turned his attention toward Reza. "Captain Gard, you are charged with the murders of Job Kahane Nathan, President of the Confederation, and Dr. Deliha Rabat. How do you plead?"

Reza said nothing. He knew he could kill Borge at this instant, but his son's life likely would be forfeit, and any chances he might have of saving the Empire – and the Confederation – would be lost forever.

Borge frowned. "Silence is entered as a plea of guilty." He turned to Jodi. "Commander Jodi Mackenzie, you are charged with conspiring with Captain Gard to murder Doctor Rabat and President Nathan; further, you are charged with the despicable murder of Tanya Buchet. How do you plead?"

"Go fuck yourself," she spat.

Borge snorted in disgust, then turned to the new Chief Justice, another of his latest appointees, Anton Simoniak. "Your Honor, if you please."

Simoniak stepped up to the podium. "Due to the barbaric nature of these crimes and the subsequent bloody escape of the accused, the court was compelled to conduct their trial *in absentia*," the Chief Justice stated flatly, as if bored by the supposition that they could possibly be anything but guilty. "The call for justice was unanimous." He looked down upon the condemned. "You have both been found guilty, as charged, on all counts." Turning to Borge, he said, "The recommended sentence is death, Mr. President, to be carried out immediately."

Enya opened her mouth to speak, but found Braddock's hand over her lips.

"Don't," he whispered urgently, "or you'll find yourself condemned along with them." He looked around urgently, afraid that someone might have noticed their exchange. No one was paying them any attention. Good. "There's nothing you can do for them now."

She angrily pulled his hand away, ashamed that he was afraid to speak out against this madness. And she was even more ashamed that she herself remained silent. Braddock was right, she thought as she watched the tragedy unfold before her. There was nothing to be done for them.

Borge nodded gravely as the justice stepped back to his position among the rest of the luminaries on the dais. "I concur with the verdict," he said, "and with the sentence. However, with the power vested in me as president, I hereby commute the sentence until Operation Millennium has been completed and our fleets return home." His eyes bored into Reza. "I want these traitors to witness the destruction of the evil that has washed our galaxy in human blood for the last hundred years, to see the power of God's vengeance before they see the gates of Hell!"

Like a surging tide, the assembly roared its venomous approval.

* * *

From where she stood on a catwalk, high above the fateful ceremony, Nicole did not hear the thousands of voices shouting from below. The only sounds perceptible to her mind were the strange whisperings, the chill in her body, that had been her frequent companions since the day Reza had

pressed a bloody hand against hers, showing her things that no other human
– save him – had ever seen.

She had watched him from her catwalk perch like a peregrine in a cage,
wanting to help, but unable. She felt his heart, his soul, and the pain and
rage that spilled from him now threatened to bring tears to her eyes, harsh
action from her clenched hands.

Below her, the verdict having been pronounced and the crowd's lust for
vengeance temporarily sated, Reza and the others were led off to the ship's
brig, enduring the humiliation of being spat upon and cursed like molesters
of children.

Just before they passed through the blast door that led to the ship's
internal transport system, the huge female warrior looked back, and up. For
just a moment, an incalculable instant, her eyes locked with Nicole's.

Help him, Nicole read in the woman's eyes as plainly as if she had
spoken the words aloud. *Help my son.*

And then she was gone.

Clutching the railing so hard that her knuckles were bled white, Nicole
waited for the trembling to stop before she made her way unsteadily back to
her cabin. She knew what must be done, almost as if by instinct. Guided by
powers that she did not understand, she began her preparations as soon as
her cabin door closed behind her.

The fact that what she was about to do would be considered high
treason never even occurred to her.

•

TWELVE

As she stood at the podium of the conference room, Admiral Laskowski took smug satisfaction in the looks of grim submission on the faces of L'Houillier and Zhukovski. There was no longer any question of who was really in charge now. The man who sat at the head of the conference table had decided that issue when he had personally approved of Laskowski's plan, and reinforced it with the fourth star he had given her, promoting her on the spot to full admiral for her role in discovering the Kreelan homeworld. Technically she was still junior to L'Houillier, but that was a mere technicality. He and Zhukovski had only pushed forward their retirement dates by arguing against her strategy. And now, here they were, mere spectators to the operation that she had devised, that she was now in charge of in all but name, reviewing it for her president's pleasure.

It was all her dreams come true.

"Mr. President," she began, "the attack plan is fairly simple, necessarily so because of the huge number of vessels involved."

This brought a barely audible grunt from L'Houillier. They had lost another ten ships to collision at the last navigation checkpoint. Zhukovski's great eyebrows knotted as a frown chiseled itself from his glowering face.

Laskowski cast L'Houillier a disparaging look, but said nothing. *You are finished, old man,* she told herself. "As I was about to say, sir, the three battle groups – Lysander, Ulysses, and Heraklion – will jump into the system simultaneously from three different vectors.

"Lysander, the main battle group of which *Warspite* is the flagship, will engage the Kreelan main body that now orbits the homeworld. Our job will be to pin down the Kreelan fleet, and if possible destroy it en masse. Once that has been accomplished, we will proceed to neutralize the homeworld itself through orbital bombardment and, if and when appropriate, Marine landings."

Borge nodded magnanimously. His ignorance of military strategy and tactics allowed him to be properly impressed.

"Ulysses," she went on, "smaller than Lysander, will execute a similar operation against the moon that has been identified in orbit around the primary target.

"We don't have detailed information on the defenses for either target, but we don't believe at this time that planetary defense will be a major factor in the engagement: our primary threat is the enemy fleet."

This brought a raised eyebrow from Zhukovski to L'Houillier. The latter only shook his head in tiny, hopefully unnoticed movements. *Merde*, Zhukovski could imagine him saying. To himself, he thought: *We know nothing of this system other than the fact of its existence and that many Kreelan warships are already there. And already we have made potentially fatal assumptions about it.*

"The third group, Heraklion," Laskowski continued, her voice slowing as she sought to impress the president with the third group's real significance, "is the smallest of the three, but carries the greatest destructive power of all our forces. Should it be necessary and you authorize it, Mr. President, this group will employ thermium weapons against the planets in the system, and the kryolon devices we have brought along can help ensure... a final solution to the Kreelan problem."

"I've heard of the thermium devices," Borge said, intrigued, "but not of the kryolons. What are those?" He had not been briefed on the full array of military hardware prior to the fleet's sailing, but such details he found utterly fascinating.

"Kryolon bombs are proverbial 'ultimate weapon,' *Gospodin Prezident*," Zhukovski rumbled, interrupting Laskowski's monopoly on the man's attention. "They were designed many years ago, to destroy star of enemy system, and thus planets in orbit. They have been in carefully guarded storage for these years, until very recently." He paused. "None ever has been used, even operationally tested, and so true power of weapon is not known." He did not add that he thought with all his heart and soul that those weapons should have been destroyed long ago, rather than fall into the hands of a madman like Borge.

"Really?" Borge asked, his mind already contemplating the ramifications for his reign after he had defeated the Kreelans. *No system would dare oppose me while I have control of such weapons*, he thought. *And, perhaps*, he thought hopefully, *more could be built*. That was an option worth pursuing, but now was not the time.

Turning his attention back to Laskowski, who stood simmering at the head of the table after Zhukovski's interruption, he asked, "And how do you plan to employ these weapons, admiral?"

"Sir," she said, shooting Zhukovski a frigid glare, "we have brought them as an insurance policy. If you do not feel that the issue of the Kreelan problem has been resolved with the use of the fleet in conventional operations or with the thermium devices, the kryolons are a way for you to resolve the situation... utterly and permanently." She was careful to phrase her words in such a way as not to imply the possibility that the fleet could fail. She was sure that her plan would work.

"Very good, admiral," Borge said contemplatively. "Very good. Thank you." Then, looking at each of the faces clustered around the table, he said, "Well, if there is nothing else, ladies and gentlemen...? No? Then this meeting is concluded. Please inform me when we are within thirty minutes of jumping into enemy territory. Thank you all, and carry on."

The attendees stood and filed out, eager to get back to their stations and away from the cloying political atmosphere that shrouded Borge and those closest to him.

As they left, a huge Marine officer entered the room, shouldering aside the departing officers with little regard to their rank or stature. Thorella.

"And what good news do you have for me, general?" Borge asked as the last of the attendees had departed and the doors hissed shut.

"I split up the prisoners as you requested, sir," Thorella said, smiling. "I had Mackenzie transferred to the *Golden Pearl* where we've had Camden locked up." Eustus had not been on the shuttle that brought Reza and the others to *Warspite's* hate-filled landing bay. He was a gift from Borge to Thorella, a political pawn that had been lost through the administrative cracks in the fleet's preparations to attack the Empire. It was a gift that the younger man planned to enjoy immensely. "I'll have to give her credit," he said, shaking his head in wonder, "she certainly took her last flight in class. What a ship! No wonder you took it over for your personal quarters."

Borge chuckled. "Rank hath its privileges, my friend," he said, thinking of what was going to happen to Mackenzie at young Markus's hands. All of the prisoners would be set aside for Thorella's pleasure. He had certainly earned it.

As if reading his mind, Thorella asked, "What about Reza and the two blues?" He wanted them most of all.

"In time, Markus, in time. I shall not deprive you of your rewards. But his public visibility makes him a very valuable political commodity, much more so than Mackenzie or that cretin Camden. So you shall have to have your fun with them until Reza's *raison d'être* is no more."

Thorella nodded. It was what he expected, and it would do. For now. "Is there anything else you want me to work on in the meantime?"

Borge shook his head. "No, my friend. The wheels have been set in motion, and now we must simply wait." He smiled. "I suggest that you retire to our new ship and... enjoy the wait."

His pitch black eyes twinkling, Thorella thanked his master and left. Behind him, Borge quietly laughed to himself.

* * *

"Are you sure this is the right place?" Enya asked quietly, her eyes darting up and down the corridor to see if they had been followed.

"This is where he said–" Braddock did not get the chance to finish as the stark gray metal door to one of two dozen container storage rooms lining the corridor suddenly hissed open.

"Quickly," a heavily accented voice said from the darkness beyond, a dimly seen hand gesturing for them to come in. "*Voiditye*. Enter."

Exchanging a worried glance, Enya and Braddock did as they had been ordered. The door closed behind them, the lock bars automatically sliding into place to hold the door closed.

"Admiral?" Braddock asked the shadowy figure looming in front of them.

"*Da*," Zhukovski's voice replied. The darkness was suddenly peeled back a meter or so as he turned on a small electric lamp that stood on a hexagonal container squatting between the three of them. Beside it was a device with shifting numbers and tiny waveforms on its display: an anti-surveillance unit. "Forgive choice of place for meeting," the admiral said, gesturing about them at the shadowy stacks of containers and pallets, "but circumstances dictate... radical approach to most basic problems."

"Why are we here, admiral?" Enya asked cautiously. "Surely, this is not some crude joke?"

Zhukovski allowed himself a humorless smile. "I most sincerely wish that it was joke, young lady," he told her, leaning against the container with his good arm, "but things are most serious, and – I fear – out of control. You see, Admiral L'Houillier and I believe that fleet is on course for rendezvous with disaster. Admiral Laskowski, fleet operations officer, has illustrious president's ear, and has convinced him that our fleet can destroy Kreelans." The smile flickered away. "And, for insurance, we have kryolon bombs to finish job."

"Lord of All," Braddock whispered. "I thought those were only a... a myth. I'd heard about them – everyone in the fleet has – but I never thought they were real. My God, I thought the thermium bombs were horrible enough..."

"They are real, young Councilman," Zhukovski said ominously. "All too real."

Enya suddenly interrupted. "What are these things?" she demanded, not sure that she really wanted to know.

Braddock turned to her. Even in this light, she could tell that he was pale, and she began to feel afraid. "They're doomsday weapons, Enya," he told her. "If rumor holds true, any one of those bombs can destroy a star, setting an entire system aflame, destroying every planet in its orbit." He looked at Zhukovski, who nodded.

"But why would anyone build such weapons?" Enya asked, horrified at the magnitude of it.

"Simple," Zhukovski said. "They were designed for time such as this, when only apparent solution to conflict is stellar genocide. And that might not be bad idea if only one weapon existed. But there are over a dozen, exact count even I do not know because of stringent security." He eyed the other two. "Slight overkill even for Kreelan homeworld, *da?*"

Braddock's insides turned to ice. "A dozen of those things controlled by Borge..." He let the thought drift off into the darkness of the abyss it promised.

Enya finished the thought for him. "No planet in the Confederation would be safe, ever again, from the threat of total destruction," she whispered. "Borge would hold absolute power over everyone. And if they have some now, they could build even more."

"There is worse." The old admiral looked at the floor, then at Enya. "Your young Camden is under arrest," he said softly. "He was charged with treason, and is being held in location that I have not yet discovered." He looked into Enya's eyes. "Sentence was by presidential order: he is to be put to death, along with Gard and Mackenzie."

"No," Enya breathed. "No! I don't believe it! Borge cannot get away with such a thing! I'll–"

"He can, *dorogaya,*" Zhukovski interrupted gently but forcefully, "and he will, unless he is stopped. Borge's insanity knows no bounds, and all those around him have begun to fear him. That is why we must meet like this, because nowhere else is safe. People fearing for their own welfare will gladly point finger at someone else to escape suspicion. This fear has become fire, fanned by winds of Reza's alleged treason and proclaimed chance by president for victory over Kreelan enemy. And if what I believe is true, Reza and others – including Camden – will not survive coming encounter. Borge will have no more use for them; having won his great victory and returning home like Caesar, they will disappear, no doubt in unfortunate accident."

"And the Council is just as bad," Braddock said. "They're all terrified of him... including myself." He clenched his fists. "But, what can we do?"

"Kill him," Enya said quietly. She had lived her entire life under oppressive human rule, and knew that any cruelty visited upon humanity by the Kreelans had been inflicted a thousand-fold by Mankind upon itself in times past and present. *And future*, she thought bleakly, a vivid image playing in her mind of Erlang's sun exploding, obliterating her home and everything they had lived, suffered, and died for all these years.

"Enya," Braddock said uneasily, "I don't like Borge any more than you do, but he's the legal successor to Nathan, and–"

"I wonder," Zhukovski grumbled. At Braddock's questioning glance, he continued, "I have uncovered... discrepancies... in Borge's past, and in past of others who now are closely associated with him. Questionable things have been – how do you say? – tidied up. And I do not believe that Reza Gard killed Nathan. Assuming assumption is correct," he smiled at that particular turn of phrase, "hypothesis leaves obvious question of who did?"

"Thorella," Braddock murmured to himself, thinking of how he and Borge seemed to work together a bit too closely, and how so much of what the younger man did was concealed in shadows, out of sight. From what he himself had seen, and from what he had heard from Reza and Nicole over the years, the man certainly had what Braddock considered an antisocial personality, to say the least. "Borge had the motive," he went on, thinking aloud. "He never made any secret about his ambition to become president, although he had hardly advocated assassination to get there. He and Nathan had been friends for years."

"Reza and Thorella gave him both the opportunity and the instrument he needed," Enya joined in. "Reza was the perfect scapegoat, the one person no one would believe because he had been raised in the Empire, and it would be easy to label him a turncoat and a traitor. And enough people in key positions knew that if Reza had really wanted to, he could easily have killed Nathan. No security system could stop him."

"But Thorella was the actual killer," Braddock continued. "With Borge's backing, he could have gained access to the security system and somehow reprogrammed the sentinel monitors to show Reza killing Nathan." He shook his head. He knew that what they were thinking was pure speculation, but there did not seem to be any other explanation, and too many of the known facts fit the theory all too well. "Lord of All," he whispered.

"Almost perfect crime," Zhukovski said quietly. "If we allow him to succeed, he will have begun with murder of President Nathan what could be murder of millions of people, whether we win or lose in coming battle."

"Are you planning a coup, admiral?" Braddock asked. In his heart he knew the answer, and from the grim set of Enya's jaw he saw that she had already thrown her lot in with whatever Zhukovski had in mind, but he had to ask the question. For the sake of posterity, if nothing else.

Zhukovski suddenly looked uncomfortable. "Councilman, I have served Confederation for many years," he said slowly, "and always have I served civilian leaders. That is not only tradition and written law; I believe with all my heart that it is best way, best for all people in Confederation. So do many other officers who are not content with present leadership. They are not fools, they can see darkness in future, but they are bound to laws that have kept Confederation and its predecessors free." He looked squarely at Braddock. "There will be no military coup," he said firmly. "But... senior officers in Navy and Marine Corps will support new civilian leader." He paused. "They will support you."

"*Me?*" Braddock almost laughed. "Why me?" he said.

"Because there is no one else they would trust, Tony," Enya told him. "You know that as well as I."

Zhukovski nodded. "You are only survivor of purge that has swept vestiges of previous government away, Councilman. You have done well in your time in office, and fact that you are well-decorated Marine does not hurt either. You hold respect of officers and enlisted alike." He shrugged. "If you will not accept, then we must face destiny with Borge at the helm."

"That doesn't leave me much choice, does it?" Braddock asked quietly.

The old admiral shook his head. "None, councilman," he said. "None, if you wish to save Confederation from tyranny."

"Erlang is with you," Enya said, giving Braddock a reassuring squeeze with her hand. Turning to Zhukovski, she asked, "What must we do?"

THIRTEEN

"Ma'am," the Internal Security guard said uneasily, "I can't just let you in there!"

"Then you can explain to President Borge why his instructions were not carried out, sergeant," Nicole said icily. "I'm sure he would be most sympathetic to your concerns." When the man hesitated, she shook her head as if pitying the poor sod, knowing what was in store for him, and turned on her heel to leave.

She had taken all of two steps back toward the main door to the brig when she heard him call from behind her, "Captain, wait!"

She didn't stop.

"Ma'am, wait, please!"

This time, she did turn around. "What is it, sergeant?" She could see a small film of perspiration on the man's forehead, and she could swear that she could feel his fear. But that was impossible, of course. Wasn't it? "You've already wasted enough of my time."

"I've reconsidered your orders, captain," he said nervously. "I mean, there's no need for... That is, if the president himself sent you down, I don't see any reason why there should be anything wrong."

Nicole frowned, but said nothing.

Gesturing toward the mantrap that sealed the brig cell in which Reza and the two Kreelans were being kept from the rest of the brig, the sergeant told her, "Step into the chamber there, and I'll tell you when it's safe to move into the cell. If they give you any trouble, just give a yell and we'll zap the bastards."

"Very well," she said, moving through the narrow doorway and into the gleaming half cylinder that protruded from the wall. The force field grid hissed on behind her, barring the only exit.

"Stand by," the guard said. A moment later, the cylinder began to rotate, and the opening she had come through sealed. For a long moment she was in a completely enclosed tube that she knew was armed with all sorts of devices to disable and – if need be – to kill a potential escapee. It was not a normal accessory on warships, of course; the regular brig was more than enough to handle the average sailor who was sent down here after captain's mast, or even a Kreelan prisoner, had there ever been any before now. No, this was something that had been specially installed in a rush before *Warspite* had sailed for Erlang. Borge had known there would be use for it.

Suddenly, the force field that guarded the cell side of the contraption came into view, and beyond the blue-green electronic haze of the force field stood Reza.

The cylinder stopped rotating around her, having fully unmasked the opposite door. "Okay, captain," the sergeant said through the man trap's intercom, "the grid's going down... now."

The field suddenly dissipated, leaving behind it only a slight scent of ozone. Without hesitation, she stepped across the threshold to the far side, the oddly misshapen reflections she cast on the polished walls of the chamber following her like silent alter egos.

As she stepped into the cell, the force field snapped on again behind her, and she could hear the cylinder rotate again, sealing her in.

"Nicole," Reza said softly, his swirling green eyes both mournful and pleased. He had known she was coming.

"I... I had to see you," she said unnecessarily, wanting to reach out and embrace him. But that would have condemned her in the ever-present eyes of the security cameras, and then she would be of no help to him at all.

"I knew you must come," Reza whispered.

A young but proud voice suddenly asked in the New Tongue, "Who is this animal, Father?"

Reza smiled at his son. "She is my friend of many, many cycles, Shera-Khan," he told him. "Do you understand what *friendship* is?"

The boy nodded. The priestess had taught him what she knew of the concept, what she had learned from Reza as he was growing up; among the Kreela, such relationships did not exist, for they were all bound by their very blood and spirit to the Empress. "I am honored to meet you, friend-of-my-father's," Shera-Khan told Nicole in Standard.

"Thank... thank you," Nicole replied, flabbergasted. She turned to Reza. "This is your son?" she asked incredulously.

"Yes," Reza told her, his own sense of awe undiminished at the miracle that stood in their midst. "His name is Shera-Khan."

"Is she of the Blood, my son?" Tesh-Dar suddenly asked, speaking in the Old Tongue as she lay in her bed, her eyes closed. Her voice was soft, but still carried the power of command that Reza had known since the first time that he had heard her speak.

"She is, my priestess," he admitted. He suspected that Tesh-Dar was greatly disappointed that he had shared the fire that flowed in his veins with another who was totally alien to the Way. "She and I have known each other since before I came to the Way. When I returned to them, I needed someone who could... understand who and what I was. I chose her."

"Bring her to me."

Reza turned to Nicole, who was utterly confused at the rapid exchange, not a word of which she could understand, except something that sounded like "friendship."

"What is wrong?" Nicole asked. "What are you talking about?"

"Do not fear, Nicole," he told her. "There is nothing wrong. The priestess – her name is Tesh-Dar – wishes to... become acquainted with you." He took her hand and guided her past Shera-Khan to the great warrior who lay on the hard bed that protruded from the cell's wall.

The two of them knelt down next to Tesh-Dar, who continued to lie still.

"Is she dying?" Nicole asked.

"Yes," Reza responded sadly. "The warriors – the clawed ones among our race – do not atrophy before death as humans do. Their bodies remain strong until very near the end. But when the time comes to die, everything fails at once, and quickly – usually a matter of days or a week – is it over."

"I am so sorry, Reza," Nicole told him. "I–"

Tesh-Dar's eyes opened, startling Nicole with their intensity, and before she could react both of the warrior's huge hands were cupped gently around Nicole's face. The Kreelan's flesh felt warm, hot, against her skin, and Nicole began to feel faint, as if the blood to her brain had been cut off. She felt herself floating, drifting above a world that she knew she had seen before. Looking down at her arms, she saw that they were sheathed in black armor, and at the ends of her fingertips were silver claws. The flimsy uniform that she was accustomed to wearing was gone.

And in her heart, in her blood, burned the fire of the Bloodsong. She had sensed it before, as a deaf person might sense the vibration of music, but now she felt it as it was meant to be and was overcome by it, became a part of it. Every cell in her body burst into a roaring flame, joining the symphony of infinite harmonies that intoxicated her senses, that overwhelmed her brain.

The tide of the song crested, then slowly began to ebb. At last it began to fade away, and she felt the warmth of the mourning marks spreading down her face, blackening her blue skin like the falling of night over the plains of Wra'akath. She felt around her neck, her fingers touching the collar that she had worn since her youth, an oath of her own honor toward the Empress and Her Children, and of the Empress's love for her.

"Nicole," a voice spoke softly from a distance, from somewhere beyond the horizon and the rising Empress Moon. It was a voice she knew. It was the voice of someone she loved.

"Reza?"

"Come away now, Nicole," he told her in the Old Tongue. He stood beside her now. "Take my hand."

She reached out for him, taking his hand as he had asked. "Do we have to leave, Reza?" she asked, looking over her shoulder, back at the mystical world that had been like home to her in her dreams for so many years.

"Yes, Nicole," he told her gently. "This world belongs to others," he said. "You must return to yours, where you belong."

Sadly, Nicole turned away from the golden light that reflected from the spires of the Great City, and suddenly found herself falling... falling...

"Nicole."

Her eyes flew open and she sucked in her breath in a gasp as if she had been thrown into freezing water. The Homeworld – if that is what it had been – was gone, replaced by surroundings and sensations that should have felt more familiar than they did.

"Rest easy," Reza said, his hand gripping her shoulder gently.

"You have chosen your companions wisely, my son," Tesh-Dar told him as she released Nicole. Her own eyes blazed with the heat of the fire that had burned in her heart her entire life, save the last few agonizing days since the Empress's heart had closed itself away from Her Children. The feeling was at once invigorating and monumentally depressing, for she realized that she might never again feel it before she passed into the unknown darkness where once the Ancient Ones had sung Her glory, but now lay silent as a timeless tomb. "As were you, she, too, is worthy of the Way."

"Captain!" an alien voice suddenly intruded. "Are you all right in there? Do you require assistance?"

"No," Nicole managed, shaking off the last of the vision, or whatever it was. "No, I am fine."

"I think it's time you came out, ma'am," the voice of the ISS sergeant said. His tone told her that her made-up orders and threats were wearing thin. Behind her, the mantrap began to cycle open.

"We shall speak again," Reza told her. "Soon."

Nicole nodded. "*Oui, mon ami.* Soon." Without another word, she stepped into the cylinder, her eyes fixed on Reza as the force field snapped on and the door swiftly closed.

FOURTEEN

Eustus regained consciousness face down, his cheek pressing numbly into what had once been a priceless original Persian rug that was now soaked and stained with blood from the half dozen cuts in his face.

"Camden," he heard someone saying urgently, "can you hear me?"

He tried to say "Yes," but it came out through his battered lips and swollen jaw like "Memph." He tasted blood and spat out the glassy remains of what had once been an upper incisor.

He felt himself being rolled over, and he groaned involuntarily from the pain. Mostly bruises, he thought automatically, his mind long accustomed to categorizing the type of pain his body felt. No spearing pain or grating bones; nothing was broken. But the pain of the bruises and contusions were enough to bring tears to his swollen eyes.

"Jesus, Eustus, you look like hell." Forcing his swollen eyes just a little wider while trying to blink away the tears, Eustus could barely make out the dark-faced form hovering above him.

"Commander... Mackenzie?" The face nodded. "Where are we?"

"We're aboard the *Golden Pearl*," she said as she tore a strip of her undershirt off and began to blot away some of the blood from Eustus's face. "It's the ship that Reza and I took from Earth. But that's a story for another time. What the devil happened to you, Marine? Who did this to you?"

"Don't know for sure," he slurred. "Looked like ISS types, but that couldn't be."

Jodi looked at him strangely. "Yes, I'm afraid it could, Eustus," she told him. "You were arrested, I take it. Do you have any idea why?"

"They wanted me to kill Reza," he told her.

"Who? Who did?"

"Don't know." He winced as she accidentally blotted over a particularly nasty gash, where one of his assailants had landed a blow with a set of brass knuckles. "The commodore ordered me to do it, but I don't know where exactly the orders came from. All I know is that she didn't seem to care for them any more than I did." He had known that Marchand was putting on an act. She was too good an officer to have done otherwise.

"I guess you refused, didn't you?" she asked.

He nodded, feeling his neck muscles spasm with the effort. "Yeah, I gave them the 'hell no' routine, and found myself charged with treason for refusing to commit murder. Imagine that." He shook his head, careful not to interrupt the rhythm of the blacksmith's hammer banging in his skull. "After you and Reza were taken off a while ago," he went on as Jodi slowly helped him into a sitting position, "they brought me here and half a dozen goons in ISS uniforms paralyzed me and then took turns remapping my face."

Jodi smiled. "It's a definite improvement, Camden."

Eustus managed a weak smile. "Thanks loads, commander." He suddenly turned serious. "Commander, I'm not one normally prone to foul language, but just what the fuck is going on?"

"Maybe I can fill you in," came a voice from the doorway. Silhouetted was a huge man in a Marine uniform, with four other, darker, forms behind him.

"Thorella," Eustus hissed.

"That's General Thorella to you, Marine," he shot back icily as he and four ISS guards entered the room, sealing the door behind them. Just before it closed, Eustus glimpsed two more figures outside. "It seems you still have a lot to learn about basic military etiquette."

"That's a pretty big word for a Neanderthal like you, general," Jodi said. She came to her feet, standing between Thorella and his men, and Eustus, who was still unable to stand. "Or should I call you by your real name... Anton Borge?"

Thorella laughed. "Don't be an idiot, commander," he told her casually as he took another step closer. "Anton Borge died a long, long time ago, the victim of a tragic accident." The smile. "As you know, of course."

Jodi felt chilled under his black, lifeless stare. Except that it wasn't lifeless. Not this time. There was a ripple, a crawling twinkle, like light reflecting from oozing crude oil, or a parasite boring its way just below dark and dank soil, that she saw there now. "You'll never get away with what you've done, Anton," she told him, standing her ground. "You're going to hang."

"I don't think so," he said quietly, eerily, as he stepped closer. "And you should not be so concerned with the past as with the present... and the immediate future."

"You bastard," Eustus growled. He recognized the men with Thorella as the ones who had beaten him. "You're behind all this, aren't you?"

"I see you need another lesson," Thorella said pleasantly. Before either Jodi or Eustus could react, Thorella landed a sharp kick with his rough-soled boots on the left side of Eustus's head, sending him sprawling across the floor.

"Jesus!" Jodi exclaimed. "Thorella, for the love of God—"

"You still don't understand what's happening, do you?" Thorella said, turning his attention from Eustus and back to her. "This isn't some petty boot camp game, Mackenzie. This is life and death, and I get to play God."

The dark form that she had seen wriggling in his eyes had transformed itself from a burrowing maggot to a glistening hydra, filled with hate and lust.

"You're insane," she said, her voice faltering as she took a step back, away from him. "Bug-fuck crazy."

"Funny you should mention that word," Thorella said, his smile gleaming dully. "*Fuck*, I mean. I've heard that you've never had a man. Well, my dear, this is your lucky day. You're going to have a bunch of men, all at once." He nodded his head at the four men with him who now seemed a lot closer than they had been only a moment before, and they all wore the kind of smile that the lowlifes she had encountered saved only for particularly attractive women.

"No!" Eustus shouted from behind them, weakly propelling himself at the knot of men that was closing around Jodi.

"Hold him," Thorella said contemptuously as two of the ISS men easily deflected Eustus's attack and pinned his arms painfully behind his back. "Make him watch. You never know, Camden," he said congenially, "you might learn something." He turned back to Jodi. "Now, bitch, you can have this easy, or—"

Jodi chose that moment to strike, aiming a kick at Thorella's left knee, her bellow of fury mixed with stark fear filling the room.

Thorella dodged it without noticeable effort. While Jodi was good, having learned her skills the hard way, in combat, Thorella had had years of close combat training and field experience, and was one of the most physically fit human beings in existence.

"—or the hard way," he concluded. A huge fist arced out like a steel piston, striking her right collarbone, which snapped with a nauseating crunch.

Jodi screamed, her left hand reflexively reaching for the source of the electrifying pain that flashed through her body. Thorella casually reached out and grabbed her hand, spun her around, then brutally yanked it up and backward, forcing her hand almost to her neck and nearly dislocating her shoulder. Slamming her face-first into the wall, he took a handful of her hair in his other hand and began to rhythmically smash her face against the unyielding plastisteel, leaving smears of blood from her torn lips and battered nose on the antique white finish.

As she began to slide down the wall, battered senseless, her legs losing their strength, he took the opportunity to land a fist over each kidney, smiling to himself as he heard the satisfying snapping of some of her ribs.

"Stop it!" Eustus was screaming. "Stop it! You're killing her!"

He let go of Jodi, who slid to the floor in a groaning heap, and turned to Eustus. "That's the idea," he said happily before landing a fist in Eustus's solar plexus. Eustus collapsed in a gasping heap.

"Oh, look at that," he said, mocking Jodi as she tried to crawl away from him. "What's wrong, commander? Did I upset you? Here, let me help you." He reached out and took another handful of Jodi's hair, yanking her to her feet. "How do you feel, commander?"

"Fuck... you... asshole," she sputtered, blood trickling down her chin.

"A woman with spirit, gentlemen," he said to the others, who nodded approvingly. "But I'm afraid, my dear, that it's you who are going to get fucked in the asshole." With an easy movement, he slammed Jodi up against a polished oak table.

"No," she whispered. "Please, don't..."

"What's the matter, Mackenzie?" he cooed as he removed his illegal Kreelan knife from an ankle sheath. "You want this, I know you do. A good fucking from a man will do wonders for a dyke bitch like you." He inserted the knife blade at the back of her pants and started to cut. The sharp edge whispered down the cleft of her buttocks, parting the heavy material of her uniform and underwear like they were paper. When the blade reached the inseam, he stopped. Jodi felt the cold steel disappear.

"Goddamn you, Thorella," she whispered, tears welling in her eyes as her body quivered with helpless rage and fear. "God damn you to hell."

Thorella said nothing. Instead, he pulled her back a ways from the table and reinserted the blade, this time in the front of her pants, the blade cutting toward her crotch. He was leaning heavily against her now, and she could feel his throbbing erection against her exposed buttocks.

"Help, me, Father," she whispered to herself. "Please." She tried to struggle away, but Thorella was too strong. "Please..."

The blade left a thin trace of blood as it just barely cut the skin on its way down her quivering belly to her pubic mound, and then down, down. With a tiny hiss, the material parted. Thorella roughly pulled the halves of her pants down each leg with his knife hand while his other held her head pinned to the table.

"Thorella," Eustus rasped, "please don't do this. I'll do anything you want..."

"You'll do anything that I want anyway, Camden," Thorella said harshly, his breathing now labored. "And after I fuck her, I might just do the same to you."

Too rushed by his raging lust to use the knife, Thorella dropped it to the floor and used his bare hands to rip open the back of Jodi's blouse and its built in bra. He tore away the fabric, ripping it from her body to let it fall to the floor like trash. His free hand groped for her breasts, squeezing them hard, bruising the tender flesh, pinching the nipples until they bled.

Jodi bit her tongue to keep from crying out. She tasted a fresh surge of copper as blood flooded her mouth. *Think of something*, she ordered herself desperately. *Do something...*

But there was nothing to be done. She felt Thorella's hand working at his pants, freeing the pulsating serpent within. She grunted in agony as he forced himself into her with a brutal thrust, crushing her thighs against the table's edge.

The last thing she heard was Eustus, screaming for Thorella to stop, his voice oddly muffled by Thorella's frenzied panting.

But then her mind shut down, locking itself away in a tiny place where light and love ruled over the darkness of men's hearts, and the world was still kind.

FIFTEEN

From the end of the flag bridge where the main view screen was located, Borge began his speech to the ships that had reached their final rendezvous point before making the hyperspace jump that would take them to the Kreelan homeworld.

"Men and women of the Fleet," he began, his face beaming with what was both genuine sincerity and a maniacal belief in his vision of his own empire-to-be, "this day shall be one not long forgotten in the history of the Confederation. For a century have we found ourselves locked in mortal combat with an alien enemy, an enemy who attacked us for no reason, and who attempted to exterminate our people, an attempt that has been in vain. We have paid our way in blood to the threshold where we now stand, and it is time now to make the enemy pay in kind a thousand-fold." He turned to L'Houillier. "Admiral, you may give the word."

L'Houillier did not hesitate. "Prepare to jump," he ordered. He exchanged a glance with Zhukovski, who stood unobtrusively near one of the bridge's three exits.

A moment later, Zhukovski quietly disappeared.

Amid the cheering throughout the three thousand ships of the great fleet, klaxons blared to announce the imminent jump into hyperspace. The pilots of the hundreds of fighters and attack craft that had been launched at this last rendezvous point snuggled up close to their mother ships, trying to make sure they were captured in the surrounding hyperdrive field and not left behind when the bigger ships jumped. It was a terribly dangerous maneuver, but Laskowski's plan had called for it, and the president had ordered it done.

L'Houillier turned to Laskowski. "Admiral, execute the jump," he ordered.

"Aye, aye, sir," she said sharply, turning to the battery of fleet controllers who were clustered around a myriad of consoles in a darkened alcove at the rear of the flag bridge. "Execute!" she snapped.

A moment later, under control of the *Warspite's* straining navigational computers, thousands of human warships disappeared from their dark and lonely rendezvous point, leaving behind nothing but ripples in the fabric of empty space.

* * *

The jump was a short one, Reza noted silently. He felt the first tremor in his flesh that had always announced to him that they had bridged the gap between normal space and what was beyond, followed a few short minutes later by the second tremor indicating their return to normal space.

"We have arrived," he told Tesh-Dar and Shera-Khan. "We are home. It will soon be time for us to depart this place."

"The animals will not allow us to leave, my son," Tesh-Dar noted. For some reason she could not explain, her health had markedly improved since her joining with Reza's human friend. Perhaps it was the breath of purity that flowed from the woman's vision, a legacy that Reza had left her when his blood had mingled with hers; perhaps it was only the final gasp of her body as it sought to stave off Death for but a while longer. *No matter*, she counseled herself. *I shall do all in my power to return Reza to Her, and to see that I die with honor, in battle.* "We shall have to fight them. The oath you swore to not spill the blood of your birth must be broken by deed as much as word."

"And so shall it be," Reza answered. "My honor do I forfeit for Her sake." He looked away. "No sacrifice may be too great."

He felt Tesh-Dar's hand on his arm. "Your honor is your love for Her, Reza," she told him gently. "Your debt to your forebears have you paid, ever since the very first day that you returned to them from the Empire."

"I am with you, Father," Shera-Khan told him quietly, but with a solemnity in his voice that Reza would always remember. His son would be a great warrior someday. If only he survived.

"You honor your mother well, my son," he said.

The lights suddenly dimmed, and the entire hull reverberated with artificial thunder.

"The battle is joined," Reza said, coming to his feet. "Soon, now. We must be prepared."

* * *

"*Merde*, admiral," L'Houillier shouted, "I ordered you to disperse the fleet! We are packed in here like sardines!"

"But–"

"Another word and you are relieved," he snarled. "You can go and have your beloved president relieve me of duty, but until then you are under my command and by God you will follow my orders!"

Such an exchange normally might have wrought complete, dumbfounded silence on the flag bridge. But even the curses of the Grand Admiral were lost in the frantic hubbub of the flag and ship's bridge staffs as they sought to make order out of the chaos that had erupted when the Armada dropped back into normal space after the last jump.

In the background was the main flag bridge viewscreen, and what it showed no human eyes had ever before witnessed, nor would they again. An assemblage of Confederation warships that swarmed through the skies of the alien homeworld, clashing with an equal, if not superior, armada that bore the runes of the enemy that Humanity had been fighting for nearly a century. Dozens of ships, most of them Kreelan, had already died, their death throes marked by flaring explosions that left nothing behind but slagged hulks and clouds of iridescent gas. Tens of thousands of energy bolts, crimson and green, joined hundreds of ships in the blink of an eye, bringing death to some, victory to others. And amid the great warships darted clouds of fighters.

But the human ships were at a great tactical disadvantage. In the initial deployment formation that Laskowski had chosen, the conical groups of human ships could only bring their forward batteries to bear, while many of the Kreelan ships, disorganized as they were, could bring their entire broadsides into action against the invaders. On the oceans of ancient Earth, this had been known as "crossing the T." It was a disastrous disadvantage that L'Houillier was desperately trying to redress.

"Aye, aye, sir," Laskowski responded woodenly, for the first time sensing that all might not go as she had planned. Without another word from L'Houillier, she turned to the operations section and began barking out the Grand Admiral's orders, feeling not so much resentment as a growing sense of fear as they fought to reorganize the fleet.

Slowly, ever so slowly, the three huge task forces began to change their shape, from the roughly conical formations in which they had arrived to a series of great staggered wedges, their courses altered to bring as many batteries to bear on the enemy as possible.

L'Houillier watched the tactical display with his fists knotted at his sides. He had agreed to Zhukovski's plan, but he was determined to fight his fleet as long as there was some possibility of victory. Even the crippling of the Kreelan fleet would suffice, if it were not at the cost of his own.

On the great screen, the number of engagements doubled, then trebled. The Kreelans were fighting back, but weakly. L'Houillier allowed himself a faint ray of hope. There was every chance that his fleet would inflict far more damage on the enemy than they themselves would sustain.

Perhaps, he thought, we might even win.

* * *

Zhukovski was beginning to feel the chill of panic rising in his throat. The corridor that ran through the outer hull and separated two banks of massive storage rooms was empty. *Where the devil was Braddock?* he wondered. "You can think of nowhere he might be found?" he asked Enya again.

"No, admiral," she said, equally worried. "He said he would meet us here, as agreed. He only wanted to speak with Nicole, to wish her luck on her mission, before he met with us."

Zhukovski's head whipped around. "Mission?" he snapped. "What mission? Carré was not to fly. Personal orders of Grand Admiral himself after she ferried a fighter aboard. *Chyort voz'mi,*" he cursed. "Come! We check her cabin."

"But that's all the way across the ship!"

"You have better idea?" he asked over his shoulder. "Come! We waste precious time."

Unable to think of any alternative, Enya rushed after him. Her footsteps were lost in the cascade of godlike hammer blows that was *Warspite's* batteries engaging the enemy.

* * *

"Sarge," one of the guards whispered, "look."

Sergeant Ricardo Estefan, ISS, looked up to see Nicole Carré step through the blast doors and into the brig. She brought with her a large flight bag, obviously full, and she was wearing a strange expression.

Standing up, he said, "I'm sorry, ma'am, but the president ordered that no one – especially you – be allowed to see the pris–"

His sentence was interrupted by the bark of the blaster that suddenly appeared in Nicole's free hand. Set on stun, it was still powerful enough to send the one hundred-kilo sergeant reeling against the wall, unconscious.

The four others on the guard detail were already reaching for their weapons, but Nicole was faster, much faster. In the blink of an eye, all four had been blasted to the floor, unconscious.

Working quickly, Nicole shut down the monitoring devices and entered the security override code she had coaxed from an ISS officer who had wanted a physical reward for the information. She had not disappointed him, although it had not been what he had been expecting. He still lay unconscious and bleeding in his cabin.

With a hum, the mantrap began to cycle open. The force field within had been shut down completely.

Shera-Khan and Tesh-Dar emerged from the opening, Nicole wondering how the two had squeezed themselves into the tiny chamber.

"Sergeant Estefan," a belligerent voice suddenly spat from the control panel. "I'm not getting a reading from your monitors, and I show that the mantrap's been opened. What's going on?"

"Where is Reza?" she asked Shera-Khan urgently, as she took an electronic key from one of the unconscious guards and removed their explosive collars. The door to the mantrap slowly began to cycle back into the cell. *Too slow, too slow!* she thought frantically. She could see in her mind the two Kreelan warriors and herself exposed and vulnerable out here, with Reza trapped in the revolving cylinder as a dozen ISS guards burst in, shooting.

"He remains within," the boy replied.

Nicole saw that Tesh-Dar seemed to have regained something close to what must be her awesome natural strength, as she moved immediately toward the door to the corridor to watch for intruders, her muscles rippling beneath the leatherite armor. Without a word, she jammed a sliver of metal she had taken from somewhere in her armor into the door slot. It would not be closing on them unless they wanted it to.

"Estefan!" the voice shouted. "Respond!"

"Come on, come on!" Nicole urged the maddeningly slow cylinder. She could just see the edge of the opening when the mantrap suddenly stopped turning.

"Security alert, Brig Four!" the voice bleated over the ship's intercom. "ISS detachments to the brig, on the double! Intruder alert! Intruder alert!"

"*Merde!*" Nicole hissed. She tried the code again, but the controls had been overridden, probably somewhere in engineering, and she did not know enough about the systems to try a manual override. Behind her, the motors driving the door to the brig whined in futility against the metal Tesh-Dar had wedged in the doorway, trying to prevent their escape. "He is trapped! We have to—"

Her jaw went slack as she watched Reza walk through the ten centimeter-thick chromalloy of the mantrap, his body passing through the metal as if it were not there at all. The explosive collar was already gone from around his neck. She had no idea how he could have removed the otherwise foolproof device.

Before she could say anything, Reza said something to Shera-Khan, who immediately rushed to Tesh-Dar's side, a shrekka clutched in his claws.

"We must go," Reza told Nicole, taking her by the arm.

"Reza... wait," she managed, gesturing toward the flight bag. In a way, what she had seen did not surprise her; she knew from her dreams that – in his world, anyway – such miracles were possible. But here, now...

Without waiting for her to explain, Reza opened the flight bag. He knew instinctively that she would not have brought it without good reason, and sensed her confusion at what she had just witnessed. But explanations would have to wait. For all the infinite age of the Universe, they were running out of time.

Inside he saw the deep black of his Kreelan armor and, beneath that, the glittering of his weapons. His sword.

"In Her name," he whispered. Looking up, he said, "Thank you, Nicole."

"You are... welcome, *mon ami*," she said as he hastily stripped out of his uniform and donned what long ago had been his second skin. He had made crude adjustments to it over the years, and while it did not fit as it should, as the clawless ones would have made it, it was still comfortable. It felt right.

In less time than Nicole could believe, Reza was ready. With but a proud glance at her adopted son, Tesh-Dar moved quickly into the corridor, one of the guards' weapons clutched in her huge hand, her own weapons locked away in a security vault somewhere else in the ship.

When she signaled it was clear, Reza asked Nicole, "Where are we to go?"

"The only place we can get transportation off the ship," Nicole said, leading Reza into the corridor, her own weapon held before her. "Hangar deck."

* * *

After ringing at Nicole's cabin and receiving no answer, Zhukovski opened the door with his command override.

The door slid open to reveal Tony Braddock sprawled in Nicole's bunk.

"Tony!" Enya gasped as the two of them rushed into the room, the admiral closing the door behind him after casting a wary eye about the corridor to make sure no one had noticed them.

To be discovered now would be disaster, he muttered to himself. Around them, *Warspite* shuddered and boomed as the battle raged. *Good luck, my friend*, he silently wished L'Houillier.

"What happened?" Enya demanded as she shook Braddock back to consciousness.

"Nicole..." he rasped, "stunned me."

"Why, councilman?" Zhukovski demanded. "Why would she do this? What does she plan to do?"

"Reza," Enya knew the answer instantly. "She's gone to free him, hasn't she?"

Braddock nodded stiffly. He felt like someone was pricking him with a million needles. The feeling was not exactly painful, but it was hardly pleasant, either. "That must be it," he managed, shaking his head to clear it. His vision gradually began to clear. He took a breath of air through his nose, trying to clean out the sharp smell of ozone that was a peculiar side effect of being stunned.

"We must stop her," Zhukovski said. "They will know—"

"Security alert, Brig Four!" the ship's intercom announced. "ISS detachments to the brig, on the double! Intruder alert! Intruder alert!"

"That tears it," Braddock said, getting to his feet. He went over to a cabinet boasting a cipher lock, punched in some numbers, and opened it.

"What are you doing?" Enya asked.

Braddock withdrew two blasters. "Jodi was always paranoid that Nicole should have something to protect herself with," he told them. "She gave these to her on her birthday a few years ago, and Nicole promised Jodi she would keep them with her." He shook his head. "Nutcases, both of them. Thank God."

After checking to make sure the weapons were loaded and carried a full charge, he handed one to Enya, keeping the other for himself. Zhukovski wore his own sidearm.

Zhukovski opened the door, leading the other two out into the corridor. "Where do you think she will go?" he asked Braddock.

"Where else would a pilot go?" he replied. "Hangar deck."

* * *

Nicole had led Reza and the others through a maze of passageways and service tunnels to avoid being spotted by the alerted security teams and the damage repair crewmen whose duties required them to move through the ship while at battle stations. They were only a few yards from the last set of blast doors separating them from the hangar deck when *Warspite* shuddered and her metal body screamed in agony. The four of them were hurled against the bulkhead as the battleship recoiled under a direct hit, the already dim corridor lights flickering, dying.

Even as the echoes of the hit died away, Nicole could hear the sound of thunder beyond the blast door. The red tell-tales on the control panel told her all she needed to know.

"Hangar deck has been hit! It's venting air to space!" she shouted above the howling of hangar deck's air supply whirling away into vacuum on the other side of the bulkhead, just as the dim red emergency lights flickered on.

"Behind us!" Shera-Khan warned as several dim shapes appeared from the crimson murk of the corridor.

In the blink of an eye, a shrekka appeared in Tesh-Dar's hand, its lethal blades already tearing into their target in the elder warrior's mind. The muscles of her arm tensed in a pattern no less precise, yet infinitely more elegant, than any machine could have calculated.

Evgeni Zhukovski would have died had Reza not been an arrow's breath faster than his priestess.

"He is a friend," he told her as his hand gently touched her arm. He did not have to grab her or restrain her. She reacted instantly. Her arm relaxed. Slightly.

"Tony!" Nicole exclaimed, her face a mask of anguish as her husband embraced her. It had nearly killed her to stun him, but there was no way she could have explained what she had to do, and she did not want him to be associated with her crime. Then she noticed Zhukovski. "Admiral! What are you doing—"

"We have no time for unnecessary words, commander," he cut her off. Nodding to Reza, then to the two Kreelans, he said, "After forty years in Navy was I ready to commit mutiny, commander. This day even that has gone awry. Now we are all fugitives, with no way to escape." He gestured to the blast doors.

Warspite took another hit, worse this time. They found themselves curled up on the floor against the starboard bulkhead, a cloud of dust in the air from the shock.

Zhukovski noted with alarm that *Warspite's* return fire was starting to lose its cadence, becoming more random, sporadic. Fire control was breaking down. "Flagship is hurt," he told them. "Badly, I think."

Reza felt a minute fluctuation in the artificial gravity. It was a very, very bad sign. "Engineering has sustained damage," he told them. "Our warships" – Kreelan warships – "must be concentrating on *Warspite*. We must get away, and soon." He turned to Nicole. "What is left on this ship that could get to the moon orbiting the Homeworld?"

"The captain's gig, but that is all the way forward."

"Then that is where we must go."

"But Reza," Nicole said, "we will have to go through the main corridors! There will be no way to avoid the security patrols."

He glanced at Tesh-Dar, then turned to Nicole, his face a grim, alien mask. "They shall not stop us."

"There may be another way," Zhukovski growled. He stood at the wall, scrutinizing a miniature data display he held in his hand. Reza could see the trace of a smile, well hidden in the older man's beard, shining in the crimson light of the battle lanterns. He looked like Satan himself. "Borge has sent for *Golden Pearl*, as I thought he would," he told them. "He is abandoning ship."

"If we could get to it first..." Enya mused. The thought sent a chill up her spine. They were actually trying to make their way to the enemy's capital. But to do... what?

She shook her head. Whatever it was they were about to attempt, it was the only thing left that they could do.

"They are going to attempt docking at main gangway airlock," Zhukovski repeated from the interface. "We have less than eight minutes to get there."

"Let's move it, then," Braddock said gruffly.

Had Jodi been there, she would have recognized the voice of the hard-bitten gunnery sergeant who had looked after her on a backwater world, seemingly so long ago.

* * *

The battle was not going well, President Borge lamented angrily. He was furious at the failure of Grand Admiral L'Houillier and *Warspite's* captain to keep the ship – and himself – safe from peril while annihilating the enemy. He would have had them both shot, but the second Kreelan salvo to penetrate *Warspite's* failing shields had speared through the hull and destroyed the bridge. It was only a stroke of divine intervention that Borge had been in his private quarters, watching the battle develop with the Confederation's chief leaders: his own subordinates.

"I'm sorry, Mr. President," Laskowski reported over the comm unit that Borge held in his hand. "The reports are true. Ships throughout the fleet are picking up gravity spikes: more Kreelan ships are inbound." Her face was blackened and bloodstained. She happened to have been on her way back from the intel section to the flag bridge when the latter was blasted into wreckage. Had she passed through one more blast door on her short journey, she would have been dead. Like L'Houillier and the others. This was the worst moment in her life, the most difficult thing she had ever done. "I suggest we withdraw, sir. Immediately."

Borge's face flushed red on its way to purple. "We will do no such thing, admiral!" he snapped viciously. "We are winning! Your own estimates," he shook a handful of flimsies at the comm unit, "say so! We will return to Confederation space victorious or not at all," he went on softly against the background of firing and periodic hits absorbed by *Warspite's* thousands of tons of armor. "And if you or anyone else suggests such a traitorous idea again, I will have you shot. Do you understand, admiral?"

Laskowski choked back her fear. The honeymoon, it seemed, was over. "Yes, sir," she replied carefully. "In that case, I request permission to transfer my flag to *Southampton*. Sir. *Warspite* will be untenable soon, and the flag bridge is gone."

Borge grunted. Furious as he was, he could hardly deny that request as he made his own way to another vessel to carry on his crusade, forging humanity's future upon the ruins of the Empire. "Very well, admiral. Carry on." With that, he snapped off the comm link. "Bloody incompetents," he cursed to his aide, absently handing her the comm unit.

"Don't be concerned, sir," the woman said soothingly as she retrieved the device and stowed it carefully in the black case that also contained the control codes for the kryolon weapons that were stowed aboard another ship. Curiously, no one knew – except for the president himself – which ship that was. "We knew there would be some losses on our side. This is simply a minor inconvenience."

The two of them followed a squad of ISS guards, and behind them was a trail of senators and council members – his trusted lieutenants – that made up the bulk of the Confederation's government, corrupt though it now was.

"It is sloppy work, Elena," Borge said as they followed the guards around yet another bend in the long march to the gangway, "and there is no excuse for sloppiness. Not in my–"

"Look out!" someone shouted as a hail of crimson bolts came blasting down the corridor, followed by several shadowy blurs that Borge did not realize were Kreelan shrekkas.

Without hesitation, he pushed his aid and latest lover into the line of fire, her body absorbing three energy bolts that would otherwise have found him. Rolling to the floor with the agility of one well accomplished at escaping from tight situations, he snatched the black case from her still-twitching hand and began to crawl through the sudden panic that now filled the corridor, heading for the airlock.

More and more weapons fired as two more squads of ISS guards who had pushed their way through the mewling politicians joined the fray. The deck filled with smoke and the smell of charred flesh and freshly spilled blood, the muzzle flashes surreal in the dim red glare of the emergency lighting.

"Where's the president?" Borge could hear someone screaming hysterically. "Where's the pres–" The voice was cut off in the crackle of a blaster firing from somewhere down the corridor that ran perpendicular to the main gangway.

On the floor, like a man caught in a burning building, Borge could see clearly, unhindered by the cloying smoke of burning flesh, cloth, and plastic that now blinded anyone standing upright. Smoke from the *Warspite's* mortal wounds now filled the decks of the dying ship. The flashing red and yellow coaming lights around the main gangway airlock drew him like a moth to a flame, and he smiled grimly as he low-crawled his way toward it, dragging the all-important case along with him. He had no idea who had started the shooting, perhaps some disgruntled crewman who was jealous that they could leave this doomed hulk while he could not, but it did not matter: Borge would make it. He would reach the airlock where the *Golden Pearl* was even now docking. He would survive.

But Borge was not a patient man. As the airlock loomed closer, he rose from his crawl and into a crouch, using his legs to propel him faster than could his knees and elbows crabbing along the floor.

Again *Warspite* rocked from a hit, sending Borge sprawling to the deck, the precious case falling from his grip to bang and slide a few meters back the way he had come as the thunder of the great ship's armor being penetrated crashed through her hull.

"Dammit!" he cursed as he regained his bearings in the smoke-clogged gangway, his right knee ringing with pain from where it had smashed against the bulkhead when he fell. He started back for the case, lost in the haze–

–and stumbled over something. Looking down, he saw the body of a child at his feet. A Kreelan child.

His blood suddenly ran cold. *Reza's son*, a tiny voice in his mind informed him, quite unnecessarily. And where his son was, Reza was no doubt close by. Borge reacted quickly, doing what any politician of his caliber would have done. Seizing the dazed child by the hair with one hand, he drew his personal blaster with the other, pressing the muzzle against the boy's head. Then Borge put his back up against the wall to prevent any surprises from behind.

It was only then that he noticed the unnatural stillness in the corridor. The fighting had stopped. Only the subaudible thrum of the ship's engines and a periodic salvo of her guns now and then broke the silence.

"Gard!" he shouted into the swirling smoke. "I've got your boy, half-breed! Do you hear me?"

"I hear you." Reza's cool voice came from somewhere in the choking smoke roiling through the corridor. "Which is surprising, to hear the voice of a dead man."

Borge's brittle laugh cut through the air. "If I'm dead, so is your boy, Reza. Don't believe I won't kill him if you make me."

"Just like you killed Markus Thorella?" Zhukovski's voice accused from the fog. "Only this time, there will be no body to substitute, no fortune to collect for personal benefit."

"But there is a fortune, you short-sighted fool, a fortune in victory, a fortune in power that you could not possibly comprehend." Borge began to back cautiously toward the airlock, dragging Shera-Khan with him. Not quite so dazed now, the boy began to struggle, and Borge did not want to harm his insurance too soon. "Make him stop trying to break free, Reza, or I'll kill him right now," he warned.

A few words spoken in Kreelan from the darkness seemed to calm the boy. Perhaps too much.

"That's better," Borge said. "Now, there's a case sitting in the corridor somewhere near you. I want it. Now."

"What is in it?" Reza asked quietly. Borge could swear that his nemesis was speaking right into his ear, but there was no one to be seen.

"None of your business," Borge snapped. "Just hand it over."

The case suddenly skittered along the floor, coming to rest at Borge's feet. "Pick it up," he told Shera-Khan.

The boy did not move.

"Pick it up, damn you," Borge hissed as he pushed the muzzle harder against Shera-Khan's temple.

As Shera-Khan leaned down to do as he had been told, a hollow thump, followed by the airlock coaming flashing green, announced the arrival of the *Golden Pearl*.

"I'm going to see your planet burn, Reza," Borge shouted into the smoke, although his eyes were still riveted to the inboard airlock hatch and the telltales on the control panel. The outer lock was cycling open. Only a minute left before he was free from this floating coffin. "If you manage to make it to a lifeboat, you might have a chance to see it for your–"

Shera-Khan bolted from his grasp, slashing at his arms with his claws as he leaped into the smoke-shrouded darkness.

"Little bastard!" Borge cursed, raising his weapon to shoot the boy in the back.

As his finger convulsed on the trigger, a huge shadow suddenly materialized from the mist between the gun and the retreating boy. The blaster's energy bolt caught Tesh-Dar squarely in the middle of the chest, flaring her armor white with heat as it penetrated to the aged and dying flesh beneath.

But Borge was not to receive a second chance. One shot was all he would get. As if taking candy from a comatose child, Tesh-Dar slashed out with one hand, her claws severing Borge's arm at the wrist.

Borge opened his mouth to scream, not in pain, for he felt none yet, but in fear. He saw Tesh-Dar as the incarnate devil of his nightmares, the bogeyman come to horrid life. Her mouth opened to reveal fangs that could rip his throat open, but that was not Tesh-Dar's way. She did not care for the foul taste of human blood. Instead, she plunged the talons of her other hand into his ribcage. As she lifted him from the floor, his jaw hanging open in a scream of terrified agony, she let out her own roar of anguish and pain, and righteous vengeance upon an evil that fed upon its own kind. Slowly did her fingers close, drawing her talons together around his furiously pumping heart. He clawed at her hand, his throat now making hollow gagging sounds as his lungs filled with blood and collapsed. With one final, titanic heave, Tesh-Dar tore his heart, still beating, from his chest. She threw her head back and roared in triumph, crushing the disembodied organ in her Herculean grip.

And then, like a great stone pillar with a tiny but mortal flaw, she collapsed to the floor, her bloodied hands covering the still-smoking hole in her own chest.

Reza was there to catch her, and he gently, lovingly, lay her down to rest. "My priestess," he said softly. "My mother—"

She signed him to silence before putting a hand against his face. He held it in one of his own to ease the trembling he felt in hers. "My son," she said softly, "the Race is in your hands, now; our salvation is in your love for Her. Go to Her now... quickly. You must save Her... or we all shall face eternity... in darkness." A tiny tremor ran through her, and her hand clamped painfully around his. "May thy Way be long and glorious... my beloved son."

The strength passed from her hand as her eyes closed, her spirit fleeing her body for what should have been paradise, but without the Empress's light could only be a cold and terrifyingly lonely Hell. A Hell he had seen for himself.

"Reza," Enya whispered behind him, "why... why did she do this? Why didn't you stop her? You could have killed Borge without... without this."

Reza gently unclasped the band and its honors from around Tesh-Dar's neck. Now that her life had passed from her body, the ancient living metal clasp surrendered to his trembling fingers. "She did it because it was her Way," he told her softly.

"I do not mean to intrude on emotional discussion," Zhukovski interjected, "but time becomes short. Security will be here any mom–"

The airlock at the end of the gangway suddenly cycled open to reveal four ISS guards in battle dress.

"Where's the pres–" one of them began before seeing Borge's mangled body and the three humanoids in Kreelan armor.

The ISS sergeant's observation of the gory scene was cut short long before he or his men could raise their weapons. His eyes had just shifted from Borge's body to Reza when Shera-Khan's shrekka sheared his head cleanly from his torso. The head toppled to the deck like a bowling ball, the armored helmet clattering to a stop near one of the other guards' feet. The now headless torso spasmed as if in surprise, and a fountain of blood from the severed carotid artery sprayed the lock's ceiling before the corpse toppled backward into the airlock.

Nicole shot two of the others, while Braddock finished off the last.

"Let's go," Braddock said tightly, gesturing toward the waiting gangway into the smaller ship as he watched the blast doors down one of the other corridors start to cycle open. "More bad guys are on the way."

His last sentence was punctuated by a sudden burst of rifle fire that filled the corridor with crimson and emerald beams of lethal energy as a score of ISS guards rushed through the doors.

"I will cover you!" Zhukovski shouted into Reza's ear, and with his good hand he snatched up a pulse rifle from one of the fallen guards, training it with evident skill on the men advancing upon them. Zhukovski shot one, then another before he was forced back against the wall under a hail of return fire.

"Admiral, we can't leave you!" Nicole shouted above the riot of gunfire that was becoming uncomfortably accurate, as she loosed her own barrage on their attackers.

"Get on that ship, Carré!" Zhukovski shouted furiously. "That is direct order!"

After a moment's hesitation, everyone started toward the airlock, stumbling backward through the smoke and stench of ozone and scorched flesh as they sought the safety of the *Pearl's* main airlock, all the while firing back at the approaching guards.

"You, too, Reza," the old admiral said. "My work is done in this life. You have much yet to do. Good luck, my friend." With a devilish grin, without fear or remorse, he turned his attention back to his chosen enemy.

Reza wanted to thank him in some way, but there were no words. He said a silent prayer to the Empress for this man whose courage would have been the envy of the peers, then turned to make his way to the *Pearl*.

As he passed Borge's body, he noticed the black case that had been the focus of the dead usurper's final moments. Wondering what the man could have considered so important, he picked it up by the bloodied handle before dashing up the textured metal ramp and into the airlock.

The armored door slid closed behind him as Zhukovski's final battle raged toward its inevitable conclusion.

Sixteen

Reza immediately sensed that something was wrong; the aura of his surroundings had changed, darkened, as soon as he set foot inside the *Golden Pearl* and the airlock had cycled closed behind him.

Nicole, Tony, and Enya had already dashed for the cockpit, a muffled scuffle announcing that the *Golden Pearl* had just had a change in flight crew. Reza felt the *Pearl* lurch as she separated from the dying *Warspite*. In seconds, the sleek ship was accelerating toward the Empress moon as Reza had instructed, dodging through the web of energy fire and torpedoes from the massive battle raging around them.

"What is it, Father?" Shera-Khan asked in a whisper as Reza drew his sword. His own hand reached instinctively for one of the remaining shrekkas. He did not have his father's special senses, but he could sense the change in him, even without hearing his Bloodsong, as he could sense that hot had turned to cold.

"I know not, my son," he replied quietly as he set down the black case on a nearby table to leave his hands free for fighting. "Something is amiss; beware."

Together, the two warriors warily advanced down the chandelier-bedecked hallway that led toward the library.

* * *

The first thing Jodi became aware of was an unfamiliar taste in her mouth. There was blood, to be sure. But there was also something different, something she had never tasted before, but from descriptions she had heard from other women, she had no doubt as to what it was. Semen.

Forcing back the nausea that rose in her throat, she feebly spat the sticky substance from her mouth, along with some blood and the debris from a broken tooth. The effort resulted in a red-hot lance of pain from her stomach and ribs, and it was all she could do to keep from moaning aloud. The mixture of blood, semen, and enamel bubbled from between her lips to ooze down the side of her face in a warm, coppery stream.

With what seemed a titanic effort, she managed to pry one eye open, the other resisting her will with the force of the swelling that had deformed the right side of her face. Beyond the panorama of the carpet, stained with her own blood, she saw the blurred image of a combat boot, then its mate as it slowly swam into focus. For now, the vision of the two boots on the bloody rug was the extent of her world.

"Shouldn't Cerda have checked in with us?" a voice from somewhere above asked in a high, nasal voice. "Maybe we should go check on the president, or something."

"Shut up," said another, deeper voice, one familiar with being in charge of any situation. "If you want to brown nose, just butt snorkel with Cerda and keep away from Borge. Treak," he called to a third, "go forward and see what the hell's going on. Find out what we're supposed to do with this trash." A boot prodded Jodi's buttocks, but she only felt a vague pressure, nothing more. She was numb below the waist, and a tentative command to curl one of her toes disappeared into darkness, unheeded. Her lower body was paralyzed.

"Sure, sarge," someone answered casually, and she heard heavy soles clump toward an exit, a door slid open—

—and then all hell broke loose.

"Look out!" someone cried as a lion's roar ripped through the room, followed by her captors screaming and shouting. A few shots thundered out, and Jodi could see a rush of booted feet running toward the door.

And there was another sound, one she recognized instantly as the lethal whisper of a shrekka whirling through the air. One man's scream was cut off in mid-sentence, and Jodi heard two distinct thumps as his severed head and then his body hit the deck. She also heard the distinct rhythm of a blade scything through the air, armor, and flesh with equal ease.

The Kreelans have boarded, she thought, her hopes for rescue dying, replaced now by the hope that her torment would soon be ended.

Suddenly, the sounds of fighting were gone, and the only sign visible to Jodi that a battle had raged was the curling smoke that stung her single good eye.

A sandaled foot stepped into her view, and she closed her swelling eye, waiting for the final blow to come. If nothing else, she thought, the Kreelans had never sought to make humans suffer, as other humans did. Whatever their motives for war, it was to fight and die. To kill the enemy or be killed oneself. The desire for torture and suffering that Man inflicted upon others of his own kind was absent in the hearts and minds of the Kreelans. Death would come quickly, now, painlessly.

"Jodi?" she heard a hoarse whisper from lips she had once kissed.

"Reza?" she said, not willing to believe that her luck, perhaps, was finally turning, and for the better. "Is it you?" She tried to lift her head enough to see his face. The pain that was her reward left a moaning cry in her throat and a savage, flaming agony shooting up and down her spine.

She felt his hands tenderly grip her shoulders, but for a long time she could say nothing, a scream of raw pain issuing from her throat like a wall of water exploding from a breached dam as he tried to turn her over. After a time, it subsided into a dull throb that pulsed with every beat of her heart, and her mind was finally able to command her tongue to form words that Reza might hear, might understand.

"I... I think my back's broken, Reza," she whimpered. She hated the way she sounded, helpless, terrified, but she could not deny, even to herself, that it was true. "Thorella..." She cringed at the sound of the man's name, even from her own lips, "Thorella beat me... he..." She could not say what else he had done to her.

"Hush," Reza said, biting back the wave of black rage that rose in his soul. "Be still. I will—"

"Father," Shera-Khan called from the next room, his voice conveying concern, apprehension, but no fear; there was no threat to him in there. "There is another like her in here."

"What..." Jodi rasped, "what did he say?"

"Nothing," Reza lied. "Be still."

Uncoiling like a snake about to strike, Reza covered the distance to where his son stood in three paces.

"Eustus," he whispered, his heart catching in his throat. His friend hung in the air, suspended from the heavy chandelier above. His tormentors had tied his elbows together behind his back with a thin metal cable, pulled so tight that it had cut into the flesh of his arms, and then hoisted him from the ground. Then they had beaten him with what could only be a Kreelan grakh'ta, the whip with seven barbed tails like the one that had once scourged Esah-Zhurah's back.

Handing his sword to his son, he said, "Cut him down." Then he held onto Eustus's motionless body while Shera-Khan sliced the cruel metal wire that bound his father's friend. Ever so gently, Reza carried him into the other room, laying him next to Jodi so he could tend to them both. With a claw of his right hand, he severed the wire that bound Eustus's elbows, letting his shoulders and back spring back into something like their normal position.

Eustus let out a groan.

"Reza," Jodi asked, "what's going on? What is it?" Lying as she was, she could not see any of the three other living people in the room, only two of the mangled bodies of the ISS men who had raped her. Somehow, it was not as comforting a sight as she had at first thought it would be.

"It is Eustus," he told her as he pointed out to Shera-Khan a medikit that hung on one of the bulkheads. The boy immediately scrambled to retrieve it.

"How... how is he?"

"Alive," Reza said softly, fighting to keep his hands from trembling with the anger coursing through his veins. Thoughts of dark vengeance intermingled with compassion for his injured and beaten friends, friends who had become his family in this strange world that called itself humanity.

Taking the medikit from Shera-Khan, he told the boy in the New Tongue, "Go to the flight deck and get help. Tell them that Jodi and Eustus are aboard, and are hurt badly."

Shera-Khan nodded in acknowledgment, then bolted for the flight deck at a dead run.

In the meantime, Reza tore open the medikit and began to do what little he could until the others could help him get their friends into the ship's sickbay.

SEVENTEEN

Above the Kreelan Homeworld, ships danced and died. But the one-sided slaughter of Kreelan ships that had been the hope of the now-deceased President Borge had become far fiercer than anyone, except Reza, could have predicted. The Kreelans did not fight with their usual expert skill, but they fought with the tenacity of cornered tigresses, and the tide of slaughter was beginning to turn against the invaders.

And yet, despite the carnage that was gutting both of the great fleets, the humans had managed to secure a tenuous perimeter around the solitary moon. Since the heavy ships and their big guns were still engaged with their Kreelan counterparts, and so could not be brought to bear for an orbital bombardment, the task force that had been assigned the moon had begun to disgorge hundreds of dropships. Thousands of Marines were deploying to attack the single built-up area on the moon's surface, a mountainous city that dwarfed the greatest such construct ever conceived by Man.

Leading them was recently promoted Major General Markus Thorella.

"Sir," reported one of the comms technicians, "the Third Fusiliers have landed at–" he read off coordinates that corresponded to a flashing blip on Thorella's tactical display "–and report no enemy present, no resistance. Colonel Roentgen reports 'proceeding toward primary objective.'"

Thorella frowned. He should have been elated that his troops were making such swift progress, but the lack of all resistance – of even sighting any Kreelans at all – thus far on the moon fundamentally disturbed him, especially since this was the fifth regiment on the ground, and the previous four had made nearly identical reports. "Advise all assault elements," he said, "to proceed with caution."

He turned to his deputy division commander for maneuver, the woman who was directly responsible for coordinating the activities of the units disembarking from the ships and moving on the ground. "This is too bloody strange," Thorella told her. "That place should be crawling with Kreelans, confused ones or otherwise. Where could they all have gotten to?"

"Withdrawn to ambush sites?" she suggested.

Thorella shook his head. "No, that's something we would do. The Kreelans prefer head-to-head fighting, whatever the terms."

"But this must be an extraordinary situation for them," she pointed out, simultaneously directing another regiment toward its destination on the moon below, the stylus in her hand marking the destination, which was then sent over the data link. "If Reza Gard can be believed, they've never faced an invasion before."

Thorella considered the thought. "No," he concluded, more to himself than for the other officer's benefit. "Something else is going on, but what?" He had to know, he thought to himself.

Turning to the command ship's captain, he snapped, "Get us down there, now."

* * *

"There is nothing more we can do for her now," Reza said quietly as he finished programming the ship's autodoc to do what it could for Jodi. "We can ease her pain, but that is all." With the help of the automated ship's surgeon, Reza had managed to numb Jodi's spine above the point where it had been severed, confusing her brain into believing that the great nerve pathway merely slept, and was not utterly destroyed halfway down her back, just below her heart. A more general painkiller shielded her from the many other points of damage that would have brought overwhelming pain as the shock slowly wore off.

"Will I be all right?" Jodi asked softly, unexpectedly regaining consciousness, if just for a moment.

"Yes, my friend," Reza replied as he watched the monitor, but he did not – could not – turn to face her. "You will be as good as new." He looked at her then and tried to smile. Failed.

Jodi smiled up at him. She knew he had just told the first lie of his adult life, and she felt honored somehow that he had done it for her, to make her feel better.

"I tried to stop them," Eustus said bitterly. His injuries, less severe than Reza had at first feared, had been dealt with quickly by the ship's electronic surgeon. He still carried terrible bruises, but that affected his looks more than his health. His greatest injury was guilt at not having been able to help Jodi, at having to helplessly watch the things they did to her. His own pain was nothing. Even without his second sight, Reza could feel the guilt feeding on his friend's soul. "But—"

"Eustus," Jodi said, opening the one eye that was not swollen shut. Sleep was not far away, a drug induced coma that would save her from the pain, but she would not let that stop her from comforting her friend. "Eustus," she said again, reaching out with a hand which held only broken fingers, now dead to any further sensation, "it's not your fault. It's Thorella's. If you want to blame someone, blame that bastard, not yourself."

Eustus took her hand in his as if it were an intricate, delicate sculpture of blown glass. "Jodi..." he closed his eyes, fighting the tears.

"I will find him," Reza told her quietly. "I swear in Her name that he shall not escape me again."

Slowly, she shook her head. "No, Reza," she whispered. "We've come too far... given up too much, for you to throw it away in an act of revenge. You have to save your Empress, and give your own people – and ours – a chance to survive. Ships and people are dying out there, and you're the only one who can stop it." Her mangled lips managed a smile that tore at Reza's heart. "Besides, you have a son to look out for now. What will happen to him if you throw your life away after Thorella?"

That thought had not occurred to him; he had not yet really begun to think like a father, to realize that until Shera-Khan well understood the Way and how to follow it, he, Reza, must guide him. And it would take both of them to save the Empress.

"The truth do you speak," Reza admitted grudgingly.

"Reza," Nicole called through the ship's intercom, "we are hitting the atmosphere. I need you to guide me."

"Coming," he answered immediately. He felt most sorry for Nicole: the only one among them qualified and able to pilot the ship, with Braddock keeping her company, she had to remain at the helm as her best friend lay grievously injured, dying. But there was nothing to be done. The ship's autopilot was not good enough to bring them unscathed through the maze of ships blasting at one another. Only Nicole's skill had made that possible, and even so, the *Pearl's* hull now sported a score of burn marks where salvoes from human and Kreelan ships alike had grazed her hull through the weakening shields.

"Good... luck," Jodi said, as the ship's computerized surgeon boosted the level of painkillers in her system. She closed her eyes, and her mangled hand, still clutched carefully in Eustus's own, released its tiny, childlike grip.

Reza's sandaled feet were silent as Death upon the deck as he made his way forward, Shera-Khan close behind him, leaving Eustus and Enya to tend to Jodi. He did not look back.

The view from the *Pearl's* flight deck brought tears to Reza's eyes. The Imperial City, Her home for thousands of generations, lay burning. Dim, almost forgotten memories from his youth of another shattered world, of a young boy orphaned by strangers from the sky, clouded his mind's eye.

Streamers of flame reached as high as mountains, as hundreds of assault boats and fighters swarmed over the great buildings and spires. They fired their weapons randomly, and dropped bombs and cluster munitions into any portal or avenue that could have harbored any Kreelan defenders. Pillars of smoke blocked out many parts of the city, but Reza's imagination easily filled in the blanks. *Over one hundred thousand years,* he thought bitterly, *tomorrow shall be nothing more than smoldering ash.*

"Father," Shera-Khan said from behind him, the boy's hand gingerly touching Reza's shoulder. His voice was brittle with fear. Never before, even during the Great Chaos before Keel-Tath's ascension, had harm come to the Empress Moon. But now Shera-Khan and Reza were witness to its systematic destruction.

Reza put a hand over his son's, to reassure the boy as well as himself, although he said nothing; he did not trust his voice not to display the fear he himself felt.

Can Esah-Zhurah still be alive? he wondered. *And what if she is? What is even the Empress to do against... this?*

"How is Jodi?" Nicole asked from beside him, her voice carefully controlled. She had stopped worrying about either Kreelan defensive fire or being attacked by the scores of human ships prowling about. From the chatter she had been monitoring from the landing force, the Kreelans on the surface were offering no resistance at all, and the other human ships had not been alerted to the *Pearl's* escape. But she had not stopped worrying about Jodi.

"She..." Reza paused, not sure how to tell her. Death and suffering had been his constant companions since childhood, but this was different. Simply blurting the wounding truth was somehow impossibly difficult. "If we do not get her to a healer soon, she will surely die," he finally said. "The ship can only ease her pain, no more."

"And if we take her in time to someone who can help her," Nicole finished for him, "the Empress will die, and we will all be finished."

Reza only nodded.

Nicole stared through the viewscreen at the glowing hell below that was rushing up to meet them. "We have no choices left, Reza," she said grimly. "If there is a chance of you stopping this battle, this war, we must take it, no matter what the cost to ourselves." She looked at him hard, and he thought he saw a glimmer of Esah-Zhurah's strength in her eyes, and he wanted desperately simply to reach out and touch her, that he might touch a tiny part of the woman he loved. But he could not, dared not. "The tide of the battle is changing," she told him. She had been keeping watch on the tactical display as a staggering increase in the number of human ships was added to the casualty list, while fewer and fewer Imperial ships were being destroyed. "More Kreelan warships are arriving all the time, just as you predicted. The main battle group, most of our ships, is scattered, cut off from its jump point. They are being torn apart. Our only hope now is through you. Just show me the way."

Just as they emerged from another pillar of smoke, Reza saw their destination. "There," he said, pointing to a crystalline pyramid that rose over five kilometers in the sky. "The Throne Room is at the top of the Great Tower. That is our destination. We must find a landing bay as high up as possible."

"Reza, this is not a fighter, remember," Nicole reminded him as the computer scanned and rejected most of the bays as being too small. "We cannot land in a shoe box."

"Could we not use the Empress's portal?" Shera-Khan asked, pointing to a large bay complex that also happened to be the highest on the tower. "It will lead us directly to the Throne Room."

"It is closed, Shera-Khan," Nicole said, looking at the information the computer was showing from the scanners.

"No longer," the boy announced, touching his collar in a peculiar fashion. "Behold."

Less than two kilometers away now, the iris door of the great portal suddenly began to open, exposing a warmly lit bay that could have held a dozen ships the size of the *Pearl*, but that now lay empty and barren.

"All who are taught to fly as I have been are given a special device to open the portal," he explained proudly, "that any may serve Her when She calls."

"Well do you serve Her this day, my son," Reza said. He did not know until that moment that Shera-Khan had been trained as a pilot, no doubt under Tesh-Dar's tutelage. He only mourned that he had never known him until these last few desperate hours. *How much I have missed.*

With a precision that matched the grace of the big yacht, Nicole brought the *Pearl* inside the bay. She moved the ship in as far as she could to avoid damage from the raiding ships outside, and to put them closer to the many doorways that lay within. From her last glance at the tactical display of the fleet's desperate plight, every second would count against them from now on.

"Shall I close the portal?" Shera-Khan asked, his hand at his collar.

"No," Nicole advised, just as Reza was about to say the opposite. "We may need to leave quickly."

If we fail, Reza thought silently, *we will have nowhere to go.* "Let it be, then," he said. "We must go."

The others were waiting for them at the main hatch.

"Reza..." Nicole said, her gaze straying down the main hall toward the sickbay.

Reza nodded. "We shall wait for you," he told her as he slammed his fist down on the button to open the hatch and drop the ramp to the deck below. He did not offer to go with her; their farewells to one another would be a private matter.

"I will not be long," she told him.

Nicole entered the sickbay knowing what she would find, but not really prepared for it. To do that would have been to do the impossible. She bit back a small cry as she looked at what had become of Jodi's beautiful face, now little more than a hideous mask of torn flesh, glued loosely to a bruised and battered skull.

"Oh, Jodi," she whispered. "What have they done to you..."

Her friend opened her eyes in the way someone might when returning to the world from a vacant but pleasant dream. "Nikki," she said, "you shouldn't be here... you don't have time..."

"I have always had time for you," Nicole told her, tears flowing freely down her cheeks. She gently touched what looked like an unbruised spot on Jodi's cheek. "And I always will."

"I love you," Jodi said simply. They were words she had said to Nicole a thousand and more times in her dreams and daydreams, but never once in the flesh. She loved her too much to drive her away.

Nicole had no words to answer her. Instead, she leaned forward and kissed Jodi gently on her tattered lips. "I will be back for you, Jodi," she whispered. "I promise. Then... then we will have time together, to talk about things."

Jodi tried hard to smile, but her beaten face made it look more like a grimace. "I'm not going anywhere, babe," she said. "But you'd better. You've wasted enough time on me. Good luck, Nikki."

With bitter tears burning her eyes, Nicole quickly left to join the others at the ramp.

Time was running out.

EIGHTEEN

"Where is everyone?" Enya whispered. They had been moving through the halls of the Great Tower toward the Throne Room for what seemed like half an hour, and they had not seen a single Kreelan – alive or dead – anywhere. Rooms and alcoves that were obviously meant to be occupied stood open and empty, and the halls through which they crept were eerily silent, devoid of any sound at all except the occasional boom of a bomb exploding somewhere outside, or perhaps a stray energy bolt from an attacking fighter. The invading Marines had apparently assumed the tower would be the most heavily defended position, and so had not attacked it directly. But, if the rest of the city were like this, they would make their way here very quickly, indeed.

"I am not sure," Reza answered uneasily as he saw the bluish glow from the Throne Room grow stronger with each step. His second sight told him that the entire Imperial City was dead. Or, more exactly, he thought with a tingling in his spine, the city was completely lifeless: none of the millions of Her Children who had once lived and toiled here in Her service remained. Except in the Throne Room. From there, and there alone, did he sense the faintest tremor of life.

"The Empress," he whispered to himself. "Let it be She."

"Could the Marines have already gotten here?" Enya asked.

"No bodies, no sign of firing," Braddock answered. He felt vulnerable in the business suit he usually wore under his councilman's robe, no Marine combat dress having been handy. But the blaster in his hand reassured him, and his political self had easily stepped aside to let the old Marine inside take charge. "It seems as if they just vanished into thin air, walked off a cliff or something."

Eustus, walking backward most of the time to keep an eye on whatever might be behind them, took the opportunity to turn around and add his two bits to the whispered conversation. "Then what happened?"

He almost blundered into Enya, who stood with the others at the massive doors to the Throne Room. None of them, except for Shera-Khan and Reza, who had both been inside before, had any idea of what to expect, other than something ornate, something alien. They had been awed by the halls through which they had come, the walls rising tens of meters to crystalline domes overhead, any one of which human architects could only dream of. But the Throne Room, hundreds of meters across and as many high, its hectares of sloping and curving walls graced with the work of artisans who had lived and died millennia before Michelangelo, overwhelmed them into stunned silence, immobility.

And in the great room's center, at the literal heart of the Empire, stood the Throne itself, poised upon a pyramid of steps that formed the watermark of the Empire's social ranking, the guiding weave of its cultural fabric. But She was not there. Instead, an unholy wall of cyan light, a kaleidoscope of turbulent lightning, encircled the great dais that stood above the highest steps, blocking the Throne itself from view. And only then did Reza understand why there was no one left in the city.

"It is as Tesh-Dar feared," he said quietly. "They are gone, all of them. Dead."

"Who... who is dead?" Nicole managed. She was not quite as stunned as the others, for she carried Reza's blood in her veins, and had seen this place before in her dreams. But to actually be here...

"The inhabitants of the city, of this moon," he explained bleakly. "All of them are dead."

"How can that be?" Eustus whispered, still unable to tear his eyes away from the incredible wonders that lay before him. "How did they die? Our Marines didn't kill them. Where did the bodies go? There must have been... well, millions living here. They couldn't have just disappeared!"

"Yes," he said, "they could have." Reza nodded toward the light that swirled as if something alive dwelt within. "They tried to reach Her, the Empress, through that," he explained quietly, "to save Her, to save the Empire itself. But the light..." He paused, a chill creeping up his spine. "The light is the essence of the guardians of the First Empress's spirit. It is a barrier, a fire that burns hot as the sun."

"Like in the cave, on Erlang..." Enya said slowly.

"You're right," Eustus murmured, a chill running down his spine at the eerie glow. "The light – it looks the same."

"But why here?" Nicole demanded. "Why now?"

"Because this was to be the time the circle closed," Reza told her, "the time when the First Empress's spirit rejoined with us, and fused Her Own power with that of the living Empress."

"That's what was in the crystal heart," Enya said quietly, "the spirit of this First Empress." She had no idea how such a thing was possible, but she had once read that the technology of an advanced civilization would seem like magic to more primitive people. And the Empire had been around for a very, very long time. Humans had been plying the stars for hundreds of years. The Kreelans had been a spacefaring race for *thousands.*

"Yes, the crystal heart," Reza said, "the vessel containing the spirit of the First Empress, whose power – and spirit – Esah-Zhurah also inherited, making Her the most powerful Empress, the most powerful Kreela, ever born. But with her heart and spirit broken, all the Empire was cast into darkness." He looked again at the swirling wall of light that blazed defiantly above them. "And that is the power of the Imperial Guard," he told them. "You saw their physical remains in the chamber on Erlang. Now do you witness the power of their spirit."

"Then what are we supposed to do?" Braddock asked. "Won't it kill you, too?"

"My blood is Her blood," he said cryptically. "My heart is Her heart, my spirit Her spirit. And my love shall be Her love, Her life." He turned to Nicole. "I must challenge them, to fight them as is our Way. If I do not survive," he told her, "I would ask that you and Tony... care for Shera-Khan."

"I will fight beside you," Shera-Khan proclaimed fiercely, his talons tightly gripping his sword in want of battle.

Reza held the young warrior's shoulders, his own talons digging into the hardened metal of Shera-Khan's armor as he met his son's gaze with his own. "I am your father," he told him softly in the rapid lilt of the New Tongue, "and you are my son, blood of my blood, flesh of my flesh. Proud am I of you, of what you are, and of the great warrior you will become as you follow the Way. Many battles have you yet to fight, and great victories shall you win for Her honor. But not this day. Not here, not now. This battle was preordained upon the deathbed of Keel-Tath in a prophecy that has passed from mothers to their daughters for thousands of generations, and this is the day of reckoning." He smiled at Shera-Khan, the Kreelan way, wishing he could wipe away the black stripes of the mourning marks on his son's face as he might the salty streaks of his own tears. "To fight are we born, I know," he told him, softer still, "and so it is difficult not to seek out the Challenge that to your heart calls. But patience is a skill well-suited to the warrior, Shera-Khan, and patience this day must be yours."

Shera-Khan nodded as Kreelans do, and said, "What shall become of me should you... not return?"

Reza nodded toward Nicole and Braddock. "They are my peers, fellow warriors of my old race; they are my friends, my family. The woman carries my blood in her veins, the blood of the Empress; our ways are not alien to her. Should I fail you, should the Empress die, you must go with them, for they will care for you with the love I would show you, that your mother held for you since the day of your birth. They shall guide you to the Way."

Shera-Khan lowered his head. "It shall be as you wish, Father," he said quietly, knowing that, if his father failed in his mission, his life would be meaningless, his spirit without hope of redemption in the Afterlife. But this weakness he would not show the warrior priest who called him Son.

"I love you, my son," Reza said, suddenly finding the boy in his arms, embracing him fiercely. "May thy Way be long and glorious."

With a final hug, the two separated. "Follow me," Reza said to the others as he began to climb the steps he had not seen since he was a young man.

Like tiny but determined ants climbing a great mountain, the six of them ascended the ancient stone stairway toward Hell.

* * *

"Have you been able to hail them?" Thorella snapped at the assault command ship's captain.

"No, sir," he answered. "I only get the IFF beacon, nothing else."

Thorella chewed his lip nervously. They had picked up the *Golden Pearl's* signature heading down to the surface. *Why is it here?* he wondered. He could understand the president's desire to bring the ship down to witness their victory, although he considered such a vain action to be nothing short of stupid. But why would it wind up inside a landing bay right at the top of what the Navy had considered an impregnable tower? Why had the president not contacted him to tell him what he was doing? And why had they left no one in the ship to monitor communications?

"It doesn't make any sense," he said. Turning to the comms officer, he said, "Contact *Warspite*. I want confirmation that the president got on board the yacht."

There was a beat of silence in the little ship's combat center.

"Well?" Thorella demanded angrily.

"*Warspite's* gone, sir," the captain said quietly. How many thousands of sailors had died in these last hours, he thought, and this fool was not even aware of the destruction of the fleet's flagship. "We won't be getting any confirmation – or anything else, for that matter – from her. *Southampton's* flying Admiral Laskowski's flag, now. She's in overall command."

"Contact *Southampton*, then!" Thorella ordered, angered by the man's impertinence. The significance of what he had just said, that the Confederation fleet had lost its flagship, was lost in the immediacy of finding out what had happened to the president.

A few moments passed, in which the necessary inquiries were made. "*Southampton* cannot confirm the president's safe transfer to the *Golden Pearl*," the comms officer announced. "They only know he was supposed to board her."

That clinched it. "Take us into that landing bay," he ordered the ship's captain, "and set us down beside the yacht. Lieutenant Riggs," he said to the leader of the command ship's platoon of Marines, "I want your platoon standing by to secure this ship from attack, but no one is to enter the *Golden Pearl* without my express permission." There were things in the yacht that he would rather not have the Marines see, lest they start asking awkward questions. "Is that understood?"

The ship captain nodded unenthusiastically, convinced the Marine general had just lost the last of his marbles, while the Marine second lieutenant, fresh from training and eager to please, barked a hearty, "Yes, sir!"

It took only a few minutes for the command ship to reach its destination. Thorella had already gone over the status of his units with the ops officer. He had hoped that there would be at least a single regiment free to leapfrog up to what looked like undefended high ground. But they were all heading to their primary and secondary objectives, already a long way from their dropships.

Thorella would be on his own.

NINETEEN

The climb up the steps had left the humans out of breath by the time they reached the top. When Enya had asked the question of the practicality of an elevator, Shera-Khan shook his head in a practiced human gesture.

"The Empress ascends to the throne each day step by step," he told her in Standard, "a symbol that She favors none, that She loves all of Her Children. Great warrior or simple porter of water, the highest among the peers or the lowest, She considers the needs of each on Her way to the throne."

"I wish our own leaders cared as much for their people," Braddock murmured.

But any thoughts of the climb vanished when they reached the great dais. The view, like being atop a mountain peak overlooking a forest of priceless art, would have been stunning were it not for the malevolent wall of cyan light that swirled in front of them. The thunder of bombs exploding outside, in the city, reverberated throughout the great dome just as the first hint of smoke reached them, here at the pinnacle of the Empire's heart.

"I can feel them," Nicole murmured as she looked into the swirling blue wall before them. She wrapped her arms around herself to ward off the sensation of unseen eyes watching her, unblinking, hostile.

"You must wait here," Reza told them as he drew his sword. He, too, could feel them, the Guardians. He felt a surge of heat through his body and heard the faint strains of the lonely solo that had been his Bloodsong for longer than he cared to remember. *This shall be my final Challenge*, he knew. "No matter what happens," he told them, "do not go into the light. Do not so much as touch it. If I fail..." he paused, "If I fail, return to the ship as fast as you can and try to return to human space. There will be nothing left for you here but death."

"Reza," Nicole said softly beside him. He turned to her, and was met by warm lips pressing against his. "Good luck, Reza," she said, then stepped back with the others.

It was time. Without hesitation, he stepped forward into the eerie wall of light.

* * *

The place, he knew well: the temple of the Desh-Ka, high upon the mountain of Kular-Arash. But it was not the ancient ruin where in his youth he had been transformed into something more than a man, where he had bound himself to a woman not of his race. No, the temple in which he now stood was new, immaculate, filled with the power of the great warriors who dwelled there. This was the prize of their warrior civilization in its youth, its full glory.

Standing in the sand of the great arena, the glare of the sun was shaded by the dome that would last for another hundred thousand years. Reza saw that he was not alone. Before him, standing like a pillar at the far side of the arena, was a lone male warrior.

"Tara-Khan," Reza breathed. He did not need to see the symbols inscribed on the other warrior's collar to know his name or who he was. He was known to all Kreela who had come after him, for he was the greatest of the warriors ever to have fought for Her honor, in all the days of the Empire. He had been Keel-Tath's love, Her life. And here, in this place that was a dream that could yet draw blood, he was Her guardian, the last of the host She had taken with Her.

The warrior nodded. "Indeed," he said in a voice of ages-long sadness, "it is so."

Beyond Tara-Khan, Reza could see the dais at the head of the arena, where the world of the real and that of the spirit converged. And on it lay a figure in white. "The Empress," he whispered, his heart falling away at the sight of Esah-Zhurah's still body. She lay upon the dark marble altar at the center of the dais, draped in Her white robes, the thin gold collar gleaming from around Her neck. Reza could see the black mourning marks that ran from her eyes like rivers of sorrow against the snow white hair that lay in carefully coiled braids around her shoulders. Her breast rose and fell slowly, slowly, as her lungs labored on, and Her broken heart forced life through unwilling veins.

Turning back to Tara-Khan, he challenged, "And by what right do you stand before me?"

Tara-Khan's eyes followed Reza's to the still form of the vessel of Keel-Tath's spirit. "I stand here as Her last guardian and protector, an instrument of Her will," he said quietly. "This is my honor, Reza, to defend Her. The others are gone now. Only I remain." He turned his eyes back to Reza. "Long have I slept beside Her spirit in the Darkness until this, the day of redemption, of the final combat. It is my honor to see that you are worthy."

"And if you slay me this day," Reza asked, "what is to become of Her?"

"The Empress shall perish," Tara-Khan rasped miserably, "and with Her the Empire, our very souls cast into the pit of emptiness from which there shall be no escape for all eternity." He smiled. "But do not fear, young one," he said. "I have listened to your heart, your spirit; your love is true. But this, your final covenant with Her, must be made afresh in blood. This is as She long ago willed, and so shall it be."

"Let me pass, Tara-Khan," Reza implored him. "There has been enough death this day. Let me reach Her, that the lost may be saved, that the Empire shall not perish."

Setting his hand upon the grip of his great sword, whose blade had slain countless foes in ages past, Tara-Khan replied, "Fated by Her own hand were you to be here this day, to fulfill the Prophecy. But beware: there are no guarantees. I can pass none until they are proven worthy, until they can best my sword."

As the fire spread through his veins, his eyes taking in his dying Empress, his love, one last time, Reza hissed, "Then let it be done."

And the thunder of clashing swords filled the arena.

* * *

Thorella cautiously made his way up the ramp into the *Golden Pearl*, his sidearm held at the ready, his finger tensed on the trigger. Behind him, Lieutenant Riggs's Marines waited uncertainly in their defensive perimeter around the yacht, the roar of the command ship still loud in their ears as it reversed course, abandoning them in the huge hangar as it sought to avoid a possible ambush. None of them were thrilled with the idea of being stranded up here, still so far from even the closest regiment should they need help.

On his solitary reconnaissance, Thorella was completely uninterested in what his men thought. He was concerned only with what he found – or did not find – on the *Golden Pearl*. It did not take him long to find the bodies of the flight deck crew, holes drilled neatly through their chests by hand blasters. Even more cautious now, he went on to find the butchered remains of the ISS guards that he had left to take care of Mackenzie and Camden. Still, there was no sign of anyone who was still alive. Could Mackenzie and Camden have somehow taken over the ship and brought it here? *Impossible*, he thought to himself. *But, still...*

Slowly, sweat beading on his brow, he reentered the main corridor and began to make his way aft, toward sickbay and engineering.

"Sir," Riggs reported excitedly from outside, "the patrol we sent up the main hall has detected a small group of the enemy not far from here." To Riggs, the enemy was anyone who was not specifically designated as friendly.

"Details?" Thorella growled, annoyed that his concentration was being diverted from his search of the ship, but somehow relieved that someone had finally seen some activity from the Kreelans.

Riggs patched through the patrol leader. "It appears to be some kind of, I don't know, a royal hall or something, sir," reported the staff sergeant who was leading the patrol. "It's huge, like nothing I've ever–"

"The enemy, sergeant," Thorella snapped. "Tell me about the enemy!"

"Uh, yes, sir," the woman replied. "Five individuals, sir. At the very top of a big, I don't know, a pyramid, like." Pause. "But I could swear that four of them look like our people."

"What do you mean, 'our people?'" Thorella demanded. Any thoughts of exploring the *Golden Pearl* further were rapidly fading.

"Humans, sir," said the staff sergeant, reporting what she could make out through her image enhancers. "Two males and two females. One of the males is in Marine combat dress, one of the females in Navy uniform. The two others are in civvies of some kind. But the fifth one is definitely Kreelan, but she looks kind of small."

"About the size of a human teenager?" Thorella asked, his face contorting into a rictus of ice-cold rage.

Pause. "Now that you mention it, yes, sir, that's what she looks like. A young Kreelan–"

"Get them!" he choked.

"Sir?" Riggs cut in over the confused staff sergeant.

"You heard me!" Thorella raged as he whirled, running back down the corridor toward the hatchway. Now he knew what had happened to Borge: he had never made it off the doomed *Warspite*. "Get them! They're renegades, they killed the president!" Thorella did not need a body for evidence. He knew for sure that Borge was dead. Precisely how he had gotten that way was of no further concern. All that mattered now was that his own ascension to power was finally cleared of the last obstacle, his despicable father. He just needed to be sure that Reza Gard and his accomplices were noted in the history books as President Borge's murderers, and himself, the avenger. "And I want them alive!" He would not be denied the fulfillment of his long-lived vendetta.

Outside, Riggs felt his blood turn to ice. Such an outrage could not go unpunished. Two presidents, murdered? It was unthinkable. "Yes, sir! Sergeant Khosa," he ordered, "open fire! Pin them down, but do not – repeat, *do not* – shoot to kill. We're on our way."

* * *

Nicole stood close behind Shera-Khan. Lightly, she put a hand on his shoulder. He did not flinch away. "Do you... feel anything, Shera-Khan?" she asked as they all stared into the light that swirled and writhed like a living thing.

He shook his head. "I am empty," he said bleakly. "I cannot hear my father's song; I cannot touch his soul."

"How will we know if he's successful," Eustus asked, "or... if he fails?"

"If the Empress dies," Shera-Khan said, "this–" he gestured toward the light, "–will be no more, and Darkness shall fall upon the sun. All shall end; there shall be no more."

"Shera-Khan," Braddock said quietly, "I've known your father for a long time, and I know how much he loves her, and I know how much you must love her. But, even if she dies, the universe will still go on. You'll still be alive and well, and–"

"You do not understand," Shera-Khan interrupted. "She is not an individual. She is all of us. Our souls and spirits are bound to Her. Even now, now that I cannot feel Her or any others of my kind, should She perish, I shall surely die also. With Her last breath, so shall the Empire perish from the Universe. My father bade me come with you should he fail; he did this out of kindness and hope. But should the Empress perish, so shall I; so shall all my kind."

Braddock and Enya still did not understand, but Nicole did, and she drew Shera-Khan closer to her. "He will win the Challenge," she said, a tingling sensation running through her chest at the words. "He must."

"Hey," Eustus said from behind them. Unable to watch the eye-searing light anymore, he had turned to study the rest of the throne room. Now, as he watched Riggs's Marines darting in through the entrance they themselves had used, advancing on the great stairway, he almost wished he hadn't. "I think we've got company."

"Who–"

"Down!" Eustus cried, throwing the others to the floor of the dais just as a hail of energy bolts blasted chunks from the stairway below and ricocheted from the crystalline dome above.

* * *

Reza hissed as Tara-Khan's sword slashed through his armor, drawing blood from his shoulder.

"Well do you fight, young one," Tara-Khan told him through gritted teeth, for Reza's sword had found its mark on occasion also, "but still do you have much to learn."

For what seemed like hours the two had fought, caught in a cycle of desperate attrition, one to save the future, the other to slaughter imperfection, unworthiness. Both were perfect in their craft, unable to inflict a decisive blow, only able to harm. To hurt, to bleed.

"I have learned much already," Reza hissed. His sword swung through space with a power and speed that left thunder in the air as the great blade sought Tara-Khan's neck. It was perfectly timed, the razor's edge keening as it sought the older warrior's flesh.

Instead, it found only falling water.

"What?" Reza stammered in confusion. Tara-Khan had disappeared. Only a pool of water, rapidly sinking into the sand, was left where he had been standing. Warily, he stepped closer, prodding the wet sand with his foot.

A flutter caught his eye. *The Empress*, he thought. *She moved!* But as he studied Her, he knew it must have been an illusion. She was still as the stone upon which She lay. If he did not save Her soon, that was how She would forever remain. Pushing Tara-Khan from his mind, he took a step toward Her. Every second he waited was a grain of sand slipping through the waist of a cosmic hourglass. And so few grains were left, he thought. So very few.

Another step.

Where was Tara-Khan? He whirled about suddenly, his sword cutting a protective arc, but Tara-Khan was nowhere to be seen. There was only the cryptic stain upon the sand, quickly fading. Surely, he thought, Tara-Khan had not conceded, not in silence, without a word?

He took another step toward Esah-Zhurah, the Empress. And another. Closer to Her now, he could hear the slow, shallow rustle of Her breathing, could smell Her hair, and his insides began to tremble. The trickle of warm blood that ran down his side from his shoulder felt like a caress, as when her hand had touched him lovingly, when he had held her close. So long ago, he thought. So very, very long ago.

He was close to Her now, his sword ready at his side, but his eyes were filled with the image of Her face. She had become his world, the very Universe. The song that had turned his blood to fire sang still, not for battle, but for love, for Her.

At the dais, now. Climbing the steps. The sound of his feet through water. Her face, turned toward him—

Water?

– as if watching him, Her eyes closed...

He did not see the water stir as he passed, heard nothing as it rose and took shape and form, silent as a still pool as metal, flesh, and bone emerged.

His inner alarms clamored and his body reacted with the strength of a tiger and the speed of lightning, but it was too little, too late. With a triumphant roar, Tara-Khan attacked. The great blade speared through the side of Reza's armor, embedding itself deep within him in a searing flash of pain.

In agonized rage, Reza swung his own weapon at Tara-Khan's unprotected head, but again it found nothing but water.

I have failed, he thought miserably, as Tara-Khan rose again, his sword ready to strike.

"You fought well young one," the elder warrior said, "but you are not The One. You are not worthy of Her love, and thus shall you perish." The sword fell.

Water, the thought flashed through Reza's mind as the blade hissed through the air. *Water... and ice...*

At the last instant, Reza threw himself forward, sinking his claws into Tara-Khan's armor as the sword whistled past above his head. Laughing at Reza's desperate attempt to save himself, Tara-Khan did as Reza had hoped. His body melted into water, his essence slipping through Reza's fingers.

But they were no longer in the arena.

* * *

"Look out!" Enya cried, as an energy bolt sheared an elephant-sized chunk of the great glassine dome from the slender frame above.

With a jerk of his head, Braddock saw the huge glass fragment falling toward him. Twisting desperately to the side, he tried to get out of its way, but he was too late. With a crash that shook the dais itself, Braddock disappeared beneath the mass of crystal as it exploded into a million tiny shards.

"Tony!" Nicole screamed as she crawled through the debris toward him, the crystal fragments lacerating her hands and knees. She reached out to take hold of the glass shell that covered Braddock's body like the transparent lid of a coffin.

"No!" Shera-Khan cried, batting her unprotected hands away from the razor sharp edges. "Let me." Sensing a lull in the firing from below and using his armored hands and diamond-hard talons, he struggled to lift a fragment of the crystal that covered Braddock's body, but was unable to move it. It was far too large, too heavy.

Nicole slid up next to him, keeping her head down and out of the line of fire. Above them, the dome began to disintegrate, huge chunks falling into the throne room as the structure began to lose the last of its integrity.

"Tony," she whispered, peering at his smashed body through the clear crystal. His face, his coat, his hands were covered with blood. Blood was everywhere. "No," she moaned. "Please, Tony," she whispered, "You cannot die!" But she had seen death enough times to recognize it. And Tony Braddock was dead.

As Shera-Khan watched helplessly, Nicole laid her head on the crystal that covered her husband and began to silently weep.

On the other side of the dais, separated by the circle of blue light from the others, Enya and Eustus continued to fire at their attackers, trying to keep them pinned down.

"There are too many of them!" Enya shouted above the thunder of the guns.

"You have a talent for understatement, my love," he replied as he sent a round into a careless Marine's leg. He was trying desperately not to kill any of them, only to injure them or keep their heads down. The ISS guards were one thing; they were as much an enemy as the Kreelans had ever been. But the Marines were his people, his family. "Nicole," he bellowed, "how are you doing?"

Only the guns below answered him.

"Nicole?" he called again. They had been able to hear each other before. "What the hell are they doing over there?" he asked Enya as he turned, ready to skirt around toward the other side, where the other three of their little band had posted themselves.

The ugly snout of a blaster suddenly thrust itself into his face.

"Drop it," a voice growled from behind a combat helmet. Eustus saw that where the nameplate had been on the man's armor, there was nothing now but a still-hot scorch mark. "Both of you. Now."

Hesitating for just a moment, Eustus did as he was told. They had lost.

Behind him, Enya asked quietly, "Eustus?" She still held her weapon, clenched in her left hand.

"Drop it," Eustus told her. He heard the weapon clatter onto the cold stone floor.

"Where are the others?" Eustus asked.

"Shut up," the Marine snarled as three more armored figures appeared from the other side to surround them. The Marine motioned with his blaster toward where he had left Nicole, Braddock, and Shera-Khan. "Move it. Now."

Eustus led Enya around the cylindrical wall of light, ignoring the vicious shove the Marine gave him as he passed. As he walked, he heard something crunching under his feet, like glass. And then he saw Nicole slumped over a huge mass of crystal, Shera-Khan on his knees beside her, a Marine covering them with his rifle. A pool of blood seeped from beneath the crystal.

"Sweet Jesus," he whispered. "Nicole, what hap–"

A huge Marine slammed an elbow into Eustus's jaw, sending him sprawling dangerously close to the light. Through the stars dancing through his brain, he smelled hair burning, and a prickling sensation told him that it was the hair on his arm, being burned into plasma by whatever energy governed the barrier.

"Eustus!" Enya cried as she grabbed at his ankles, pulling him away from the shimmering wall. "You could have killed him!" she snarled at the figure looming behind her.

"He's a traitor," Lieutenant Riggs sneered over the suit's PA system, "just like you. I don't know why General Thorella wants you alive, but he does." He grimaced at all of them, a look of utter disgust diluted only with hatred, not caring that they could not see his expression behind his helmet. "And I follow orders." A booted foot kicked at Braddock's crystal sarcophagus.

"You bastard!" Nicole shrieked, leaping to her feet, her blood suddenly blazing with a fiery alien rage.

Shera-Khan watched in amazement as this human woman, this friend-warrior of his father, struck out at the animal in armor. She moved as if she had talons, with the deadly grace and speed of a warrior priestess.

Riggs was caught off-guard, and his head rang against the inside of his helmet as her hands slammed against his armor with a strength he never would have guessed at by looking at her. But sheer mass, if nothing else, was on his side, and he recovered quickly. As one armored fist fastened itself around one of Nicole's wrists, the other rose to smash her in the face.

In that instant, Shera-Khan sensed a tremor pulse through his body, and he knew that if he did not act, Nicole would be dead.

Like a tiger he leaped, his arms outstretched, his claws reaching not for Riggs, but for Nicole.

* * *

Reza fell to his knees upon the ice, his face already a cherry red from the freezing wind that howled over the great glacier at the south pole of the Homeworld, a place so cold that spit froze solid before it hit the ground.

Forcing his eyes open against the frigid wind, he saw Tara-Khan's face, frozen in a nightmare state that was half flesh, half ice. One eye was still fully formed, staring at him in astonishment, while the other was stretched, elongated like a broken yolk as it had begun to flow toward the ground. The mouth, misshapen, skewed, was open, but what emotion might have been conveyed there was unimaginable, horrible. His arms and sword had liquefied, falling to fuse with what was left of his legs, now mannequin-like sculptures in ice that had become one with the glacier.

And Reza's hands, which had been holding onto his opponent's armored chest, were now locked in an icy grip, fused inside Tara-Khan's partly-solidified torso, water and ice, flesh and blood.

With a cry of desperation, Reza broke his hands free, falling backward onto the ice, Tara-Khan's cooling blood-water on his hands. Struggling against the gale and his own rapidly ebbing strength, he stood up, facing what remained of Tara-Khan.

"May you find peace in Her name," he said to the nightmare face. Then, with his hands clasped together, he smashed the frozen warrior's head from his shoulders, sending frozen bits of ice and flesh across the plain of white.

He turned toward the sky, toward the Empress moon, which hung low on the horizon. *Running out of time*, he thought, his vision starting to turn gray from the blood that poured from the gaping wound in his side, his limbs numb from the cold. As his breath froze into crystals around his mouth, disturbed only by the small trickle of blood he had coughed up from his punctured lung, he closed his eyes, picturing the dying Empress in his mind.

After a time that was not time, he opened his eyes. The arena was dark around him, the walls hidden in shadow. Even the sky through the dome above was darkened, invisible to his failing vision. Only around the Empress was there a halo, an aura, of gently pulsating cyan light that faded as he watched, its power failing with Her will to survive.

Willing his dying body to move, he struggled toward her, his sandals dragging his frostbitten feet through the sand. He stumbled, fell against the stone of the dais, then dragged himself forward, up the steps on his hands and elbows, fighting pain, fighting time, fighting a cursed fate.

He made it to the top, facing the stone slab on which She lay. Around him now was darkness, as if the world itself was shrinking down upon Her, and even She was falling into shadow as the light around Her pulsed, faded.

"No," he moaned, forcing himself to his knees, crawling to Her side, leaving a trail of blood in his wake. Shaking off his gauntlets, he reached forward with trembling hands to touch Her, felt the coolness of Her skin, the silence of the spirit that cried for release from its pain. "I am here," he told her as he willed her to wake, to rise. "Please, my Empress, you must not die."

Then it was that he saw something clutched in her left hand, something about the size of his fist, and now black as coal. The crystal heart.

Not really knowing why, following an instinct that had been planted long ago in a race that was not his own by birth, he pried the scorched crystal from her hand, noting the scar on her palm that matched his own.

Drawing the dagger of the Empress, the one that Esah-Zhurah had given him so long ago, he joined his hand to hers, the cold metal between them. Once before had he done this with the woman who owned his heart; now he would do it with the woman who owned his spirit, and the spirit of his adopted people.

"With my last breath," he whispered to her, "do I give thee life, my Empress." He pulled the knife between them, feeling the pitiable trickle of warmth that welled from his numbed hand, then closed his bleeding palm over hers.

As the world faded toward darkness, he gently kissed her lips. The tingle of memory, of what once had been, surged through his mind as he touched her. Closing his eyes, he laid his head upon her breast. He rested next to her on the cold stone slab, his life rapidly draining away into the empty shadows where once the dais had been, where now the Darkness of Forever reigned.

"I love you," he whispered. The last of his strength did he give that his hand could hold hers. He hoped that the tiny spark of life that remained in his body would be enough to rekindle Her own.

His heart beat slower, ever slower. And then it was still.

He did not feel the quickening of Her breath, or the sudden warmth of Her breast beneath his gray, frozen cheek. He did not see as once again the crystal heart began to glow beneath the blood, his own, that coated it and had penetrated it as had Keel-Tath's millennia ago.

Beside him, the Empress awoke.

* * *

The Marine who had been guarding Shera-Khan spun around as the boy lunged toward Riggs, the projected sight reticle in the Marine's helmet tracking the boy with smooth precision. The Marine's finger tensed on the big weapon's trigger just as a jagged bolt of lightning streaked from the maelstrom that was the center of the dais, incinerating him with more heat than could be found on the surface of a star.

Shera-Khan slammed into Nicole, knocking her from Riggs's grasp just as the world exploded around them. The big Marine, caught off guard by the boy's attack and the blinding bolt of lightning, stumbled backward and fell off the dais just as another bolt crackled through the air where he had just been standing.

"What the hell?" Riggs cried as he went over the edge, landing hard on his back and then scrabbling madly to keep from rolling down the hundreds of steps that lay below. He saw as in a nightmare that the barrier had dissolved into a hydra of lightning that snapped and bit at the air over the great dais, its energy prickling his skin. He watched, dumbfounded, as the seething monster struck again, a blinding tentacle lashing out at another of his Marines. A flash and a roar crashed through Riggs's brain, loud enough to deafen him even with the suit's passive aural dampers. Blinking away the spots that peppered his vision, he saw nothing left of the Marine but a scorch mark on the stone.

"What's going on in there?" Riggs heard Thorella's voice through the pandemonium around him, his voice barely audible over the boosted voice link.

"I don't know, sir," the young lieutenant shouted back in a panic, rolling down another step as the deadly storm that turned and wheeled above him struck down yet another of his people, and then another. "We're getting killed up here!"

"Goddammit!" Thorella screamed into the radio from where he stood far below, at the entrance to the throne room. Looking up, he saw what looked like a lightning-whipped tornado whirling around the apex of the enormous pyramid of stairs, blinding flashes of light reflecting from the surrounding dome like a gigantic strobe. "Give me a proper report, lieutenant!" he shouted again. "What is happening? What do you see?"

Hauling himself up on his elbows, Riggs peered over the last step, his eyes coming just above the stone floor of the dais. "Jesus," he whispered to himself as he saw what awaited him. There, at the very center of the dais, stood a Kreelan woman clothed only in simple white robes. Her hands were lifted above her, and Riggs's eyes widened as he saw the lightning dancing from her palms, enveloping her in a swirling aura that was so bright that it hurt his eyes to look directly at her.

She looks like an angel, he thought to himself before the woman turned her burning eyes upon him. *An angel*, a hysterical voice in his mind echoed as he lost control of his bladder, a blade of fear cutting through his stomach. *An angel of death.*

He tried to push himself back down the stairs, away from her, but it was far too late. One of the dancing bolts of lightning arced from her hands, vaporizing Riggs in the blink of an eye.

* * *

Feeling Shera-Khan motionless close beside her, Nicole shivered on the floor as a roaring tide of energy coursed through her body, as if she had suddenly become a human conduit for raw, pure power. And then she heard the voice that was not a voice, but was more like a blast of sound through her brain, a single thought exploding inside her skull. A curtain of fire swept through her veins, scorching her flesh. Agony. Ecstasy.

"My Children..."

* * *

Even from his distant vantage point, Thorella was nearly blinded and deafened by the forces that gripped the throne room. He watched as Riggs's entire platoon was wiped out by what looked like nothing more complex, nothing less devastating, than lightning. He had no doubts that had he chosen to make the trek up those ancient stone steps, he, too, would now be dead.

But Thorella was a survivor, and always had been. "Marine One," he called the command ship that was orbiting somewhere overhead, "we need an emergency evac down here now!"

"On our way, sir," came the tinny reply.

"Move it," Thorella snapped as he turned to head down the hall toward the landing bay.

But, as he did so, he saw out of the corner of his eye the ship as it passed over the dome, low, too low. Thorella was about to shout a warning when a bolt of lightning shot upward through the dome, reaching a blazing claw toward the ship. In a blinding flash the ship exploded, leaving nothing but burning fragments whirling away from an expanding cloud of gas as its remains streaked out of sight, leaving behind a trail of sooty smoke.

Then the lightning surged into the structure of the dome itself, the blinding veins of cyan working their way through the stone and crystal like water through a plant thirsting for water, leaving in their wake a shimmering fluorescence.

Thorella ran alone from the carnage behind him. He ran for the *Golden Pearl*.

* * *

Enya was deafened by the sudden silence. The thunder and lightning that had exploded all around her were gone. The gale force winds that had swept over the dais were still. The great dome was silent, as was the city beyond. The bombs had stopped falling. Her whole body was shivering with fear, her eyes tightly closed. Eustus lay unconscious in her arms. His breathing was ragged. Against her better judgment, she opened her eyes.

The Marines were gone. There was nothing left of them but a faint trace of burned plastic and the stench of scorched flesh. While the blue fire was also gone, the throne room still glowed with eerie light that highlighted the scene of devastation that was the once pristine dais.

Nearby, Braddock's lifeless body lay entombed by the slab of crystal that had fallen from above. Next to him Nicole and Shera-Khan lay equally still. Enya was suddenly afraid, afraid that she was alone with whatever power now haunted this place.

It was then that a phantom stepped from the smoke that still clung to the dais. Enya's skin prickled as she saw the white braids that framed the blue skin of the Kreelan woman's face, proud and unblemished now by the black marks that she had worn for so many years. Her eyes blazed with wisdom and the power of her unfathomable spirit, just as the sleek muscles beneath the white robes belied her physical strength. Upon her head was a tiara, glittering with gemstone fire. With a liquid grace that seemed unlikely, unnatural, perhaps, as if her feet did not quite touch the floor, the woman made her way to where Nicole lay, and knelt beside her.

Enya stared as the woman delicately extended a hand to touch Nicole's face, and saw the scar across the Kreelan woman's palm, the blood-red talons.

She is Esah-Zhurah... The Empress, she thought silently, her eyes wide with awe.

Nicole stirred at the woman's touch, and the Kreelan spoke, but not in any language that Enya would ever understand.

* * *

Nicole's mind struggled against the rising sea of voices that threatened to drive her insane. The fire that had filled her blood had left her heart racing without cease, her body filled with adrenaline, but with no way to dissipate it. She lay helpless, her spirit dissolving in the maelstrom that roared within her.

And then she felt a touch, the sensation that someone had placed a hand on her face. But it was more than that. Amid the infinite mass of clamoring souls into which she was falling, the touch offered a rallying point, a focus. Then she heard a voice, felt a powerful mind lead her own back to order and purpose.

"Be not afraid," the Empress whispered soothingly in the Old Tongue. "All shall be well, my child. All shall be well."

"And what of my love?" Nicole heard herself ask in the same language, as the great choir burning in her veins began to subside and her mind began to reassert itself. "Death has taken all I have ever held dear. It has ruled my past, and now has it claimed my future."

"I know of the fondness your kind has for miracles, child," the Empress said gently. *"Behold."*

* * *

Enya watched as the Empress rose and went to stand beside Braddock's body. With a gesture of her hand, as if she were lifting an invisible feather, the massive block of crystal that pinned him to the dark stone began to tremble, then rose from the floor. A flick of the Empress's hand sent it spinning away across the throne room to shatter against a distant wall.

She then cupped her hands together as if she were holding water, and Enya watched in open-mouthed wonder as the pulse of the Kreelan monarch's life force took shape between her palms, bathing all of them in an eerie cyan glow. She opened her hands to reveal a ball of light just smaller than one of her fists that, as if it possessed a will of its own, floated down toward Braddock's lifeless chest. It hung over his heart, growing larger, diffusing as it sent innumerable tendrils all over his body to envelop him in a shroud of blue fire that swirled and shimmered. In a moment, the glow began to fade, then disappeared.

Braddock's chest rose. With a groan, he rolled partway over, rubbing his eyes with the heels of his hands.

"Tony!" Enya cried.

"Enya?" he asked, perplexed. "What the hell? Nicole? Nicole!" Nicole knelt beside him, motionless, as if in a trance. He had no time to say any more as the Empress took careful hold of his hands and gracefully pulled him to his feet.

The shock of realizing whom he was facing hit Braddock like a hammer in the face. His mouth opened, but no sound came out.

"You have little time," the Empress told him in Standard. "You are now the supreme ruler of your people," She said as if She had known him all his life, "and if you are to save the remains of your great fleet, you must withdraw them with all haste. I will also allow you to retrieve your warriors here, in this place. Your ships will not be menaced so long as they do not attack My Own. But you must hurry."

"What about Nicole?" he blurted, his mind struggling to catch up with the whirlwind of events, many of which he suddenly realized he had missed completely. "I won't leave her."

"No harm to her shall come, I promise you. But I have need of her yet, and shall send her on to you when all is made right again."

"What do you mean?" Braddock demanded, concerned now, uncertain.

"Remember my words," the Empress said with finality, "and preserve your people." Before Braddock had a chance to breathe another word, he was gone. Vanished.

The Empress turned to Enya, but her eyes focused on Eustus's unconscious form. Without warning, his head still cradled against Enya's breast, Eustus seemed warm, far too warm, as if he had instantly developed a raging fever.

He suddenly opened his eyes. "Lord of all," he whispered, as the heat dissipated as quickly as it had come. "It's her."

"Are you all right?" Enya asked, relief flooding through her, overcoming the strange mixture of fear and elation at what the Empress could do, had done.

"Yeah, I think so," he replied, his attention riveted upon the Empress. Enya saw that the bruises that had covered his face were gone: the Empress had healed him completely. "I feel a little shaky, but I'll be okay."

"Yes," the Empress said, "indeed you shall. But your talents are required elsewhere. You must go to the place where your warriors shall gather, and help see them safely away from here upon the ships that even now are approaching. Several of your strange devices used to aid in this task are there, awaiting you."

"Beacons?" Eustus thought aloud. "Where did you get–"

"Eustus," Enya hushed him gently, "later." She did not understand much about the alien woman who stood facing her, but she had seen enough to grasp the incredible power she wielded, as well as her sincerity. But one question could not be set aside. "Does the war end here? Or tomorrow will we once again be enemies?"

Emulating the human gesture she had learned from Reza in their childhood, the Empress shook her head. "Never again after this day shall our two races meet," she replied solemnly. "The ancient prophecies this day shall be fulfilled, and so shall end the Way of the First Empire. And just as the coming dawn shall bring the first day of the Second Empire, so, too, shall the Way of your own people take a new, brighter course."

"And what of you?" Enya asked. "What of your people? And Reza, what of him?"

The Empress turned to where Shera-Khan now stood, content, his face no longer streaked with black. "We are something much more than we have ever been," she replied gently. "And Reza... awaits me." She bowed her head. "We shall remember you. Always."

And in the Empress's eyes, Enya fully understood those words. Gazing upon a face whose soul was thousands of generations old, Enya realized that "always" to these people truly meant forever.

"Farewell, and thank you..." was all Enya had time to utter before the throne room suddenly disappeared, to be replaced by a huge landing bay somewhere else in the city and an odd assemblage of human equipment, the beacons, that Eustus was feverishly working on. Moments later, as she stood watching, the first Marines arrived.

* * *

The Empress turned Her attention to the remaining human figure that still knelt upon the dais. "That which was shared with you, child," She said gently in the Old Tongue, "must now be returned."

Seemingly weightless, Nicole rose to her feet, her eyes fixed on the Empress. Her heart raced not with fear, but with joy at Her voice, Her command.

The Empress's hand closed gently around hers, and the Kreelan monarch led her to a point on the dais where there stood a crystal spire that Nicole dimly recognized as not having been there before, and saw at its apex the crystal heart aglow with blue flame. She did not feel the claw that gently drew against the skin of her palm, did not feel the warmth of her own blood as it welled up from her flesh. She watched as the Empress's hand placed her own against the pulsing crystal heart.

"Reza," Nicole gasped as she touched it, as her blood melded with something that was not merely a structure of inert mineral carved by artisans whose bodies had turned to dust countless centuries before, but was alive and had a spirit, a soul. A soul she had known for most of her life. Like a river swollen by monsoon rains, Nicole felt the alien spirit that Reza had shared with her so long ago rush across the living bridge that had been made between her hand and the crystal vessel. The fire in her blood, numbed by the Empress's empathic touch, flickered and died just as the last of the alien voices fell silent. And then all was still. All was as it should have been, as it had been before Reza had shared his blood with her. In a way that would take her many years to understand, she was terribly saddened at the silence that suddenly filled her, the same silence and isolation that Reza had faced all of his adult life.

Exhausted, drained, she staggered back from where the crystal was now rippling with blue fire, the details of the heart's surface lost in a cyan glare. She collapsed to the floor, her eyes fixed on the blinding radiance that began to grow, expand. She knew that her eyes must be blinded by such brilliance, but she felt no pain, and dared not turn away from what was now unfolding. There was no heat, no sound. There was only the light, and the figure of the Empress standing close by, staring into the center of the tiny star that burned beside the throne. The Empress lifted her arms, hands outstretched, as if beckoning to someone.

And then Reza stepped from the light, traversing a passage that linked the here and now with some other realm that Nicole felt she had once known, but that was now a universe beyond her mortal understanding. The palms of the two lovers touched, their fingers entwined, and the Empress drew him into an embrace that left no doubt of their love for each other, the queen and her knight, man and woman, husband and wife. Behind him, the pathway closed, the light fading away until the only trace left was the afterimage that flickered in Nicole's eyes.

The crystal heart was gone.

"Nicole," Reza said quietly, suddenly kneeling next to her.

"Reza..." she shook her head, not knowing what to say, or how. His armor gleamed as if new, the Kreelan steel black and infinitely deep as the great rune – she tried in vain to remember what it signified – glowed at its center. His eyes were alight with a fire that she had never seen, with the power of life, of fulfillment.

"Father Hernandez once told me that he believed in divine miracles," she said. "I was never sure I could believe in such things... until now."

Reza smiled and took her in his arms. Holding her close to him as a brother might a beloved sister, he said, "My life, my happiness, do I owe to you. And whatever the future may bring for you and your people, Nicole, remember that I shall always love you. Always."

He kissed her, lightly, on the lips, and she put a hand to his face, her fingers tingling at the warmth of his skin.

"*Adieu*, Reza," Nicole said quietly.

"Farewell, my friend," Reza said, and then in the Old Tongue, "and may thy Way be long and glorious."

And suddenly, he was gone. Nicole felt a cold chill blow over her, and a mist clouded her vision for a split second, as if the world had suddenly gone out of focus and then come back. In the blink of an eye, she found herself staring at the dumbstruck bridge crew of the battlecruiser *Sandhurst*.

"Captain Carré!" someone exclaimed. Turning numbly toward the speaker, she saw old Admiral Sinclaire rushing toward her, his ruddy face reflecting wonder, confusion, and concern. "What in blazes...?"

But Nicole's first thought was not about where she was or how she had gotten there. It was about someone she had left behind.

"Jodi..."

TWENTY

Being rich, regardless of how it had come about, had had its advantages for Markus Thorella. Among the many other pleasures he had experienced as a young man, he had learned how to pilot a starship. He was not as competent or as experienced as the Navy crews who flew as part of their careers, but he could fly.

The flight controls of the *Golden Pearl*, in fact, were much the same as the yacht his father had once bought for him so many years ago. Thus, his escape from the strange disaster that had befallen Lieutenant Riggs's platoon was all but assured, even without the ill-fated command ship to extract him. The *Pearl* was waiting in the landing bay, almost as if it had been meant for his use.

Unfortunately, escape was all he could manage for the moment. He could not get back into the battle yet, for he was unable to raise any of the nearby human ships on the *Pearl's* data link, with the net result that he was cut off from the rest of the fleet. It seemed that he could receive information, but could not transmit anything. He had to assume that the onboard comms package was malfunctioning, and that the IFF system probably would not work. Without that, the *Pearl* would be singled out by any nearby human warship as an approaching enemy and blasted out of space. All he could do was curse and wonder what was wrong with the ship.

For lack of any better ideas, Thorella steered to sunward, toward the volume of space that was nearly empty of ships while he pondered what he should do. From what he saw on the tactical display, it did not take a tactical genius to understand that the human fleet was now being slowly reduced to a scattering of flaming hulks, cut off from escape by an incoming tide of Kreelan warships. Hundreds of human ships already had been destroyed, and many more were damaged or dying as Kreelan warships surrounded them and pounded them into plasma.

It was then that a familiar voice came over the comm link, accompanied by a determined face in the holo display.

"Ships of the Fleet," the voice declared, "this is Councilman Braddock of the Confederation Council. As the senior surviving member of the council, and by law the president for this emergency, I hereby order all combat units to withdraw immediately, repeat, immediately. All Marine elements now on the Kreelan moon are ordered to rendezvous at your primary pickup zones. Follow the beacons that have been set up for you. You will meet no resistance, so move as quickly as possible. All troop transports are to retrieve their landing contingents from the Kreelan moon; you have been guaranteed safe passage as long as you do not fire on any Kreelan vessels. I repeat: you are safe as long as you hold your fire. Once you recover your troops, you are ordered to immediately withdraw to Confederation space at the best possible speed." The face paused for a moment, as if listening to something off-screen. "Detailed orders are now being forwarded over the fleet command links. Follow them to the letter. Good luck and Godspeed. That is all."

The display went blank.

Before Thorella's widened eyes, the terrible ballet of ships underwent an immediate and profound change. Suddenly, the Kreelans were ferociously attacking some ships while blatantly ignoring others. The pattern made no sense to him until he realized that the ships that were mysteriously immune to attack were lightly armed Marine transports – empty – headed back down to the moon from which he had just escaped. Kreelan ships maintained weapons lock on the human ships, but made no move to attack. The only ships being attacked were those that continued to return fire. Soon, even they were left alone as their commanders realized that the councilman's words were, on the surface, at least, true.

"This is impossible," Thorella hissed angrily as he saw human battleships winking off the tactical display as they jumped into hyperspace. In but minutes, the only capital ship that remained was *Sandhurst*, Sinclaire's flagship, and the carriers that were busy recovering the Marines under the watchful eyes of the Kreelan fleet. It was a sight no human could ever have foretold, and one that many would never be able to accept as being anything other than legend or fantasy.

To Thorella, it was nothing less than cowardice. Treason.

After the initial wave of anger caused by those thoughts, he realized the full implications – for himself – of what had happened. Camden and Mackenzie had obviously survived to tell their stories, and with Braddock as the senior councilman and acting president (unless someone else more senior happened to show up, which Thorella thought was unlikely, at best), Thorella's future back in Confederation space would be exceedingly grim. His ambitions, his destiny, were blown away as if by a battleship's guns.

In a daze, he left the cockpit, not even bothering to put the ship on autopilot. *It doesn't matter*, he thought. *Nothing matters now*. He wandered aft, toward the parlor and the liquor cabinet. The *Pearl* carried only the finest, he noted bitterly as he hefted a bottle of eighty year old scotch. None of that syntho crap for her passengers! He did not even bother with a glass, but removed the cap and lifted the bottle in a mock toast to his own failure and impending demise. Then he took a long swallow, his body nearly numb to the burning liquid's passage. Like a child with a favorite teddy bear, he carried the bottle to the overstuffed chair next to the artificial fireplace and collapsed into it, drained. Finished.

It was only after he had polished off a third of the bottle that he noticed the black case perched on a table on the far side of the room, near the door. Something about it was vaguely familiar, but through the fog of alcohol and depression, he could not quite place where he had seen it before. Intrigued as he could be in his present state, he mustered enough energy to get up. Not quite walking, but not staggering, either, he made his way to the table and the mysterious case. He ran a finger over the top, noting the perfectly smooth surface and the material's excessive strength.

Could it be? a tiny voice somewhere inside his skull cried. He picked it up, feeling the weight in his hand.

"I can't believe it," he whispered to himself as his heart began to race with excitement. Dropping the bottle of expensive scotch, he set the case back down on the table – carefully, oh, so carefully – and examined its latching system. "Ohmygod," he breathed, his body quivering as if in the throes of orgasm.

There was no mistake. It was the kryolon weapon command console. The fools, he thought, had somehow gotten hold of it, and then left it behind! That was the only reason he had not recognized it sooner: his mind could not accept the possibility that it had simply been left here, unattended.

Suddenly, his fortunes had changed yet again. He thought of *Sandhurst* standing by, watching over the recovery of the Marines, and Braddock and the others on board her.

"Thank you, God," he said aloud, a blasphemy coming from such lips.

Despite what Laskowski had briefed to the General Staff about the weapons being distributed among several ships, the entire arsenal had secretly been put aboard the ill-fated *Warspite*, with two of them being transferred to the *Golden Pearl* during Gard and Mackenzie's short-lived incarceration aboard the flagship.

Only three people had known the launch codes: Borge, who was now dead; Admiral Laskowski, who had recently gone down with the *Southampton*; and Thorella. He was now the only living human being who could launch the two remaining weapons.

And launch them he would.

* * *

Jodi forced her eyes open against the pain and drugs that were gradually working their way out of her system after her forced separation from the autodoc. She had to see what Thorella was doing, had to know what scheme he had come up with that had changed his somber mood to one of disquieting elation.

Wedged into a chair at the main engineering console in the *Pearl's* engine room, Jodi was managing to hold out, minute by minute. She had been asleep in the sickbay when Thorella came aboard, and the transition to flight had awakened her. She had called out for Nicole, for the others, but no one had come. Thank the Lord of All, she thought, that she had not used the ship's intercom. That would have brought Thorella right to her.

No, she had sensed that something was wrong, and had managed to pull herself out of her bunk and crawl to a monitor. From there, she could view the cockpit. It took her a long time to be sure that she would not scream at the sight of the thing that sat at the controls. Not long after that, she decided to act.

The first thing she had to do was to get out of sick bay and find a place that would be relatively safe if Thorella decided to prowl around. The second was to find a way to neutralize whatever threat he might pose to both her and the others, wherever they might be. After a moment's consideration, her knowledge of the *Golden Pearl* led her to the engineering section all the way aft as the best place to fulfill both requirements. After that, she only had to figure out a way to get there.

It did not take her long to realize that she would never make it on her own. Now separated from the autodoc, the pain that poured into her brain was agonizing, and it was only sheer willpower and a badly bitten tongue that kept her from crying out, perhaps letting Thorella know that he was not alone on this ship.

As she lay panting, trying to rally some strength, she remembered the ship's complement of service drones. Carried by many starships, such drones were the ship's handymen, performing many of the more monotonous maintenance tasks. They were neither aesthetically attractive nor particularly intelligent, but they more than made up for it in brute strength and reliability.

Pulling herself back up to the ship's comm console, Jodi waited for the pain to subside again before she began entering the commands that she hoped would bring one of the machines to her without attracting unwanted attention. A sailor would pay no attention to a passing drone, subconsciously knowing that the machine was merely setting off to check on some subsystem or other. A psychotic Marine, however, might take more notice.

Minutes passed as Jodi fought to keep from passing out, waiting for the drone to arrive. She had no way from this panel to monitor its progress; besides, she was more interested in keeping an eye on what Thorella was doing, which was, mercifully, nothing. For the moment.

Finally, after what seemed like hours, she was rewarded with the smooth humming of a drone entering sick bay, obediently coming to a stop in front of the chair where she had been sitting, waiting.

With another burst of effort, Jodi managed to drape herself over the boxy machine's back, its impellers instantly compensating for her weight.

"Engineering," she gasped, ignoring the flecks of blood that flew from her lips.

With nothing in the form of acknowledgment, the drone retraced its path out of the room and silently headed aft, hauling her along with it.

Once in engineering, the first thing Jodi had done after locking the door behind her was to make sure that Thorella could not communicate with the outside world. She had no idea what he was up to, why he was on this ship, but she had no intention of letting him get into more trouble – or causing any. Then she disabled his maneuvering controls. That took a while, during which she heard Tony Braddock's fleet broadcast.

His voice and his words told him that Nicole must be all right, too. The thought made her feel better, but it did nothing to improve her health. She was bleeding again, inside. And there was no autodoc here to help her.

Jodi watched with grim amusement as Thorella lost himself in depression at Braddock's words. To see him crushed, defeated, was a small victory, enough to bring a smile to her battered face, and with that accomplished, her body demanded rest, and she passed out into dark oblivion.

She woke up some time later to see him tinkering with a strange black case that he had found, and she was instantly worried by the change in his demeanor. She should not have been afraid, she told herself, because he could not access any of the ship's systems from outside this compartment, and there was no way he could get in here without blowing through the hardened bulkhead.

"What are you doing, you bastard?" she whispered as she watched his fingers fly over the console that was revealed to be inside the case. "What is that thing?"

A pair of flashing lights on the control panel suddenly caught her attention: TORPEDOES ARMED, the display said.

"Wait just a minute," she hissed. "Computer," she barked, "weapons status?"

"All weapons under local control are in standby mode," the synthesized female voice answered smugly. "No targets designated, no–"

"Then why are the torpedo status lights showing that they're armed?"

"Torpedo tubes one and two are not under local control," the computer answered as if Jodi were an idiot.

"Then who controls them?" Jodi felt a bead of sweat slip down her back.

"That information is classified."

"Do tubes one and two have targets?" she asked, frantic now as she watched the status display changed from simply armed to ready.

"Affirmative."

"What are the targets?" Jodi yelled at the console.

"That information is classified."

"Goddammit," Jodi shouted helplessly, "what the fuck isn't classified?"

"Tubes one and two were reloaded with unserialized weapons while we were docked with *Warspite*," the machine answered suddenly.

"What weapons?" Jodi asked. "Special weapons? What kind?"

"That information is–"

"Shut up!" Jodi shouted angrily. "Show me a theoretical torpedo trajectory based on current ship's vector and torpedo launcher alignment." She could not get the computer to tell her what the real target was, but maybe she could dupe it into giving it to her anyway.

"One moment." And then the holo screen showed the sector of space near the sun. A red line arced out from the icon that was the yacht, following a trajectory right into the sun.

"What the hell..." Jodi whispered to herself. Suddenly, she understood. She had heard the tales, but had never believed them until now. *Kryolon warheads*. And Thorella controlled them. Her blood turned to ice in her veins.

"Computer," she ordered, "shut down all power to weapons–"

The ship shuddered. Again.

"Torpedoes one and two away," the computer announced cheerfully. "Power-down to weapons systems commencing... Completed. Weapons successfully powered down."

Too late! Jodi cursed herself. On the holo display, the two weapons followed the computer's projected course with unsurprising precision.

There was only one thing left for her to do now, she thought. It would no doubt cost her life, but there was no choice. She reactivated the datalink, hoping that Thorella would not catch on until it was too late.

"All ships, all ships, this is the *Golden Pearl*..."

* * *

"Weapons launch!" *Sandhurst's* tactical officer cried, his eyes following the trajectories of two torpedoes launched from the small ship trailing behind the rest of the retreating fleet. For the last hectic forty minutes – it had seemed like hours – his primary job had been to keep human ships from firing on Kreelan ones, and for the most part he had been successful.

"Who?" Admiral Sinclaire demanded.

"It looks like that yacht, sir, the *Golden Pearl*," the tactical officer replied quickly as his fingers stabbed angrily at his console, "but I'm not getting an IFF response, no datalink, and no voice, either. She's not responding at all."

"What's she targeting?"

"Don't know, sir. There aren't any Kreelan ships in that quadrant." Pause. "The torpedoes are headed right into the sun."

What the Devil? Sinclaire thought. He had just gotten the fleet back into some kind of order, strange as it was, and he was not about to let things fall back into chaos, especially with the Marine transports still en route back from the Kreelan moon.

He was about to ask something else when the comms officer suddenly shouted, "Fleet emergency broadcast, admiral!"

"On screen!" Sinclaire demanded immediately. He was shocked by what he saw.

"All ships, all ships, this is the *Golden Pearl*."

"Jodi," Nicole whispered, fighting to keep the tears of rage held in check at the sight of her friend's mutilated face, guilt surging through her for abandoning Jodi in her hour of need.

"This is Admiral Sinclaire aboard *Sandhurst*. Go ahead, commander."

"Sir," Jodi said thickly, obviously in excruciating pain, "you've got to get the fleet away from here as fast as you can. You're all in great danger."

"Commander, the Kreelans have given us time–"

"It's not the Kreelans, sir," she interrupted him, "it's the weapons General Thorella, who's aboard this ship, just launched. You should be tracking two torpedoes, heading into the sun." A nod to Sinclaire from the tactical officer. Two maroon streaks were rapidly making their way across the holo image of this part of the system to the star at its center. "I think they're fitted with kryolon warheads." She paused in the sudden silence that enveloped *Sandhurst's* bridge.

"Thorella launched these things?" Sinclaire managed to say with what felt like someone else's tongue, so shocked was he to be hearing this. "On whose authority?"

She gave him a bitter smile through blood-caked lips. "His own, of course," she rasped. "He's never needed anyone else's."

"I am coming to get you, Jodi," Nicole said suddenly. She had made a quick mental calculation from the tactical display. "I'll be there in twenty minutes."

"Nicole," Tony said from behind her, putting a hand on her shoulder. She shrugged it off angrily.

Jodi shook her head slowly, wincing at the pain the movement caused. "You can't risk it, Nicole. There's no time. And... I don't think I'll last that long now, anyway." A bitter smile.

Sinclaire could feel the hair on the back of his neck stand on end. *Kryolons, of all things. Could it be true?* More to the point, could he discount the possibility? And what could he do about it? *Run like hell*, he told himself, a shudder rippling up his spine. "Mister Zhirinovski!" he bellowed to the acting fleet operations officer.

"Sir?"

"How much longer to jump?"

"We should be ready in seventeen minutes, sir." Five assault transports were still coming in; their carriers would jump as soon as they were aboard, and *Sandhurst* would follow them out, the last human ship to leave. The only ones now being left behind would never be coming home, anyway, their drives dead, their life support failing. There were simply not enough able ships left to rescue all the stragglers.

Sinclaire turned on his tactical officer. "How long before the torpedoes reach the corona?"

"Just under two minutes, sir," he replied, noting that the torpedoes had now run out of fuel and were coasting on toward their target. "If what I've heard about the kryolons is right, we'll have about fifteen minutes from initiation of the kryolon reaction – that'll be upon detonation in the corona – to the first stellar debris reaching us here." He looked helpless for a moment. "But that's just a guess."

"Better than nothing, lad," Sinclaire said quickly. "Zhirinovski, you've got ten minutes to get the other ships out of here. Tell the transports to push it past the limit. If they're not back aboard by then, they get left behind." Five minutes was not much of a safety margin, but it was all he could give them.

"Aye, sir!"

"Captain Jorgensen," Sinclaire spoke into the comm link to the ship's bridge, "we've got a problem."

"Sir?" the captain answered immediately, her attention riveted on the old sailor's face in the screen.

"Have *Sandhurst* ready for her jump in ten minutes, captain. The Kreelan sun may be... unstable. We're pushing up the timetable."

"Aye, admiral," Jorgensen answered. "We're ready any time, sir."

Sinclaire nodded.

"What about her?" Nicole demanded quietly, nodding toward Jodi's image. Her eyes were closed, head down.

"She's right, lass," Sinclaire said as gently as he could. "You couldn't get there in time to help her. You'd only die, too. Perhaps... keeping her company might be best. No one likes to go out of this world alone, and Lord knows she's earned what little comfort any of us can provide."

Nicole nodded in resignation, now welcoming Braddock's arm around her shoulder. But she looked up suddenly at Jodi's voice.

"Nicole," she said in a whisper, "It's Thorella. I think he's coming..."

TWENTY-ONE

Reza did not have to see what was taking place throughout the Empire; he could sense it. He was spiritually reconnected with Her Children, with the Bloodsong again echoing in his veins. He could again sense Her will, and knew that a great Change was about to take place, something that would alter his people forever and take them to the next step in their evolution as a species. Wherever they were, warriors and clawless ones waited for the rapture that they knew was about to come, only moments away now. Even the hapless males that had been evacuated from the nurseries knew that something was happening, for while they were witless creatures with but a single function in life, they, too, were bound to Her will. And in their own way, they felt the tremor in the life force that bound them all to one another, that was the endless thread of life that the Kreela called the Way. While they did not realize it in their blissful ignorance, they had been redeemed, and the glory and honor that had once been theirs was about to be again in the new form that was soon to come.

But Reza's mind was yet troubled, for there remained one task for him to complete. He did not have to ask his Empress for what he desired, for in Her great wisdom, She already knew.

"I know of the one you seek," She told him. "Do this thing and return to Me, my love. For our time here grows short; the new dawn is soon upon us."

"I shall not be long, my Empress," he replied, his hand fastened about the handle of the ancient sword Tesh-Dar had once given him.

"Let it be done."

And Reza vanished.

* * *

Jodi's plan would have worked completely had she only remembered to turn off the display monitors on the drones like the one that had brought her to engineering. She had finally cut Thorella off from accessing any of the other systems on the ship. But she had forgotten that one little thing.

Thorella was laying on his back, his head and shoulders buried in the ship's central computer core in a vain attempt to figure out what was ailing the *Pearl* when one of the idiot machines came up to him, intent on dislodging this odd parasite from its electronic parent. Thorella kicked at it in fury, not understanding or caring what the machine was trying to do, and accidentally turned up the volume control on the machine's internal voice relay.

"Thorella launched these things?" he heard someone say. "On whose authority?"

"His own, of course," came a choked reply. "He's never needed anyone else's."

Thorella did not need to hear any more.

"Mackenzie," he hissed, withdrawing himself from the computer's innards and pushing past the single-minded drone. His blaster in hand, he quickly made his way aft, to the one section of the ship he had not taken the time to check.

Engineering.

* * *

Jodi saw him on the monitor outside the door.

"He's here," she sighed, trembling inwardly. "Oh, shit." She tried to hold the blaster she had taken from the small weapons vault near the door, but her broken fingers could not hold it right. Even with both hands.

"Jodi," Nicole said from very, very far away, "can he get to you?"

He stood in front of the door, looking straight into the video pickup. Smiling.

"I don't think so," she said. But then he held up what could only be a coded magnetic key, and she watched in horror as he swiped it across the door's access panel. She had no way of knowing, but Borge had made sure Thorella was provided with a proper commander's key for the ship that could open any door. "Oh, shit," she moaned. "Yes, he can get in..."

"Jodi, try to–"

The door slid open.

"Game's over, bitch," Thorella said quietly as he leveled his blaster at her stomach. He would make sure she died, but he did not want to hurry her along too much.

"Fuck you, you bastard son of a who–"

Something unexpected happened just as Thorella squeezed the trigger. There was a blast of frigid air, a moving shadow, a high keening sound that Jodi thought she had heard before. But only the gun that was pointed at her mattered, the gun with a bore that seemed as big around as an irrigation pipe.

In a slow motion dream she saw Reza appear out of thin air to her left, his mouth open in a snarl of rage that she could not hear, his arm held out before him as if... as if he had... thrown something? In front of her, only a few paces away, she watched Thorella's face glow in the backlight of the blast his weapon made as it fired. But there was something odd about it, she thought, odd about his hand, the weapon. It took her an eternal moment to realize that they were no longer attached to his arm. Thorella's hand, still clutching the gun, was falling – so slowly falling – toward the deck, the stump of his arm now shooting blood at her instead of searing energy. Curious, she followed the crimson stream, noting with some small surprise that it intersected a gaping hole where her abdomen had once been. She touched the ragged edge with a numbed hand. Warm. Wet. *Oh, God.*

Reza stood still a moment, stunned by the horrible misfortune of his timing. *A second sooner,* he raged to himself, *and I could have saved her.* He turned his attention to Thorella. "I should have killed you a long time ago," Reza said softly through the smoke that rose around them from the shot that had smashed Jodi's body.

"You have to take me back for trial," Thorella cried as he tried to hold the stump of his arm with his good hand, Reza's shrekka having severed it just below the elbow. He nodded toward the screen where Nicole's horrified face still looked on. "You can't kill me," he gloated, "not with the whole fleet watching. It'd be murder."

"Enough." Reza had long debated how he would kill Thorella: slowly, the way he deserved to die for all the evil he had done, or quickly, mercifully. Reza decided on the latter, not to show Thorella mercy, but because he could simply stand this horrible pestilence no more.

But just as he was about to take Thorella's head with his sword, he heard a voice that tore open his heart.

"Reza..."

He turned to look at Jodi's pleading face. He hesitated, only a fraction of a second, but it was enough for Thorella to bolt through the still open door and disappear down the corridor.

"Reza," Jodi whispered. "How...?"

"Do not speak," he quieted her as he momentarily pushed Thorella from his mind. He cradled her gently as he fought not to look at what was left of her once beautiful body. For the first and only time in his adult life, he sincerely hoped there somewhere was a Hell like old Father Hernandez had believed existed, and that Thorella would fall there to burn forever. If nothing else, Reza would make sure that he would get to find out. "There is yet time. I can take you to the Empress. She can heal you–"

"No," Jodi shook her head weakly. "It's better this way, Reza. I think... my number's come up... I ought to take it like a lady." She looked up at him. "Tell me... Nicole will be... safe?"

He nodded. "She will. For always. The Empress will let no harm come to her. Ever."

Jodi smiled. *Nicole would be safe.* That was all that mattered.

"Reza?" Nicole's brittle voice called from the display beside him, yet from hundreds of thousands of leagues away. "You've got to get out of there."

"I cannot leave Jodi–"

"Reza," Nicole interrupted him, "your sun is going to explode any minute now. You've got to get out! We did not know how to tell you, we only found out for ourselves from Jodi before... before..."

"The Empress knows of this," he told her. "It is part of our future. We await it. But it is time for you and the others to leave here, Nicole." Reza felt a ripple in his bones. It was about to happen. "Quickly." He looked at her one last time. "May thy Way be long and glorious, my friend."

"Detonation!" someone cried on *Sandhurst's* bridge. On the main viewscreen, the Kreelan sun flared with crimson brilliance as its corona began to blow outward and the deeper layers of the stricken star began to expand behind it.

"Jodi..." Nicole said, but Jodi was no longer there to talk to. The image had suddenly filled with static. Both of her best friends were gone.

* * *

Aboard the *Golden Pearl*, Reza watched Nicole's image fade as the dying star's energy was released, destroying the data link to *Sandhurst*.

"Reza, you've got to leave me," Jodi implored him quietly. "Please."

Still holding her gently, he could feel the life running from her body like the last grains of sand from an hourglass. "Do not fear for me," he said softly as he kissed her hair. "I promised that I would always be there for you, remember?" He closed his eyes, his heart aching for her. "I won't leave you now," he whispered.

"Thank you, Reza," she sighed, cradled against his shoulder. "I... love you."

"I love you, too, Jodi," he told her softly, fighting back his tears as he felt her spirit slip away, leaving her body an empty shell. After kissing her tenderly on the lips, he gently laid her body down on the deck.

With a fleeting glance at the display on the engineering console that showed Thorella on the flight deck, Reza smiled grimly at his enemy's fate, trapped alone on a ship that was doomed by his own hand.

Then he conjured in his mind a vision of his waiting Empress, his love, and vanished from the *Golden Pearl* to join Her.

All alone now, Markus Thorella hammered at the *Pearl's* useless command console as the wall of fire from the exploding star rushed forward to claim him. He was still howling in fear and rage as the ship was torn to atoms.

* * *

"Jodi," she heard a voice call in the darkness. It was a voice Jodi recognized, one that she had once loved.

"Tanya?" she called, not sure where she was, growing afraid.

"Yes, darling," Tanya answered from beside her, taking Jodi's hand. "Don't be afraid. Everything's all right now." Jodi felt the warmth of Tanya's lips on hers, and suddenly saw her face, young and beautiful as it had once been, but without the shadow over her soul. "Come on," Tanya told her, smiling as she led Jodi by the hand toward a golden glow the color of a sunrise. "Everyone's waiting for you."

And together they stepped into the light, leaving the darkness behind forever.

* * *

"The *Golden Pearl's* gone." On the tactical display, Nicole watched as the sphere of superheated matter blotted out the tiny icon that had once been a ship and her friends, but that also meant the end of Thorella's reign of terror. The shock wave reached out ever further, consuming everything in its path.

"Zhirinovski, how many ships are left behind us?"

"None, sir. We're the last."

"Captain Jorgensen," Sinclaire called to the ship's captain, "are your boats all aboard?"

"Yes, sir."

"Very well. Stand by for jump."

"Radiation is in the yellow, admiral," the ops officer warned.

"A moment," Sinclaire replied, his attention riveted to the chaotic scene on the tactical display. He wondered at the Kreelan fleet now clustered around the homeworld and its strange moon. There were tens of thousands of ships now, some of them unbelievably huge, and more were still jumping in. *Lord of All*, he thought, *why don't they jump out? The Kreelans on the planet are doomed, but at least the ships could save themselves…*

"Jesus," someone whispered as the stellar matter's first tendrils brushed the homeworld. The main viewer and tactical display suddenly went dark.

"Overloaded," someone said somberly.

"Captain Jorgensen," Sinclaire ordered, his last act before he would allow exhaustion to overtake him, "take us home."

* * *

The star that had warmed and given life to their world was dying, but even in its death it served the needs of the Empress. Having blinded the primitive electronic eyes of the humans, who were not yet prepared to understand, She made ready to take Her Children on the next part of the journey that was their eternal Way.

The vast fleet of ships was arrayed to capture the necessary energy from the exploding sun and focus it like a great lens upon the Empress moon and the Empress Herself. Reaching out with Her mind and spirit, bending the massive influx of energy to Her will, She opened a gateway in space-time that would not even be theorized by humankind for another fifty-thousand years. As one, Her people – every soul spread across the ten thousand suns of the Empire – passed through it on their first step toward the next phase of their evolution. Had humans witnessed it, they would have thought it nothing more and nothing less than magic.

Beside Her, Reza looked back through the closing portal, wondering at what had been, what could have been. He mourned Jodi's death, and wondered about Nicole, feeling a sense of emptiness that he would never again be able to see her or speak to her.

"Fear not, my love," his Empress told him, her voice warming his soul as She embraced him, Her green eyes glittering with love. "You will see her yet once more..."

EPILOGUE

Nicole rose at eight-thirty, three hours later than was her custom on a workday. But today was special, a day that had become something of a ritual over the years. Today was the tenth anniversary of the Great Expedition, ten years since the Armada had returned home from battle with the Empire. Ten years since Jodi had died. And Reza. And so many others. It was a Confederation holiday, but Nicole would not be participating in any of the official functions with her husband, the president. In other times, perhaps, it would have been expected for a spouse – especially a woman – to participate in such affairs, to look dutifully somber before the media, but Nicole had paid her dues. She was a patriot, and had the scars and dead friends and family to prove it. Hers was a time of private contemplation. Shockingly, the people of the Confederation had respected this melancholy quirk without the heartless scrutiny that was usually turned upon public figures that did not quite fit the mold, and Nicole respected her people all the more for it.

She rose and showered, welcoming the soothing warmth of the hot water on her face, thankful for such a luxury, and content in the knowledge that the many throughout the Confederation who did not have such a simple thing as this someday would. For nearly a century, humanity had labored for simple survival. But now, with the war over, men and women were again free to look ahead, to plan and build for the future. They would not have to wonder if incoming ships bore Marines who promised salvation, or an alien horde that promised death. No longer would every resource have to be devoted to the making of war; while war and the chance of it would always be with them, for a while at least the young could grow old without the constant threat of death in combat. They could again take up art and philosophy, learn to love again, and do all the many things that made humanity something special in the Universe, something worth saving. There would always be wars, she knew, but there would also be sailors, Marines, and soldiers of the Territorial Army to protect the Confederation, for humankind had learned its lesson well. But now there was room for more, for humanity to again be human.

Sitting before a mirror now, she applied Navy regulation makeup, a process that was at once simple and difficult. Simple, because there was very little that regulations allowed; difficult, because she had become used to putting on more as the years had gone by, a token surrender, perhaps, to the inexorable advance of age. There were definite wrinkles now, but not too many, she decided. Some gray in her hair, but not too much. *Natural highlighting*, she thought with a smile. Time had treated her well these last years, and if anything she had become more beautiful with each birthday, at least if she was to go by Tony's compliments. She smiled into the mirror. A much younger woman's face smiled back.

That part of her ritual complete, she went to the bedroom that had been dubbed the house's official "junk" room. It was where all the flotsam and jetsam of life that was too valuable to throw away, yet not immediately significant enough to display from day to day, found a permanent resting place. In the closet she found her Navy dress black uniform in its environmentally controlled bag. Carrying it back to their bedroom, she laid it out carefully on the bed, running her hands over the smooth synthetic fabric, her fingers tracing the gold braid that proclaimed her a commodore, her last promotion before retirement. The rows of medals, including the Confederation Medal of Honor that would have made an old Marine colonel she had once known very proud, indeed, were bright against the dark fabric. The genuine leather boots that Tony had given her one year for Christmas gleamed like Kreelan armor.

She put the uniform on carefully, religiously, savoring the feel of the silk lining against her skin, the authoritarian firmness of the boots on her feet. She thought of how Reza used to dress when he had returned from the Empire, of the ritual it was for him each morning as he donned his armor and waited to meet the rising sun. Her heart became heavy at the thought, but she did not push it away. Today was reserved for him, for all of them, and she welcomed the pain of the memories as best she could, in their honor.

Standing before the full-length mirror, she appraised herself critically, glaring at herself as she might a subordinate in a formal inspection. She nodded to herself in approval. All was well, indeed perfect. She had never had it re-tailored, and it still fit as it had ten years ago, despite having had two children since then.

The children, she thought, a smile clearing her face of the fierce commodore's glare: Jodi Marie and Reza Georges Braddock, whose first names honored Jodi and Reza. Neither Nicole nor Tony could think of a more fitting way to honor their fallen friends.

She thought of the children now, no doubt standing beside their father as he read the ceremonial speech for today, which was different from those he had written for this day over the last ten years, and each of those different from the others. There had been enough pain, enough courage all those years ago to fill such eulogies anew for centuries to come.

Placing her cap just so upon her head, Nicole said good-bye to the servants and the Secret Service agents – none would accompany her this day – and stepped into the aircar that awaited her.

The pilot said nothing to her during the flight. One of Reza's troops from the Red Legion, Warren Zevon had finished his tour with the Marines and, on the recommendation of Sergeant Major of the Marine Corps Eustus Camden, had been accepted as Nicole's personal secretary and bodyguard. He took care of the administrative part of her public life and gave her the one precious gift that was so hard to find: extra time. Time for her family, time for herself. Zevon was not normally so quiet, but he knew that her thoughts were on the past, and he gave her privacy through his silence. He, in turn, nurtured his own remembrances of his friends now lost, of his old commander, of good times and bad.

Their destination was the small village of Hamilton, where a woman Nicole had never known had left a legacy beyond her own death in what had come to be known as the Fleet Shrine. A simple obelisk of black granite, polished smooth, in the center of a great and peaceful garden, the Fleet Shrine was not the most elaborate of the many war memorials on Earth and the rest of the Confederation, nor was it the most popularly known. But the words etched into the granite made it very special to Nicole, and it had become part of her ritual.

As she walked toward the obelisk through the garden of blooming flowers, she again read the words inscribed in the polished black granite:

> To Those of the Armada Who Never Returned Home:
> Your Sacrifice Shall Not Be Forgotten

Then, in smaller letters:

> Dedicated to Commander Jodi Ellen Mackenzie,
> Whose Hour of Need Led to My Salvation

The name of the woman who had arranged for the monument to be constructed and who had left millions of credits to the Service Relief Fund was not inscribed in the granite, although Nicole knew her name: Tanya

Buchet. It had been a strange thing, she recalled: the Buchet woman had died mysteriously just before the Armada had left for Kreelan space, yet the instructions for the shrine had been part of her will. What her relationship was with Jodi, Nicole did not and would never know, but it was obvious that Jodi had been close to her heart.

In another strange coincidence, Jodi had been Tanya Buchet's sole beneficiary, and, in turn, Jodi had left her entire estate to Nicole. So, in the end, Fate had left Nicole rich beyond her wildest dreams. But she and Tony had decided that the money that Nicole had inherited would be put back into reconstruction programs on Erlang. She and Tony had each other and the children, in a galaxy that was, for the moment, safe to live in. She could ask God – or the Empress – for nothing more.

Sitting on the bench that faced the inscription, Nicole let her mind wander, just as Zevon wandered through the garden, lost in his own thoughts, but with one eye glued to Nicole in case she needed his protection. She sat that way for a long time, looking into the blackness of the granite, thinking of the past, and sometimes just not thinking at all.

She thought perhaps that she might have fallen asleep for a moment. For when she next opened her eyes something told her that her surroundings had somehow changed. Zevon still strolled through the gardens, more or less where she last remembered him; the sun had not moved appreciably, so not too much time had passed; the birds still sang. Everything seemed to be as it had been. And yet...

She suddenly looked up at the obelisk, into the shimmering blackness of the granite, and there he was, with the Empress and Shera-Khan – an adult warrior now – standing beside him.

"Reza," she breathed.

His image nodded, as if he was not accustomed to the gesture, but the warmth of the smile on his face was more than human.

"All is well, my friend," she heard him say, but his mouth did not form the words; he spoke directly to her mind. "On this day we celebrate the Last Ascension, Keel-Tath's return to us and our greatest journey upon the Way. And we wished to share this moment with you, to leave you something in remembrance of me, of us. For after this day, we shall never be able to return; we shall forever be... beyond this place, this time."

Nicole fought for words as she stood up and carefully approached the obelisk, unwilling to believe but unable to deny what she was seeing. "Reza, your planet was destroyed! How... where... where are you?"

"That is not important, child," the Empress, who had once been Esah-Zhurah, told her gently. "This, however, is." She held Her hand forth, Her fingers curled around something nestled in Her palm.

Nicole, eyes wide with disbelief, reached out toward the image in the obelisk, and drew back as she felt something placed in her cupped hands by the alien fingers that shimmered from the face of the stone.

It was the eyestone from the collar that Esah-Zhurah had once worn before becoming Empress. It was a deep, gleaming blue, engraved with the rune of what Nicole suddenly remembered was the order of the Desh-Ka, the oldest of all those that had ever served Her.

"To your name shall we always sing our praise," the Empress said. "Fare thee well, daughter."

Nicole looked up just in time to see the images fading, dissolving like a reflection in a pool into which a rock has been thrown.

"*Adieu*, Nicole," Reza said, as if from far away.

And then their images were gone. Nicole put a hand against the obelisk, but it was solid, unyielding as it should be. *I must have been hallucinating*, she told herself.

But then she felt something in her hand: it was the eyestone with the rune of the Desh-Ka carved in its center. It was real.

"Nicole?" Zevon asked from beside her. He had become worried when she had approached the obelisk and acted as if she were talking to it. "Is anything wrong?"

"No," she replied with a smile at his concerned expression. She closed her hands over the eyestone, glad in her heart at the knowledge that Reza and his people had somehow survived. It seemed to her that things this day were right in the world, and that tomorrow would dawn yet brighter than today. "Everything is fine, dear Warren," she told him, taking his arm and leading him from the obelisk and out into the flowering gardens. "Come, it is time for us to go home."

If You Enjoyed Final Battle...

The *In Her Name* saga continues with *First Contact*, the first novel in a hard-hitting trilogy about how the human-kreelan war began. You can also get *First Contact* as part of *The Last War*, a trilogy collection that also includes *Legend Of The Sword* and *Dead Soul*.

To give you a taste of what's to come, here's the first chapter from *First Contact* - enjoy!

* * *

Captain Owen McClaren was extremely tense, although a casual observer would never have thought so. Commanding the survey vessel *TNS Aurora*, he was one of the best officers in the fleet, and to his crew he had never appeared as anything but calm and in control. Even when one of the ship's newly refitted reactors had suffered a breach during their last run into dry dock, McClaren's deep voice had never wavered, his fatherly face had never betrayed a hint of fear or apprehension as he personally directed the engineering watch to contain the breach. A man of unusual physical and moral courage, he was the perfect captain for the exploratory missions the *Aurora* and her sister ships mounted into distant space, seeking new homes for humanity.

McClaren had made thousands of jumps in his twenty-year career, but every one was like the very first: an adrenaline joyride. As the transpace sequence wound down to zero, his heart would begin to pound and his muscles tensed like spring steel. It wasn't fear that made him react that way, although there were enough things that could go wrong with a jump to make fear a natural enough reaction.

No, what made the forty-three-year-old former middleweight boxing champion of the Terran Naval Academy hold the arms of his command chair in a white-knuckle grip wasn't fear. It was anticipation. To *Aurora's* captain, every jump, particularly out here in uncharted space, was a potential winning lottery ticket, the discovery of a lifetime. No matter where the *Aurora* wound up, as long as she arrived safely, there was bound to be a wealth of astrogational information to help human starships travel ever farther from Man's birthplace: Earth.

On rare occasions, precious habitable planets were to be found. Finding such systems was the primary goal of the survey ships. McClaren was currently the fleet's leading "ace," with twelve habitable planets to his credit in return for nearly fifteen years of ship-time, sailing through uncharted space.

"Stand by for transpace sequence," the pilot announced, her words echoing through every passageway and compartment in the *Aurora's* five hundred meter length.

McClaren tensed even more, his strong arm and back muscles flexing instinctively as if he were back in the ring, preparing to land a solid upper cut to the chin of an imaginary opponent. But his calm expression never wavered. "Very well," he answered, his dark brown eyes drinking in the growing torrent of information on the navigation display.

"Computer auto-lock engaged," interjected a faux female voice reassuringly. McClaren always had to suppress a grimace: the one thing he had never liked about *Aurora* was the computer's voice. It reminded him too much of his first wife.

For the next few seconds, the crew was little more than excess baggage as the ship's computer guided the transition from hyperspace back into the Einsteinian universe with a precision measured in quadrillionths of a second. While the bridge, which was buried deep in the *Aurora's* core habitation section, had no direct observation windows, the wraparound display depicted the eerie streams of light that swirled around the ship in complete detail. But what the human eye saw in the maelstrom of quantum physics beyond the ship's hyperdrive field was an illusion. It was real in one sense, but in another it wasn't. Space and time as humans commonly understood it did not exist in this realm. As the captain of a starship, McClaren had to understand both the theory and the practical application of hyperspace and the means to travel through it. But he was content in the knowledge that he never could have come up with the breakthroughs that allowed this miracle to happen: he stood on the shoulders of the scientific giants who had made the first test jump into hyperspace long before he was born.

While in hyperspace, the display would normally show the computer's assessment of the relative location of stars and other known celestial waypoints as the ship moved along its straight-line (relatively speaking) course. But McClaren always cleared the display to show what was really outside the ship just before they dropped back into normal space. It was a sight he never tired of.

"Ten seconds..." the computer's voice began counting down to the transition. "Five...four...three...two...one....sequence initiated. Hyperspace Engines disengaged."

The display suddenly shifted, the swirling light streams condensing into a bright yellow sun against a background of stars. McClaren knew that the system had several planets; gravitational perturbations observed from their last jump point had confirmed that much. The question was whether there were any orbiting at a distance from the star where water could exist as a liquid. For where there was liquid water, there was the possibility of carbon-based life. The trick now was to find them. Planets were huge close up, but in the vast expanse of a star system they seemed incredibly small.

"Engineering confirms hyperspace engines are secure, sir," the executive officer, Lieutenant Commander Rajesh Kumar, reported. "Engineering is ready to answer all bells, and the ship is secured for normal space."

Nodding his thanks to his exec, McClaren turned to the most important person currently on the bridge: the navigator. "Raisa, what's the word?"

The navigator looked like she would have given McClaren a run for his money in the boxing ring. Big-boned and heavily muscled, Lieutenant Raisa Marisova had in fact been a champion wrestler in her college years. But it was her genius at stellar astrogation that had won her a place on the *Aurora's* all-volunteer crew.

"Well..." she murmured as she rechecked her readings for what McClaren knew was probably the fifth time in the few moments the ship had dropped back into normal space. Raisa was always able to confirm the ship's emergence point so quickly because her calculations for pointing the various telescopes and other sensors at known stars to make a positional fix were always so precise. "It seems we are...right where we are supposed to be," she said as she turned and smiled at her captain, "give or take a few meters. We're above the ecliptic plane based on our pre-jump survey information. Now it's up to the survey team to find your next habitable planet, captain."

McClaren grinned, then opened a channel to the entire ship. "Well, crew, it looks like we've made another successful jump, and emerged right on target. The bad news is that we're even farther out in the Middle of Nowhere. But that's what they pay us for. Great job, everyone." The last few words were more than just a token verbal pat on the back: he truly meant it. Unlike most transits that took regular ships into hyperspace for a few days or even a week or two, the *Aurora* routinely made jumps that lasted for weeks or months. While McClaren's crew made it look easy, he knew quite well that an amazing amount of planning and preparation went into every jump, and his crew followed it up with painstaking diligence every moment they were in hyperspace. It wasn't just that they didn't want to wind up somewhere other than where they had planned, or because their captain expected perfection. It was because they had no intention of settling for second best. Period. "Everybody gets an extra round on me when we get back to the barn. Carry on."

The bridge crew grinned at one another: the captain ran up a huge bar tab on every mission, but he never failed to deliver when the ship made port.

They had no way of knowing that all but one of them would be dead in a few short hours.

* * *

The stranger's arrival was no surprise to the Imperial warships that orbited the Settlements on the third and fourth planets from the star. While even the greatly advanced technology of the Empire could not track ships while in hyperspace, they could easily detect the gravity spikes of vessels about to emerge in normal space. The stranger had been detected many hours before, as measured in the time of humans.

While this system was at the distant edge of the Empire, far from the Homeworld and the Empress, its defenses were not lacking: of the dozens of starships in orbit around the two settled worlds and the hundreds plying the asteroid belt, four were battlecruisers built within the last century. Humans might have considered them old, until they understood that the warriors of the Empire had sailed among the stars for over one hundred thousand of Earth's years. Even the most ancient of Her warships still plying the void between the stars was tens of thousands of years more advanced than the arriving stranger. Humans would barely have recognized them as starships.

But the warriors charged with protecting this far-flung system had no way of knowing the primitive nature of the incoming stranger. Nor would they have cared. The Empire had encountered other sentient races over the millennia, and the first contact protocol was no different now than it had been in ages past: the stranger would be greeted with overwhelming force.

In unison, the four enormous battlecruisers left orbit for the gravity anomaly at maximum velocity, safe behind shields that could protect them from titanic energy discharges and made them all but invisible to anything but direct visual observation.

Behind them, smaller warships and the planetary defense systems prepared to welcome the new arrival should it prove more than a match for the great warships sent to greet it.

* * *

"Bridge, this is Survey..."

Captain McClaren frowned despite himself. He knew that Lieutenant Amundsen's survey team worked fast, but they had been in-system less than fifteen minutes. It often took days for them to identify the orbits of any planets in the temperate zone unless they had extensive perturbation data on the star or stars in the system. And that they rarely had: humanity's rapid expansion to the stars didn't allow for years-long observations of any given star. His frown deepened as he took in the expression on Amundsen's face in the comms display. The normally very reserved man was uncharacteristically excited. And just as frightened. "What is it, Jens?"

"Sir..." Amundsen began, his pale blue eyes darting away momentarily to another display. "Captain...we've confirmed not just one, but *two* planets in the temperate zone..."

"Hot damn!" McClaren couldn't help himself. One planet that might have liquid water was miracle enough. Their pre-jump analysis had suggested there was one, but two had been too much to hope for. "That's fantastic!"

"Sir...they're both inhabited," Amundsen said in hoarse whisper. Normally a quiet man, often more at home with the stars and planets than his fellow human beings, the volume of his voice dropped with every word. "We didn't have to find their orbits. We found them from their neutrino and infrared readings." He paused. "I've...I've never seen anything like this. Even Sol system doesn't have this level of activity. The two planets in the temperate zone are highly industrialized. There are other points of activity throughout the asteroid belt, and on several moons orbiting a solitary gas giant. We have also observed ships through the primary telescope. Hundreds of them. They are...nothing like ours."

The captain sat back, stunned. *First contact*, he thought. Humans had explored thousands of star systems and endless volumes of space, but had never once encountered another sentient species. They had found life aplenty on the hundred-odd discovered worlds that would support human life or could be terraformed. From humble bacteria to massive predators that would have been at home with Earth's dinosaurs, life in the Universe was as expansive as it was diverse if you looked long and far enough. But no one had discovered a single sign of sentient life beyond the mark *homo sapiens* had left behind in his celestial travels.

Until now.

"Jesus," the captain breathed, conscious now of the entire bridge crew staring at him. They hadn't heard Amundsen's words, but they immediately picked up on the captain's reaction. "XO," he ordered, pulling his mind back to the here and now, "let's have the first contact protocols." He looked pointedly at Kumar. "I want to make damn sure these folks understand we're harmless."

"Aye, sir," Kumar replied crisply as his fingers flew over his terminal. "Coming up on display one." A segment of the bridge wraparound screen darkened as the standing orders for first contact appeared.

"Lieutenant Amundsen," McClaren ordered, "let's see some of these ships of yours on display two."

"Sir." Amundsen's face bobbed about slightly in the captain's comms terminal as he patched the telescope feed to another segment of the main bridge display.

"Lord of All," someone whispered. The *Aurora's* primary telescope was nearly ten meters across, and dominated the phalanx of survey instruments mounted in the massive spherical section that made up the ship's bow. Normally used to search for and map stellar and planetary bodies, it could also be pressed into service to provide high magnification visuals of virtually anything, even moving objects that were relatively close, such as nearby (in terms of a stellar system) ships.

But what it showed now was as unlike the *Aurora* as she herself was unlike a wooden sailing ship. While the *Aurora* was largely a collection of cylindrical sections attached to a sturdy keel that ran from the engineering section at the stern to the instrumentation cluster at the bow, the alien ship displayed on the bridge display was insectile in appearance, her hull made up of sleek curves that gave McClaren the impression of a gigantic wasp.

"Why does the focus keep shifting?" Marisova asked into the sudden silence that had descended on the bridge. The alien vessel shimmered in the display as if a child were twisting an imaginary focus knob for the primary telescope back and forth, taking the image in and out of focus.

"That's what I was about to say," Amundsen answered, McClaren now having shifted the survey team leader's image onto yet a third segment of the bridge display. Before he had seemed both excited and frightened. Now it was clear that fear was crowding out his excitement. "That is one of at least four ships that is heading directly toward us from the outer habitable planet. The reason you are seeing the focusing anomaly is because the ships are moving at an incredible velocity, and the telescope cannot hold the image in alignment. Even what you see here has been enhanced with post-processing." He visibly gulped. "Captain, they knew we were coming, hours, possibly even a few days, before we arrived. They knew right where we were going to be, and they must have left orbit before we arrived. They *must* have. It's theoretically possible to predict a hyperspace emergence, but...we now know that it's not just a theory." He looked again at one of his off-screen displays, then back to the monitor. "I don't know exactly what their initial acceleration rate was, but they're now moving so fast that the light we're seeing reflected from their hulls is noticeably blue-shifted. I estimate their current velocity is roughly five percent of C."

Five percent of the speed of light, McClaren thought, incredulous. Nearly fifteen thousand kilometers per second. And they didn't take much time to reach it.

"I'm trying to estimate their acceleration rate, but it must be-"

"A lot higher than we could ever achieve," McClaren cut him off, looking closely at the wavering image of the alien vessel. "Any idea how big she is?"

"I have no data to estimate her length," Amundsen replied, "but I estimate the beam of this ship to be roughly five hundred meters. I can only assume that her length is considerably more, but we won't know until we get a more oblique view."

"That ship is five hundred meters *wide*?" Kumar asked, incredulous. *Aurora* herself was barely that long from stem to stern. While she was by no means the largest starship built by human hands, she was usually the largest vessel in whatever port she put into.

"Yes," Amundsen told him. "And the other three ships are roughly the same size."

"Christ," someone whispered.

"Raj," McClaren said, turning to his exec. "Thoughts?"

"Communications is running the initial first contact sequence now." He turned to face the captain. "Our signals will take roughly thirty minutes to reach the inner planets, but those ships..." He shook his head. "They're close enough now that they should have already received our transmissions. If they're listening." He looked distinctly uncomfortable. "If I were a betting man, I would say those were warships."

McClaren nodded grimly. "Comms," he looked over at Ensign John Waverly, "keep stepping through the first contact communications sequence. Just make sure that we're listening, too."

"I'm on it, sir," the young man replied. Waverly seemed incredibly young, but like the rest of *Aurora's* crew, he did his job exceptionally well. "I'm well versed in the FCP procedures, sir. So far, though, I haven't come across any emissions anywhere in the standard spectrum, other than what Lieutenant Amundsen's team have already reported. If they use anything anywhere in the radio frequency band, we're sure not seeing it. And I haven't identified any coherent light sources, either."

So, no radio and no communications lasers, McClaren thought uneasily. Even though the aliens knew that company was coming, they had remained silent. Or if they were talking, they were using some form of transmission that was beyond what *Aurora* was capable of seeing or hearing. Maybe the aliens were beyond such mundane things as radio- and light-based communications?

"How long until those ships get here?" McClaren asked Amundsen, whose worried face still stared out from the bridge display screen. *Aurora* herself was motionless relative to her emergence point: McClaren never moved in-system on a survey until they knew much more about their environment than they did now. And it made for a much more convenient reference point for a rapid jump-out.

"At their current velocity, they would overshoot us in just under three hours. But, of course, they will need to decelerate to meet us..."

"That depends on their intentions," Kumar interjected. "They could attack as they pass by..."

"Or they could simply stop," Marisova observed quietly. Everyone turned to gape at her. "We know nothing about their drive systems," she explained. "Nothing about those ships registers on our sensors other than direct visuals. What if they achieved their current velocity nearly instantaneously when they decided to head out to meet us?"

"Preposterous," Amundsen exclaimed. "That's simply not possible!"

"But-"

"Enough, people," McClaren said quietly. "Beyond the obviously impressive capabilities of the aliens, it all boils down to this: do we stay or do we go?" He looked around at his bridge crew, then opened a channel to the entire ship. "Crew, this is the captain. As I'm sure most of you are now aware, the system we've entered is inhabited. We're in a first contact situation. The *only* first contact situation anyone has ever faced. So what we do now is going to become part of The Book that will tell others either how to do it right, or how not to do it if we royally screw things up. I'll be completely honest with you: I'm not happy with the situation. We've got four big ships heading toward us in an awful hurry. They could be warships. I don't blame whoever these folks are for sending out an armed welcoming committee. If it were my home, I'd send some warships out to take a look, too.

"But I'd also make sure to send some diplomats along: people who want to talk with their new neighbors. What bothers me is that we haven't seen anything, from the ships or the two inhabited planets, that looks like any sort of communication. Maybe they're just using something we can't pick up. Maybe the ships coming our way are packed with scientists and ambassadors and they want to make it a big surprise. I just don't know.

"What I do know is that we've got about three hours to make a decision and take action. My inclination is to stay. Not to try and score the first handshake with an alien, but because...it's our first opportunity to say hello to another sentient race. We've been preparing for this moment since before the very first starship left Earth. It's a risk, but it's also the greatest opportunity humanity has ever had.

"So here's what we're going to do. We've got a little bit of time to discuss our options before our new friends reach us. Department heads, talk to your people. Get a feel for what they're thinking. Then all department heads and the senior chiefs are to meet in my ready room in exactly one hour. I'll make the final decision on whether we stay or go, but I want to hear what you all have to say. That is all." He punched the button on the touchpad, closing the circuit.

"In the meantime," he told Kumar and Marisova, "get an emergency jump sequence lined up. Pick a destination other than our inbound vector. If these ships come in with guns blazing, the last thing I want to do is point them back the way we came, toward home."

On the display screen, the alien ship and her sisters continued toward them.

* * *

The four battlecruisers sailed quickly to meet the alien vessel, but they hardly revealed their true capabilities. While it was now clear that the alien ship was extremely primitive, those who guarded the Empire took nothing for granted. They would reveal no more about themselves than absolutely necessary until they were sure the new arrival posed no threat. The Empire had not lasted through the ages by leaving anything to chance.

Aboard the lead ship, a group of warriors prepared for battle with the unknown, while healers and other castes made ready to learn all there was to know about the strangers.

They did not have much longer to wait.

* * *

There was standing room only in the captain's ready room an hour later. At the table sat the six department heads, responsible for the primary functional areas of the ship, the *Aurora's* senior chief, and the captain. Along the walls of the now-cramped compartment stood the senior enlisted member of each department and the ship's two midshipmen. The XO and the bridge crew remained at their stations, although they were tied in through a video feed on the bridge wraparound display.

The emotional tension ran high among the people in the room, McClaren could easily see. But from the body language and the expressions on their faces it wasn't from fear, but excited anticipation. It was an emotion he fully shared.

"I'm not going to waste any time on preliminaries," he began. "You all know what's going on and what's at stake. According to the Survey Department," he nodded at Amundsen, who was the only one around the table who looked distinctly unhappy, "the ships haven't changed course or velocity. So it looks like they're either going to blow by us, which I think would probably be bad news, or their technology is so radically advanced that they can stop on a proverbial dime."

At that, the survey leader's frown grew more pronounced, turning his normally pale face into a grimace.

"Amundsen?" McClaren asked. "You've got something to say. Spit it out."

"I think Lieutenant Marisova was right," he said grudgingly, nodding toward the video pickup that showed the meeting to the bridge crew. But McClaren knew that it wasn't because Marisova had said it. It was because he was afraid to believe that what she said could possibly be true, or even close to the truth. "I don't believe they could accelerate to their current velocity instantaneously, but even assuming several days' warning - even weeks! - the acceleration they must have achieved would have to have been...unbelievable." He shook his head. "No. I believe those ships will not simply pass by us. They will slow down and rendezvous with us sometime in the next two hours, decelerating at a minimum of two hundred gees. Probably much more."

A chill ran down McClaren's spine. *Aurora* had the most efficient reactionless drives in service by any of the many worlds colonized by Mankind, and was one of the few to be fitted with artificial gravity, a recent innovation, and acceleration dampers. She wasn't nearly as fast as a courier ship, certainly, but for a military survey vessel she was no slouch. But two hundred gees? Not even close.

"Robotic ships?" Aubrey Hannan, the chief of the Engineering Section suggested. "They could certainly handle that sort of acceleration."

"It doesn't matter," McClaren interjected, gently but firmly steering the conversation from interesting, but essentially useless, speculation back to the issue at hand. "From my perspective, it doesn't matter how fast the aliens can maneuver. We're not a warship, and I have no intention of masquerading as one. It's clear they have radically advanced technology. That's not necessarily a surprise; we could have just as easily stumbled upon a world in the pre-atomic era, and we would be the high-tech aliens. Our options remain the same: stay and say hello, or jump out with what I hope is a fat safety margin before they get here." He glanced around and his gaze landed on the junior midshipman. "Midshipman Sato, what's your call?"

Ichiro Sato, already standing ramrod straight against the bulkhead, stiffened even further. All of nineteen years old, he was the youngest member of the crew. Extremely courteous, conscientious, and intelligent, he was well respected by the other members of the crew, although his rigid outer shell was a magnet for good-natured ribbing. Exceptionally competent and a fast learner, he kept quietly to himself. He was one of a select few from the Terran Naval Academy who were chosen to spend one or more of their academy years aboard ship as advanced training as junior officers. It was a great opportunity, but came with a hefty commitment: deployed midshipmen had to continue their academy studies while also performing their duties aboard ship.

"Sir..." Sato momentarily gulped for air, McClaren's question having caught him completely off-guard.

The captain felt momentarily guilty for putting Sato on the spot first, but he had a reason. "Relax, Ichiro," McClaren told him. "I called this meeting for ideas. The senior officers, including myself, and the chiefs have years of preconceived notions drilled into our heads. We've got years of experience, yes, but this situation calls for a fresh perspective. If you were in my shoes, what would your decision be? There's no right or wrong answer to this one."

While Ichiro's features didn't betray it, the captain's last comment caused him even more consternation. He had been brought up in a traditional Japanese family on Nagano, where, according to his father, everything was either *right* or it was *wrong*; there was no in-between. And more often than not, anything Ichiro did was *wrong*. That was the main reason Ichiro had decided to apply for service in the Terran Navy when he was sixteen: to spite his father and escape the tyranny of his house, and to avoid the stifling life of a salaryman trapped in the web of a hegemonic corporate world. Earth's global military services accepted applicants from all but a few rogue worlds, and Ichiro's test scores and academic record had opened the door for him to enter the Terran Naval Academy. There, too, most everything was either right or wrong. The difference between the academy and his home was that in the academy, Ichiro was nearly always *right*. His unfailing determination to succeed had given him a sense of confidence he had never known before, putting him at the head of his class and earning him a position aboard the *Aurora*.

That realization, and his desperate desire not to lose face in front of the captain and ship's officers, gave him back his voice. "Sir. I believe we should stay and greet the ships."

McClaren nodded, wondering what had just been going on in the young man's mind. "Okay, you picked door number one. The question now is why?"

"Because, sir, that is why we are here, isn't it?" Loosening up slightly from his steel-rod pose, he turned to look at the other faces around the room, his voice suddenly filled with a passion that none of his fellow crew members would have ever thought possible. "While our primary mission is to find new habitable worlds, we really are explorers, discoverers, of whatever deep space may hold. With every jump we search for the unknown, things that no one else has ever seen. Maybe we will not find what we hope. Perhaps these aliens are friendly, perhaps not. There is great risk in everything we do. But, having found the first sentient race other than humankind, can we in good conscience simply leave without doing all we can to establish contact, even at the risk of our own destruction?"

The captain nodded, impressed more by the young man's unexpected burst of emotion than his words. But his words held their own merit: they precisely echoed McClaren's own feelings. That was exactly why he had spent so much of his career in survey.

"Well said, Ichiro," he told the young man. The two midshipmen on either side of Sato grinned and nudged him as if to say, *Good job*. Most of those seated at the table nodded or murmured their agreement. "So, there's an argument, and I believe a good one, for staying. Who's got one for bailing out right now?"

"I'll take that one, sir," Raj Kumar spoke up from the bridge, his image appearing on the primary screen in the ready room. "I myself agree with Midshipman Sato that we should stay. But one compelling argument for leaving now is to make sure that the news of this discovery gets back home. If the aliens should turn out to be hostile and this ship is taken, or even if we should suffer some unexpected mishap, Earth and the rest of human space may never know until they're attacked. And we have no way to let anyone know of our discovery without jumping back to the nearest communications relay."

That produced a lot of frowns on the faces around the table. Most of them had thought of this already, of course, but having it voiced directly gave it more substance.

Kumar went on, "That's also a specification in the first contact protocols, that one of the top priorities is to get word back home. But the bottom line is that any actions taken are at the captain's discretion based on the situation as he or she sees it."

"Right," McClaren told everyone. "Getting word back home is the only real reason I've been able to come up with myself for leaving now that isn't tied to fear of the unknown. And since all of us signed up to get paid to go find the unknown, as the good midshipman pointed out, those reasons don't count." He turned to the woman sitting to his left. "Chief, what's your take?"

Master Chief Brenda Harkness was the senior enlisted member of the crew, and her word carried a great deal of weight with McClaren. Completely at odds with the stereotype of someone of her rank, she was a tall, slim, and extremely attractive woman in her late thirties. But no one who had ever worked with her for more than five minutes ever took her for granted: she was a hard-core Navy lifer who never dished out bullshit and refused to tolerate it from anyone else. She would move mountains to help anyone who needed it, but her beautiful deep hazel eyes could just as easily burn holes in the skin of anyone foolish enough to cross her.

"I think we should stay, captain," she said, a light Texas drawl flavoring her smooth voice. "I completely agree with the XO's concerns about getting word of this back home, but with the alien ships so close now..." She shook her head. "I can't imagine that they'd be anything but insulted if we just up and disappeared on them."

"And the crew?" McClaren asked.

"Everyone I had a chance to talk to, and that was most of them, wanted to stay. A lot of them are uneasy about those ships, but as you said, we just happen to be the 'primitives' in this situation. We'd be stupid to not be afraid, sir. But I think we'd be even more stupid to just pack up and go home."

All of the other department heads nodded their agreement. Each had talked to their people, too, and almost without exception the crew had wanted to stay and meet with the aliens.

It was what McClaren expected. He would have been shocked had they come to any other conclusion. "Okay, that settles it. We stay." That brought a round of bright, excited smiles to everyone but Amundsen, whose face was locked in an unhappy grimace. "But here's the deal: the XO and navigator have worked out an emergency jump sequence, just in case. We'll spool up the jump engines to the pre-interlock stage and hold them there until we feel more confident of the aliens' intentions. We can keep the engines spooled like that for several hours without running any risks in engineering. If those ships are friendly, we get to play galactic tourist and buy them the first round at the bar.

"But if they're not," he looked pointedly at Amundsen, "we engage the jump interlock and the navigation computer will have us out of here in two minutes." That made the survey leader slightly less unhappy, but only slightly. "Okay, does anybody have anything else they want to add before we set up the reception line?"

"Sir..." Sato said formally, again at a position of attention.

"Go ahead, son."

"Captain, I know this may sound foolish," he glanced at Amundsen, who was at the table with his back to Sato, "but should we not also take steps to secure the navigation computer in case the ships prove hostile? If they took the ship, there is probably little they would learn of our technology that would be of value to them. But the navigation charts..."

"It's already taken care of, midshipman," Kumar reassured him from the bridge with an approving smile. Second year midshipmen like Sato weren't expected to know anything about the first contact protocols, but the boy was clearly thinking on his feet. Kumar's already high respect for him rose yet another notch. "That's on the very short list of 'non-discretionary' actions on first contact. We've already prepared a soft wipe of the data, and a team from engineering is setting charges around the primary core." He held up both hands, then simulated pushing buttons down with his thumbs. "If we get into trouble, *Aurora's* hull is all they'll walk away with."

And us, Amundsen thought worriedly.

* * *

The alien ship had activated its jump drive. While primitive, it was clearly based on the same principles used by Imperial starships. Such technology was an impressive accomplishment for any species, and gave the warriors hope that once again they had found worthy adversaries among the stars.

But the aliens would not - could not - be allowed to leave. Together, the battlecruisers moved in...

* * *

"Jump engines are spooled up, captain," Kumar reported from his console. The jump coordinates were locked in. All they had to do was engage the computer interlock and *Aurora* would disappear into hyperspace inside of two minutes.

"Very well, XO," McClaren replied, his eyes fixed intently on the four titanic ships, all of which were now shown clearly in the main bridge display.

Suddenly the ships leaped forward, closing the remaining ten million kilometers in an instant.

"What the devil..." McClaren exclaimed in surprise, watching as the alien vessels just as suddenly slowed down to take up positions around his ship.

"Sir," Kumar exclaimed, "they must've picked up the jump engines activating! I recommend we jump-"

"Execute!" McClaren barked, a cold sliver of ice sliding into his gut. Then he jabbed the button on his command console to open a channel to the crew. "General quarters! Man your battle stations and prepare for emergency jump!"

"Interlock engaged," came the unhurried and unconcerned voice of *Aurora's* navigation computer. "Transpace countdown commencing. Primary energy buffer building. Two minutes remaining."

McClaren looked at his command console, willing the countdown to run faster. But it was a hard-coded safety lock. There was no way to override it.

"Navigation lock confirmed-"

"*Captain!*" someone shouted.

McClaren looked up at the screen as a stream of interwoven lightning arced from the bow of the alien ship that had taken up position in front of them, hitting *Aurora's* spherical sensor section. Its effect was instantaneous.

"*Jesus!*" someone screamed as what looked like St. Elmo's fire suddenly exploded from every control console and electrical system on the ship. The dancing display of electric fury went on to cover everything, even the clothing of the crew. The entire ship was suddenly awash in electrical discharges.

But it clearly wasn't simple electricity. There was no smoke or heat from overloaded circuits, and no one was injured by whatever energy washed through the ship and their own bodies. Surprised and frightened, yes. But hurt, no.

Then every single electrical system on the ship died, plunging *Aurora's* crew into silent, terrifying darkness.

* * *

Having subdued the alien ship's simple electronic systems, the lead warship made ready the boarding party that had been awaiting this moment. While the great warship's crew now knew the layout of the alien ship and all it contained, including the aliens themselves, down to the last atom, the boarding party would be sent without this knowledge. They would give themselves no advantage over the aliens other than the surprise they had already achieved; even that, they would have given up if they could. They wished as even a field as possible, to prove their own mettle and to test that of the strangers. In this way, as through ages past, they sought to honor their Empress.

As one, the thirty warriors who had bested their peers in fierce ritual combat for the right to "greet" the strangers leaped into space toward the alien vessel. Thirty warriors pitted against seven times as many aliens. They hoped the odds would challenge their skills.

* * *

"*Calm down!*" Chief Harkness's voice cut through the sudden panic like a razor. At her assigned jump station in the survey module inside the spherical bow section, Harkness had immediately clamped down on her own fear in the aftermath of the terrifying electrical surge that apparently had killed her ship. She had people to take care of, and she was too much of a professional to panic. "Listen to me," she told the seven others in the cramped compartment. There were still a couple of them moaning in fear. "Listen, goddammit!" she snarled. That finally got their attention. Of all the things in the ship they might be afraid of, she would be the first and foremost if that helped them hold it together. "Get your heads screwed on straight. The ship's hull hasn't been ruptured. We've still got air. That's priority number one. All the electrical systems must've been knocked out, which is why the artificial gravity is gone, along with the lights." The darkness was disorienting enough, but being weightless on top of it was a cast iron bitch. She was actually more worried that the emergency lighting hadn't come on. Those weren't powered by the main electrical system, and their failure meant that something far worse had happened to her ship than a simple, if major, electrical blowout. "You've all experienced this before in training. So relax and start acting like the best sailors in the Navy. That's why you were picked to serve on this ship." She paused to listen, relieved to hear that the sniveling had stopped, and everyone's breathing had slowed down a bit.

"Now, feel around for the emergency lockers," she told them. "There should be three in here. Grab the flashlights and see if the damn things work." While they could survive for some time on the available oxygen, the total darkness was going to give way to fear again if they didn't get some light.

"Found one, chief," someone said off to her left. There was a moment of scrabbling around, the sound of a panel opening, then a bit of rummaging.

Click.

Nothing.

"Fuck," someone else whispered.

"Try another one," Harkness grated.

"Okay-"

Suddenly she could see something. But it wasn't the ship's lighting or one of the emergency flashlights. It was like the walls themselves had begun to glow, throwing a subdued dark blue radiance into the compartment.

"Chief, what is this stuff?" one of the ratings asked quietly, her eyes, visible now in the ghostly light, bulging wide as she looked at the glowing bulkheads around her.

"I don't know," Harkness admitted. "But whatever it is, we can see now." The compartment was now clearly, if softly lit. "So let's use it and find out what the hell's happened to the ship."

Then something else unexpected happened: the gravity returned. Instantly. All eight of them slammed down on the deck in a mass of flailing limbs and passionate curses. Fortunately, they all had been oriented more or less upright, and no one was hurt.

"Shit," Harkness gasped as she levered herself back onto her feet. "What the *hell* is going on..."

That's when she heard the screaming.

* * *

The warriors plunged toward the alien ship. They wore their ceremonial armor for this ritual battle, eschewing any more powerful protection. They soared across the distance between the ships with arms and legs outstretched, enjoying the sight of the universe afforded by the energy shields that invisibly surrounded them and protected them from hard vacuum. They needed no devices to assist in maneuvering toward their target: theirs was a race that had been plying the stars for ages, and their space-borne heritage led them to a fearless precision that humans could only dream of.

They were not concerned about any pathogenic organisms the aliens carried, as the healers who would be sent once the ship had been subdued would take care of such matters. The scan of the alien vessel had revealed an atmosphere that, while not optimal, was certainly breathable.

There was no warrior priestess in this system to bear the honor of leading them in this first encounter, but no matter. The senior warriors were well experienced and had the blessing of the Empress: they could sense Her will in their very blood, as She could sense what they felt. It was more a form of empathic bonding than telepathy, but its true essence was beyond intellectual understanding.

As they neared the ship, the warriors curled into a fetal position, preparing to make contact with the alien hull. The energy shields altered their configuration, warping into a spherical shape to both absorb the force of the impact and force an entry point through the simple metal rushing up to meet them.

The first warrior reached the hull, and the energy shield seared through the primitive alien metal, instantly opening a portal to the interior. The warrior smoothly rolled through to land on her feet inside, quickly readjusting to the gravity that the crew of the warship had restored for benefit of the aliens. The energy shield remained in place behind the warrior, sealing the hole it had created in the hull plating and containing the ship's atmosphere.

In only a few seconds more, all the other warriors had forced themselves aboard the hapless vessel.

* * *

The screaming Chief Harkness heard was from Ensign Mary Withgott. Her battle station was at a damage control point where the spherical bow section connected to the main keel and the passageway that led to the rest of the ship. The damage control point was on the sphere's side of a blast proof door that was now locked shut. She could open it manually, but wouldn't consider it unless she got direct orders from the captain.

"Ensign!" one of the two ratings with her shouted as a shower of burning sparks exploded from the bulkhead above them. The two crewmen stared, dumbstruck, as someone, some alien *thing*, somersaulted through a huge hole that had been burned through the hull and into the damage control compartment.

A blue-skinned nightmare clad in gleaming black armor, the alien smoothly pirouetted toward the two crewmen, exposing fangs between dark red lips. Its eyes were like those of a cat, flecked with silver, below a ridge of bone or horn. The creature's black hair was long and tightly braided, the coils wrapped around its upper shoulders. The armored breastplate had two smoothly contoured projections over what must be the alien equivalent of breasts. While Withgott had no idea what the alien's true gender (if any) might be, the creature's appearance was such that Withgott had the inescapable impression that it was female, a *she*.

The alien stood there for a moment, meeting Withgott's frightened gaze with her own inscrutable expression. Then the sword the alien held in her right hand hissed through the air, cleanly severing the head from the nearest crewman. His body spasmed as his head rolled from his neck, a gout of crimson spurting across the bulkhead behind him.

Withgott screamed, and kept on screaming as the alien turned to the second crewman with the ferocious grace of a hunting tigress and thrust the sword through the man's chest.

Then the fanged nightmare came for Withgott.

SEASON OF THE HARVEST

What if the genetically engineered crops that we increasingly depend on for food weren't really created by man? What if they brought a new, terrifying meaning to the old saying that "you are what you eat"?

In the bestselling thriller *Season Of The Harvest*, FBI Special Agent Jack Dawson investigates the gruesome murder of his best friend and fellow agent who had been pursuing a group of eco-terrorists. The group's leader, Naomi Perrault, is a beautiful geneticist who Jack believes conspired to kill his friend, and is claiming that a major international conglomerate developing genetically engineered crops is plotting a sinister transformation of our world that will lead humanity to extinction.

As Jack is drawn into a quietly raging war that suddenly explodes onto the front pages of the news, he discovers that her claims may not be so outrageous after all. Together, the two of them must face a horror Jack could never have imagined, with the fate of all life on Earth hanging in the balance...

Interested? Then read on and enjoy the prologue and first chapter of *Season Of The Harvest*. And always remember: *you are what you eat!*

* * *

PROLOGUE

Sheldon Crane ran for his life. Panting from exhaustion and the agony of the deep stab wound in his side, he darted into the deep shadows of an alcove in the underground service tunnel. Holding his pistol in unsteady hands, he peered around the corner, past the condensation-covered pipes, looking back in the direction from which he'd come.

Nothing. All he could hear was the deep hum of the electric service box that filled most of the alcove, punctuated by the *drip-drip-drip* of water from a small leak in one of the water pipes a few yards down the tunnel. Only a third of the ceiling-mounted fluorescent lights were lit, a cost-saving measure by the university that left long stretches of paralyzing darkness between the islands of greenish-tinged light. He could smell wet concrete and the tang of ozone, along with a faint trace of lubricating oil. And over it all was the scent of blood. In the pools of light stretching back down the tunnel, all the way back to the intersection where he had turned into this part of the underground labyrinth, he could see the glint of blood on the floor, a trail his pursuer could easily follow.

He knew that no one could save him: he had come here tonight precisely because he expected the building to be empty. It had been. Almost. But there was no one to hear his shouts for help, and he had dropped his cell phone during the unexpected confrontation in the lab upstairs.

He was totally on his own.

Satisfied that his pursuer was not right on his heels, he slid deeper into the alcove, into the dark recess between the warm metal of the electric service box and the cold concrete wall. He gently probed the wound in his side, gasping as his fingertips brushed against the blood-wet, swollen flesh just above his left hip. It was a long moment before he was sure he wouldn't scream from the pain. It wasn't merely a stab wound. He had been stabbed and cut before. That had been incredibly painful. This, however, was far worse. His insides were on fire, the pain having spread quickly from his belly to upper chest. And the pain was accompanied by paralysis. He had lost control of his abdominal muscles, and the sensation was spreading. There was a sudden gush of warmth down his legs as his bladder suddenly let go, and he groaned in agony as his internal organs began to burn.

Poison, he knew.

He leaned over, fighting against the light-headedness that threatened to bear him mercifully into unconsciousness.

"No," he panted to himself. "No." He knew he didn't have much time left. He had to act.

Wiping the blood from his left hand on his shirt, cleaning it as best he could, he reached under his right arm and withdrew both of the extra magazines he carried for his weapon, a 10mm Glock 22 that was standard issue for FBI special agents. He ejected the empty magazine from the gun, cursing himself as his shaking hands lost their grip and it clattered to the floor.

It won't matter soon, he thought giddily as he slumped against the wall, sliding down the rough concrete to the floor as his upper thighs succumbed to the spreading paralysis, then began to burn.

Desperately racing against the poison in his system, he withdrew a small plastic bag from a pocket inside his jacket and set it carefully next to him. He patted it with his fingertips several times to reassure himself that he knew exactly where it was in the dark. His fingers felt the shapes of a dozen lumps inside the bag: kernels of corn.

Then he picked up one of the spare magazines and shucked out all the bullets with his thumb into a pocket in his jacket so he wouldn't lose them. Setting down the now-empty magazine, he picked up the tiny bag and carefully opened the seal, praying he wouldn't accidentally send the precious lumps flying into the darkness. For the first time that night, Fate favored him, and the bag opened easily.

Picking up the empty magazine from his lap, he tapped a few of the kernels onto the magazine's follower, the piece of metal that the bottom bullet rested on. He managed to squeeze a bullet into the magazine on top of the corn kernels. Once that was done, he slid the other bullets into place, then clumsily slammed the magazine into the weapon and chambered a round.

He took the bag and its remaining tiny, precious cargo and resealed it. Then he stuffed it into his mouth. The knowledge of the nature of the corn made him want to gag, but he managed to force it down, swallowing the bag. Crane suspected his body would be searched thoroughly, inside and out, for what he had stolen, and his mind shied away from how that search would probably be conducted. His only hope now was that his pursuer would be content to find the bag, and not think to check Crane's weapon. He prayed that his body and the priceless contents of his gun's magazine would be found by the right people. It was a terrible long-shot, but he was out of options.

His nose was suddenly assaulted by the smell of Death coming for him, a nauseating mix of pungent ammonia laced with the reek of burning hemp.

Barely able to lift his arms, his torso nearly paralyzed and aflame with agonizing pain, Crane brought up his pistol just as his pursuer whirled around the corner. He fired at the hideous abomination that was revealed in the flashes from the muzzle of his gun, and managed to get off three shots before the weapon was batted from his faltering grip. He screamed in terror as his pursuer closed in, blocking out the light.

The screams didn't stop for a long time.

* * *

CHAPTER ONE

Jack Dawson stood in his supervisor's office and stared out the window, his bright gray eyes watching the rain fall from the brooding summer sky over Washington, D.C. The wind was blowing just hard enough for the rain to strike the glass, leaving behind wet streaks that ran down the panes like tears. The face he saw reflected there was cast in shadow by the overhead fluorescent lights. The square jaw and high cheekbones gave him a predatory look, while his full lips promised a smile, but were drawn downward now into a frown. The deeply tanned skin, framed by lush black hair that was neatly combed back and held with just the right amount of styling gel, looked sickly and pale in the glass, as if it belonged on the face of a ghost. He knew that it was the same face he saw every morning. But it was different now. An important part of his world had been killed, murdered, the night before.

He watched the people on the street a few floors below, hustling through the downpour with their umbrellas fluttering as they poured out of the surrounding buildings, heading home for the evening. Cars clogged Pennsylvania Avenue, with the taxis darting to the curb to pick up fares, causing other drivers to jam on their brakes, the bright red tail lights flickering on and off down the street like a sputtering neon sign. It was Friday, and everyone was eager to get home to their loved ones, or go out to dinner, or head to the local bar. Anywhere that would let them escape the rat race for the weekend.

He didn't have to see this building's entrance to know that very few of the people who worked here would be heading home on time tonight. The address was 935 Pennsylvania Avenue Northwest. It was the J. Edgar Hoover Building, headquarters of the Federal Bureau of Investigation, the FBI. Other than the teams of special agents who had departed an hour earlier for Lincoln, Nebraska, many of the Bureau's personnel here at headquarters wouldn't leave until sometime tomorrow. Some would be sleeping in their offices and cubicles after exhaustion finally overtook them, and wouldn't go home for more than a few hours over the next several days.

A special agent had been brutally murdered, and with the addition of another name to the list of the FBI's Service Martyrs, every resource the Bureau could bring to bear was being focused on bringing his killer to justice. Special agents from headquarters and field offices around the country were headed to Nebraska, along with an army of analysts and support staff that was already sifting through electronic data looking for leads.

Everyone had a part in the investigation, it seemed, except for Dawson. In his hand, he held a plain manila folder that included the information that had been forwarded by the Lincoln field office. It was a preliminary report sent in by the Special Agent in Charge (SAC), summarizing the few known facts of the case. In terse prose, the SAC's report described the crime scene, the victim, and what had been done by the local authorities before the SAC's office had been alerted. And there were photos. Lots of photos. If a picture was worth a thousand words, then the ones Dawson held in his shaking hands spoke volumes about the agony suffered by the victim before he died. Because it was clear from the rictus of agony and terror frozen on Sheldon Crane's face that he had still been alive when—

"I'm sorry, Jack," came a gruff voice from behind him, interrupting Dawson's morbid train of thought as Ray Clement, Assistant Director of the Criminal Investigative Division, came in and closed the door. It was his office, and he had ordered Dawson to wait there until he had a chance to speak with him.

Ray Clement was a bear of a man with a personality to match. A star football player from the University of Alabama's Crimson Tide, Clement had actually turned down a chance to go pro, and had instead joined the FBI as a special agent. That had been his dream since the age of ten, as he had once told Jack, and the proudest moment of his life had been when he'd earned his badge. Jack knew that a lot of people might have thought Clement was crazy. "I loved football," Clement would say, "and I still do. But I played it because I enjoyed it. I never planned to do it for a living."

Over the years, Clement had worked his way up through the Bureau. He was savvy enough to survive the internal politics, smart and tough enough to excel in the field, and conformed to the system because he believed in it. He could be a real bastard when someone did something stupid, but otherwise worked tirelessly to support his people so they could do their jobs. He wasn't a boss that any of his special agents would say they loved, but under his tenure, the Criminal Investigative Division, or CID, had successfully closed more cases than under any other assistant director in the previous fifteen years. People could say what they wanted, but Clement got results.

When he had first taken over the division, Clement had taken the time to talk to each and every one of his special agents. He had been up front about why: he wanted to know at least a little bit, more than just the names, about the men and women who risked their lives every day for the

American Taxpayer. They were special agents, he'd said, but they were also special human beings.

Jack had dreaded the interview. Whereas Clement could have been the FBI's poster child, Jack didn't quite fit the mold. He was like a nail head sticking up from the perfectly polished surface of a hardwood floor, not enough to snag on anything, just enough to notice. Outwardly, he was no different than most of his peers. He dressed the same as most special agents, eschewing a suit for more practical and casual attire for all but the most formal occasions. His well-muscled six foot, one inch tall body was far more comfortable in jeans and a pullover shirt, with a light jacket to conceal his primary weapon, a standard service-issue Glock 22. While he had no problems voicing his opinions, which had sometimes led to respectful but intense discussions with his superiors, he had never been a discipline problem. He was highly competent in the field, and was a whiz at data analysis. At first glance, he seemed like what he should be: an outstanding special agent who worked hard and had great career prospects.

But under the shiny veneer ran a deep vein of dark emptiness. Jack smiled, but it never seemed to reach his eyes, and he rarely laughed. He was not cold-hearted, for he had often displayed uncommon compassion toward others, especially the victims, and their families, of the crimes he was sent to investigate. But he had no social life to speak of, no significant other in his life, and there were very few people who understood the extent of the pain that lay at Jack's core.

That pain had its roots in events that took place seven years earlier, when Jack was serving in the Army in Afghanistan. His patrol had been ambushed by the Taliban and had taken heavy casualties before reinforcements arrived. Jack had been badly wounded, having taken two rounds from an AK-47 in the chest, along with shrapnel from a grenade. The latter had left its mark on his otherwise handsome face, a jagged scar marring his left cheek. That had been rough, but he was young, only twenty-six, and strong, and would make a full recovery from his wounds.

What had torn him apart was what happened back in the States. While he lay unconscious in the SSG Heath N. Craig Joint Theater Hospital in Bagram, his wife Emily was kidnapped while leaving a shopping mall not far from their home outside Fort Drum, New York. Emily had her own home business, and they had no children, so no one immediately noticed that she'd gone missing. Four days passed before a persistent Red Cross worker who had been trying to get in touch with Emily about Jack's injuries contacted the provost marshal at Fort Drum. Two military policemen went to the house, and when they found it empty, they contacted the local police.